JESS

Book four of *The Book Club* novels

Jess's Story

ALI FISCHER

HYPERBOLE PUBLISHING

Copyright © 2024 Ali Fischer
All rights reserved
Paperback ISBN 978-1-7397308-3-3
Published by Hyperbole Publishing
Cover Design by Spiffing
Editing services by Dark Bear Media

This is a work of fiction. Any similarity between the characters and situations within its pages and places or persons, living or dead, is unintentional and coincidental.

No artificial intelligence (AI) has been used to write this novel.

DEDICATION

To anyone that wants to just run away from it all… and have a 6'4" sex god chase them. This one's for you.

PLAYLIST

I have curated a playlist where each song matches the mood of the chapter. Links can be found on my website www.alifischer.com. For ease, here are the QR codes:

For Apple Music users:

For Spotify users:

CONTENT WARNINGS

This novel contains:
- Primal kink scenes, including breath play/hand necklaces
- Paternal neglect/maternal dietary regulation
- Parental pressure/expectations
- Abduction
- Sexual assault without penetration
- Off-page violent rape scene description
- Assault and battery of the FMC
- Spitting
- Self-loathing
- Graphic sexual scenes
- Masturbation

Please note that this is a work of fiction and is not an instruction manual for the safe practice of Primal/BDSM. Your safety is important, and so is your consent.

Fear is just excitement without breath.

Fritz Perls

CHAPTER 1

JESS

Fall in Line (feat. Demi Lovato) – Christina Aguilera

'Is that what you're wearing?' Jess's mother looked down her nose at her as she poured the tea, which was no mean feat since she was a good three inches shorter than Jess.

Jess cast her eyes over her outfit as she entered the garden room and suppressed the desire to respond with, 'No shit, Sherlock,' as she'd learned from an early age, smart-mouthing her mother got her nowhere, or more specifically, it got her whisked off to boarding school. She took a breath and pushed down her frustration.

'Yes, mother, this is what I'm wearing.' It was an unseasonably warm day, so Jess wore her natural linen trousers, a white crewneck T-shirt, and her favourite beaded necklace she'd bought from a market stall in St. Tropez. She felt comfortable for once and didn't understand why her mother was worried about her outfit choice. They were only having tea, for Christ's sake. Or at least she hoped they were only having tea. Oh God, what did her mother have planned?

Jess crossed the garden room, collapsed into her favourite chair, and soaked in the beams of sunshine that flooded the space through the glass walls. This was her favourite place to sit and read. Looking out over the acres of land, she'd often imagine what it would be like to feel free. She'd lose herself in the latest novel her friends in the book club had chosen and forget her troubles. Forget she was the star of her own Rapunzel retelling. Only in her version, a handsome prince wouldn't save her. She was eternally stuck with the villain.

Her mother's curt tone interrupted her thoughts. 'You'll need to change. I'll lay something more appropriate out for you.' Her mother bristled and straightened her already perfectly straight bottle-green cardigan.

Jess didn't want to ask, already guessing the answer, but she had to play her mother's game. 'Why do I need to get changed?'

She swallowed, waiting for the inevitable as her blood heated under her mother's stare.

Her parents had always controlled her, micromanaging her every move, but they stepped it up a gear when they demanded she move back home after allowing her to live in one of their properties in a nearby village. It was while she was living there that she met her best friend, Sarah, and they started a smutty book club. Her parents swiftly took away her freedom when they claimed it made little sense for her to be living in a property they could rent out to someone else for a huge sum. Jess didn't believe their reasoning. It was obvious they saw her living her own life, and didn't like it.

It probably didn't help that one of her friends was involved in a manslaughter incident, then moved to London to specialise in designing sex dungeons for people's homes. Oh, and her best friend was a victim of revenge porn and ended up in the national newspapers.

So here she was, back at the family home, being treated like a puppet to heighten her parents' status.

'I asked you to join me so we might discuss the plan for this evening.' She puffed out a frustrated breath. 'Jessica, have you forgotten we're entertaining the Wilberforce family this evening?'

Fuck.

She'd totally forgotten they were entertaining Will and his stuck-up parents. She hoped her silence told her mother all she needed to know.

Her mother poured a cup of tea as she chastised her. 'I knew letting you move to London was a mistake. You move away from home for five minutes and forget where your duties lie.'

She watched in silence as a sliver of lemon was dropped into the cup of black tea and thrust into her hand. She wasn't allowed milk or sugar; both were fattening and uncouth.

'Mum, I didn't forget entirely. I thought it was tomorrow night.' It took all her self-control not to roll her eyes. Who organised a dinner party on a Thursday?

Her words went unheard as her mother carried on. 'I don't know what's going on with you lately, but you should know your father and I do not approve. First, you cut your beautiful long hair, and now you're off gallivanting around London getting up to God knows what. We have a reputation to uphold, Jessica, and your wayward behaviour is not going unnoticed.' Her mother lowered her voice and hissed, 'There are rumours you're working for an S-E-X hotel.' Her mother's face paled with horror.

Jess ran her fingers through her golden shoulder-length hair and suppressed the desire to scream. The temptation to throw the shit tea across the room and tell her parents to back off was almost too much to bear.

The usually open and spacious room was closing in around her. But she couldn't move. Couldn't escape it. 'I cut my hair because I was sick of it being so long. I wanted a fresh look, more suitable for a woman in her mid-twenties. It was time for a change. And I'm not off gallivanting around London working in a sex hotel.' She tried to put a lid on her barely contained rage. 'I'm running a successful business and making a name for myself in the art industry. I'm supplying the art for a hotel opening in London. Maybe don't believe all the petty gossip you hear.'

She decided it was best not to mention that this hotel had kink-themed rooms that catered to people's more specialised tastes in the bedroom. That would probably kill her mother off.

Her mother sipped her tea before she placed the cup heavily on its saucer. 'I don't know why you insist on carrying on with this art nonsense. You'll be kept plenty busy when it comes time to marry, and then you simply won't have time to run a business. You'll be expected to help run the household and raise your children.' She watched as her mother's eyebrows rose. The movement was barely visible thanks to years of regular Botox injections, but Jess could spot it. 'Or have you forgotten everything you were taught in finishing school?'

Jess put her cup down on the glass side table and stood. 'I have no intention of giving up on my career. This is the twenty-first century. Women have equal rights.' She went to leave the room, but her mother's words halted her in her tracks.

'You will do well to remember your place, Jessica. Put a lid on your attitude and wipe that look off your face. Your father has worked hard to give us everything we desire, and you will do as you are told. Will is very much looking forward to seeing you tonight, so be on your best behaviour. Do I make myself clear?'

'Abundantly,' she said through gritted teeth.

Georgina's shoulders sagged. 'Jessica, please understand that I am just trying to help you. I want what's best for you.'

Jess ignored her mother's parting comment. She didn't believe for one second that her mother would ever do what was best for her. Her mother cared about one thing, and one thing only. Herself.

Jess changed into the simple maroon dress her mother had picked out for her. Tailored to perfection—the unforgiving fabric restricted her ribcage and made eating impossible. She questioned whether her mother did that purposefully to prevent her from overeating, or if it was just a lucky coincidence.

Of course, the outfit came with flesh-coloured stockings and a pair of nude heels. She rolled her eyes as she studied her reflection in the antique gilt-edged mirror that dominated one wall of her bedroom. Who did her mother think she was?

Her mother, Georgina Chatwin, liked to enforce the same strict dress code with her daughter that the royal family adhered to. Her parents got themselves on the guest list for any event with royal attendance, their sights set on the princes as potential husband material for Jess. Georgina was livid for weeks when the last suitable prince was married off. The way her mother scowled at her afterwards made Jess think she held her personally responsible.

From an early age, it was made abundantly clear that Jess's role in life was to represent her parents at social events, get married, and produce heirs. She was lucky her father didn't force her into taking over the family business—a private bank specialising in all things horse racing, from providing financial backing to managing the owners' accounts.

Her mother would tell her that was the plus side to having a uterus. Her job was breeding, like one of their prized mares. She was to give them a grandson so *he* could continue the family business.

No pressure then.

She didn't want to end up like her mother. She saw the sadness behind her eyes most days, vying for her husband's attention, knowing she was a constant source of disappointment because she didn't produce a son. Jess knew that feeling all too well. She had grown up seeing the disappointment in her father's eyes every time he looked at her. She didn't choose to be a girl, but she suffered for it anyway.

Jess told herself she just needed to smile and get through tonight. She'd be back in London for the opening night of the hotel soon, and that would afford her a few days respite from the crushing claustrophobia of being at home.

Jess sat at the table, feigning interest in the conversation going on around her. Georgina had placed her next to Will—no surprise there—while her mother and Camilla Wilberforce sat on the opposite side. Her father, Peter, took the head of the table and Frank Wilberforce sat at the opposite end. The staff had set the table with the finest bone china, crystal glasses, and silver cutlery shined to within an inch of its life. Fresh flower arrangements adorned the centre and filled the room with the heady scent of roses.

The formal dining room was like something out of a Regency romance movie. Deep red rugs covered the polished mahogany floors. Portraits of previous Chatwin residents hung from the walls and plush velvet curtains framed each of the windows. It felt stuffy and old-fashioned and Jess hated every square metre of it, but to her parents, the room spoke of their wealth and breeding.

Pompous twats.

'Jess, darling, are you listening?' Jess's mother was glaring, or at least trying to.

She blinked and cleared her mind, getting herself into her role. 'Sorry, I was miles away.'

'Will was asking you a question.' Georgina kept her tone lighthearted, but Jess knew she was in for a telling-off as soon as their guests were out of earshot.

She turned her attention to the man next to her. Will Wilberforce was only a couple of years older than her and had recently celebrated his twenty-eighth birthday. Thankfully, Jess was in London, so couldn't attend his party. From what she'd heard, she was glad to miss it. There was nothing worse than partying with a group of entitled pricks with more money than sense.

It was obvious Will's attire hadn't been chosen by his mother, as his outfit was nothing like his father's. His father wore a tailored, three-piece tweed suit, whereas Will dressed in navy chinos and a half-zip sweater, the collar of a check shirt visible beneath.

Country boy chic.

He'd slicked back his mousy brown hair, which was poker straight and entirely unremarkable, much like everything else about him. He was dead behind his pale chestnut eyes, and she would describe his jawline as weak. His shoulders sloped, and she knew without seeing it that he was pigeon chested. He was the definition of S.D.E—small dick energy.

She plastered on a smile. 'Sorry, Will. Please, do go on.'

Sorry, Will. Please, go fuck yourself.

He cleared his throat. 'I was asking what it is you're doing down in London. You're spending a lot of time there.' His tight-lipped smile contradicted his attempt at a breezy tone.

Jess could read between the lines. His nose was out of joint because she hadn't made herself available for his party. Gossip said they were an item, and as such was expected to show her face at such a big event.

'Some clients have hired me to curate art for a new boutique hotel they're opening soon. They want to support local artists, so I'm having to spend a lot of time there.' She kept her tone neutral and devoid of the excitement and pride she felt at her achievements. It wouldn't do well to let these people know how much she loved her job. They'd only use that against her somehow.

He scrunched up his face. 'It's nice to have a hobby, I suppose.'

Her mother's glare told her to keep her mouth shut. She took a sip of her water and considered her response. Opting for an easy life, she pushed aside her fantasy of throwing her drink over him. 'Oh, it's not a hobby. It's my career.'

A condescending smile crept across his face. 'Well, I guess you should enjoy it while you can.' He looked over at his father as they smirked at each other.

Her blood heated as the rage simmered under the surface. 'Oh? Is there a time limit on my career?'

Will shrugged. 'Well, I assume you won't have time for it, you know, once you're married and all that.'

Was he putting on the hoity-toity accent, or did he always speak like that? She hadn't paid attention to anything he'd said before, but he had her full attention now. 'Wha—'

'Shall we go through to the parlour for some sherry?' Georgina piped up, clearly not wanting Jess to cause a scene. Before Jess could respond, the others had thrown their napkins to the table and were ready to leave.

'Jess, will you take a walk with me around the grounds? I'd like to talk?' Will's mouth said talk, his eyes said grope. He lowered his voice and said, 'Come on, you know we need to play the game, keep the olds happy.'

'Oh, what a lovely idea. You two go along, although we can't promise to save you any petits fours.' Georgina's forced laugh sounded like nails being dragged on a chalkboard. Jess knew full well that her mother didn't eat the delicate sweet treats their chef prepared, but you could be damn sure that Jess would be sneaking into the kitchen to polish them off as soon as she got out of her ridiculously restrictive outfit.

Jess faced Will as he leant his elbow on the back of his chair, his free hand in his pocket like he was posing for a magazine shoot for *'Britain's Rich & Desperate.'* Christ, this pathetic excuse for a man wasn't even the worst her mother had tried to set her up with. 'Come on, then.'

As they reached the door out onto the lawn, Jess kicked off her heels and slid her feet into her sliders. Sensing she was going to feel uncomfortable for this part of the evening, the least she could do was limit some of the pain.

She hoped to God he was going to keep his hands to himself.

Little Willy: Jessica, thank you for last night. It was a surprisingly enjoyable evening. I have some advice for you. Play along. Our lives will be a lot easier when our parents aren't breathing down our necks.

CHAPTER 2

JESS

The Boy Is Mine (a-cappella) - Ariana Grande

Sarah: How's it going at home?

Jess: As expected.

Sarah: I'm scared to ask…

Jess: For today's Sunday Lunch I will be entertaining Will Wilberforce and his parents, again.

Sarah: Is Will at least hot?

Jess: You have a one-track mind.

Sarah: I do, but I love the track it's on. Answer the question.

Jess: He's one of the better ones. He's wearing clothes from this decade at least.

Sarah: There you go! It's not all bad then. I hope it goes okay. Only a week before you're back.

Jess: Counting down the days...

Jess sighed as she pocketed her phone and strolled down to her mother's stables. The air was crisp, and the morning dew darkened her chocolate brown nubuck riding boots.

This was her favourite time of day. The house staff were busy getting ready for Sunday lunch. Her mother was at the local spa for her regular treatments, and her father was playing golf. Her shoulders relaxed and her breathing evened out.

After the predicted scolding from her mother about manners, she waited for her parents to retire to their rooms—that's right, rooms. Plural. They slept apart. Romance was dead and buried in her family home—and made a beeline for the kitchen. The chef knew Jess all too well and had left a plate of petits fours out on the large marble island that dominated the room. He'd also prepared her a steak sandwich with the leftovers, and as she was wearing her elasticated waisted pjs, she had no problem polishing them off with a large glass of chilled milk on the side.

What Georgina didn't know wouldn't hurt her.

But her mother's voice was never far from her mind.

You'll get fat if you eat all that.
No one will want you if you let yourself go.
Your job is to look pretty and marry well.

So, here she was on a Sunday morning getting ready to ride out her frustration and burn some calories on her favourite horse, Teddy. He belonged to her mother. All the horses in the stables belonged to her mother, but she didn't like to ride. As with all things Georgina Chatwin, they were for show.

The Earl that lived locally was re-homing Teddy, as he didn't have what it took to make it on the racing circuit. Jess could relate to that. Bred for a task and found lacking. She fell in love instantly and convinced her mother to take him in. To have a horse from the Earl's famous bloodline of racehorses would make her look good at the tennis club. So, it was a done deal.

Plumes of steam billowed out of his nostrils as he huffed a hello. He rested his head on her shoulder as she tickled his neck. 'Good morning, gorgeous boy. Are you happy to see me?'

He grunted as he nudged at her shoulder. 'Come on, let's get you saddled up. I want a long hack today. I hope you've had your fill of hay this morning.'

As she got Teddy ready for the ride and strapped her helmet on, she reflected on her texts with Sarah. She longed to be back with her friends. They'd all been through their fair share of shit, and yet they'd come out the other side happier and stronger for it. In her opinion, they had it all: loved unconditionally by hot men, money, successful careers, and beautiful to boot. She'd socialised with some of the country's wealthiest people and yet she never saw such pure happiness as she did when she spent time with her friends.

Since being hired by Steele Interiors—the company run by her friend Lucy, a fellow member of the book club—she felt like she belonged somewhere and had a purpose in life. Lucy's clients, the Lombardis, respected her opinions and were so impressed with her standards they hired her to revamp their personal art collection. So why didn't she feel happy?

Maybe she didn't deserve happiness. Maybe she was a murderer in a past life and this was her punishment. Forced to breed with the toffs of Britain. That didn't feel right, but how else could she explain the card she'd been dealt?

And then she felt like a total dick.

'Oh, poor little rich girl. Daddy doesn't love you enough, but you live in a country manor, on acres of land with a stable full of pure-bred horses. What a pity,' she mumbled as she checked the straps on the saddle for the last time. Teddy nudged his nose at the pocket of her jacket, knowing full well she always had a packet of mints for him. She pulled out the packet, ripped it open and placed a chalky sweet in her hand. His mouth tickled her palm as he gently took it from her. 'Right, time to stop moping. Let's clear away some cobwebs.'

As she walked him out of the stables and around to the mounting block, she felt like maybe life wasn't so bad.

'Welcome everyone, to the grand opening of Luxe. We'd like to thank you all for attending. Your support is so important to us.' Charlotte Lombardi stood mid-way up the stairs that led out of the main foyer of the hotel. Her sexy Italian husband, Rob, was close by, a look of pure admiration and love in his eyes.

'We must also thank the exceptionally talented people at Steele Interiors and Spencer and Black Associates. Without you, this wouldn't have been possible. There aren't a lot of building and design companies out there that can take the visions of two kinky buggers and turn them into a reality. So, let's raise our glasses and say cheers to them.'

Jess raised her glass of champagne in a toast and cast her eye around the room full of people as Charlotte continued her speech. She spotted Sarah leaning into her boyfriend while they exchanged hushed words.

James Spencer was one half of Spencer and Black Associates and Sarah's new Dom and soulmate. A warm sensation filled her heart as she saw him reach up and tuck her auburn curls behind her ear as he whispered something to her. Sarah had been through so much and to see her glow with happiness was amazing. She was truly happy for her friend but couldn't help but wonder if she'd ever find such happiness herself.

She noticed a few party guests taking photos of the artwork that hung on the walls. Artwork that she handpicked to reflect the theme of every room in the hotel. Pride swelled in her chest and pushed out any feelings of longing for love. She could make her own happiness. Her focus would be on building a name for herself in the art world. She didn't have time for a man, anyway.

'Hey, you. You look deep in thought.' Jess turned to face Imogen, who'd joined her in the corner. She looked as stunning as ever. Her chestnut hair fell in loose waves, framing her face, accentuating her rich, chocolate brown eyes. Her style echoed the Art Deco theme of the hotel perfectly, like she'd picked out the fitted silk dress to match the colour of the emerald-green walls. The Bardot neckline showed off her ample breasts and peachy skin.

'I was just taking a moment. I rarely get to spend the evening surrounded by people appreciating the artwork I source.' Her eyes lit up as she smiled at her friend.

'It feels good, doesn't it? You should be proud of what you've achieved. The pieces are stunning.'

Jess wasn't very good at accepting praise. It wasn't something she was used to. Throughout her life, every accomplishment was met with a comment from her father about how she could do better. But she was determined not to think about her parents while she was away from home. That was future Jess's problem.

'Thanks, hun.' She looked over Imogen's shoulder. 'Where's Cam?' Cameron Black was the other half of Spencer and Black Associates and Imogen's husband. Their path to each other had been traumatic and ended with Cameron fighting for his life in hospital after being stabbed by Imogen's ex-boyfriend. Love conquered evil, and in the words of Beyoncé, Cam put a ring on it.

'He's grabbing us all another drink. We're letting our hair down tonight, Jess, so make sure you have a great time.' Her eyes glinted with excitement.

His ears must have been burning as before Jess could respond, a fresh glass of champagne appeared in front of her face. 'Here you go, ladies. The good news is that James and Sarah aren't drinking; he has a surprise in store for her tonight, which means more for us.' Cameron wiggled his eyebrows as he wrapped his arm around Imogen's shoulders. Jess guessed that surprise involved a trip to their favourite kink club.

Jess loved her friends, but her heart ached for what they had.

She downed her glass of champagne, discarded the empty and brought her fresh glass to her lips. Tonight, she was drowning her mixed emotions. She was full of pride, jealousy, and mourning the life she was missing out on.

'My goodness. It must be our lucky night. Look what the cat dragged in.' Cam raised his glass to someone on the other side of the room. Jess leaned around him to see what all the fuss was about. Her breath caught in her throat at the man who'd just walked in. The rest of the room seemed to blur into the background as her gaze zeroed in on the large, imposing frame.

Julian was Cameron's cousin, and he didn't skip the line when the family's hotness genes were handed out. In fact, she was sure he got in line twice. He was at least six foot four inches tall, the tallest out of their group of friends, and as her aunt always used to say, 'built like a brick shithouse.'

God rest her soul.

His hair was the same rich dark brown as Cameron's, but was longer and sat in dishevelled waves. A five o'clock shadow gave him a gritty look and his simple outfit of a white shirt and black trousers gave away the fact he'd come straight from the restaurant he co-owned with Cameron.

Cameron was a silent partner, leaving the running of the restaurant to Julian. Which, she assumed, suited Julian just fine, as it had been quite apparent to Jess when she first met him, he preferred to be in control. He worked tirelessly to ensure the standards of his restaurant were impeccable. Every dish they turned out was worthy of a Michelin star.

Jess first met Julian at a dinner party hosted by Cameron, and she was instantly attracted to him. How could she not be? He was beautiful. Chiselled to perfection. There was a spark between them that excited her.

He asked her out on a date, but it didn't amount to much when Jess's parents dragged her back home and Julian worked every hour available. There wasn't room for a relationship to blossom, but that didn't stop him from taking her breath away and causing an aching between her legs that crippled her.

Their eyes met as he made his way over to Charlotte Lombardi. She watched as he greeted her like an old friend, a kiss gently pressed on each of her cheeks. Charlotte gripped his upper arm as she spoke to him. Jess felt ridiculous at the sudden pang of jealously that shot through her.

What the fuck was wrong with her tonight? She hated that she'd been reduced to wallowing in self-pity, feeling jealous of her friends, and now she was jealous of a woman touching a man that wasn't hers.

'Hey, Jess. You doing okay?' Imogen's eyes were full of concern as she turned her attention away from Julian.

'I'm good. Really. I just wasn't mentally prepared for how hot he'd look tonight.' She pressed a palm to her forehead. 'Christ, he's rolled his shirtsleeves up, Jen. How is a single female meant to resist that? Have you seen his forearms? He should have to carry a licence to have those out in public.'

Imogen's soft laughter filled the space. 'That is true. He wins the forearms competition.'

'I'll pretend I didn't hear you talking like that about my cousin.' Cam said with a smile. 'I think you two would make a great couple, Jess. Want me to sack him from the restaurant so he has more time on his hands?'

'Who's getting sacked?' A head popped up behind Cam, making Jess and Imogen jump.

'Bloody hell, James. You scared me.' Imogen's hand flew to her chest as she gripped onto her glass of champagne with the other.

'Sorry. I just wanted to let Jess know not to expect Sarah home anytime soon. Will you be okay getting home?'

'Of course. Have a great time.' She was looking forward to having some time to herself back at Sarah's apartment. Jess had been living with Sarah while she was working in London on the hotel project, and she'd got used to the freedom it afforded her, but it wasn't often she was there on her own. In one way or another, there was always someone around.

'Great. Now tell me, who's getting sacked?' James glanced around the circle they'd formed, a look of intrigue on his face.

'No one. Cam was just offering to sack Julian so I could go on a date with him. Bit extreme, so I politely declined.' Jess raised a mocking brow and smiled at Cameron, who winked in response as he sipped from his glass.

Jess wasn't aware of the rest of the conversation. She nodded along at what she hoped was at the right times, her attention firmly back on Julian, who was now talking to Sarah.

Was it a coincidence every time she looked his way, their eyes met? And did she imagine the hungry look in his eyes? She felt like prey with the way he fixated on her. Her skin prickled, the tiny hairs standing on end and her heart raced like it was getting ready to run. And that was nothing to what was happening in her knickers. She shifted her feet to dispel the inappropriately timed arousal. It wasn't successful.

She couldn't explain or understand the effect this man had on her, and that made her situation worse. Growing up, she'd never wanted for anything, her parents buying her everything in place of love, and yet she couldn't have the one thing she desired now. This was too cruel.

James slapped Cam on the back. 'Right, I'm off to work the room. Cam, I think you should do the same. We can drum up a lot of business tonight. These guests are loving what we've done with the place.' James may be the joker of the pack, but he was passionate about his business and worked hard. He'd earned every award and deserved the success. The excitement in his eyes brought a smile to Jess's face.

'Agreed. See you ladies later.' Cam pressed his lips to Imogen's temple before strolling off into the crowd.

Imogen watched her husband saunter off while chewing her lip. She snapped out of her dreamy expression and announced, 'I need the loo. I'll be back in a second.' Before Jess could offer to join her, she'd vanished. The reason for her sharp exit became abundantly clear as Julian approached.

'Hi.' One word. All he said was one word, and her legs felt weak. His voice was deep and smooth, but with a raspiness as if he'd recently woken up. Her mind drifted to how he'd look first thing in the morning, sleep-mussed and groggy. She bet he still looked perfect.

'Hi, Julian. How are you?' Her voice came out higher than normal. She cleared her throat, hoping he didn't notice.

He slipped a hand into the pocket of his trousers. 'I'm doing well, thank you. The restaurant's great, but I'm still getting grief from Cam about dropping my hours.' He shrugged. 'Same old, same old. I love what you've done with the art here. Charlotte's very impressed. Apparently, a few of the guests have already made her offers to take some of it home with them.'

Her eyes widened. 'Really? That's insane. Maybe I should work the room too.' She looked around, chewing her lip, feeling torn. It would be a prime opportunity to attract new clients, but she didn't want to leave Julian.

'I wouldn't worry. There's a stack of your business cards on the reception desk and people are grabbing them like hot cakes. Your work speaks for itself. I'd love it if you worked your magic at the restaurant.'

Her spine straightened as she glanced over in the direction of the reception desk, and her cheeks heated at the prospect of working with Julian.

'I'd love to. Let me know when.' She cast her eyes down as she said, 'It'd be nice to see you.'

Christ, she really was lonely and desperate, and now she'd advertised the fact.

'Tonight is your lucky night. Sarah has kindly put me in charge of getting you home safely.'

'She did what?' Oh, God, that was embarrassing. 'I can look after myself.' She willed her cheeks to stop flushing. The heat radiating off them was a dead giveaway.

'I think it's safe to say she had an ulterior motive.' His eyes softened as they flicked between hers. 'Our friends won't rest until we're married off.'

She shook her head and sighed. 'It seems everyone is looking to marry me off.'

He crouched slightly, bringing himself to eye level with her. 'Hey, I was only joking. I feel like I've hit a nerve there. Do you want to talk about it?' Up close he was simply stunning, from his chiselled cheekbones to his strong jawline darkened with stubble. Julian's colourings were almost identical to Cameron's, but being this close to him, his eyes—solely focused on hers—let her see the flecks of gold that caught the light.

She breathed in his scent, clean and fresh and deliciously masculine. What she wouldn't give to have one night with him; the things she'd let him do. Her hand rested at the base of her throat as her fingers stroked along her collarbone before squashing that train of thought. She didn't need another complication in her life. It was useless anyway. Someone like Julian would never live up to her parents' expectations. That was another reason she hadn't tried to take their friendship any further. A restaurant manager wasn't good enough for a daughter of the Chatwins, even if he did co-own it. He knew nothing about banking, and she assumed he knew less about horses. He wasn't featured in Britain's most eligible bachelor list, and he certainly didn't have any royal connections. Not that she knew of, anyway. But she couldn't admit her parents' exacting standards to anyone.

If her friends knew the real reason she was still single, they'd disown her for her family's prejudice and snobbery alone. Sarah knew some of what Jess had to put up with, but she kept so much to herself. Her family embarrassed her, and that ate away at her. The last thing she wanted to do was subject Julian to her vacuous parents and their narcissism.

She blinked, hiding the sorrow from her eyes and pasted on a smile, wafting her hand through the air. 'Oh, no, I'm fine. My parents are just hassling me about settling down.' It was only a white lie.

He nodded as he straightened. 'My parents gave up on that a long time ago. They soon realised their nagging only made me do the exact opposite. You'll know when you find the right person, and that's not something to rush, or force.' He looked around the room where people had moved into the main function room where the Lombardis had moved all the tables to the side and turned the space into a disco, complete with a flashing dancefloor. Jess's favourite. 'How about we join the others and dance our troubles away?'

She'd never seen Julian dance before, but it was an offer too good to refuse. She nodded in agreement as he linked his arm with hers. 'Let's go have some fun.'

CHAPTER 3

JULIAN

Living Proof - Bon Jovi

Jess paused in the car seat with her hand on the handle as she said, 'Thank you for giving me a lift home.' Julian had danced the night away with Jess, but made sure his hands remained in a platonic position. The desire to grip her hips, her arse, and pull her body into his was torture, but apparently, he was a masochist as he kept up the pretence of friendship all night long.

In a past life, he'd become an expert at reading a woman's body language, and he had an inkling she was holding back on him, too. Her pulse visibly throbbed in her neck and her nipples were pert under her simple yet elegant dress. He desperately wanted to know what sound she'd make if he were to tweak one, maybe bite down on it and make her scream. But that was Julian from the past. Chloe, his ex, had made sure that version of himself was firmly locked away. He couldn't afford for him to come out to play.

'You're more than welcome. Wait there.' He rounded the car and opened the door for her. 'Allow me to walk you to your door.' She took his outstretched hand as she glanced up at her apartment. Her hand felt so small, so fragile in his.

'That's very gentlemanly of you, but it's only just there.' She pointed with her free hand. Her head volleyed between him and her apartment, as if weighing up her options. 'Unless you'd like to come up… for a drink?'

He wanted so much more than a drink, but he wasn't right for Jess. He could never be the man she deserved. It wasn't a secret that her parents had high hopes for her future husband, that much he'd gleaned from how Sarah would talk about them, and while in the future he might tick their boxes, he wasn't the right man for her.

'I would love to, but I agreed to meet the boys for breakfast in the morning and I'm exhausted.' The disappointment on her face crushed him. He didn't want her to think he didn't like her that way, but maybe that was for the best. 'Apparently, I've neglected them recently, so I'm booked into a hotel tonight. I need to get there to check in before the desk closes.' She nodded in understanding, but the ache in his heart remained.

As they took the few steps up to the main door to Sarah's apartment, Jess said, 'You should have got a room at Luxe. It's crazy that we've just spent the night there at the opening party and you're staying somewhere else.'

'Yeah, well, Charlotte tried to get me to stay, but I wanted somewhere quieter.' He didn't want to explain that he tried not to associate with the Lombardis and their like anymore. His days of running around with the kink community were over.

He leaned against the stone wall and stuffed his hands into his pockets. He found himself doing that a lot around Jess. It was the only way to stop himself from reaching out and running his fingers through her enticing silky blonde hair. A strand always seemed to be loose, goading him to reach over and tuck it behind her ear.

He loved her long, blonde locks and was mildly disappointed when she cut it shorter. Images of him wrapping it around his fist flashed in his mind, like it did every morning in the shower. If only she knew how many times she'd featured in his fantasies while he stroked his cock.

He cleared his throat as he turned his mind to other thoughts. It wouldn't do well for her to see his growing erection while he was trying to act like he wasn't interested.

'I hadn't realised you knew Rob and Charlotte.' She shook her head. 'What a small world. How is it that you know them?' She clasped her hands in front of her, letting her small clutch bag dangle from her wrist. She'd made no move to get her keys from the bag, like she was interested in what he had to say, and was in no rush to leave him.

He shrugged. 'They were good friends with an ex of mine. We used to see each other a lot at parties and stuff. I didn't feel right mixing with them after we broke up. Charlotte convinced me to go to the hotel opening, and since it was you guys who worked on the hotel, I couldn't really refuse. It's the first time I've seen them since…' He didn't want to get into that right now. 'Well, just in a long time.'

Jess nodded her head before taking her keys from her bag, looping the keyring over her thumb and flicking them back and forth. 'I get that. The benefit of never having a boyfriend is that I don't have to deal with all the shit that goes with a breakup. Was it a bad break up?' She blinked rapidly as she blurted, 'Bugger. Sorry. I shouldn't have asked that. It's none of my business. You don't have to answer that.' She looked absolutely mortified.

He didn't want to answer the question, but he also didn't want her feeling bad. 'Don't worry about it. It was just one of those things, you know? She loved to play hard to get until she discovered it was the thrill of the chase she wanted and not the man that came with it.' That was all he could say. Hopefully, it was enough.

Her perfect button nose crinkled. 'Ah. That is a bit shit.'

He laughed, scratching at his jaw. 'You could say that.'

'Well, I guess I'd better let you go and get your beauty sleep before your breakfast date with the boys. I wouldn't want to be responsible for you turning into a beast.' Her eyes flashed wide.

How little did she know how close to the truth she was. 'It's been great to see you, Jess.' He stepped closer and she wrapped her arms around him. It took him a second to comprehend what to do, but he recovered quickly and draped an arm around her bare shoulders. He pressed a kiss to the crown of her head and inhaled the floral scent of her, committing the aroma to memory. Roses, lavender, and sunshine.

It was over too soon as she stepped back. 'Thanks for being such a gent, Jay. I'll see you soon.'

He watched as she crossed the threshold, wiggled her fingers in a small wave, and closed the door behind her. He stayed staring at the door for a few seconds, not really sure why. Maybe he thought she'd open it again and come running into his arms like in the movies, but his life wasn't like that.

He wasn't sure what woke him up, the raging hard on or his phone alarm. Either way, he was awake, erect, and full of pent-up energy. He dressed quickly into his gym gear, stuffed his feet into his trainers, and made his way down to the hotel gym. That was another reason for not staying at the Luxe the night before. They didn't have a gym. The facilities at Luxe catered for a very different style of physical exercise and, as he was no longer partaking in that part of his life, he opted to work out his frustration in the gym.

He put in his earbuds, already blasting his favourite playlist, and turned the treadmill on. As he built up a steady rhythm, he felt his brain switch off as it focused on the pounding of his feet on the rubber conveyor. He tapped at the control screen, increasing the speed until he maxed out. His muscles screamed, drowning out the thoughts of Jess whirring around his mind.

When his body couldn't give anymore, he slowed down to a steady jog. Sweat poured from his skin, his clothes clung to every muscle as he towelled down the machine and made his way to the weights. It would never be enough, though. His body always craved more of what he refused to give it.

'Here he is. We took the liberty of ordering you a full English. Hope that's okay?' Cameron clapped Julian on the back as he joined them at their table in the greasy spoon cafe that was untouched by London tourists. It served the best cooked breakfasts in the city.

'That's perfect, thanks, Cam. Did you all have a good night?' He took his seat and gulped down the bog standard black filter coffee that was waiting for him.

Tom nodded over to James, who was sitting with a glazed expression. 'This one had one hell of a night. He hasn't been able to wipe that smirk off his face or form a coherent sentence all morning.' He combed his fingers through his dirty blond hair as he winked over at James. 'It's safe to say he won't forget last night for a long time, if ever.'

Julian knew all too well how a good night in a kink club could change a man's life. And not always for the better. 'I'm happy for you, mate. But feel free to spare me the details.'

'Oh, come on, Jay. You know you want to hear all about how James got fuc—' Before Cameron could finish his sentence, plates of deliciousness were placed on the table. Julian spent the majority of his time serving haute cuisine to discerning customers, but in his opinion, you couldn't beat a perfectly cooked sausage.

'Here you go, lads. Four breakfasts with all the trimmin's. Enjoy,' said the waitress as she stepped back. The four of them had been coming here for as long as they could remember, and the same cockney lady served their breakfast every time.

'Would you mind not blurting out the private things Sarah and I got up to last night in the middle of a cafe?' James had come out of his stupor, no doubt roused by the smell of the perfectly cooked greasy fry-up in front of him. Cameron rolled his eyes as he tucked into his food.

Julian wasn't interested in the details, he only had one thing on his mind. 'How was Sarah this morning?' He kept his eyes on his plate, slicing bacon and dipping it in the yolk of his fried egg. He didn't mean Sarah; he wanted to know how Jess was, but couldn't risk being so blatant. He'd never hear the end of it.

'Knackered. We got back to her place early this morning so I left her sleeping. Last night was epic, but fuck me, do I ache.' James rolled his shoulders as he slathered his sausage in ketchup.

Tom leant back in his chair. 'She and James had an evening with Mrs Jones last night.'

'Mrs Jones? She works at Katia's club, right?' Julian had heard Tom talking about her before.

James gulped his coffee and said, 'Yeah. She's the Den Mother and a Dominatrix. She's been mentoring Sarah. She challenged me in a Dom competition and I lost. She ended up domming all of us, her sub, Roxy included. It was fucking hot. Turns out I'm a switch and I love group scenes.' He slowly shook his head in wonder. 'Mate, I did some crazy shit last night.'

'James, you're always doing some crazy shit.' Cameron laughed.

'You know what I mean. Sure, I've had threesomes with other women before, but this was different. It was hardcore.' He looked around and leaned in closer to the others. Lowering his voice, he asked, 'Any of you ever have your prostate milked? That shit is insane.'

Julian looked down at his eggs and pushed the plate away having lost his appetite. 'Mate, I'm thrilled for you, I really am, but I do not need to hear about your prostate being milked while I'm eating.' Julian was no prude, but he had his limits.

'Oh, sorry. Good point. I won't say another word.' James's glazed expression returned to his face while everyone focused on the food in front of them.

Tom wiped his mouth with his paper napkin and asked, 'How did it go with Jess last night? Sorry we bailed on you. Lucy was knackered.'

'Don't think I didn't know what you were all up to.' It was painfully obvious to Julian that his friends were relentlessly trying to set him up with Jess. He couldn't even be mad at them for it; she was perfect. Cameron, Imogen, Tom, and Lucy all made their excuses fairly early on in the evening, leaving Julian alone with Jess on the dancefloor. He wasn't usually one to dance, but it was the only way he could think of being close to Jess without having to find conversation topics that didn't revolve around how much he craved her.

Cam held his hands up in surrender. 'Hey, Imogen was genuinely tired. Her hormones are all over the place since she came off the pill, and it's knocking her for six. Women have it rough, you know?' He bowed his head. 'I'm exhausted and I'm just on the sidelines. Can you all keep your fingers crossed that my boys do their job soon?'

'Good luck, mate.' Tom patted Cameron on the shoulder. 'You'll get there in the end. You just wait until pregnancy hormones kick in. Then you'll be fucked, and not in a good way.'

Cameron groaned as James's attention turned back to Julian. 'Don't think you're off the hook with all this baby talk. What happened with you and Jess?'

'Nothing. We danced. We drank. I took her home and went back to my hotel room… alone.' He missed off the part about him being erect for the entire drive across the city and having to sort himself out in the shower—twice—before he had any chance of falling asleep. And then he dreamt of Jess, on her knees begging for more.

Shit. He was getting hard again.

'I'm disappointed in you mate, you missed your opportunity there.' James raised his brows and pursed his lips.

'All right, guys. You can stop meddling in my private life now.' He appreciated the gesture, but it only served to rub it in his face. He wanted her. He couldn't have her. Simple as that.

'We're worried about you. You've not been with anyone since Chloe.' Cameron paused, as if realising he needed to tread carefully. 'I hate to see you alone because of that woman.'

'I'm not alone because of that woman. I'm alone because I'm busy running our successful restaurant.' He allowed a flash of anger before cooling it. Cameron was looking out for him like he'd done ever since they were little. He just didn't know all the details.

'You can't keep using that excuse. The restaurant is doing so well that it's a licence to print money. You can afford the best staff and yet you insist on being there all the time. You need to start living your life again.' Cameron lowered his voice. 'You can't keep living in the past. Chloe is out of your life now and you need to let it go.'

Julian ground his jaw, pissed off that he'd been called out on his bullshit excuses. Cameron was right; he'd put all his efforts into the restaurant and hidden away from the world. He didn't want to get hurt again.

Couldn't get hurt again.

From an early age, Julian knew he was different from the other boys at school. Different to Cameron. His favourite playground game was Kiss Chase. The girls would always ask him to play because he was so good at it. He loved to chase them. To hear them squeal and run was exhilarating. He liked to chase them into the playing fields and let them hide in the bushes. Nothing made him feel more alive than when he'd jump out in front of them when they thought the coast was clear.

The other boys would try to catch the girls as quickly as possible, just to get to the kiss. The kiss itself usually consisted of a quick peck on the cheek with everyone goading them on. Girls were, after all, smelly and annoying at eleven years old. But not to Julian. He wanted to prolong the chase for as long as possible. His heart would be ready to explode before he caught them. Kissing them wasn't the priority. Instead, he'd wrap his arms around them and swing them around until they were laughing too hard to speak.

The kissing came later.

Chloe liked the thrill of the chase. She pushed Julian to go further, to be rougher. He explained his limits and discussed safe words, but it wasn't enough for her. He refused to give in to her demands, and she thought she was ready to find what she wanted elsewhere.

She misjudged. But he couldn't think about that now.

Julian blamed himself, and she let him. Before he knew what was happening, she was bad-mouthing him to anyone who'd listen. He shut himself away, removing himself from the scene. He focused on the restaurant. He needed to keep his mind and body busy. If he was left to his own devices for too long, his needs and desires would creep back in. And he couldn't have that. He couldn't risk failing someone he loved ever again, so, it was easier to never love again.

He looked around the table at his friends. All of them had women in their lives who had suffered heartbreak and trauma. They understood what it meant to be vulnerable and how hard it was to trust someone again, but he couldn't tell them the extent of what he'd been through. What he blamed himself for.

He'd head back to the restaurant and try to put thoughts of Jess aside.

The problem was, like a pressure cooker, at some point he was likely to explode.

CHAPTER 4

JESS

Smile - Christina Perri

'What are you staring at?' Curled up in a ball on her sofa, Sarah cradled a cup of tea in her hands. Her unruly copper-coloured curls resembled a bird's nest, and her cheeks were glowing. She blinked at Jess, waiting for a response.

'I'm just processing. Did you really let Roxy ride James's face while you rode his ding-a-ling?'

Sarah nearly spat her tea out, catching herself so only a dribble escaped her mouth. She swallowed before blurting, 'Ding-a-ling? What are you, twelve? I rode his cock, Jess. I rode it like a jockey at the Grand National, let me tell you.'

Jess shivered in mock horror and covered her ears. 'Please make it stop. Please make it stop.' She burst into laughter as Sarah threw one of the many cushions at her. 'James is officially a client of mine now, Sarah. I can't think about his dick. From now on, we'll have to use ding-a-ling.'

'Hun, his cock is a pierced masterpiece. There is no way I'm referring to it like that. Anyway, believe it, baby. Last night happened and I can't wait to do it again. It's amazing how he's adapted to Dom life. He's a natural. But when Mrs Jones asked if he'd switch and let her lead the scene, well, it was amazing.' Sarah's eyes misted over as she looked off into the distance. Jess sat in silence, waiting for her friend's moment to be over.

Sarah eventually shook her head, blinked, and said, 'Anyway, it's safe to say we're hooking up with Mrs Jones and Roxy again soon.'

She took a sip of her tea. 'You haven't told me how it went with Julian last night. Did you get on okay?'

Jess was surprised it had taken as long as it had for Sarah to start the inquisition. Mrs Jones must have really done a number on her. She tucked her hair behind her ears. 'We had a very pleasant evening, thank you. Surprisingly, he asked if I wanted to dance. I don't think we left that dance floor all evening.'

Sarah grabbed another cushion and hugged it to her chest. 'Oh, tell me more. Did you do some dirty dancing?' She wiggled her eyebrows suggestively.

'No. He was the perfect gentleman. He's a great dancer, actually. Astonishingly supple hips for a man of his size. His hands didn't stray to my arse once.' Much to her disappointment.

Sarah fiddled with the zip on the cushion. 'Oh. That's a shame. I was really hoping that leaving you two alone in a kink hotel would get the ball rolling.'

'Honestly, you all need to give up on us. You know he wouldn't survive two minutes with my parents. It wouldn't be right of me to start something with him that couldn't go anywhere.'

Sarah tapped her fingertips against her lips and avoided eye contact.

'Go on. Say it. I know you're dying to.' Jess crossed her arms across her chest, preparing for the truth bomb.

'I'm massively overstepping, so I'm not sure I should say it.'

Jess let out a guffaw. 'When has that ever stopped you?' Nerves fluttered as she wondered what Sarah was about to say. Her best friend had never been backward about coming forward and the fact she was second-guessing if she should speak up had her worried.

'Okay, I'll say it but will caveat it by reminding you it's coming from a place of love.'

'Just get on with it.' Jess rolled eyes.

'When are you going to tell your parents to fuck off and start living your life for you? Your father pretends like you don't exist most of the time, and your mother wouldn't know what maternal instinct was if it punched her in the face.' Sarah cast her eyes to the floor and lowered her voice. 'And I really wish it would punch her in the face.'

Jess's eyebrows rose as her head reared back. 'Shit. You didn't hold back at all on that one.' Jess knew her friend was right, but the words stung. She lived knowing that she wasn't good enough, but to hear that it's obvious to others felt like a punch to the gut.

'I'm sorry, hun. I want what's best for you, and I think living at home isn't it. Why don't you move here with me and tell your parents to go fuck themselves?'

As tempting as it was, she knew her parents would find a way to get her to move back home. They had a hold on her she couldn't explain, and it drove her insane. 'That's a great suggestion and all, but what about when you move in with James? You won't need this apartment and James won't keep on paying for it if you're not in it.'

Sarah pouted. 'He might. And who's to say I'm moving in with James? It's still early days between us.'

Jess rested her elbow on the back of the sofa, her head in her palm. 'I can guarantee you'll be moving in with him in a matter of weeks. As soon as you've tied up everything here, you'll be in his bed quicker than I can say ding-a-ling. It's fine, honestly. I can take care of myself. I've done a good job of putting off the suitors they keep bringing over for lunch. I'll work my charm, or lack thereof, on Will and he'll get bored and leave me alone. Then I'll have some respite for a few months while my parents start the process over again. Eventually they'll get the message and leave me alone… or die.' Jess grabbed her mug of tea and blew across its surface as if she didn't have a care in the world.

Sarah's jaw dropped as her eyes bugged out of her head. 'Jess! Your master plan to get out of this situation really shouldn't be waiting for your parents to die. You'll waste your whole life waiting for that to happen. Why do you keep doing as you're told?'

Jess released a frustrated breath as she gripped her hair at the roots. Every word Sarah spoke was the truth, but she didn't need to hear it. 'Because they're my parents, Sarah. They're the only family I've got.'

After Sarah agreed to stop nagging her—for the time being—Jess packed her bags and boarded the train home.

Jess had refused her parent's offer to have their driver pick her up from the station. That was just another way they'd control what time she travelled back, and she wanted to eke out the last remaining minutes of her freedom.

As she let herself in, the house was blessedly silent. She smiled to herself and took her bags up to her bedroom, relishing the peace and quiet. No doubt her parents had gone their separate ways; her mother to the tennis club or spa and her father to the golf course. She guessed she had a few hours to herself, so she changed into her riding gear and headed outside.

Her mood improved further as she reached the stables. Teddy's head was sticking out of his stable door, and his excited whinnies warmed her heart. At least someone was pleased to see her.

If she moved away from home, she had to consider what to do about Teddy. She couldn't leave him here. He'd go crazy without a daily ride and her mother couldn't care less. The local riding school used the other horses, but they didn't want to use Teddy. He didn't fit the bill. Was it sad her soul mate was a horse?

She rode him out for miles, until her thighs burned, and she'd finished listening to the current book club novel. The escapades of the characters made her laugh out loud and forget her troubles. Who knew a paranormal, why choose with demons, demi-gods, and a dragon shifter could be so hot and hilarious at the same time? She wondered if she should take Sarah up on her offer to go to the kink club and partake in some group action. Maybe she needed to live a little before being forced to fulfil her role. Get enough fabulous cock action in one night, enough to last her a lifetime. Or would that just be setting herself up for a future filled with disappointment?

The signal on her phone was too poor to download the next book in the series, so she turned back home, opting to relax in her jacuzzi bathtub until her fingers and toes wrinkled.

The clip-clopping of Teddy's hooves on the concrete floor of the stables soothed her soul and reminded her of why she kept coming back home. She loved the land her home afforded her. She didn't even mind the smell of horse manure; it was a damn sight better than the shit she had to deal with from her parents.

She gave Teddy a quick brush before settling him back into his stable and topping up his hay. As she said goodbye to him, she overheard someone talking. She put her finger to her lips, telling Teddy to be quiet, and then questioned why she'd done that. He was a horse, for crying out loud.

She recognised the hushed voice as her father on the phone and wondered why the fuck he'd be down here to take a call. The signal was rubbish, for starters.

'Yes, I understand your frustration, Frank, but you know as well as I do that these kids today don't do as they're told. As a nation, we've raised a generation of entitled brats who want everything and give nothing in return.'

He's silent for a few seconds before holding the phone away from his ear, pacing back and forth, pinching the bridge of his nose.

'I'm trying, but she won't co-operate. I blame her friends. They're filling her head with ideas above her station.'

Her heart pounded as she craned her neck trying to get closer to hear more clearly. Was he referring to her? Was he talking to Frank Wilberforce about her?

After another beat of silence, he carried on. 'Have you considered that perhaps Will could work harder to woo her? Would it kill him to make an effort with his appearance when he sees her? He has to make up for his lack of charm somehow.'

He nods as he listens to whatever Frank is saying. 'Yes, but we want her to marry him, Frank, and for that to happen, it would be helpful if she did so willingly.'

She reared back, eyes wide. Holy fuck! They expect her to marry Will-the-wanker Wilberforce. Her father's words faded into the background and all she could hear was the blood pulsing as her heart pounded with anger. She squeezed her eyes shut and focused on her breathing. As she regained her composure, she brought her attention back to the conversation.

'Yes, of course I'm grateful for the upfront investment, Frank. An insurance sector at the bank would indeed be beneficial to us both... Yes, I know she's part of the deal. I'm working on it, okay? I had hoped Georgina's meddling would've produced results by now, but it looks like I'm surrounded by useless women... Yes, Frank, I will get it sorted. One way or another. In the meantime, tell that son of yours he needs to step up his game.'

Jess covered her mouth to stop the gasp escaping her lips. What. The. Actual. Fuck? One way or another? What exactly did he mean by that?

Breathe. Breathe, she repeated as she watched her father hang up. On silent tiptoes, she retreated into the stables as her father made his way up to the house.

Her plans to take a long bath went on the back burner as she chose to take her anger and frustration out on the broom and sweep out the stable block. She didn't want to risk bumping into her father until she'd had time to process what she'd heard and calm down. It wouldn't do her any favours to go storming up to the house in her current state. She needed time to plan how she was going to tackle this.

Jess had always assumed her parents were trying to move themselves up the social ladder with their choice of men they introduced her to. They were all highly regarded and wealthy. But what they also had in common were their business backgrounds. Maybe her parents weren't just trying to marry her off to someone wealthy, they were interviewing for potential investors. She'd never felt more like her father's chattel than she did at this moment. She wasn't his daughter, she was his property. A depreciating asset to be sold while it still held its value. Just the thought of it made her sick to her stomach.

An hour later, the stables were spotless, and her arms ached as much as her thighs. She made her way to the house and quietly walked through the hallways until she was safely ensconced in her bedroom.

After cleaning herself up, wrapped in a fluffy white towel, she stood and surveyed her bedroom. Her mother had chosen everything in there, from the wardrobe of perfectly tailored clothes to the luxurious one-thousand thread count bed sheets. Very little of what she owned reflected who she was. Her parents carefully orchestrated everything to fit with the image they wanted to portray, so it shouldn't come as a shock that they'd map out her future as carefully.

Not feeling hungry, she changed into her pjs and slipped under the covers, balling herself into the foetal position, her knees tightly tucked to her chest. As she lay in the dark, her anger grew into a fiery ball of rage, sitting heavy in her stomach.

The snippets of her father's conversation replayed in her mind as she tried to understand why she was being married off. It had to have something to do with an investment. Perhaps the bank was in trouble? It made sense. The economic climate wasn't great, and horse investors were declining in numbers. People were moving their money to whoever could offer the best returns, and private banks weren't doing so well.

If Frank Wilberforce was willing to invest and bring his insurance company into the mix, that would bolster her father's bank balance and allow him to enter a market that was still doing well. Everyone needed insurance, after all. What she couldn't fathom was why she had to be part of the deal? Was Will in on it, or was he just as much a victim as she was?

She rolled over, relishing the feel of the cold end of the pillow, and as she pressed her face into it, her mind dreamt up every possibility.

Peter Chatwin held two things in high regard: money and appearances. It was obvious now when she thought about it. Chatwins Bank must be close to financial ruin and that would bring shame to his family's name. He would rather sell off his daughter in a business deal than look like a failure.

How could her father stoop that low? He'd never win any awards for his skills as a parent, but she never would have expected this.

What were her options? Should she go along with her father's plans and help save the family business, or should she get out? Take her savings and disappear. She might not like her father very much, but he was the only one she had.

A single tear scorched her face as it slipped down her cheek and soaked into the pillow, no longer cool and comforting below her. It felt like an impossible situation to be in. Was this her chance to finally get her father's approval? She instantly hated herself for thinking that.

She'd never felt wanted growing up, but now he needed her. It didn't feel good, and it came at too high a price, but Jess knew she couldn't walk away from the situation. She didn't see a way out, or a happy future, but for the time being, her life was her own, and she intended to live it.

CHAPTER 5

JULIAN

Monster - Imagine Dragons

Julian rubbed the sleep out of his eyes, clutched his takeaway coffee in one hand, and slid the key into the lock of the restaurant door. They didn't open until the evening service on a Monday, but he wanted to get ahead on the prep and sort out issues with their supply chain. He also didn't want to be alone with his thoughts at home.

And by thoughts, he meant fantasies about Jess. No matter how hard he tried, he couldn't stop thinking about her. Couldn't stop imagining himself sinking his teeth into her delicate neck and leaving his mark.

Fuck. He was hard again.

His dick ached so fucking much. Uncontrollable erections hadn't been a problem for him since he was a teenager. He clenched his jaw as he closed the door behind him and locked it. Anger coursed through his veins that his ex-girlfriend, if he could call her that, had reduced him to a hormonal teenager, unable to get any relief from the overwhelming need to dominate. Punishing workouts and masturbation simply weren't enough to sate the beast.

He brought his cup to his mouth, draining the last of the espresso, throwing the empty in the bin as he walked into his office.

Pausing, he took a moment to relish the silence. He slowed his breathing, trying to switch gears from Jess obsessed to responsible businessman. He savoured this time alone in the restaurant. It wouldn't be long before his team arrived, and the quick, sharp sound of knives hitting chopping boards, clinking cutlery and chatter would fill the empty space, and he wouldn't have time to think, let alone pine for a woman he couldn't have.

He pulled his chair out, sat down, and slid closer to the desk, clicking on his mouse to wake up his computer before he typed in his password. All the while, his dick demanded attention, straining at the zipper of his black trousers, like a pipe about to burst.

He groaned as he rubbed at his crotch, willing it to go down, knowing he was wasting his time. It wasn't going anywhere. Sitting back in his chair, Julian unbuttoned his trousers, and slid the zip down. His dick released itself from his boxer briefs and stood to attention, giving him a moment's relief from the ache that had built up.

Closing his eyes, he pictured Jess in his arms as they danced at the hotel. Her body pressed against his chest, feeling her nipples through her tight dress. He ran his thumb through the pre-cum leaking from him, spreading it over the crown. He tightened his grip and stroked.

'Fuck.' He sucked air in through his teeth as he felt the welcomed pressure building at the base of his spine. He'd make this quick, not wanting to draw it out. It was pointless anyway; the relief would be short-lived.

Nothing satisfied him anymore. Chloe had made sure of that. No longer comfortable running in his usual circles, he'd turned his back on his regular players. As a result, he no longer had a sub. No one to play with. He'd tried going on a date after Chloe. They'd gone back to her place, and to give her credit, she tried everything to bring him pleasure, but in the end, he faked his orgasm and left. He'd made her come three times, so at least his conscience was clear. After that, he knew he'd never find pleasure like he had before.

He couldn't risk getting it wrong again. Couldn't risk choosing the wrong partner.

His imagination was the only place he could be himself. He turned his thoughts back to Jess, but this time, she was running.

Her hair flowing out behind her as she sprinted toward the woodland. Her fevered skin glistened with perspiration and his body thrummed with adrenaline at the thrill of the chase.

'That's right, baby. Head for the trees. I like it when you hide from me.' He muttered the words as he stroked, his pace increasing until he felt his balls tighten and the base of his spine tingle.

He imagined Jess darting between the trees, frantically listening for his approach. She doesn't know he's already there, lurking. He could hear the leaves and fallen branches crunching under her bare feet. The scent of damp soil and moss kicked up from her movements, filling his lungs. Any second now.

His heart thundered as she passed too close to him. He stepped out from his hiding place, a scream tearing from her lips as he wrapped his arms around her shoulders, bringing them crashing to the floor.

He twisted as they fell, taking the brunt of the impact, but he quickly flipped her onto her back, his legs between hers as he tugged her skirt up. Without warning, he ripped her knickers off, yanked open the fly of his trousers releasing his straining cock and slid into her in one quick motion.

He groaned with pleasure as he gripped his dick, imagining how her tight pussy would feel, stroking hard and fast as his muscles tightened and his balls contracted. He covered his crown with his free hand, catching his spend. Panting, he allowed his head to fall back.

Reaching for the tissue box on his desk, he cleaned himself and zipped his trousers. Screwing the tissues into a ball, frustration already creeping its way through his veins like a virus, he carried them through to the bathroom, flushing the evidence of his desperation down the toilet.

Staring at himself in the mirror, he washed his hands.

'Fucking loser.' He gripped the edge of the sink with both hands as he dropped his chin to his chest.

It wasn't enough.

He needed more.

He needed Jess.

'Hey, boss. You're here early.' Julian had been sorting out paperwork in his office for an hour before his door swung open and his head waiter walked in.

'Hey, Sam. You're early yourself.' He looked up from his screen with a smile. Sam was a good guy, dependable. He always turned up to work early, his short black hair always perfectly in place and his face clean shaven. He liked to keep fit and filled his white shirt and black waistcoat well, and his shoes shone with polish. It hadn't escaped Julian's attention that the diners were usually ladies when he was on the lunchtime shift.

'Not early enough, it seems. I was hoping to come in and sort out some of the paperwork for you.' He turned to the door and looked back at Julian.

'Take a seat, Sam. What's on your mind?' Julian could read people like a book, and he knew Sam had something to say.

'Okay.' He took the seat opposite Julian and rubbed his palms on his thighs. 'I'm just going to come straight out and say it.'

His eyebrows bounced as he said, 'Please do.'

'I want more responsibility.'

'Okay. Keep talking.' Julian leaned back and clasped his hands together on his desk.

'I do a good job for you. I've never let you down. You know you can trust me. I graduated top of my class and I think I'm ready for a new challenge. I want to be the assistant manager.'

'You think you're ready, or you know you're ready?' Julian knew he was ready, but he needed to hear him say it.

'I know I'm ready. I've been offered a job at a restaurant in town, but I don't want to leave here. I love working for you and I love how passionate you and everyone else are about this place. I want to be a bigger part of it. I know you struggle to hand over control, but I can't be head waiter forever. I'm going to propose to my girlfriend, and I want to show her I'm worthy.'

Julian waited for Sam to take a breath before speaking, wanting to be sure he'd got everything off his chest. 'Is there anything else you wanted to add?' He had to admit, he was impressed Sam had come to him with this. It would have been easy for him to take the other job, a position that was already waiting for him, instead he came to Julian, determined and prepared, and asked for what he really wanted. Julian could respect that.

Sam shook his head and puffed out a breath. 'No. I think that just about covers it.'

'Okay.' Julian nodded his head.

'Okay? As in, you'll give me a promotion?' Sam gripped the arms of the chair.

'Yes. You're right. I can't afford to lose you. You've been with us from the start, and you've proved yourself many times. Cameron has been nagging me for a while to take a step back, and I've been too stubborn to agree.' Julian walked around his desk to meet Sam and held out his hand. 'Congratulations. You're now officially the Assistant Manager of Four Corners.'

Sam stood as he shook Julian's hand with vigour. 'Wow. Thank you. Thanks. I didn't think it would be that easy.'

Julian laughed. 'I'll sort the paperwork and get your pay rise sorted. How does an extra ten grand suit you?'

'Fuck off.' Sam clapped his hand to his mouth. 'Sorry, boss. What I meant to say was, that is acceptable, thank you.'

Creases formed around Julian's eyes as he smiled his first genuine smile in a long while. 'You're welcome. Your first challenge in your new position is to find out why our lobster supplier hasn't delivered the goods so far today.'

He bowed his head. 'Consider it done.'

'Good. And then you can sort the recruitment for a new waiter.'

As Sam closed his office door, he picked up his phone and dialled Cameron.

'Hey shithead, how are you?' Cameron really needed to drop that nickname.

'I'm good, thanks. I have news.'

'I'm all ears.'

'I've promoted Sam to assistant manager so you can stop nagging me.'

'About bloody time. He's the right man for the job. Does that mean you're going to take my advice and get a life?'

Julian pinched the bridge of his nose. 'Can we take it one step at a time?'

He could hear Cameron sigh before he spoke. 'Do you want me to come meet you for lunch? It's time you told me what happened between you and Chloe.'

He was right. Cameron was always bloody right. He wasn't sure he was ready to tell him everything. He looked up to him like a big brother. They were close, and they'd always been there for each other, but he didn't think anyone would understand what happened, not even him.

'Not today. I've got some shit to sort out here and a new menu to plan.'

'I'm not backing down on this. How about you join me and James tonight? It's been months since you last came to our lads' night and it'll give Sam a chance to manage the restaurant without you breathing down his neck.'

It was clear that Julian wouldn't be able to get out of this. 'Okay. I'll see you tonight,' he said with a resigned sigh, but his lip curled into a half smile. Part of him was happy to be going out.

Cameron's local village pub was quiet even for a Monday night. Their usual table by the fire was available as they placed their orders at the bar. Julian had to admit, it was nice to have a night off and let someone else worry about executing the perfect dinner service.

He was never truly off the clock, though. He caught himself checking out the furniture, thinking that maybe it was time to upgrade his chairs in the restaurant.

He liked the atmosphere of this pub. It was a more relaxed vibe; classy and refined, but not ostentatious. The food was delicious, and the cask ale was poured to perfection. He wondered if he ought to build a bar at the back of his place, offer his patrons a cocktail before they dined.

'Dude, I can see the cogs turning. Stop it. We're here to talk shit and put the world to rights, not pick up business ideas.' James handed Julian his pint of ale and they walked over to their table.

They took their seats, Julian flanked on either side by James and Cameron at the small round table. They sat in silence as they took long swigs of their drinks, the white foam collecting on their top lips.

Cameron closed his eyes and shook his head. 'That hit the spot. I needed that.'

'What's up with you?' Julian couldn't believe that perfect Cameron could ever need a beer.

James laughed. 'Haven't you heard, mate? Jen is running him ragged. They're at it like rabbits. I'm surprised his dick hasn't fallen off.'

Cameron winced. 'Shh. Don't let it hear you talk like that.'

Julian contained his laughter. He was hardly one to talk; his dick wasn't too happy with him either. 'I'm not sure what's worse. Too much sex or not enough.'

'Definitely not enough. Cam is just being weak. There is no such thing as too much sex.' James raised his eyebrows.

Cameron gave James a side eye before he said, 'Speaking of not enough sex, Julian, what's going on with you? Talk.'

He hadn't even finished his first drink and he was being grilled. Now he knew how his lobsters felt.

Julian shrugged. 'I don't know what to do.'

James turned to face him. 'About what? You know, you can talk to us about anything. This is a judgement-free zone.' James waved his hand in a circle over the table.

'I appreciate that.' He blew out a breath. 'I can't stop thinking about Jess.' There, he'd said it. He might not mention that when he thinks of her, she's mostly naked and her hair is wrapped around his fist. That might be a step too far, even for this judgement free zone.

Cameron rolled his eyes. 'Tell us something we don't know. You should ask her out. You don't have any excuses now you've promoted Sam.'

He did have one excuse left, and that was the problem. This one wasn't so easily solved. 'I can't. I'm not good enough for her. I'm not a good man.'

James put his pint down and looked at Julian with a shocked expression. 'What the actual fuck are you talking about? You're an amazing bloke, Jay. We love you.'

'I agree with James.' Cameron leant forward. 'You have got to stop letting Chloe win. I may not know the details of what went on with you two, but I *do* know you have to put it behind you.'

Julian's shoulders slumped forward as he sagged in his seat. 'It's not that easy. I'm not like you two, okay? I'm not normal.'

Cameron scoffed. 'What's that supposed to mean? You're perfectly normal.'

He raked his fingers through his dishevelled waves. 'I'm not. I can't just go on a date. I need more than that.' He didn't know how to explain what he needed, and he wasn't sure he particularly wanted to share his deepest secrets with these two, but at the same time, it was eating him up inside and if he couldn't trust his cousin or mate, then who could he talk to?

'What do you mean, you need more than that?' asked James. His soft tone suggested he genuinely wanted to understand rather than being dismissive.

Julian felt his blood heat and his cheeks colour. 'I like kink. I have certain needs that aren't to everyone's liking.'

James shrugged. 'That doesn't make you abnormal, Jay. I, for one, can tell you with confidence that kink is excellent. Would it help if I told you some of my sexy shit?'

'Oh god, here we go. I'll go and get another round of drinks in. I think we'll need it.'

As Cameron went up to the bar to order another round, Julian downed what was left in his glass, preparing for James to spill the beans.

'I get why you think we wouldn't understand. Until a few months ago, I probably wouldn't have understood kink at all. I'm the one who turned Sarah down because she wanted to explore something that I thought was messed up. But I was wrong. I opened up my mind and I'm glad I did.'

'Did I miss any of the details?' Cameron asked as he carefully placed the fresh drinks on the table.

'Nope, I'm just getting to the good parts. Cheers.' James raised his glass and took a sip. 'I love who I've become. Sex was great before, but now it's off the charts. Turns out, I love to dominate Sarah. Pain can be pleasurable when done right, and I've learned to love dishing it out, but I'm also a switch. It felt so good to turn my brain off and not have to worry about anyone else. I just let Mrs Jones do whatever she wanted with us and it was fucking mind blowing.' He leaned in and lowered his voice. 'If it wasn't for kink, I wouldn't know how much I liked my arsehole being played with. Trust me, gents, if you've not tried it, give it a go.'

'Fucking hell, James,' Cameron muttered as Julian shook his head, a smile on his face. James wasn't one to mince his words.

James continued, unperturbed. 'Anyway, what I'm trying to say is, being kinky isn't wrong. Come on Jay, we can't help you if we don't know what we're dealing with. Are you into wearing nappies or something? It's okay if you are, it's not cool to yuk someone's yum.'

Cameron's brow creased as he looked over at James. 'Mate, what the fuck are you talking about?'

James shrugged, palms face up. 'What? Each unto their own, and all that. All I'm saying is we shouldn't judge people's kinks.'

Julian crossed his arms across his chest. 'You two aren't going to stop, are you?'

They both shook their heads as James said, 'Nope.' Popping the P.

'For the record, ageplay isn't my kink. I love the thrill of the chase. I like to hunt my women like they're prey. I don't make love. I'm not like Tom, giving pleasure over and over again. I take it. Or at least, I did until Chloe.'

This moment felt monumental. A weight lifted from his chest as he admitted his darkest secret, but his body tensed, waiting for the judgement to land. After a beat, he glanced up at his friends to see their reactions. Cameron took a sip of his drink and James was smiling.

'Don't tell Sarah you're a primal Dom. That's her favourite and I don't want to have to beat you up for stealing my woman.'

Well, that went better than he expected. They didn't make him feel like a monster and that encouraged him to keep talking.

He took a breath. 'I *was* a Dom. I'm not anymore. I can't bring myself to do it.' And there it was. The final truth laid out for all to see. He was broken. Saying the words out loud didn't feel cathartic. Putting voice to his feelings only worked to reinforce them in his mind. He picked at the beer mat, taking his frustration out on the soggy cardboard.

'What exactly happened with Chloe, Julian?' Cameron's face was full of concern.

Julian felt a wave of nausea roll through his stomach as he formed the words. 'We loved CNC roleplay, but she wanted to take it further and I wasn't comfortable doing that.'

Cameron held up his hand. 'Hang on. What's CNC?'

James spoke up before Julian could answer. 'Consensual non-consent. It's exactly what it says on the tin.'

Cameron formed an O with his mouth. 'That makes sense. Imogen is always talking about it, but I was always too scared to ask.'

Julian carried on talking. 'It's not for everyone and it has to be managed properly.'

Cameron nodded. 'I get that. So, what did Chloe want?'

He looked around for anyone eavesdropping and scooted forward in his chair. Dropping his voice, he said, 'She wanted me to drug her. She wanted to be unconscious while I fucked her. I know of people who do it, but I'm not one of them. I'm not comfortable when I don't know what the other person is thinking. To me, consent can be taken away at any point. It doesn't matter if I'm balls deep in a woman. If she says her safeword, I'll stop. I like it rough, but only if my partner wants it, and I don't know that if they're not even conscious. Plus, I like the chase, and unconscious people don't tend to run very far.'

James let out a whistle. 'I've read about it, but to be honest, I always thought it was mainly kept to the pages of dark romance novels. I can see why you said no to her. That's a tricky one to get right.'

'Exactly.'

Cameron furrowed his brow. 'I don't understand what the problem is. She wanted something you didn't, and you said no. Shouldn't that have been the end of it?'

'Yeah. And it was. She walked away. Problem was, she walked into the arms of a man willing to give her what she wanted. He wasn't so bothered about limits and safewords. He was a pure sadist. Two weeks after we broke up, I got a phone call from the hospital. I was still listed on her phone as the emergency contact.'

'Shit. What happened?' Cameron ran his hands through his hair.

'Turns out she'd asked him to drug her. He did. And he had a great time doing whatever he wanted with her. What she hadn't banked on was that he liked to watch, too. He brought his mates in, and they all had a go. There wasn't a part of her body they didn't abuse.'

'Fucking wanker,' James hissed out.

'She made a full recovery, physically, but mentally she never got over it. She blamed me. She told our mutual friends I let her down because I wouldn't give her what she needed. That I was a poor excuse for a Dom and a man. That shit tends to get into your head.' He rubbed at his temples, squeezing his eyes shut against the memories.

'Mate, I know what you're going through. I blamed myself for what happened to Sarah—'

'Yeah. You blamed yourself. So you can see how everyone blamed me for what happened to Chloe.' He hung his head, sucking in a breath to calm his emotion. 'Some strangers found her in an alleyway and called an ambulance. The fuckers left her for dead. You should've seen the state they left her in.' He shook his head, rubbing at his chest in an attempt to ease the heartache. 'I can't unsee that shit. She was barely recognisable. If I'd have given her what she wanted, she would've been safe. I have to live with that. What I want…' He shook his head. 'What I need is wrong. It's messed up. I'm in the same category as that fucked up scumbag that raped her, and then watched as his mates did the same.' His voice broke as tears fell from his eyes.

He quickly swiped at them with the sleeve of his hoodie as the waitress brought their food over. She glanced at him, but quickly looked away, not even asking if they wanted anything else before making a hasty exit.

Cameron cleared his throat, his eyes glassy with unshed tears. 'You are not in the same category as that arsehole. You set your limits, and you stuck to them for a reason. She chose to ignore them. Chloe isn't stupid, Jay. She knew what she was getting into, and that was what thrilled her. That's not your doing. No one is to blame for what happened to her apart from the men who did that to her. You broke up because you didn't want the same things as her.'

James cleared his throat. 'Yeah, mate, you're a primal Dom, which is quite literally a different beast than what she wanted. You're not like those other men, not in the slightest.'

Julian heard their words, but they didn't sink in. After Chloe left the hospital and spouted her side of the story, Charlotte Lombardi tried to tell him the same, that it wasn't his fault, but he didn't believe her either.

James carried on. 'It took a lot of convincing for me to believe that it wasn't my fault that Sarah was the victim of revenge porn. If I'd have just said yes to her.' James jabbed his finger at his chest. 'If I'd explored BDSM with her instead of sending her on her merry way, she would never have ended up in Dominic's dungeon and on PornCentral. But I wasn't ready for that. I might have done more harm than good if I'd have given it a go.' He stabbed his index finger in the palm of his hand. 'Instead, I went away and researched. I did everything I could to be the man she needed, and I don't regret any of it. Do I wish she hadn't gone through what she went through while I sorted myself out? Of course. But I can't change the past.' He wrapped his arm around Julian's shoulder. 'It's not your fault. Do you hear me? It's not your fucking fault.'

'I can see that what we're saying is going in one ear and out the other, but you need to believe it. You're one of the good ones. You deserve to be happy. So does Jess, and despite what you think, you can give her that,' said Cameron.

He wanted that to be true. A weight had lifted when he admitted what had really happened. He'd been carrying it around for so long, blurring the lines of reality and his perception of what had happened. 'Come on, guys. You know Jess. She's perfect. Too perfect for someone like me. I don't think I can deny my needs forever. I feel like I have a beast lurking below the surface, and I can't risk letting it loose on Jess. I'd break her.'

'Don't judge her before getting to know her. I've spent the last few months reading what they read in their book club, and I can tell you with good authority that Jess always requests the primal romance books. I think she'd surprise you. It's always the quiet ones you have to watch.' James nodded his head before stuffing a thick-cut chip in his mouth, which he must have instantly regretted as he started puffing and fanning his hand at his open mouth. 'Fuck! That's hot. Sorry, carry on.'

'And what do I do about her parents?'

'You're not suggesting you fuck them in the woods too, are you?' James pursed his lips. 'Although it might be the most effective way to remove the stick they have up their arses.'

Julian's laughter felt lighter than it had done in months. 'No, I'm not suggesting I fuck her parents. I was referring to their desire to marry Jess off to a rich toff.'

'First of all, I don't think you should worry about her parents,' Cameron said as he put his knife and fork down. 'And second, you've spent so long trying to make a name for yourself in your own right that you've forgotten who you are. I think it's about time you remembered.'

CHAPTER 6

JESS

Bad Thoughts - Rachel Platten

'Can you come and stay at my house for the weekend? We're hosting the book club and Cam wants the lads over, just like old times.' Imogen had called Jess, giving her a break from wallowing in her bedroom hideaway where she had successfully avoided her parents as much as possible. Her plan was working well so far, but she knew it wasn't a long-term solution. She was already going mad and it had only been three days.

She stretched her legs across her bed and rolled onto her side, gazing out of the large bay window. 'I'd love to. I've spent the last few days slobbing around in my pyjamas and I need a change of scenery.' It would also mean she couldn't be forced to entertain Will.

'Great. It's going to be such fun. Cam is making paella again.'

Jess remembered the last time he'd cooked his favourite dish for everyone. It was the night she'd met Julian, and he'd hand fed her a Padron pepper. The pepper wasn't hot, but he was. A familiar heat pooled between her legs as she remembered how his thick thigh brushed up against hers as they all sat around the table.

'Jess, you still there?'

'Shit, sorry. My mind wandered for a second. I clearly need to get out of the house.'

As predicted, her mother wasn't pleased when she strolled out of the front door on Saturday afternoon, overnight bag in hand. Jess had a hard time giving a shit. A weekend at Imogen's was exactly what she needed.

Her tyres crunched over Cameron's gravel driveway, reminding her of home. Only here, she didn't get a sinking feeling in the pit of her stomach from the sound. She was excited for the weekend ahead chatting about books and all things book boyfriend.

She flipped down the visor, checking her reflection in the little mirror. Knowing they weren't going anywhere, she'd opted for light makeup, skinny jeans, and an oversized sweater with '*Buy me books and tell me I'm a good girl*' written on it.

She rubbed away some smudged mascara and ran her fingers through her hair, allowing herself one more minute of wallowing over the mess her life had become before she straightened her spine, flipped up the visor and pushed the dread to the deepest part of her soul. She was going to forget her worries and live her life as much as possible, right up until she couldn't any longer.

From the collection of cars already parked, she knew everyone else had arrived, which was good news for the four bottles of champagne she'd pilfered from her father's cellar. What he didn't know wouldn't hurt him.

Imogen dashed out to greet her in slippers, leggings, and a similar book themed sweater. Her hair was piled on top of her head in a messy bun. She reached out and took the clinking bag of booze as Jess grabbed her overnight bag.

'Hey, you. Are you okay? I didn't want to interrupt that moment you were having in the car.' Imogen's face was etched with concern.

Jess decided not to tell her friends that she'd overheard her dad selling her off. Until she could figure out exactly what was happening, and how she was going to handle it, she was keeping it under wraps. For now, she wanted to carry on as normal—no, scratch that—better than normal. Fuck her parents and their ideals.

'Oh yeah, I'm good. Mum wasn't best pleased to see me getting away for the weekend. You know how she is; she likes to always know what I'm up to.' Jess rolled her eyes.

'Ugh, annoying. Well, you're here now and you don't have to worry about her.' She peeked inside the carrier bag. 'Looks like you're on a mission to get pissed. I'll get these in the chiller. In the meantime, James is making cocktails, want one?'

'Yes, please. It's safe to say I have a thirst on.'

Imogen led the way through the house to where the others had congregated in the kitchen. After the obligatory kiss on everyone's cheeks, Cameron took her bag up to one of their guest rooms.

'James, would you mind making Jess a Bellini while I pop her champers in the fridge?' asked Imogen.

'My pleasure. It's the least I can do, as she's the star of the moment.' That caught Jess's attention. She looked over at James, who was looking particularly hot in his glasses, a plain white T-shirt and grey jeans. His hair was free of product and the waves flopped gently to the side.

She blinked away her thoughts, wondering why she was suddenly lusting after James. She cleared her throat, 'What do you mean by star of the moment?'

Jess watched as James poured the prosecco into the peach juice. Her mouth watered. 'We've been inundated with requests from new clients, all requesting your services. We're going to have to discuss paying you a retainer or making you a full-time employee of Spencer and Black.' He smiled as he passed the gently fizzing drink to her.

'Wow, that's amazing.' Her heart thrummed with pride until the moment she remembered it could all be for nothing. Everything she'd worked so hard to build was there for the taking, and yet it no longer felt as thrilling as it once had. Her future was planned out in front of her, the clock ticking on her career and her happiness.

She threw back the contents of her glass, the sweet fizz calming her spiralling thoughts. She reminded herself that what was to become of her was future Jess's problem. For now, she was going to drink, eat, talk about sexy fictional characters, and pretend everything was normal. She shoved the empty glass into James's hand. 'Can I have another one of those? I need to grease my wheels.'

James's eyebrows rose, but he simply nodded and poured another. The second drink was suspiciously more peachy than the last.

'Is everything okay, Jess?' It was Lucy's turn to look concerned as she leant on the counter, one arm wrapped around Tom's waist as she daintily sipped on her cocktail. 'Hun, I asked if you were okay.' All eyes were on her as Lucy repeated her question.

With a quick shake of her head, she replied. 'Yeah, totally fine. I just need to regroup after getting away from my parents. You know how they get under my skin sometimes. I need to hit reset.' She glanced over at the wine fridge. 'Is the fizz chilled yet?'

Cameron pulled a bottle of vodka from the freezer as he said, 'I think you need something stronger.' He ran his palm over his chin. 'Not that I recommend using drink to solve problems, obviously, but sometimes it's warranted. How about I make you a round of espresso martinis before we head off to watch the rugby?'

Sarah clapped her hands together. 'Perfect.'

They all took tentative sips of their freshly made cocktails, careful not to spill any as they carried them through to the living room. Since Imogen moved into Cameron's house, she hadn't changed his décor. The only addition she'd made was their beautiful wedding portrait that hung over the fireplace. It caught Jess's eye as they sat down. She ignored the mix of emotions that washed over her. She doubted she'd ever look that happy on her wedding day.

Sarah grabbed a cushion and hugged it to her chest as she pulled her legs under her. 'Before we talk books, I have to share some news. If I don't tell you now, I'll burst.' Sarah was almost bouncing in her seat.

Rolling her hands, Lucy encouraged Sarah to keep talking. 'Come on then, spill the beans. I'm not even going to attempt a guess.'

Sarah puffed out an excited breath. 'You know Katia is holding another masquerade ball at K's next month?'

'I didn't, but go on,' Imogen piped up. Imogen and Jess didn't go to the members only kink club that Tom's friend, Katia, owned.

'The theme is fantasy and James has sourced custom-made costumes.'

'Oh shit, do I need to step it up a gear and get something new to wear?' Lucy looked a little put out.

Sarah shook her head with a smug look on her face. 'No need. You won't be able to beat what we're wearing.'

Jess wasn't going to the ball, but she was desperate to know what James had sorted. 'Get to the point, for fuck's sake.'

She leaned forward, eyes wide. 'He's had wings made. Full on, handmade wings.'

'No way!' Imogen paused with her glass halfway to her lips.

'I shit you not.' Sarah sat back in her seat, a look of triumph on her face. 'He had his made from black feathers, and because I'm his angel, mine are white, and obviously smaller. He looks so fucking hot wearing them that I can't control myself. His wingspan is impressive, if you know what I'm saying,' she giggled.

'Flipping heck, Sarah, that's amazing.' Jess meant it. 'Sexy romantasy cosplay. You are living the dream.'

'I am. I can't believe I walked away from him. I'm never making that mistake again. He's literally perfect.' Sarah flopped back into the plush cushions, releasing a long sigh.

Jess squeezed Sarah's arm as a feeling of genuine happiness came over her. 'Shall we stop there before you tell us all about his pierced ding-a-ling again?' Sarah stuck her tongue out in response.

Imogen walked over to a wooden bookcase and pulled out four paperbacks. 'Actually, ladies, I have a gift for you all. I got hold of signed copies of a primal romance I think we'll love. It's a novella too, so we could all read it together today. What do you reckon? I'll grab the blankets, snacks, and champagne, and we can all sit and read and discuss as we reach the end of each chapter.'

Jess loved the idea of being able to escape into another world for a few hours. 'I think that's a perfect idea.' She glimpsed the front cover. 'Oh, I've seen that all over my socials. I can't wait to read it.'

For two hours the only sound made was the occasional gasp, request for more alcohol or the crunch of sweet and salty popcorn being consumed as if it was on a conveyor belt, their attention fully on the hot storyline and not on the volume of satiating snacks consumed.

Jess turned the last page and closed the book. 'Shitting hell, Jen. That book was awe—'

Lucy waved her hand in the air. 'Don't say anything! I've got one more page to go.'

Jen and Jess glanced at each other and smiled as they patiently waited for the other two to finish. Sarah closed the book and sat in silence. All eyes on Lucy.

'Okay. Done. I think it's safe to say we failed miserably at talking about this book after each chapter.' Lucy slapped the book to her forehead. 'I need a cold shower after that.'

Sarah tutted and hugged her arms across her body. 'I need a good seeing to. A cold shower won't cut it.'

'Well, don't look at us. We can't help you there.' Imogen laughed.

'When are the boys getting back?' Sarah replied.

Jess pointed at them all. 'Oh, now hang on, girls. You can't pounce on the men when they get back. What am I supposed to do with myself?'

Sarah opened her mouth to reply, no doubt with a lude suggestion about a vibrator, when the sound of the front door crashing open interrupted.

Imogen laughed. 'That answered our question. Shall we see how drunk they got at the rugby?'

They met the boys in the hallway, rosy-cheeked and talking louder than usual.

'Hello, gorgeous ladies.' James beamed. 'Look who we found at the rugby match.' James stepped to the side as Julian walked in.

He was wearing the same green, black, and gold rugby jersey as Cameron. It hugged his hard lines to perfection and if it wasn't for the indigo jeans he was wearing, he wouldn't have looked out of place on the pitch with the other players.

'Afternoon all.' Julian kissed Imogen on the cheek. 'Thanks for having me, Jen.' He gave a slight wave to the others, and if Jess didn't know any better, she'd say he looked shy.

Tom closed the front door and slapped Julian on the back. 'Turns out, Jay has finally joined the land of the living and has handed over the reins to someone else at the restaurant.'

Julian rubbed at the scruff on his chin. 'Yeah. Tonight is his first Saturday in charge without me.' He winced as he glanced at his phone in his hand.

Cameron grabbed it and placed it on the table by the front door. 'Come on, you don't need to check your phone every five minutes. Leave it there and enjoy your evening of freedom. I'll get dinner started. James can grab everyone a beer and we'll head out the back for a quick game.'

Sarah clapped her hands together. 'Can we watch? Tom, you could make us some cocktails.' She danced the tips of her fingers together, a look of mischief on her face. 'I think it should be topless rugby. What do you think, ladies?' She turned to see their reaction.

She was met with three sets of eyes rolling. Jess was thankful no one had agreed with her. That would rub salt in her wounds as she reflected on her current position of gooseberry, only made worse by the arrival of a man she could only dream of having.

James grabbed Sarah by the waist and pulled her in for a kiss. When he came up for air, he said, 'Why don't you ladies play with us? Girls against boys?'

Lucy chewed on her thumbnail and looked at the men standing in front of her. 'Are you kidding? You'd kill us. You have to promise to be gentle. And don't go tackling me to the ground, I don't want to get smooshed.'

'Speak for yourself, Lucy. I'd quite like James to tackle me.'

Cameron shook his head as he walked towards the kitchen. 'Shall we sort the teams out later? Beer and food are the priority.'

The girls sat at the large oak island that dominated the country-style kitchen while Cameron made a start on the paella, James opened bottles of beer, and Tom made French Seventy-Fives for the ladies. Julian was clearly missing his restaurant as he easily slipped into the role of sous chef as he anticipated Cameron's every need. Jess couldn't take her eyes off him as he moved around the kitchen with grace, expertly prepping the prawns. He could easily make a living making cookery video thirst-traps on social media.

Cameron wiped his hands on a towel and took a long drink from his beer. 'Come on, the prep is done, time to play.' Seconds later, he emerged from the utility room holding a rugby ball. He pulled open the large glass doors that led onto an expansive patio area.

Imogen looked down at their bare feet. 'Don't we want to put shoes on?'

Tom shrugged. 'Stop stalling and get out here. You don't need shoes.'

Jess wiggled her toes into the grass, grateful it was at least dry, and the air pleasantly warm. Cameron tossed the ball to Imogen as he declared it was to be girls against boys. He looked at the other men and said, 'But don't be rough. This is just for fun, and I don't want to punch any of you for hurting my woman.'

James rolled his eyes. 'Your woman is safe. Don't worry.'

Jess held her hand up and chewed on her lip. 'Can I just point out that I don't have a clue how to play this game? My experience with rugby is watching from afar, and even then, I'm just ogling the players' thighs.'

Julian stepped forward, combing his fingers through his hair. 'Don't worry. All you need to do is run like hell if you have the ball and touch it down…' He looked towards the end of the garden. 'Over there, in line with that big bush thing. We'll try to get the ball off you, and score at this end of the garden. We can forget all the other rules. How does that sound?'

Jess nodded. 'Got it. Get the ball. Run like the wind, dodging you guys.'

Julian smiled and nodded.

Imogen kicked off proceedings by squealing and running away, but not nearly fast enough as Cameron wrapped his arms around her waist and took her down. Of course, he took the brunt of the landing as Imogen fell on him, laughing so hard she dropped the ball.

James snatched it up and ran to the other end of the garden with the three remaining women in chase. Imogen was busy pinning Cameron down, clearly forgetting they were playing a team game.

A blur of auburn hair dashed past Jess as Sarah collided with James. He let out a loud oof as she tackled him to the floor, not being careful about it at all.

Jess looked around to see if she had any back up as she scooped the ball up in one hand. Tom was all over Lucy, anticipating where she was going to run to next. It was all down to Jess to score.

Julian was sprinting towards her as she turned on her heel and ran as fast as she could down the lawn. She was the hundred-metre sprint champion back in her school days, so she was sure she had this in the bag. Although, she didn't drink multiple cocktails before an athletics meet, and it was taking a toll on her performance. Thankfully, it was slightly downhill, so she soon picked up speed, gravity lending a hand.

She turned to see Julian gaining on her and felt a thrill of exhilaration at the prospect of being tackled to the ground by him. She could see their try line fast approaching, but she could sense Julian was about to take her out at any second. Her heart beat out of her chest and at that moment, Jess was aware of everything. Time was moving as if in slow motion. It felt good to run. She felt free. The thrill of the chase made her feel more alive than she had felt for a long time. She wanted to be caught.

But she wanted to score more.

The only way she was going to make it was if she jumped for it. With only a few feet to go, she threw herself into the air, shrieking as she realised she was going to overshoot the try line and end up head first in the bush.

She closed her eyes, waiting for prickly greenery to rip her face to shreds, but instead of pain, massive arms wrapped around her, her face buried in a firm chest. Her landing was hard, but not painful.

She stilled; her face pressed to his chest, breathing in an intoxicating scent, made even more delicious by his body heat. Reluctantly, she pulled her face away from his pec and cracked an eye open to find herself nose to nose with Julian and her thighs straddling his.

'Oh. Hi.'

He cleared his throat. 'Hi.'

CHAPTER 7

JULIAN

Lose Control - Teddy Swims

*F*uck.
Fuck.
Fuck were the only words going through Julian's head as he chased Jess across the lawn. His vision tunnelled, focused solely on her.

His prey.

His instincts kicked in as his heart rate picked up, adrenaline coursing through his veins. He could have caught her by now, but where was the fun in that?

He was barely aware of the others around him, distracted in their couples and leaving him to stop Jess as they cheered him on, the girls singing their protests at being held back.

She still had half the pitch to run before she'd score, and he had no intention of letting that happen. He needed to get a grip and control himself, though. Remind himself this wasn't the chase he was used to. He was playing a much toned-down version of rugby in his cousin's garden. He was not in a scene.

He was not in a scene.

If he said it to himself enough, he hoped his body would listen when it came time to tackle her.

And by body, he meant his dick. Which hadn't received the memo.

She was fast. He was having to put some effort into gaining on her and for a fleeting moment he thought she might stand a chance of scoring and his chance to get his hands on her would be gone… then she leapt.

She was going too fast, but he saw it all play out in slow motion. She was going to end up headfirst in the bush, and the bush didn't look like a soft landing. Panic washed over him as his protective instincts kicked in. He couldn't let her get hurt.

He dug deep and sprinted for her. His muscles screamed as his bare feet struggled to find purchase on the grass. He lunged for her, wrapping one arm around her waist, his other hand cupping the back of her head, pressing her face to his chest and plucking her out of the air. Twisting, he took the brunt of the fall as the branches dug and scratched into his back. But he ignored the pain. All he could feel was the rise and fall of Jess's panting breaths against his chest. The feel of her warmth in his arms and the way her thighs clung to his as if in a death grip.

He lay in the bush, gripping on to her while he tried to calm his heart rate and his cock, which was easier said than done with her legs entwined with his. His every instinct wanted to roll her over and take her. But he couldn't.

His friends were no doubt feeling proud of their obvious attempt to bring them together, but they'd have no idea of the beast they'd released in doing so.

A beast he worked hard to keep buried.

He released his hand from the back of her head as she lifted it from his chest. 'Oh. Hi.'

'Hi.' It was an automatic response, one he wasn't fully aware of as he stared up at her.

Her voice was breathy and oh so bloody hot. He told himself that, of course, it was breathy. She'd just run the length of the garden. And it wasn't a small garden by any means. She was out of breath, that was all. She certainly wasn't turned on by the chase, or being tackled into a bush.

So why was she staring at his lips like she wanted him to kiss her? She chewed on her lip. Her cheeks were flushed, her breaths laboured, her pupils dilated, and he was certain she was gripping his hips with her thighs harder than necessary.

If they were in a scene—which they weren't—but if they were, her green flag would be flying high, and he'd be biting her thighs before driving himself deep inside her. Fuck, he wanted her.

'Jay, are you okay?'

Her voice was gentle and full of concern. He cleared his throat. 'Oh, yeah, I'm fine.' His eyes scanned her body as he asked, 'Are you okay?'

'Yeah. Yeah, I think so.'

He brought his hands to rest on her hips as she lifted upright, leaning on his chest. She smiled as she said, 'This counts as a score, right?'

He looked to his left, at where the ball was wedged between the branches. 'I'm afraid this doesn't count as a try. You didn't touch the ball down.'

Her pout was delightful as her brow creased. 'Semantics. I feel I should get the points for a valiant effort.' She shifted, simultaneously causing broken branches to stab at his back and his blood to flow in the wrong direction as she pressed into his groin. He winced as he felt a twig puncture his skin, but it did nothing to ease his growing erection.

'Oh shit, sorry. Are you in pain?' She jumped up and held her hand out to help him as Cameron strode over to collect the ball before he could answer.

'You all right, big man?' Cameron tossed the ball from hand to hand.

'Yeah.' He dusted off the stray leaves from his jeans, taking the opportunity to hide his semi as Jess swiped at the twigs stuck on his back. 'Jess would like a score for effort, but I reckon she should have half a point for that.'

Cameron rubbed at his chin with one hand as the other clung to the ball. 'Deal. And you get half for heroics.'

He wondered if a hero would get an erection while saving a damsel in distress. He thought not.

Before he knew what was happening, Jess pressed her lips to his cheek and whispered, 'Thank you for saving me, Jay.' Cold shivers ran across his body as images of Chloe laying battered and bruised in a hospital bed flashed in his mind.

He was no hero. He didn't save her.

His arousal dissipated as if doused in icy water. 'I'll get the dinner on.' He didn't wait for a reply as he fled.

'Hey, Jay, are you okay?' Cameron had caught up to Julian by the time he'd reached the kitchen. Julian didn't want to talk about it, so he busied himself by turning the hob on, warming the paella pan, and getting the plates out.

'We should've got this on sooner. It'll be a while before it's ready and those guys need something to soak up the booze before they hurt themselves.' He bustled around the kitchen opening cupboard doors with no idea what he was looking for, but it beat looking Cam in the eye.

'They're fine. It's you I'm worried about. What happened out there?'

Julian stopped his frantic search for nothing in particular and straightened, keeping his eyes on the pan. 'Nothing happened.'

'There's no one else here, Jay. It's just you and me. I'm not letting up until you tell me what just happened.'

His back teeth groaned under the pressure from his clenched jaw as he tried to make sense of his thoughts. 'I had a flashback.'

Cam took a step closer, as if edging his way to someone about to jump off a cliff. 'Of Chloe?'

Jay nodded.

'We've been over this. You know that wasn't your fault. You're not responsible for what someone does when they're not with you.'

He gripped the edge of the counter as he held back the emotion threatening to rip from his soul. 'You didn't see her. That image haunts me every time I close my eyes. I may not have been the one to put her in the hospital, but I could've prevented it.'

Julian flinched as Cameron rested his hand on his shoulder and squeezed. 'No, Jay, you couldn't have. You weren't meant to be together. She knew that. That's why she left. What happened after that was nothing to do with you. You have got to stop beating yourself up over this.'

He faced his cousin, pain etched on his brow. 'It's not that easy. The pain doesn't go away just because you tell it to. You can't control this, Cam. I should've given in to her and given her what she wanted. If I'd have just put aside my own fucking reservations, she would never have got hurt.' Julian knew they'd been over this, and he tried to take what he and James had said, but the guilt remained ingrained in him like muscle memory.

Cameron sighed with frustration. 'That's not true, and you know it. Chloe was fucked up. You just couldn't see it. You never would've satisfied her. She wanted something you could never give her. She didn't want to roleplay, Jay, and that was the problem. It would never be real with you. Listen to what I'm saying.' He stepped in front of him, gripping his shoulders, eyes locked on his. 'You. Were. Not. Meant. To. Be. With. Chloe. Are you listening?'

'Yes, I'm listening.' He was hearing what Cameron was saying, loud and clear.

'This is not on you. For fuck's sake, Jay.' Cameron pointed towards the garden where everyone had remained. 'There is a beautiful woman out there who is clearly smitten with you, and you've got a chance to make something real with her. You want to save someone? Save her from a lifetime of being set up with wankers her parents deem suitable.'

His breath caught as Cam's words hit home. 'Do you really think she's that into me? What if she doesn't like who I really am?'

Cameron shrugged. 'What if she does? Listen, shit-face, how would you feel if she ends up with the current guy her parents have lined up? Let's say in a month's time, she brings him to one of our get-togethers. How does that make you feel? Can you live with yourself if you let that happen because you're scared?'

And that was the crux of it. It was easier for him to blame what happened with Chloe, to use that as an excuse, than to show his true colours to Jess and have her reject him. The thought scared him, but the prospect of never finding out if they would work together petrified him.

What started out as guilt over what happened to Chloe became a shield he lived behind, but it was time to drop it. He twisted, resting his forearms on the island behind him, tucking his head in his hands. 'Fuck. I feel like I can't breathe.' His ribs gripped his lungs like an iron fist. The realisation of how he really felt hit him hard, knocking the wind out of him.

Cameron wrapped an arm around his back. 'It's okay. You're the good guy, don't forget that. You deserve your happy ever after. You've spent too long running away from who you are, Jay. You need to start living your life again.'

Julian squeezed his eyes closed, focused on filling his lungs and swallowed down the emotion as he voiced his fear out loud. 'What if I can't? I feel like I'm broken, Cam.' The question earned him a shove to the shoulder.

'No, you're not. You just need some time to adjust. You know what Jess would say?'

He gave Cameron a sideways glance. 'No, but I'm sure you're about to tell me.'

'The best thing to do when you fall off a horse is get back on it. Look, I don't know what it's like to be a primal Dom, and to have all these urges, but I do know you'll go mad if you keep denying yourself.'

Cameron says he doesn't understand it, but Julian knew otherwise. 'Mate, it's a family trait. Where do you think you get your Alpha male complex from? We're two sides of the same coin. You want to protect your mate with an animalistic need, and I want to be the one you're protecting her from. Only I can't do it anymore. And before you say it, I did try again.'

Cameron nodded as he scratched his jaw. 'Huh, I can see what you mean. That makes sense. So you've tried to get back at it?'

'Yeah. It was with the Lombardis, actually.'

Cameron's eyebrows shot through the roof. 'No fucking way?'

Julian nodded. 'They are two kinky fuckers, let me tell you. Charlotte suggested I have an evening with them at home. She thought getting back in the saddle with a couple I knew in a place I was comfortable would help. I felt good at first. Rob joined in. We worked well as a team, and Charlotte loved it when we tag-teamed, but when it came to it, and we caught her, I just couldn't go through with it. I think there being two against one set off alarm bells. All I saw every time I touched her was Chloe.'

'I had no idea. I'm so sorry.'

Julian rolled his head to the side and shrugged. 'Why would you know? I tend not to fill you in on all my kinky goings on with other couples.'

'Well, maybe if you had, you wouldn't have spent all this time thinking the worst of yourself and staying away from women. It sounds to me like you tried to run before you could walk. You need to take it slow and ease your way back into it.'

What he was saying made sense, but it didn't ease his doubts. 'Oh really, and what if I want someone that I know won't want me? And I mean the real me?'

'Then they're not the right woman for you.' He made it sound so simple. 'But I think Jess will surprise you. She's a dark horse and you should give her more credit.'

'Christ, can you give the horse references a rest now?'

The conversation came to an abrupt end as the others came crashing through the door.

Imogen came to a stop when she saw the two of them huddled together. 'Oh, are we interrupting something?'

Cameron straightened and shook his head. 'Nope, we're just shooting the shit while the pan pre-heats.'

Tom started fanning the pan with a tea towel as smoke billowed up into the extractor fan. 'Well, it's safe to say it's preheated.'

'Fuck.' Julian turned down the heat as Cameron grabbed the ingredients. And just like that, normal service resumed. Only Julian didn't feel like he had a lead weight holding him down anymore.

'Jay, your back is bleeding.' Jess pointed as he twisted his head to look.

'Oh, bollocks. So it is.' His rugby top was torn, and blood had pooled on his skin. He hadn't noticed the stinging until now.

'Let me clean it up. It's the least I can do after you saved me from the same fate.'

'I think that's a marvellous idea. I could do with him out of the kitchen while I cook. He gets in my way,' said Cameron with a smirk.

Jess grabbed Julian's hand and led him out of the kitchen before he could protest.

Not that he wanted to. Her hand felt perfect in his.

CHAPTER 8

JESS

Feels Like - Ella Mai

As Jess pulled Julian from the kitchen, she couldn't help but enjoy the feel of her hand wrapped in his massive one. They were like plates.

Sexy plates she wanted to feel all over her body.

She let out a giggle at her random thoughts.

'Is my bleeding that funny?' Julian's deep voice interrupted her thoughts of sexy crockery, which truth be told, she was thankful for as she doubted her sanity.

'Oh no, sorry. I… I was just thinking of something funny.' She had nothing. She couldn't explain this away.

'What's so funny? I could do with a laugh.'

She rolled her lips between her teeth as she opened the bathroom cabinet, looking for something to clean his wounds. 'Oh, um, I can't remember now, actually.'

He quirked a brow, clearly not believing a word she was saying, but there was no way she was going to tell him how she wanted his sexy plates all over her. 'Can you take your top off please?'

He sucked in air between his teeth as she helped him pull his top over the wound.

She felt terrible. 'I'm so sorry about this. I got a little carried away and wasn't thinking. I could feel you running behind me, and I just…' She shrugged. 'Got carried away.'

He looked down at her, which wasn't difficult as he towered over her. 'Am I that scary?'

He wasn't, but the way he towered over her, the way his voice spoke directly to her lady parts and the way he made her want to run away from everything and spend the rest of her life under him, should've scared her.

She chewed on her lip, deliberating if she should say what she wanted to.

Fuck it. She was either going to be married off and chained to the kitchen sink soon, or she'd have to disappear and run away from her life. Either way, she was very much in her grabbing-the-bull-by-its-horns era. Her parents thought they could control her every move? She'd show them.

'Yes, and no.' She shook her head. 'Sorry, I'm not making any sense at all. I enjoyed it, that's all.'

She grabbed the cotton balls and ran them under the tap, trying not to stare at the semi naked man-bear in front of her.

'You enjoyed playing rugby or... being chased?' His throat caught on the last word, catching her attention.

She didn't know how to explain it, but she was going to try. 'Not so much the rugby side, but the threat of being tackled. I wanted you to catch me, but at the same time, I didn't. It's quite an adrenaline rush. I've only ever felt like that before when I'm galloping with Teddy and we're coming up to a high fence.' She figured she should stop talking now before he thought she was a total weirdo.

Julian raised an eyebrow. 'I hope you're talking about a horse.'

Jess's cheeks blushed as she playfully swatted his arm. His big, muscular arm, corded with veins. My god, he had biceps for days. How did a chef and restaurant manager get a body like that?

'Oh, yes. My horse. Well, it's not strictly my horse. It's my mother's. All the horses are hers, but she doesn't actually ride them. Teddy is the under-dog. Well, I guess he's the under-horse, as it were, so I like to ride him. He's a bit broken, but even a broken horse deserves a good ride.'

Oh bloody hell, she was rambling. She inwardly cursed herself and snapped her mouth shut.

Julian laughed as he said, 'I couldn't agree more. Shall we get to fixing my back? I'm doing my best to look manly and unaffected but it's stinging like a motherfucker now the air has hit it.'

'Oh, shit. Yes, sorry. There was me rambling about riding and you're here bleeding.' She was totally nailing the sexy nurse persona she had originally set out to portray… not. 'Turn around.'

He smiled. 'Yes, ma'am.'

As he turned his back on her, she took the opportunity to study his body some more. And by study, she meant perv. He looked delicious in clothes. But out of them was something else. He was delectable. And wide. If he lay on top of her, he would swamp her. She wanted swamping.

Was he in proportion? Could she assume that because he had big hands, big feet and was generally, well, just… big, that he was big everywhere? At that moment, her vagina piped up with her own opinion if the fluttering was anything to go by. Jess wanted to find out. If she was forced to marry Will-probably-has-a-pencil-dick Wilberforce, then surely, she owed it to herself to have a ride on the Clydesdale horse. She was going to spend the rest of her life on a pony, for fuck's sake.

'As nurses go, you're not really at the top of your game.'

She'd done it again. She really needed to get her act together. This man was literally bleeding because of her, and all she could do was objectify him and consider having sex with him just to get one amazing shag in before her life was over. She was a shit person. That wasn't fair to Jay. Not at all. He deserved better.

'Okay, sorry. I was just getting a good look at you—it. You know, assess the situation.'

'It's a scratch, not a shrapnel wound.'

She pressed the wet cotton ball to the cut and giggled as he let out a hiss. 'Come on, big man, you can cope with a little scratch, can't you? It's not like it's a *shrapnel wound*.' She threw his words back at him.

His shoulders bounced as she heard his chuckle. 'Touché.'

She dabbed at the blood until it was all clear. 'Oh, you're right. It is just a little scratch. It's stopped bleeding. Looked worse than it was. There, all done.' Without thinking, she pressed her lips to a spot just above the injury. 'All better.'

She felt his muscles tense under her lips and pulled away quickly. 'Oh, god. Sorry. I just went into autopilot there. Our nursemaid at school always used to kiss it better. Which, come to think of it, is a bit weird.' She scrunched her face up as she thought about how school staff definitely wouldn't be allowed to kiss anything nowadays.

Julian turned to face her with a warm smile on his face. 'You ramble when you're nervous, don't you?'

Her body was overheating, and the bathroom was getting smaller. She was sure of it. 'Do I? Can't say I've ever noticed.'

He took a small step towards her, closing the gap. She looked up at him as he said, 'Yes, you do.'

This conversation was doing things to her she really shouldn't be enjoying. 'I'm not nervous. Maybe it's because I feel so bad that I got you hurt.'

He stared into her eyes for a beat too long. She was certain he knew she was talking out of her arse. She was nervous. Nervous that she wanted more than she could ever have, and that was something she'd never recover from.

He nodded. 'Thanks for cleaning me up. I'll grab a new top and meet you downstairs.'

'Oh, of course. Yes, I'll see you downstairs.' She hurried out of the bathroom, feeling foolish for hoping that was more than it was. A friend helping another friend. Nothing more. It certainly wasn't leading to a kiss. Or a quick fuck up against the sink.

So why did disappointment coil itself around her as she descended the stairs?

'Hey you. Is he all right?' Sarah looked at her with genuine concern as she thrust a glass of something pink and fizzy into her hand.

'Yeah, it was just a scratch.' She batted her hand at the comment and took a sip from the fluted glass. The cool bubbles soothed her fevered state. She took another glug. Sarah was giving her the side-eye.

'What? What are you staring at?'

Sarah smirked. 'Nothing. You just look a little flushed.' She stepped closer and lowered her voice. 'Did something happen up there?'

'What is it about people when they're happily in a couple?'

'What do you mean?'

'You all think everyone else is at it.' She waved her champagne flute through the air.

Sarah looked offended, but the twinkle in her eye said otherwise. 'That is not true. I did not think you were at it with Jay upstairs. For your sake, if you were, I'd expect you to still be up there doing it.'

Jess rolled her eyes and joined the others around the island as Julian strolled back into the kitchen. She inwardly groaned. He smelt divine and breathing him in was doing things to her. She wondered if she was in heat. She must be. The lack of sex for years had addled her brain, and seeing him topless was the final straw.

Julian gently squeezed Jess's shoulder as he walked past. 'Thanks for your help. It feels much better now.' He flexed his shoulders and back to emphasise the point.

'You're welcome. Anytime. Although I don't suppose you tackle women into bushes often.' She giggled as James spat his beer out, having just taken a sip. It didn't escape her attention that Jay shot daggers with his eyes at him.

'Hey Jay, I'm just about to serve up. Can you do me a favour and do your thing?' Cameron shouted over from the stove top as he scooped out paella onto the waiting, pre-warmed plates.

'Sure thing. Everyone, let's head to the dining room.'

Jess looked around as everyone took the same seats as before, leaving her next to Julian. She wasn't mad about that, but it wouldn't help her out with her current situation.

Julian did his thing, which apparently was pouring everyone's wine, twisting the bottle so it didn't drip and helping Cam carry the plates in from the kitchen. They worked together like well choreographed dancers. She could watch Julian in his element all night.

Julian leaned over Jess as he placed her plate in front of her, and what she breathed in was delicious. Her mouth watered and her skin warmed. She had no idea what the food smelt like; she didn't really care about that.

They chatted as they ate; the conversation flowing just as easily as it had the first time they'd sat together like this. Jess couldn't help but reflect on what they'd all been through since. They all looked so happy, and she wondered when it was her turn.

'Penny for them.' Julian's deep voice was quiet next to her.

She turned to look at him. 'Sorry?'

'Penny for your thoughts.'

She blushed at being caught out wallowing in self-pity. Her mother would have her guts for garters if she saw how she was behaving tonight. 'Oh, yes. I was just thinking about everything these guys have been through. They'll certainly have a story to tell their kids about how they met.'

The skin around his eyes crinkled as he smiled. 'That they will. Although they might need to leave out some details.' He counted off with his fingers as he said, 'Stalking, stabbing, kink clubs, dodgy deals with a mafia boss, and sex dungeons aren't really bedtime story material.'

She huffed out a laugh. 'No, they aren't really, are they? They may need to tweak their stories a little.'

Her eyes followed his hand as he raised his glass of red wine to his lips and took a sip before asking, 'What about you, Jess? What's your story going to be?'

A tragedy.

A comedy of errors.

One thing she knew was that her story wouldn't feature a HEA. It wouldn't even be a happy for now. But admitting that would not only make him ask more questions, but it would hurt.

When she was younger, she would lie awake at night, in the cold dormitory she called home, and imagine a prince would burst through the window and whisk her away. The Princess Bride was her favourite book growing up, and she desperately wanted Wesley to come to her aid. She would jump out the window, landing on Teddy, and ride off into the sunset.

But that wasn't how her story was going to go. Her father had made sure of that.

Instead of pouring out all her troubles, she simply shrugged and said, 'I have no idea.'

He stared into her eyes as if assessing her response. She held her breath, waiting for his judgement. 'I hope it's a good one. You deserve a good one.'

Did she? She wasn't so sure.

'What about you?'

'Me? I'm not destined to have a love story. I'm the beast. The villain, if you will.'

'The morally grey character?' Did Julian have a dark and dirty side? The thought of that gave her a thrill.

'Is that the technical term, is it?'

She nodded and sipped from her glass. She looked at the almost empty glass and made a mental note to drink more water. A note she would no doubt ignore.

'Yep. There are certain criteria you have to fill to get the official title, though.'

'Oh yeah? Like what?' He leaned closer, the heat from his body warming her. Or was that the wine? She was no longer sure.

'Did I hear morally grey mentioned?' Lucy's eyes lit up at the mention of her favourite type of book boyfriend.

'You did. Jess reckons I'd make a good one. She was just about to tell me the criteria.'

Sarah clapped her hands together as James rolled his eyes. 'Oh dear, you've started something now, Jay. Book Club is now in session. There are only two rules of Book Club.' James counted off the points with his fingers. 'One: you do not yuck someone's yum. Two: you do not talk about what's said in Book Club. Do you agree with those terms?'

'Fucking hell, I'm scared, but yeah, sure. I agree.' He downed the last of his wine before reaching for the bottle. He topped Jess's glass up first, before filling his own and passing the bottle along.

Cameron shook his head. 'Brace yourself, Jay. These ladies take no prisoners.'

Imogen elbowed Cam in the bicep and cleared her throat. 'Jay. Do you have any tattoos?'

He bowed his head and Jess was sure he muttered, 'Fuck. Should have known.' After he huffed out a breath, he raised it and said for everyone to hear, 'One. But I don't want to talk about it.'

Sarah's eyes lit up as Jess studied Julian's face. He didn't look particularly comfortable with this line of questioning, and she didn't want to push it but was too late to stop Sarah from blurting out, 'Oh, you know you can't say that and expect us to leave it there. Come on, is it an embarrassing tattoo of a full moon on your arse cheek? I bet it is. Or maybe a tramp stamp on the base of your spine that you got when you partied in Ibiza for the first time.'

Julian's jaw ticked as if trying to collect his thoughts, but Tom jumped into the conversation, saving him.

'Actually, it's best we leave that topic alone. Come on, what's the next question, 'cause I'm covered in tattoos and I want to know if I'm morally grey, too.'

Lucy wrapped her arm around his shoulders and nuzzled her nose along the column of his neck up to his ear. She whispered, but Jess could hear her as she said, 'You know you're the epitome of morally grey, you bad boy.'

Sputtering into her wine, Jess momentarily wondered what had happened to the girl-next-door version of Lucy, then remembered that she'd hooked up with a pleasure Dom and had become a total vixen.

'Moving along. Jay, you have the option to burn the world down to save your woman or sacrifice your woman to save the world. Which would you choose?' asked Sarah.

He turned to Jess and locked eyes with her. 'I'd burn the motherfucker to the ground. No question.'

'Oh, right answer.' Sarah did a little happy dance in her seat and James nodded along approvingly. 'Okay, final question. This one for the win.'

Julian took another sip of his wine and cracked his neck from side to side as if preparing for a fight. 'Hit me with it.'

Sarah's face was entirely too serious for this. 'Theoretically, let's say you're in a situation where Jess has to take her top off and you see her back for the first time.'

Julian raised an eyebrow and glanced at Jess. 'Why am I scared about where this is going?'

'Don't worry, you'll be fine.' Jess rested her hand on his forearm and gave it a reassuring squeeze. Or at least, she hoped that was how he interpreted the move. She'd been staring at his forearm all evening and really wanted to touch it. That reminded her, 'Jay, would you mind passing me the water?'

As he poured, the cool clear liquid glugged into her glass as she realised just how thirsty she was. So thirsty, and not just for the H2O. Sarah's voice focused her attention on the conversation.

'Can we get back to the question at hand, please?' Jay nodded. 'Good. So, you see her back, but it's covered in marks, like she's been whipped. What is the first thing you ask her?'

'As I know Jess doesn't partake in BDSM, I would have to assume that this wasn't a consensual whipping, therefore I would want to know who did this to her, so I could rip his heart out with my bare hands and feed it to him.'

The men all clapped; the women nodded in approval. Imogen raised her glass and said, 'You are officially morally grey.' She fanned her hand at her face. 'And hot.'

'Hey, you can't say that about my cousin.' Cameron grumbled as he pulled Imogen onto his lap, wrapping his arms around her waist.

'Did I do okay, then?' Julian asked Jess.

'Um, yeah. You nailed it.' Her vagina wanted to high-five him. It intrigued her that his first thought turned to BDSM.

'Everyone, can I say something?' Imogen called out.

All eyes fixed on her, and Jess wondered what she was about to say. 'I want to go on a trip with you all. As you've probably guessed, we plan to start a family, or at least try.' She squeezed Cameron's hand. 'And I want to take the opportunity for us to all go away together—our treat—for my birthday.'

'We thought it would be nice to have one last big hurrah before babies end our social lives.' Cameron laughed.

Jess's shoulders dropped with relief. For one selfish moment she thought they were announcing they were pregnant, and whilst she knew that couldn't be the case as Imogen was sitting with a glass of wine, albeit a small one, part of her thought that would be the next blow. She hated herself for thinking it, but her life was soon going to be over. When she had a baby, it wouldn't be born into a loving relationship like Jen and Cam's would be. It would be born out of duty. She would've been happy for them, of course she'd be overjoyed, but part of her would resent the life they have.

Jess knew she could never marry someone she didn't love, just to produce an heir. She didn't want a child growing up with the pressure to take over the family business and live a life according to her father's rules. She'd been through that and wouldn't wish it on anyone. And what would happen if she had a girl? She'd be forced to keep going until she produced a boy because her father was an archaic, sexist twat.

Guilt washed over her. He was all those things, but part of her still wanted his approval. That was how twisted she was. Someone could treat her so badly and she'd keep going back for more.

As everyone cheered, she realised she'd missed the big announcement, but thankfully Sarah clued her in as she danced around the table singing, 'Vegas, baby.'

Perhaps leaving the country and getting out of her father's grip would be just what she needed.

CHAPTER 9

JESS

I Know - Rachel Platten

Jess released a long sigh as the plane touched down. For the first time since she snuck out of her house at four in the morning, she could breathe again. Sneaking out and being rebellious, providing her with a much needed buzz of excitement, but she couldn't ignore the anxiety that was present, bubbling away under the surface.

Imogen organised the trip in record time, stating they didn't have time to waste as she wanted to enjoy everything Vegas offered before getting pregnant. Jess assumed she meant cocktails.

Three weeks later, they were taking their first-class seats on the plane.

Julian was told, in no uncertain terms, that saying no to the trip was not an acceptable answer. He'd reluctantly agreed but hadn't stopped checking his phone for updates on the restaurant.

Jess chose not to mention the trip to her parents. In the three weeks leading up to it, her mother had tried to set her up with Will on multiple occasions, and Jess was running out of excuses for not being available. It wasn't difficult to avoid her father; he'd spent her life being a pro at evading her.

One evening, she'd overheard her parents arguing. Her dad was livid that her mum hadn't progressed the relationship with Will, and apparently time was running out. Jess didn't like to think about what that meant, or how much time she had. And part of her wondered if it would be best if she didn't return home from the trip at all.

Maybe she could just disappear? It had worked for Imogen. Jess rolled her eyes. She could hardly say that Imogen running from her ex had worked. He'd stalked her and nearly killed Cameron. Maybe running wasn't the answer. The problem was, she was clueless about how she was going to get out of this one.

As they reached the baggage reclaim area, the men announced they'd handle the luggage, so Jess, Imogen, Lucy, and Sarah all took a seat on the metal benches that dotted the area.

Sarah stretched her arms to the ceiling and let out a long sigh. 'Ah, this is the life. We get to sit here and watch as our men do all the heavy lifting.' She was clearly eyeing up James as he hauled her suitcase from the conveyor belt. For this trip, he must have engaged holiday mode as he'd replaced his chinos with a pair of dark blue linen trousers.

Sarah licked her lips. 'He's been taking his fitness seriously. He's been working out with Cameron more in the office, and I am here for it. Fuck, he's so hot. I permanently have a hard on for him.'

Jess let out a laugh. 'Bloody hell, Sarah. You're insatiable.'

'I can't help it. He's unlocked this side of me.'

'Shut up, has he. You've always been like that.' Jess had lived her life vicariously through her best friend; enjoying Sarah's tales of her weekend antics, finding them more entertaining than her books.

Lucy leaned over them as she pressed her hand to her chest to stop her delicate white top with brocade sleeves from gaping. 'I know what you mean. I can't get enough of Tom. If he doesn't do everything topless at home, I get so annoyed. I even made him do the ironing topless the other night. Well, until he accidentally steamed his abs.' She grimaced before giggling.

'You just wait until you're trying for a baby, ladies. I'm obsessed. I was sure I was ovulating the other day, so I made him fuck me in the woods behind the office. But don't tell anyone that.' Imogen's eyes were wide as she realised she'd probably overshared.

'As much as I love hearing about your great sex lives, could we not? I'm in the midst of the driest spell ever and there's only so much I can take.' Jess straightened the collar of her pink-marl linen blazer.

'Sorry.' Sarah said as she hugged her. 'Sometimes we get carried away and forget that you're not getting any.'

Jess instantly felt guilty for complaining. She had no right to dull her friends' shine. She was only jealous. 'No, don't worry, I'm just sexually frustrated and sick of my parents cock-blocking me at every given opportunity. Unless, of course, they're the ones getting to choose the cock.'

'Well, your parents aren't here now, are they? But you know who is?' Sarah glanced over at Julian just as he lifted both his and Jess's suitcases off the conveyor with ease. If she didn't know any better, she would swear the cases were empty.

Hers wasn't empty. She was fortunate to have travelled all over the world but had never worked out the secret to packing light. Something she bitched about as she hauled her suitcase into the back of her car as she left that morning.

'This is the perfect opportunity to see if there's more between you. There is literally nothing stopping you now.' Imogen wiggled her eyebrows. Jess had a feeling Imogen was getting up to her usual tricks and meddling in love lives again.

She looked back over at Julian. He was normally tightly wound, always fretting about the restaurant, but since landing in Vegas, his demeanour had changed. A smile played on his lips and his shoulders no longer carried the tension she was used to seeing. The four men stood around, chatting and laughing at something James had just said, like they didn't have a care in the world. Perhaps he'd realised that if anything went wrong at the restaurant now, there was nothing he could do about it. This was progress.

She allowed herself a few more moments to take him in. He was stunning, even though he kept his clothing casual when not at work. But that was what drew her to him. He didn't hide behind a designer outfit, his stature spoke for itself, commanding the room wherever he was. Both women and men walking past gave him a double take, triggering an unexpected possessive streak in her. She wondered how her parents would react if she brought him home and introduced him as her boyfriend. What would her father actually do? It's not like he could physically force her to leave him and bed another. Is it?

He was the opposite of anyone they'd tried to set her up with. They were all scrawny with slicked-back hair, cashmere sweaters and tweed, whereas Julian looked every inch the man with his vintage black band T-shirt, loose fitting dark grey jeans and trainers. A hoodie was casually slung over his shoulder and his dark brown hair sat in floppy waves free from product and begging to be tugged on. Nothing about him screamed old-English, but she didn't care. He was exactly what she wanted. A psychologist would have a field day with her attraction to someone who was the exact opposite of her father in every way.

'From the way you've been eyeing up that man's arse, I'd say you're thinking what I'm thinking.' Sarah's voice broke Jess out of her reverie.

'Oh, blimey, Sarah. That really could be anything.' But at this moment, Jess didn't doubt that their thoughts were aligned.

As they stepped out of the airport into the blazing afternoon sunshine, the heat warmed her face. All four of the ladies closed their eyes and tilted their heads back to soak up the precious rays on their faces. 'Time for a Vitamin-D boost, ladies,' sighed Sarah.

The journey to the hotel was quick and as they all stepped inside the impressive lobby, the welcomed chill of the air conditioning washed over Jess's skin. 'Ah, that's better. I wasn't expecting it to be that hot out.'

James laughed. 'You're literally in the middle of a desert. What else would you expect?'

'Yeah, all right, smartie pants.' Jess stuck out her tongue and caught Julian looking at her with a smile. 'What's so funny, Jay?'

He took hold of her suitcase handle and pulled both his and hers along as he said, 'Nothing. It's just nice seeing everyone so chilled out. It's been a long time since we've all been so happy.'

She swallowed the lump that formed in her throat. 'Yeah. It's about time we were all in a good place. I can take my case, though. You don't need to take it for me.'

'I know you can. That won't stop me from taking it. Tackle it off me if you like.' He raised an eyebrow in challenge.

Jess held her hands up in surrender. 'There'll be no tackling from me, thank you. I've had my fill of that.' Total lie. She'd tackle him to the floor now if she could.

'Shame,' he replied with a smirk. Her heart skipped a beat.

They chatted excitedly as the concierge took them to their suite. As they stepped into the large open-plan living space, Imogen explained, 'I hope you like this place. It sounded perfect when I was researching. It sleeps nine, has a decent coffee machine, an infinity edge spa tub, and an immersion steam shower.'

'What the hell is an immersion steam shower?' asked Sarah, her face scrunched in confusion.

Imogen's face beamed as she said, 'I have no idea, but it sounds so fancy. Oh, and they have Bvlgari bath amenities.'

The ladies all cooed over the details as Cameron tipped the concierge and James, Tom, and Julian delivered the luggage to the rooms.

'Uh, Imogen. You know you said this suite slept nine?' Julian called out as he walked out of the room furthest away from the main living space. 'Where exactly did it say they all slept?' He rubbed at the back of his neck, his T-shirt lifting to expose a patch of defined abs and a dusting of dark hair. Jess licked her lips as she busied herself taking in the opulence of their home for the next few days.

Imogen placed her hands on her hips. 'Uh, well, in bedrooms, I guess.'

'Okay, well I can only find four bedrooms, and they all have king size beds. No twin beds.'

'Right, well, that's okay, isn't it? Because there are eight of us, and four big beds.'

Julian looked at Imogen for a beat as Jess caught on to what he was getting at.

'Jen, I think what Jay is telling you is that there aren't enough beds for three couples.' She gestured between Julian and herself. 'And two single people.'

Imogen scratched at her head. 'Oh shit. You're right. I assumed the ninth person had a single room.' She looked around as if the answer would pop out. 'There must be a sofa bed somewhere then.'

Cameron walked over with a large leather folder in his hands. 'Yeah, it says here that the sofa bed is the one near the TV.'

Imogen rubbed at her temples. 'No, Julian is huge. He can't fit on a sofa bed. Jess, why don't you and I share, and Cam can share with Jay?'

Cameron snapped the folder shut and turned to his wife. 'Sweetheart, do you remember what we're trying to achieve at the moment? I think we stand zero chance of me getting you pregnant if I sleep with my cousin.'

Her face fell. 'Oh, yeah. Um, I don't know what else to suggest.'

Jess felt terrible. It made no sense that she slept in a king size bed while the biggest member of their group slept on the smallest bed.

'I'll sleep on the sofa. Jay, you sleep in the room. Sorted.'

Julian shook his head. 'Nope. Not happening. I have slept in far worse places than a luxury sofa bed. I'll be fine. Honestly, it's all cool.'

Jess wasn't convinced, but knew it wasn't worth arguing over. She wouldn't win.

And that seemed like the story of her life.

Three hours later, they'd all unpacked their luggage and had eaten at one of the Japanese restaurants in the hotel. Jess had insisted that Julian shared her storage space, as there was no way he was going to live out of his bag. She demanded he used her en suite, too. Which had its perks when he stepped into her room wearing only a towel around his waist, dripping wet, rivulets of water trickling down the deep V poking out the top of the towel. She'd keep that image in her bank for life.

She may or may not have watched him from the corner of her eye to find the mystery tattoo, but she couldn't see it. This further confirmed her opinion that it was something embarrassing on his arse cheek. And she really wanted to see it.

His arse.

She wasn't actually that bothered about his tattoo.

'I am exhausted. Can we go to bed now?' asked Lucy as they finished eating the last of the teppanyaki.

Cameron shook his head. 'Nope. It's not late enough. We need to power through until at least eleven, otherwise we'll be out of sorts tomorrow.'

James clapped his hands on his thighs. 'The only way we're going to get through the next couple of hours is shots and dancing. It's my foolproof cure for jet lag.'

Sarah raised her hand. 'I'm up for that.'

'Good girl,' James said with a wink.

'Eh, enough of that. Save that for your bedroom,' laughed Tom, pointing a chopstick at them.

It took thirty minutes for all four men to work out how to set up the sofa bed. This may have been because of the B52 shots they'd consumed. Jess thought it looked anything but luxury. But Julian assured her it would be fine and sent her off to bed.

She lay in bed for what felt like ages, a mixture of booze, dry mouth, and guilt keeping her from slumber. After what she thought was at least an hour, she couldn't put it off any longer and decided she needed a glass of water, otherwise she'd be paying for it all day tomorrow.

She crept out of her room and tiptoed down the corridor, running her hand along the wall to find her way as her eyes tried to adjust to the darkness, the chequerboard tiled floor cool beneath her feet. Her journey was made a little easier as she crept into the living room as the floor to ceiling windows let in the bright lights of Vegas.

Her foot snagged on something and before she could stop herself, she collapsed on the floor with a squeal and a thump in a tangle of sheets. Shots of pain rang up her thighs from her knees.

'Ah, what the fuck!' She rubbed at her knees as Julian sat bolt upright.

'Shit. Are you okay?' His hands reached out to her, resting on her knees, his body heat instantly soothing her.

'Yeah. I'm okay. Just shocked. I'm sorry I trod on you. I wasn't expecting you to be on the floor in the middle of the room,' she whispered. The covers pooled at his waist, revealing his chest to her once again.

'Oh yeah.' He rubbed the back of his neck. 'Turns out the sofa bed is shit and I preferred my chances with the floor. This looked the best spot because of the rug.'

Jess tried to stand, but as she did, the covers that were caught around her ankles tugged and revealed more of Julian. A Julian that was wearing only his boxers. Words failed her. Even in the dim light, she couldn't help but bite her bottom lip at what she saw. It was the only way to stop the groan of desire from leaving her lips.

'Well, this is certainly the most inventive way someone's had a tangle in my sheets,' he said with a quiet laugh.

Her face flashed crimson. 'I'm so sorry.' Before she could think it through, she blurted out, 'Will you please just come and sleep in my bed? It's massive, so there is plenty of room for us both. If it'd make you feel more comfortable, we can build a pillow wall.'

'Do we need a pillow wall, Jess? Should I be worried you're going to fondle me in my sleep?' God, yes. His sleepy voice was as panty-melting as she'd imagined.

'What? No. I promise I won't fondle you.' She absolutely could not promise that. She wanted to fondle his pants off. 'Please. I can't sleep knowing that you're out here on the floor, for Christ's sake. We're spending five days here in a luxury suite and you're on the floor. It's not right and I won't have it.' She hoped she sounded authoritative and not bratty.

He puffed out a breath. 'Okay. I would appreciate that very much. Thank you.' He stood and held a hand out to her. He pulled her up with ease until their chests were almost pressing against each other. She could feel his body heat radiating from him, and she fought the urge to close the gap and nuzzle her face into his impressive pecs. Inhaling deeply, she filled her lungs with as much of him as she could, imagining what it would be like to be enveloped in his arms.

Safe.

She stepped back before she did something embarrassing. 'Come on, let's get to bed. I'm knackered.' Her dry mouth was forgotten as her mind focused on not groping him.

He quickly rolled the sheets up and dumped them on the makeshift bed before following her down the hall towards what was now their bedroom.

As they climbed into bed, Julian let out a groan of pleasure. 'Ah, this is much better. Thanks, Jess.'

'You're welcome.' She rolled onto her side, facing away from the sex-god beside her. Her final thoughts before she drifted off were reminding herself not to fondle him.

CHAPTER 10

JULIAN

Head Under Water (Sadler's Country Version) - Tom Walker

Julian listened to Jess breathing a slow, steady rhythm until he was sure she was asleep before rolling over to face her. He may have joked about her not groping him, but the truth was, he didn't know how he was going to last four nights in her bed and keep his hands to himself.

His groin was clearly thinking the same. He was going to need to get some more suitable sleep attire, something baggy to hide the hard-on he was bound to have as a permanent fixture. Being well endowed meant just wearing his boxers was going to get inappropriate, fast.

Over the last three weeks, he'd been psyching himself up for this trip. He'd listened to what Cameron had said and agreed that it was time he stopped living in the past, but he needed closure over what happened with Chloe. He'd called Tom for advice, the conversation they'd had replaying in his head many times since.

Tonight was no exception.

'You can't keep blaming yourself for what happened to Chloe. You set your boundaries with her, and she didn't respect them. You were right to say no. SSC, Jay. Safe, sound, and consensual. The basic rules of the community are there for a reason. The right to say no isn't just for subs. She didn't follow the basic principles and paid the price, and that isn't on you. I have two pieces of news that I think will help ease your mind.'

'Go on.'

'I know that the guy who did this to her won't be a problem for anyone going forward. He was the same guy that went after Katia's father.'

What the fuck? There really was nothing he could've done to prevent what happened to Chloe if she jumped into a drug-fuelled night with a known Russian mafia member. One that foolishly tried to take on his boss, and Tom, in the process. 'Oh fuck, that explains a lot. What was the second piece of news?'

'I asked around. Chloe is active again and is owned. She's happy. She's safe.'

Julian didn't know how to feel. He'd come some way to getting over the guilt, but knowing she was safe and happy made all the difference. If she could put her past behind her and be with someone, then he could, too.

'Jay, you can stop blaming yourself and get back to doing what you do best. Your pack misses you, you know.'

'Yeah, well, maybe I'm not the same guy I once was.'

'You will be.'

A blinding light interrupted his thoughts, but before he could locate the source, it disappeared. A few seconds later, it was back. He heard a faint vibrating noise and, leaning up on his elbows, saw Jess's phone lighting up constantly. He wondered if he should check who it was. It looked like someone was desperate to get hold of her.

It wouldn't hurt to have a peek. He could make sure it wasn't an emergency and then chuck a pillow over it so he could finally get some sleep. He carefully raised himself up and over her in an athletic side-plank manoeuvre his gym buddies would be impressed with, and plucked her phone from the nightstand.

As he turned the screen to face him, another text message came through.

Dad: Jessica, where the hell are you?

And then, milliseconds later.

Dad: I don't know what you're playing at, but you'd better get yourself back home, NOW.

> **Dad:** You have no idea the shitstorm you have created for me with this little disappearing act. How dare you leave without telling us where you are going.

> **Dad:** Your mother is worried sick. She checked the safe and your passport was gone. Where are you, Jessica?

The text messages continued to stream in. Each one was more frantic than the last.

> **Dad:** You don't get to do whatever you want, you selfish little shit. Your mother has gone to great lengths to set up this weekend. You have a duty to this family and Will is expecting you to comply. Now get home.

He gripped the phone, waiting for the next message to come through, but when the screen went black, he placed it back down on the nightstand. Her father had obviously given up.

Julian's blood boiled. How dare her father speak to her like that. He knew she wasn't exactly happy at home, but he had no idea her father was that unpleasant. Six words stood out to him, and he didn't like them. 'Will is expecting you to comply.'

He wanted to know who the fuck Will was, and what exactly he was expecting her to do. He briefly considered waking her up to question her, but no good would come of that. She was exhausted and needed to sleep.

Leaning back on the bed, he rolled onto his side as he tried to get some sleep, but instead of replaying conversations with Tom, he was planning a conversation with Jess.

As ten o'clock rolled around, he decided he'd let her sleep long enough. He reached up and clicked a button that was built into the headboard and watched as the curtains slowly opened, allowing the morning sunlight to flood the room.

Jess groaned and rolled over, attempting to wrap the covers over her. When she tugged on them and realised they weren't budging, her eyes shot open.

'Oh! Good morning. I'd forgotten where I was for a minute.' Her voice was groggy, her eyelids struggling to open, and Julian desperately wanted to wrap his arms around her and pull her close. But he couldn't.

'Good morning, sleepyhead. You slept well.' He watched in amusement as her eyes widened like saucers.

'Oh. Please tell me I didn't snore. I think I might die if I kept you awake snoring.' Her words were muffled as she kept the covers over her mouth as she spoke.

'Panic not, you didn't make a sound.'

She gave a little nod.

He scrunched his brow together as she remained hidden behind the sheets. 'Is there a reason you won't show me anything below your nose? Have you grown a second face overnight?'

Her eyebrows rose, along with the pitch of her voice. 'Morning breath. I tripped over you because I needed water, and I forgot to get some, so now my mouth feels like something has died in it.'

'Oh, I see. As it was my fault you tripped over, I'll get us a coffee and water. Stay there.'

He knew he was stalling, but he couldn't allow her to be dehydrated. That would be irresponsible of him, and some Dom instincts would never leave him. That was what he was telling himself, anyway.

He grabbed his sweatpants and T-shirt from where he'd discarded them on the living room floor before fixing a tray with coffee and orange juice.

The bedroom was empty when he returned, but he could hear the buzz of an electric toothbrush coming from the en suite.

Seconds later, a much more put together version of Jess climbed back into bed. Julian placed the tray of drinks on the bed as Jess climbed back on. He stood next to the bed, unsure of what to do with himself so focused on sipping his coffee.

'Oh, juice. That is exactly what I need right now.' She downed the entire glass before letting out a long sigh, and then her face scrunched up in disgust. 'Oh shit-a-brick. I shouldn't have done that. Orange juice does not mix well with toothpaste and mouthwash.' She flicked her tongue out and grimaced.

Julian couldn't help but laugh at the faces she was pulling. 'School girl error. Here, drink this.' He handed her the cup of coffee. 'There's creamer and sugar on the tray. Do you want either?'

She shook her head slightly as she blew across the surface of the coffee. 'I'm not a fan of creamer. It's too heavy on the calories. If I have milk, it has to be skinny.'

'Why? You don't have to worry about your weight. You should, however, be worried about getting enough nutrition, and skimmed milk is just cow piss.'

'If I think I don't have to worry about my weight, I'll soon be in a position where I have to worry about my weight.' She glanced away and muttered under breath, 'And nobody loves a big girl.'

'I'm sorry. What did you just say?' His playful mood had just gone out of the window.

She looked embarrassed, choosing to hide behind the cup of coffee. 'Oh, it's nothing. It's just something my mother always says. I don't believe it.'

He pursed his lips as he mulled that statement over. 'Remind me when we get home to have a conversation with you about nutrition and weight maintenance. I'm not about to disrespect your choices, but I highly recommend you add a splash of creamer to your coffee, if that's what you'd like to do.'

She wrapped her hands around the cup and rested it in her lap. 'No. Thank you. I actually really don't like creamer.'

He shrugged, but made a mental note to watch her closely, the need to look after her consuming him. 'Fair enough.'

He perched on the edge of the bed, careful to keep some distance from her. If he got too close, his penis would start doing the thinking, and that would be less than ideal.

Goddammit, he should have had a tactical wank before leaving the hotel for the day.

'Did you sleep well once you were in a proper bed?' She sipped her coffee.

It was now or never. 'Actually, I didn't. Your phone was lit up like the strip out there.' He nodded to the windows.

'Oh. There was me thinking I'd be doing the right thing by letting you sleep here, and I didn't. I never seem to do the right thing.' Her shoulders dropped.

There it was again. He'd been picking up on her self-deprecating comments a lot more recently, and now he knew where it stemmed from. He kept control of the rage simmering in his belly.

'Trust me, you did the right thing. This bed is amazing. I hope you don't mind, but I got worried at how often the messages were coming in, but I didn't want to wake you, so I looked at your screen.'

The colour ran from her face. 'How much did you see?' Her words were muted and filled with trepidation.

'I saw enough. Do you want to tell me what's going on? And who the fuck is Will?' He forced himself to keep his voice calm, his tone soothing. He needed her to know he was a safe space for her.

'It's nothing to worry about. He's just the latest guy my parents are trying to set me up with. They do this all the time. They'll soon realise I'm not interested and move on.'

'I saw a lot more than that in the messages, Jess. You can tell me what's going on. A problem shared is a problem halved.'

Jess finished her coffee and placed it on the nightstand. Her movements were slow and deliberate, and he could tell from the rise and fall of her chest she was straining to look calm.

'I mean it, Jess. You can talk to me.'

'Jay, just leave it. Please.' She averted her eyes, her gaze focused on the bed linen.

He wouldn't leave it. Her pulse twitched erratically under the thin skin on her wrist. Her face was flushed, but the room was cool. She might be hiding the truth, but her body was communicating loud and clear. If he was in a scene, he'd know to pull back and check in.

He slid closer to her and tentatively curled a finger under her chin, tilting her head to look up to him. 'Are you okay? And I'm not talking about a hangover or jet lag. I'm asking if you're okay, back home.'

Her chin quivered, and his heart shattered. He pulled his hand away and clenched his fists, trying to keep the tension out of his face. 'Have you talked to the others?'

Her eyes were like a deer in the headlights as she frantically shook her head. 'No. I can't talk to anyone, especially not the others. Sarah is still getting over the stress of the court case. Imogen is trying for a baby. The last thing she needs is to be worrying about me. And Lucy has been through enough. I can't bring more stress and issues to the table.'

He sat up on his knees, closing the gap between them, but he was careful not to crowd her. 'I don't want to do this, Jess, but if you don't tell me what's going on, I will speak to them. We're your friends and you know we don't suffer alone.' He felt like a dick saying that out loud after he'd so long blaming himself for what had happened to his ex and shutting himself off from the world, but in his eyes, that made him qualified to have that opinion.

She looked hurt as she stared into his eyes and it killed him to be the one to put that look there, but it had to be done.

'I don't know what to say.'

'Start by telling me the truth. Who is Will and what is he expecting you to comply with?' He didn't want to ask the next question, but he had to. 'Jess, is he forcing himself on you?'

Her head snapped up to meet his gaze. She shook her head. 'No. He wouldn't dare. He's just as much a pawn in whatever game my father is playing.'

'What game?'

She rolled her head and released a long sigh, resignation written all over her face. 'Okay. If I tell you, promise not to tell the others.'

'You know you should tell the others.'

'I mean it, Jay. If you betray my trust, I'll never forgive you. Promise me or I won't tell you anything and you can go back to sleeping on the floor.'

He didn't like it, but he'd rather know what was going on than not. 'I promise.'

'I think my dad might be in financial difficulty. I overheard him on the phone about a month ago. He was really stressed out. And he kept talking about an investment and how I was part of the deal.'

Where did Jess come into this? As far as he knew, she didn't have any involvement in her father's bank. 'Where do you and Will come in to this?'

'They want me to marry Will to grease the wheels of a merger or something. I think Will's father has handed over money for shares and I was supposed to be a bonus. I got little information from what I overheard, but that's what I'm assuming it's all about.'

Julian remained silent, not wanting to give Jess an excuse to stop talking, but it was getting increasingly difficult to prevent a violent outburst.

'Please understand that in my family's social circle, we still live by old-fashioned ideals, and one of those is that women are for breeding and looking pretty. My Dad was incredibly disappointed when I was born missing one very important body part.'

He understood perfectly what she was talking about, but that conversation was for another time.

'I was raised to be seen and not heard. I was to look pretty and be polite. My role in life is to produce an heir as soon as possible. Love doesn't come into it. Honestly, it's the reason I don't really like historical romance. They read like my diaries.' She cracked a small smile, and it broke his heart and his resolve.

He jumped up from the bed and paced around the room. 'I fucking hate them. The stuck-up, egotistical, narcissistic, pompous twats.' He stopped pacing and faced Jess. 'I'm so sorry you've had to live through that.'

'It's okay. You can't know what it's like. I don't expect you to understand.'

He understood it. He'd grown up surrounded by people just like her father. Cameron was lucky. His father was down-to-earth and moved his mother away from that world as soon as they were married. Julian wasn't as lucky. Both of his parents were from 'old money,' and he'd realised as soon as he started secondary school that he would never fit in. Later in life, he learned they were just better at hiding their debauchery.

His family was conservative but loving. And for that, he was grateful. But he could see the disappointment in their eyes when he announced he wanted to be a chef. They wanted him to be a lawyer, a banker, or the world's best brain surgeon. In the end, he walked away from the life they wished for him and set up the Four Corners restaurant with Cameron. It's not that he didn't have the money to do it on his own, it was that he didn't want to use it; he hadn't earned it.

'I don't need to understand to know that what you're going through isn't right. Have you spoken to your parents and explained that you don't want to marry Will?' He'd assumed she didn't want to marry him. He hoped to God that was the case.

'There's no point. My parents have never listened to what I say or cared about what I want. They won't start now, especially when the business is at stake.' Her lip quivered again, and she took a shuddering breath. 'I keep telling myself that I won't go along with it. My parents deserve nothing from me, but I just can't bring myself to walk away. I'm so fucked up in the head that a part of me thinks this is how I can finally earn their love and respect.'

He fisted his hands to keep them from wrapping her in his arms. He wanted to hold on tight and tell her she deserved all the love in the world, but not from people like that.

But he couldn't hold back any longer. He gently cupped her face with one hand as he shuffled closer. 'I'll help you. You're not alone in this.'

She scoffed at that. 'How can you help me, Jay?'

Good question. He didn't know the answer, but what he knew was that she wasn't marrying anyone against her will.

'Give me some time, okay? I'll think of something.'

She nodded. 'And you promise not to tell the others? I've spent my life feeling like a burden. I don't want to feel like that around my friends. They're my happy place.'

'I won't tell them.' *For now.* If shit got real and he needed some help, he'd be turning to Tom. But she didn't need to know that.

'Where's the creamer gone? Anyone seen it?' came a holler from the kitchen.

'Looks like the others are up. Are you ready to put a smile on your face and paint the town red?'

'No. But I will be after another coffee.' As he went to leave the room and give her some privacy to get herself together, she added, 'Jay, in case you weren't sure, you're my happy place too. Thank you for being here for me.'

Oh fuck. His dick stopped talking. It was his heart's turn to get in on the action.

CHAPTER 11

JESS

Edge of Saturday Night - The Blessed Madonna & Kylie Minogue

Their day had started with a lazy brunch in the hotel's rooftop restaurant, where they discussed the plans for the day. Imogen had booked them matinee tickets to see the Crazy Horse show, so they filled the early part of the afternoon messing around on slot machines before heading back to the hotel to get ready for the show and an evening spent exploring the main strip.

Julian had suggested Jess used the shower first so she could 'do all the girly shit' while he showered after. This seemed like the perfect plan.

When Jess agreed to that plan, she hadn't thought about the fact she'd be in their room getting ready with him. She also hadn't taken into consideration how good he would look, or smell, while he was getting ready.

To save any embarrassment, she'd quickly dressed in a simple black Bardot neckline dress that stopped just above her knees. It was just about warm enough in the evenings for her to not bother with tights or stockings and inwardly stuck her fingers up to her mother and her stupid dress-codes. Once she was suitably covered up, Julian came in to use the shower.

It's a wonder she managed to apply her makeup as well as she had as thoughts of a naked Julian in the shower continually distracted her and, at one point, she nearly applied mascara to her eyebrows.

She kept glancing in the mirror in the hope she'd nonchalantly catch the moment he opened the en-suite door, wrapped only in a towel.

Her hard work paid off.

It was like something out of a movie. As the door opened, steam billowed out before he stepped through it. It was better than she could've imagined. He wasn't wrapped in a towel. He was wearing just his boxers that clung in all the right places.

Holy fuck, he was packing heat.

When she'd unceremoniously tripped over him, she'd not noticed the full extent of his package, but tonight, she was very much noticing it. It was impossible not to.

Surely that wasn't flaccid?

It must have some blood in it. Maybe he'd had a wank in the shower, and this was what it looked like before it'd fully deflated?

For fuck's sake, she was rambling in her head and obviously staring at his dick. Their eyes met in the mirror, and he was most definitely smirking.

'You're looking beautiful this evening, Jess. Be careful with that mascara wand, though. You nearly took an eye out then.'

He grabbed his black jeans from where he'd laid them out ready on the bed and slipped them on.

That only made it worse.

A hot man wearing only jeans was every woman's kryptonite. Never, in the history of ever, had she found herself wishing a hot man would put more clothes on. This was ridiculous.

She quickly finished her makeup with a slick of nude lip gloss and pulled her jewellery roll from the top drawer of her dresser. Her makeup and outfit were simple so she could dress it up with some jewellery. She'd brought her favourite fancy necklace with her. A gold, chunky snake that wrapped around her neck before making its way to her cleavage. It made her feel sexy, and that was definitely how she wanted to feel tonight, especially if she was going to be on the arm of Jay. It was also her mother's least favourite, and she could never wear it around them.

Her fingers were trembling as she tried to pull on the clasp. It didn't help that she was still trying to glimpse Julian getting dressed. He pulled a simple white shirt from the wardrobe and shrugged it onto his shoulders. Before he buttoned it up, he noticed Jess struggling with her necklace.

'Want a hand with that?'

The room instantly grew hotter. She cleared her throat and said, 'Yes, please.'

He smiled as he walked over, barefoot, jean clad, and shirt blessedly open. He stopped behind her, so close they were almost touching, and ran his fingers through her hair, moving it to one side. His touch sent tingles across her, lighting her up. Gently taking the necklace out of her grip, he secured it in place.

'This looks stunning on you.' He rested his hands on her shoulders as their eyes met in the mirror once more.

'Thank you. It's my favourite. Makes me feel invincible.'

'I can see why. I'll be proud to have you on my arm this evening, Miss Chatwin.'

Kiss me. Kiss me. Kiss me, she chanted in her head, hoping the message would work its way to him. But his lips didn't brush her exposed shoulders like she hoped they would. Instead, he stepped back and walked over to the other dresser, buttoning up his shirt. Then he went and bloody well rolled the sleeves up to mid-forearm.

Was he doing this on purpose? She was certain he was. She needed to escape the room before she ruined her underwear. 'Right. I'll leave you in peace and see you out there.' She grabbed her purse and shoes, bundling them into her arms as she dashed out to wait in the living room, where she hoped there was a bottle of something, anything, open.

'Here she is. What took you so long? Anything to do with a hot, sexy beast of a man?'

'Ha-ha, hilarious, Sarah. I was struggling with my necklace, that's all.'

Sarah didn't look convinced as she poured Jess a glass of champagne.

Sarah looked stunning in a petrol-blue silk dress that floated down to the floor. The halter neck kept it in place and left her back almost entirely exposed. She suspected James had a say in what she wore tonight, as it hadn't escaped her attention that James's favourite thing to do was have a hand on Sarah's back.

In fact, everyone had scrubbed up well. They looked like they'd all walked straight off the set of a GQ photoshoot, and she wondered if she was letting the side down with her simple black dress.

Then out walked Julian. He'd styled his hair to fall in loose waves to the side. His shirt was disappointingly buttoned up, but the top two remained open, exposing just enough of his skin to keep Jess salivating. Between that and the forearms, she was glad they'd be in the dark for the next couple of hours.

Stealth perv activated.

She felt lighter, more playful since offloading onto Julian this morning and was determined to enjoy this break with her friends to the fullest. If that meant mentally undressing one of them at every given opportunity, she was okay with that. She'd allow herself to live in that fantasy for the rest of her time in Las Vegas as she had no idea what awaited her when she got home.

The thought of home sent a shiver skittering over her skin, and before she could mull over her situation any longer, she put a smile on her face and drank her champagne. She was here to celebrate Imogen's birthday and wouldn't let her parents, or more specifically her father's dodgy dealings, ruin this.

As they left the show, Julian rubbed at his eyes. 'Bloody hell, Jen. You weren't messing around with those seats, were you? I feel like I'm intimately involved with most of the cast and need to take them all out for dinner.'

He reached out and took Jess's hand in his, automatically interlacing their fingers. It felt so natural, and he clearly wasn't fully aware he was doing it. Jess had no intention of questioning it. She enjoyed feeling effortlessly wanted and wouldn't give him a reason to stop. Did that make her feel like a desperado? It did, but she'd worry about that later.

Julian looked at Imogen and said, 'I hope our plans for the rest of the evening contain fewer tits and arse.'

James shot him a look of utter disgust. 'I can't believe you just said that, mate. I don't know if we can be friends anymore.'

Julian shrugged. 'I feel like I'm at an amazing buffet table and I'm strictly nil-by-mouth.'

Jess giggled and squeezed his hand. 'I feel your pain, trust me, and I'm not even a tits-and-arse girl.'

It was James's turn to laugh as he said, 'You could be. Sarah has become rather fond of Roxy's tits, haven't you, Angel?'

Sarah sighed, looking wistful. 'Yep. They're fun to play with and taste like sunshine. Anyway, enough about that. What's next on the agenda, Mrs Black?'

Imogen's eyes lit up. 'I have a suggestion of what to do. You know how at kid's birthday parties they usually play games?'

Everyone remained silent, and if they all felt like Jess, it was out of fear of what she was about to suggest.

She carried on, unperturbed. 'Well, I'd like to play a game, and I think hide and seek would be so much fun around Vegas. What do you reckon? We should split into our couples—oh, shit, I've done it again. Sorry Jay and Jess. I mean, pairs. We pair off and the girls hide. The last couple—sorry, pair—to meet up at the cocktail bar has to pay the tab at the bar when they get there.'

Everyone looked a little confused, and Jess was no exception. Jess scratched her nose and said, 'But I thought the point of hide and seek was to not get caught first. Surely the first to the bar is the loser?'

Imogen put her hands on her hips. 'Well, yes, usually. But that doesn't work here. The race is on to find your partner, get to the cocktail bar, and drink as much as you can on the tab before the losers arrive.'

Cameron raised his hand as if in a classroom. 'Can I just say I'm not sure about you walking around here on your own.'

Tom nodded. 'I agree. Can we set some rules about where you go and how far away you go? You ladies have a habit of getting into… difficulties.' He shoved his hands in his pockets and shrugged his shoulders.

Sarah pointed her thumb at Tom. 'He has a point.' She looked around at their surroundings. 'What about if we have to stay within two casinos distance? One on each side. To be honest, my shoes hurt, and I don't fancy walking too far, anyway.'

That seemingly appeased the men of the group as they all nodded their approval. Jess caught Julian's eye and noticed something flash in them as he tilted his lips in a slight smirk. Whatever it was she saw in him, it sent shivers through her body that made her eager for the game to begin.

Imogen clapped in delight. 'Yes. I like it. Boys.' She pointed to the coffee shop near to where they stood. 'Go in there and order yourselves a shot of espresso. In the time it takes for you to order, pay, and drink it, that's how long we have to hide. Got it?'

They all nodded and said, 'Got it,' in unison.

Before they all went their separate ways, Cameron said, 'But ladies, if you see anyone even remotely dodgy come near you, scream and run away. Okay?'

Imogen gave him a squeeze to reassure him. 'Don't worry, Cam. We'll be fine.' She turned to face Jess, Sarah, and Lucy, while bouncing on her heels, said, 'Let's do this.'

Jess felt a rush of excitement at the prospect of being hunted by Julian, and whilst she didn't want to get stuck with a massive bar tab, she didn't want to be found straight away.

The others gave each other hugs and kisses, leaving Jess and Julian looking awkwardly at each other. She had to hand it to Jen; if this was a dastardly plan to match-make, it was epic.

'Okay, I'll come and find you as quickly as I can. I don't want to boast, but I'm a bit of an expert at this game,' Julian said with pride on his face.

'Oh, really?' Jess loved how carefree he was when he wasn't stressing about his business. The bottle of red wine he'd shared with her at the show helped with his mood too, as she noticed the tension in his shoulders ebb away with each glass.

'Yeah, I'm basically a professional. Don't worry about making it easy for me. In fact, hide as well as you can so it's fair to the others. I don't want to show them up.' His smile crinkled the skin around his eyes.

'Blimey, you're very confident in your abilities,' she said with a giggle. 'I shall make it nice and hard for you.' As the words left her mouth, she heard the double entendre. And from the playful grin he was giving her, it hadn't escaped Julian's attention, either.

'I'll look forward to that,' he said as he wiggled his eyebrows. He cupped her face in his hands and planted a kiss on her forehead before heading off with the others to start the game. She was never washing her forehead again. She wished he was like that with her all the time, it felt so natural that she had to remind herself it was the red wine making him so relaxed with her, and not their relationship status.

Imogen gave her an eyebrow wiggle and a smile. Even though she didn't say the words out loud, Jess knew she was thinking. 'I love it when a plan comes together.'

Jess gave herself a few seconds to watch his retreating arse, and then the girls wished each other luck and dashed off in different directions with an excited squeal.

She knew it was just a harmless game, but the adrenaline rush she experienced made her heart race as she scanned the surrounding area. She could see a cafe themed like a rainforest. Perhaps she could hide behind one of the plastic trees? She quickly discounted that as a stupid idea.

Glancing over her shoulder, she checked if she could see any of the men leaving the coffee shop. She released a breath when she saw the coast was clear and dashed over to the other side of the casino. She saw a flash of curly red hair dive behind a row of slot machines and headed further away.

Her plan was to keep moving and then backtrack to where Julian may have already checked. She smiled to herself as she scanned all around her, constantly on high alert, sure she was making it difficult for him.

She crept along the outer wall and headed for the main entrance to the casino. If she could hide near the entrance, she'd be able to see if Julian went into a casino on either side. Then she'd sneak back inside and get a drink from the coffee shop. He'd never expect her to end up there.

She was the hide and seek genius. She was sure of it.

She glanced back every few paces to make sure Julian wasn't there. To get through the main doors, she'd leave herself exposed, and she wasn't ready to get caught.

Dashing through the main entrance on the far left side of the building, she hurried along the edge, trailing her hands along the brickwork and ducked around the corner into an alleyway between the buildings.

Peering down into the alleyway left her feeling a little uneasy, so she stayed close to the front. She gripped the corner of the building, keeping watch.

This was the perfect plan.

Right until she heard footsteps.

CHAPTER 12

JULIAN

Bad Things - Jace Everett

'Did you tell Imogen that Jay is a fucking primal Dom?' asked James as he blew on his espresso, cooling it enough to knock it back.

Julian coughed out, 'Used to be. Not anymore, remember?' That earned him an eye roll from James.

Cameron shook his head as he grimaced after downing his own drink. 'Christ, that coffee is shit. They should be ashamed of themselves; it's over-extracted and overheated. Fucking amateurs.' He turned to face James. 'No, of course I haven't told Jen that. It's not my place to tell anyone about my cousin's sexual preferences. It's not like I drop it into conversation over our morning coffee and toast.'

'So where has all this hide and seek stuff come from? I'm sure this entire trip is an excuse to set Jay and Jess up.' He held his hands up, palm facing towards the others. 'I'm not mad at the chance to chase Sarah, though. If she's hidden somewhere good, it may be some time before I take her to the cocktail bar. And it'll be worth the massive tab.'

Tom laughed. 'For the love of all that is holy, please don't get caught in a scene with Sarah in the middle of this casino. That won't go down well, and I think she's had enough of being in the public eye, don't you?' Tom combed his hands through his hair as he looked out the door of the coffee shop.

'Obviously I'm not going to Dom her in the middle of this place, but I can get something started. I'm enjoying this already. Jay, I can see why you did it.' Everything about the way James was standing exuded energy. He was ready and raring to go.

Julian was enjoying it too. He could feel his body coming alive the closer it came to starting the hunt. Gearing up to find Jess felt natural. He felt comfortable in his skin, like he'd just shrugged on a well-worn jacket or hoodie. He'd already downed his espresso, which didn't help with the nervous energy building inside him.

He was itching to go after her but knew better than anyone that the wait was worth it. He wanted to build the anticipation.

He had to remind himself that this wasn't an actual hunt for him. Jess wasn't his sub. This wouldn't end the way it usually did. The closest he'd get to sex from this is if he ordered a sex on the beach at the bar afterwards.

He wanted to tell them all this was nothing compared to the real deal, but opted to keep that to himself. He didn't want to give them an opening to start a conversation, and he really didn't need another therapy session from his well-meaning friends.

Instead, he said, 'Just try to remember that we're not all coupled up and keep the PDAs to a minimum when you find them. Okay?'

Cameron slapped him on the shoulder. 'Understood. I'm sorry if you feel awkward. That's not our intention. We keep forgetting that you and Jess aren't a thing. You really should take the opportunity to—'

'Before you say it, I know. I intend to chill out on this trip and if something happens, it happens. I'm not ruling it out, but I'm not going to magically get over my issues and jump into bed with Jess. She deserves someone who's sure about what they want, and I don't know if I'm there yet.'

'I totally understand that, mate,' said James. 'I was the same with Sarah. Take your time. Jess is special and you don't want to hurt her.' He clapped his hands together and instantly changed the serious mood by saying, 'Let's go chase down some sexy women.'

The others all headed off in different directions without a plan. Julian shook his head and muttered 'amateurs' under his breath. He took a deep breath while he calmed his senses and cleared his mind. Finding a needle in a haystack took thought and consideration. Know your prey and think like they would.

He knew Jess would want to win and, in her mind, winning would mean being found last. He also knew that she wouldn't simply hide behind a slot machine and hope he didn't happen across her. She'd make it difficult for him. She'd keep moving and likely double-back on herself. And to do that, she needed a good vantage point, one where she could watch him but stay hidden. He smiled to himself as he turned his head towards the entrance of the casino. She'd want to loiter near the entrance. That way, she could see into the casino, but also see when he inevitably left to look for her elsewhere. Then she'd take her chance and run back inside, hiding where he'd already checked. Knowing her, she'd go straight to the coffee shop and order a drink, safe in the knowledge she'd outsmarted him. But what she didn't know was that he was born for the hunt.

A large group of men, no doubt at a bachelor party, were walking towards the doors. They were laughing and chatting loudly and gave Julian the perfect cover. He blended in with the crowd so he could leave the casino without Jess being able to see him.

And, bingo.

There she was, her face peeking around the corner of the brick building. Her blonde hair shining under the flashing lights that surrounded her. He rubbed at his jaw, raking his nails through his stubble as he worked out how long he'd give her.

Should he walk up to her now or let her sweat a little longer?

The decision was taken away from him as he noticed a few of the guys he'd used as cover break away from the group and walk in her direction. He didn't like how they were looking at her, or the way they shoved at each other's elbows, goading each other on.

The crowd that had given Julian the cover he needed was now blocking his path. He frantically pushed his way through them as they all looked at their phones and discussed which way they needed to go to get to their next destination, oblivious to their friends' misdeeds. As he broke through them and onto the other side, Jess was yanking her arm out of the grip of one of them.

'Hey, sexy. What's a nice girl like you doing hanging around dark corners? You look too fancy to be a hooker. Or are you one of those high-class ones? Come on, you can join our party.'

Julian didn't appreciate them speaking to her like that. Not one bit. He stepped closer, standing with his back to Jess, blocking them from reaching her again. 'I suggest you stay the fuck away from her, unless you want to get seriously hurt.' He growled the words out through clenched teeth.

'Why don't you just keep walking, fuck-face?'

He took another step closer and shook his head. 'I'm afraid I can't do that.'

The cockiest of the three curled his lip into a sneer. 'Oh, really? Why? What has she got to do with you?'

'I don't like it when other people touch what's mine.' He chanced a glance at Jess. Her eyes were wide, and not entirely with terror. He recognised the look in her eyes, and it stirred the beast he kept hidden. He'd seen it all too many times on the faces of his subs during a scene.

The scumbag laughed, the sound grating on Julian's last nerve. 'Well, then I'd say you've got a problem, *mate*,' he said with an exaggerated, and shit, British accent.

Images of Chloe, battered and broken, flashed in his mind, clouding his judgement. Jess wasn't in the same situation that Chloe put herself in, but he was past reasoning. All he could see was a group of men crowding a vulnerable woman.

'I'm not. Your. Fucking. Mate.' He could feel his nails digging into his palms as he held himself back.

Julian pulled himself up to his full height as rage took over. Adrenaline pumped through his veins as he readied himself to punch the living daylights out of this wanker. The other two weren't so brave as they backed away, joining the others who'd noticed something was going on. He stepped forward until he was almost chest to chest with him. Julian had the size advantage and knew this would be an easy fight, but he'd rather avoid losing his shit with Jess so close.

As he clenched his fist, a man dressed as Dorothy from the Wizard of Oz—obviously the groom—stepped up to them, his hands out as he said, 'Brad, for fuck's sake, leave the woman alone.' He turned his attention to Julian. 'Sorry. He gets a bit tasty when he's been drinking gin. I'll make sure he stops. Just please, don't hit him. My fiancée will kill me if he does anything to ruin the wedding photos.'

He shook his head as Jess wrapped her arm around his upper arm, gripping tightly. 'Fine. Get this twat out of my sight. Now.' The muscle in his jaw ticked as he worked to keep his anger in check. He could easily take on one or two of them, but he knew if shit hit the fan, he could find himself on the receiving end of ten drunken men and a groom in a cheap Dorothy costume trying to defend their friend. That wasn't on his list of things to do today.

Dorothy grabbed his friend's shoulder and pulled him away. 'Again, sorry. Have a nice evening.'

'I want him to apologise to my girlfriend.' He couldn't just let this guy walk away. He wouldn't let another man mistreat a woman he cared about again.

'Yeah. Yeah, of course.' Dorothy nudged at his friend. 'Say sorry to her, now.' He flicked his brown plaited wig over his shoulder, a move Julian would've found hilarious in any other situation.

The idiot stepped forward, rubbing at his face before mumbling, 'Sorry. I think I might've had too much to drink. You're lovely, and in no way do you look like a hooker. I'd do yo—'

He didn't finish the sentence as Julian's palm made contact with the side of his face, snapping the guy's head around with the force. 'You can fuck off now. And don't worry, that won't ruin the photos.'

The crowd dissipated as Dorothy shouted at them all to move on, and they found themselves alone in the alley. The sounds of the drunken party drowned out as they walked away. He gently took hold of her hand, twisting it round so he could inspect where the lout had grabbed her wrist.

He rubbed his thumb across the underside of her wrist, feeling her pulse beat. 'Are you okay?'

She nodded as their eyes met and her lips parted, her tongue darting out to moisten them.

'Fuck,' Julian muttered under his breath before he rounded on Jess, gripped her throat and pushed her against the wall.

She released a groan as his mouth smashed down onto hers, his tongue forcing her lips apart as he licked and bit down on her bottom lip. He tightened his grip on her throat as he nudged her legs apart with his knee and pressed himself against her. Need coursed through him, bringing more than just his dick to life. Every cell in his body screamed that she was his to taste. His to take.

His free hand slapped against the wall next to her head, the rough bricks pinching his skin, making it burn. With a final tug on her bottom lip, he growled, 'Tell me to stop, Jess.'

She didn't. Instead, she raked her nails through the hair on the back of his head and kissed him, sucking his tongue into her mouth. Her leg hooked around his hip, hitching her dress up her thighs, exposing her black lace knickers to him.

She breathed out a gasp as he finally released her throat, needing both his hands to grab her wrists and press them into the wall above her head. He transferred her wrists into one of his hands, holding her in place as his other roamed her body before coming to a stop at the seam of her thong.

He didn't ask permission. As he took her mouth in another punishing kiss, he slid a finger straight into her core and swallowed down her moans.

'Did that make you wet? Did you want those men to fuck you? Is that why you hid in a dark fucking alley?'

'Julian, please.' From the tone in her voice, he didn't know if she was pleading with him to stop or to carry on. Her hips rocked against his hand, giving him the answer. He slid in a second finger, his dick leaking with how tight she was. He imagined how perfect she would feel wrapped around his cock.

'I want to fuck you up against this wall, Jess. I want to tear these fucking knickers from your body and stuff them in your mouth so you can't scream when I fill you. Is that what you want?'

Her eyes widened; her pupils blown. 'Yes. I want that.'

He felt her walls grip his fingers in a pulsing rhythm, and he knew with a few more strokes he could get her off.

'Oi, get a room, you two.' A booming voice followed by a laugh echoed down the alley. Julian withdrew his fingers and covered Jess with his body as she straightened out her dress.

'Fuck. Double fuck,' Julian muttered to himself. He should've had more self-control than that. Jess deserved so much more than a quick fuck against a grimy wall, and if it wasn't for the interruption, that's where it was headed. 'I'm no better than the drunken louts.'

Jess looked up at him, shock on her face. 'What?'

'I took advantage of you. Here I am, ready to beat a man for calling you a hooker, and then I take advantage.'

'Whatever that was, I wanted it. I could've asked you to stop, but I didn't. I'm done with being pushed around, Jay.'

He hung his head in shame. 'You might think that now, but you were running off adrenaline. I know what it's like to get carried away, which means I should've controlled myself sooner. This isn't the time or place for this. I'm sorry.'

She lifted her chin as she said, 'Stop apologising. No one has stood up for me like that before. Jay, the things you said… I don't know how to explain what those words did to me.'

He swallowed the lump that formed in his throat as he reached up and gently tucked her hair behind her ear and cupped her cheek in his hand.

'You know I'll always fight for you, Jess.'

The fire in her eyes blinked out as she said, 'If there's one thing my father's taught me, it's never to back a losing horse.'

'I never lose.'

Julian marvelled at how quickly Jess outwardly recovered from what had happened in the alley as she greeted their friends with a megawatt smile. Brushing off problems was clearly a practised skill of hers, and it made him wonder what she'd lived through. Yet another reason for him to hate her father.

They'd found the others chatting loudly as they all sipped on the most obnoxious cocktails he'd ever seen. Smoke billowed out of Sarah's drink and didn't look at all pleasant.

'Ah, here they are.' James stood up and clapped his hand on Julian's shoulder. 'Not as much of an expert as you thought you were, eh?' He laughed as he handed a padded leather folder over. 'Here's the tab.'

Jess went to take hold of it, but Julian swung it out of reach, holding it above his head. 'Nope, you don't need to see this. I've got it. What's everyone having? I'll get the next round in while I'm settling this.' He waved the folder in the air.

They all called out random sounding cocktails like, *the light bulb*, *the demon's crotch*, and *The Mad Hatter's tea*.

As he and Jess waited at the bar, Jess scanned the menu that looked more like a phone book and tapped her fingers against the polished wood. 'I haven't got a clue what to get. I like the sound of a *screaming orgasm*. Sarah's *demon's crotch* looked interesting; she said it was a bit spicy.' She drummed her nails on the menu. 'Oh, I can't decide.'

'If you want my advice, I generally try to avoid a spicy crotch. That's usually a sign of something untoward. Maybe go with a *screaming orgasm*.' Julian smiled at her, hoping to give her some reassurance that everything was good between them.

Jess raised an eyebrow. 'Yes, perhaps I should order one. It's the only way I'll be getting one of those any time soon.'

Bollocks. He was proving to be a total arse-hat tonight. Why did he have to suggest that to her? He should've stuck with something safe, like a *Long Island iced tea*.

Before he could fumble a reply, she'd walked off to join the others, leaving him with the tray of cocktails and the bill.

His eyes bulged at the figure on the bill.

CHAPTER 13

JESS

Shiver – Hazlett

As Julian handed out the drinks, Jess couldn't bring herself to make eye contact with him. She politely took the glass and downed it far too quickly, but she needed something to take the heat away. Her cheeks were flaming, and her core was positively smouldering. She didn't mean to be a dick with Julian, but she couldn't help how she felt. The way he took over and pressed her into the wall, she wanted him to take her there and then. She'd never felt so alive or turned on. If they'd carried on for just a few more seconds, she would've orgasmed and the residual burning need was almost as painful as how she felt when he'd put a stop to it. In doing so, he'd added himself to the list of people who think they know what's best for her.

But that didn't stop her from wanting him. She was struggling to reconcile her feelings, and the drink was doing a good job of deadening them.

If she was being honest with herself, she didn't know what her future looked like. She had no idea what her father was up to, or what she'd be walking into when she got home, and she couldn't put Julian in the middle of it. She was falling for him, which was dangerous. Whenever she was around him, she lusted after him, but she thought too much of him to pit him against her father.

She was so confused, and his pheromones were addling her brain. And the way he gripped her throat and snogged the soul right out of her body destroyed any resolve to do the right thing and stay away from him.

'You took your time getting here. We were about to send out a search party,' Sarah said as she blew the smoke away from her drink.

'Well, I'm just a professional at hiding, I guess.' She shrugged.

'And Jay is apparently some sort of expert finder, so you did well to evade him for as long as you did.'

Jess turned to Julian as he stepped up to the tall table they were all standing around. Apparently, this bar was too trendy for stools. 'Jay, I keep hearing you're an expert finder. Please explain how you can achieve such a title?'

Pretending nothing had happened, and that she wasn't dying inside, was her coping strategy. Being in denial had worked for most of her life, so she didn't see the point of confronting her feelings now. The ramifications of it were firmly shoved into the box of things to deal with in the future. The issue, however, was that the box was stuffed to capacity.

Julian glared at James over the rim of his glass, which was no mean feat as it was stuffed with every cocktail umbrella known to man. James returned the glare with a mumbled, 'Don't look at me. I didn't say anything.'

Curious. What was going on here?

Julian cleared his throat. 'I was just really good at the game growing up, that's all.'

Jess gave him a half nod and squinted her eyes at him. 'Okaaay. Well, you did a good job finding me tonight, for I,' she pressed her hand to her chest, 'am an expert hider, as proved by us being the last here.'

Julian laughed. 'My receipt for over five hundred dollars doesn't make me feel like we won that one, but I can't argue with the facts. You were the last to be found, and in my eyes, that makes you the winner.' His expression softened as their eyes met.

Her attention was pulled away as her clutch purse vibrated in the palm of her hand. She popped it open and glanced at the text preview on her phone.

Little Willy: Jessica, I don't know what you're up to, but my father is raging and apparently it's all my fault because I can't do anything right. Care to explain what the fuck is going on? I told you before, play the fucking game. Please stop pretending you're better than the rest of us.

Quickly shutting her clutch, she mentally shook off the timely reminder of what awaited her back home. As with all his other messages, this one would be ignored.

Her heart ached with the effort of keeping the smile on her face as Julian stared at her. She was a mess. She needed a minute to collect her thoughts. 'I'm just going to pop to the loo. Back in a minute.'

She dashed off in what she hoped was the direction of the ladies' room, not waiting for her friends to offer to accompany her. As she flung herself through the door, Sarah was quick to follow behind.

'Hey, hun. Are you okay?' They stood next to each other at the sinks, talking to their reflections in the mirror. Floor-to-ceiling black gloss tiles absorbed some of the harsh light coming from the spotlights overhead, but not enough to hide the smudged mascara and lips that betrayed what they'd been up to earlier.

'I'm fine, really.' She wasn't fine. She was the very definition of not fine.

'Has something happened between you and Jay? You look like you've had your face snogged off, but you're not glowing with satisfaction. What happened?'

Jess dabbed a damp paper towel under her eyes and glanced over at Sarah. 'Can I say I don't want to talk about it and leave it at that?'

'Nope.' Sarah rested her hip on the sink, folded her arms across her face, and fixed Jess with a stare.

She thought as much.

'We may have kissed when he found me. I was hiding in an alleyway and one thing led to another, but someone walking past interrupted us. He then turned all gentlemanly and told me it shouldn't have happened, and it pissed me off.'

She was being light on the details because she didn't want them all turning the drunken blokes into more of a problem than they were, and she didn't want to mention the text from Will. 'I don't want him thinking he's doing right by me, Sarah. Have you any idea how long it's been since I've had a good fuck? Never. I've never had a good one and I know for a fact that Jay would be amazing, but just like everyone else in my life, he thinks he knows what's best for me and took the decision out of my hands.'

'Hey—'

'Sorry, I don't mean you guys, I'm just venting because… because…' She threw her hands up in the air. 'I just want to be fucked, Sarah.'

And of course, that was the exact moment someone walked through the door. She gave them a wide-eyed look, complete with smirk, before hastily locking herself in one of the toilet cubicles.

Jess squeezed her eyes shut as she released a breath. 'Bloody hell. Listen, we kissed. It was epic. I want more, but he's being nice. I don't want you all scrutinising it, so please keep this to yourself.'

It was hard to be mad at him because he was trying to look out for her, and he was, well, Julian. Perfect in every throat-gripping, panty-melting way. But Christ, she wanted him to rail her.

Sarah pulled her into a hug. 'You know Jay is a good guy. He's just trying not to fuck things up with you because he's totally in love with you. It's so bloody obvious it's painful. Give him another chance. Maybe take the bull by the horns tonight?'

When he appeared in the alley and uttered the word mine, she couldn't deny that something inside her shattered. No one had ever said anything like that to her before. No one had ever stuck up for her. Her needs, her wants, her desires were always second to everyone else's. He claimed her in the alleyway and that made her feel seen. She felt wanted and attractive, and it turned her on. The way he turned feral with her blew her mind. That she could reduce someone like Julian to behave like that made her feel powerful. She liked how that felt.

Julian was right, she was running on adrenaline, but not because she felt fear for the drunken men around her. It was because of the look in Jay's eyes and the words coming out of his mouth. Was it wrong that she was so turned on by what he was saying? Was it wrong she wanted him to chase her down and press her up against the rough brick wall of the casino?

If it was so wrong, then why did she feel gutted he put the brakes on? But she couldn't deny the relentless pulse in her core, or that there was only one man that could satisfy her need.

But none of it mattered. Every time she convinced herself to take things further with Julian, worries of what would happen when she got home would sneak into her mind. Maybe he was right to pump the brakes? Or maybe taking things further would be the answer to her problems? She was giving herself whiplash with how her thoughts were volleying from one to another.

Should she start something with Julian, or keep him out of it and do what her father wanted?

She snapped out of her confusing thoughts, and said, 'Perhaps you're right. Maybe it's about time I took control.'

'Damn straight it is. People can only control you if you let them. Remember that.'

Jess knew full well that Sarah was referring to her parents. Easier said than done.

Too many cocktails later, and the merry group piled out of the bar and onto the street. The cool night air sent a chill over Jess's skin making her shudder. Within seconds, she felt a warm, strong arm wrap around her shoulders. She instinctively snuggled into Julian's embrace.

'Are you okay?' Julian said as he rubbed his hands up and down her arms, trying to warm her up.

'To be honest, I'm not sure. It's been one hell of a night.' He pulled her closer as they made their way back to the hotel and her body couldn't help but lean into his warmth, basking in the feeling of protection he cast around her.

Kicking off her heels as soon as they opened the door, Jess let the cool floor tiles soothe her tired feet as they walked into their hotel suite. She could feel the adrenaline ebb away as tiredness washed over her. She yawned as she stretched her arms above her head.

'I'm going to head to bed, guys. I'm knackered.' She was tired. Tired of having to keep up the appearance of being happy. She wanted to grab a shower—a cold one—curl up in bed and hope sleep would give her some respite from the warring emotions plaguing her mind.

A chorus of, 'okay,' filled the space as the others bustled about pouring themselves drinks and taking a seat in the spacious living room.

'Hold up.' Julian held his hand up as he jogged over. 'I'll be through soon, okay?' He cupped the back of his neck with his hand. 'That is if you're okay with me still sharing with you? I can sleep in here if you prefer?'

'You're absolutely not sleeping in here. And no rush. Come through when you're ready.' She hoped her smile was reassuring and not maniacal.

He nodded and walked back over to where the party carried on, although a little more subdued, as it was the early hours of the morning.

After taking a shower and getting ready for bed, she slipped under the covers and stretched out. Turning off all the lights apart from the one on Julian's side of the bed, she curled up and watched as the clouds edged their way across the floor-to-ceiling window, blocking the moon that hung brightly in the dark sky.

She hadn't bothered to close the blinds. Whenever she was feeling lost or down while at home, she'd sit in her favourite chair and stare out the window. The view was uninterrupted for miles around; the vastness giving her a strange sense of security that she couldn't explain. Her view now was only interrupted by the occasional skyscraper hotel, the moon reflecting off the glass and blending into the sky like starlight. Vegas was too full of flashing lights to see any actual stars in the sky, but it didn't matter to Jess at that moment. She felt trapped and needed to see that reassuring expanse of nothing.

She closed her eyes and took some deep breaths as emotion tightened its grip on her. Tears welled in her eyes, but she didn't want to cry, to show weakness and defeat, but the dam had broken, and they spilled out against her will.

CHAPTER 14

JULIAN

Satellites - Picture This

It didn't take long for Imogen, Lucy, and Sarah to slope off to their rooms to get ready for bed, leaving Julian with three sets of eyes all staring at him.

'What?' He squinted as he leant back on the sofa, now able to spread out.

'Did something happen between you and...' James lowered his voice. 'Jess, earlier?' The others leaned forward in anticipation of his answer.

He shook his head. 'You guys are terrible. What on earth makes you think something happened between us?'

They all looked at each other and then back at Julian. James was the first to speak, as usual. 'You were gone quite a while, mate, and Jess looked a little flustered when you got to the bar. We were all just hoping you'd finally got your head out your arse and rekindled the romance.'

'Rekindled the romance?' He raised an eyebrow. He was going to have to give them something or they wouldn't leave him alone.

He stretched his arm across the back of the sofa, going for a look of nonchalance. 'No, she had a good strategy. I was impressed, but then we got delayed thanks to a few drunken idiots who tried to proposition Jess. It's all cool though, I sent them on their way.' He shifted in his seat, trying to look relaxed, and definitely not like he was hiding something.

Cameron squinted his eyes at him. 'Fuckers. Are you sure it's all good? You should've called us or something.'

'Seriously, it was nothing. I had it handled.'

He could tell his answer hadn't satisfied their lust for gossip. He feared this would be the case when he agreed to come on the trip. What was it about couples that made them want to couple everyone else up? Like their happiness wasn't enough, they wanted everyone around them to have it too. It wasn't that simple for someone like him. When you have very specific needs, you diminish the size of the pool to choose from. Add to that a fucked-up ex and you're extremely limited.

Tom took a sip of his whiskey and sucked air in through his teeth as he swallowed. 'You know I understand what's going on in your head. You doubt you're good enough for someone as amazing as Jess, but you need to believe that you are, mate. She deserves someone like you. Fucking hell, from what Lucy tells me, the men her parents keep setting her up with are crazy. You'd be doing her a service by taking her off the market.'

Everyone nodded and hummed their agreement. What Tom didn't realise, Julian thought to himself, was that taking Jess off the market would help her out in more ways than one.

He feigned a yawn and stood up, pulling at his jeans as they snagged on his thighs. 'I'm going to bed, guys. Thanks for the pep talk. I appreciate what you're saying, and I promise to not let my demons get in the way of something with Jess. See you in the morning.'

He knew if he admitted to what he did in the alley, they'd push them to take it further. He didn't want her to feel like she was being backed into a corner, and that he was her only option other than being forced into marriage. Jess's family had interfered with her love life for years, and she didn't need her friends joining in. So, he kept his mouth shut.

He tiptoed into the room and took in her form, snuggled below the covers. He made quick work of getting ready for bed, slipped into his shorts, and slid under the covers next to her. As he clicked the light off, he lay back and listened to her breathing. He desperately wanted to roll over and tug her into him. He wanted to hold her in his arms and tell her she was safe. His hands twitched with the need to touch her.

The events of the evening had triggered his primal need. It was sitting there, bubbling under the surface, trying to break free. He closed his eyes, trying to push it down. He'd have to work out in the morning and burn off the energy. That was how he coped. Since the breakup with Chloe, he'd gained a shit-tonne of muscle mass. Working out was the only way to reign in his urges, but lately, it wasn't enough, and tonight had sent him over the edge.

As he lay there, he was sure he could feel something moving. There was a barely there shift to the covers that had him leaning over Jess to check on her.

He whispered, 'Jess. Are you okay?'

He'd noticed her mood change when she checked her phone in the club. He didn't need to ask her about it; it was safe to assume it was another message from home.

She turned her head to look at him, and as he got used to the dark, he could make out the glisten in her eyes and the wet tracks down her cheeks as the faint moonlight fell across her face. She sniffed and wiped at her tears and turned away. 'Not really. I feel overwhelmed. I don't want to go home, but I can't hide from it all either.' Her lip quivered as she sucked in a shaky breath. 'I don't know how I feel. Is it possible to feel numb, and scared, angry, hurt, and betrayed all at the same time?'

He couldn't deny his instinct to pull her to him any longer. He shuffled towards her, slid one arm under her neck and the other around her waist, pulling her easily into his arms, pressing her back into him.

'You're under a lot of pressure. It's perfectly normal to be full of emotion.' She gripped his arm, tugging it into her chest.

They lay in silence as Jess allowed more tears to fall. Julian could feel them land, one by one, on his arm, and he was sure they were burning a hole straight to his heart.

'Julian.' Her voice was hoarse.

'Mmm,' he mumbled into her hair, not wanting to pull away from her to speak.

'This feels good. I don't think I've ever hugged a bear before, but I could get used to this.'

'Are you calling me hairy?'

Her giggle made him smile; she was still in there somewhere below the heartache. 'No, I just mean you're massive compared to me. I've never felt hugged so wholly and completely before.' She paused for a moment and said, 'Come to think of it, apart from you guys, I don't think I've ever been on the receiving end of a good hug before.'

Fucking hell. She was drawing every protective instinct he had to the surface tonight. He thought he'd had it bad growing up in an environment that he simply didn't fit into. He wasn't your typical posh boy, so he turned his back on his life and set up the restaurant. Fortunately, his parents allowed him the freedom to do so, for now, but Jess wasn't so lucky.

'Consider me your official hug buddy from now on.' He pressed his legs into the back of hers, connecting every part of him to her. The closeness soothed the restless part of him that ached to help her. 'It would be my honour. Now, try to get some sleep. I promise not to leave you.'

She snuggled into him, pressing herself into his chest, and he had to remind his cock that this wasn't one of those hugs although it wasn't listening and he felt the familiar tingle of it coming to life. He gritted his teeth as he thought about the least sexy thing he could.

After a few moments of comfortable silence, she moved her hips.

Please don't wiggle. Please don't wiggle.

'Jay?'

'Jess.' He kept his voice as calm as he could while he continued to think of soggy sprouts and overcooked steak.

'I'm going to blame Satan's dick for this.'

He released a gentle laugh. '*Demon's crotch.*'

She craned her neck and looked at him. 'What?'

'You keep calling the cocktail Satan's dick. It's a *demon's crotch*.'

Her nose crinkled and she scrunched her brow. 'Oh. Well, I think Satan's dick sounds better.'

She pressed her hand to his chest.

'What did you want to say?'

'I can't sleep. I don't know if this is the booze talking, or what, so if this conversation doesn't go well, can we blame it on that?'

This intrigued him. 'What do you want to say?'

'You know earlier, in the alleyway?'

'Yeah.'

'You remember how I liked the things you said… and did?'

'I do.' He didn't know what else to say, but he wanted to know where this was going. He hoped she couldn't hear his heart as it thundered in his chest.

'Um… well. Oh, no—actually, never mind.'

'Out with it.'

'I'm embarrassed.'

'Don't be. You can tell me anything and I won't judge you. I promise.'

He felt her warm exhale on his arm as she huffed in frustration. 'Out of all the feelings I have swimming around, the one that stands out the most is horniness. Is it wrong that it turned me on? Like, there I am with some drunken wanker in an alleyway, and you say one sentence and my knickers catch fire. And then you give me a textbook hand necklace and I'm gagging for you to fuck me.'

She took a second to draw breath. 'It's not normal, is it? I mean, maybe it was just adrenaline making my emotions all mixed up. Or maybe it was the excitement of hiding from you, knowing that you were out there hunting me down. Side note; that's fucking hot. Oh, and you called me your girlfriend, and I felt proud to be your girlfriend until I remembered you were just saying that to get him to leave me alone. So, then I felt like you'd dumped me and my heart broke. I'm just not girlfriend material. My parents have made sure of that.'

Julian didn't say a word. She was rambling, and he was enjoying the voyage of discovery this one-sided conversation had turned out to be.

'I thought it was a one-off when we played that game of rugby at Cam and Jen's. I've never felt my blood pump so hard as it did, knowing you were gaining on me. And let me tell you, I've done some pretty crazy things in my time, but nothing compared to how… alive I felt then. And then when Jen suggested we play hide and seek, my lady garden did a fist pump. Oh my god, I just said that out loud.' She gasped, and tried to cover her face with her hand. 'It's the drink. Satan's dick has addled my brain,' she mumbled through her hand.

Julian couldn't stop the smile from spreading across his face. It felt like all of his Christmases were rolled into one as her words replayed in his mind. Did she enjoy his primal side? Did she want it?

She was perfect. He could sit and listen to her nervous ramblings all night, but he scooted backwards and said, 'Jess, turn over and look at me.'

Not wanting to waste another second or wait for his brain to catch up with his intentions, as soon as she was facing him, he pressed his lips to hers.

She froze in his arms as he pulled away from her, worried he'd taken it too far.

'I'm sorry. I couldn't help myself,' he whispered.

Jess's breath dusted across his face in ragged pants before she slammed her lips to his. 'Don't stop. And I mean it,' she mumbled against his lips.

Their lips parted as his tongue dipped into her mouth. She tasted of salty tears and minty toothpaste, and he wanted more. She whimpered as he combed his fingers through her silky blonde hair, tugging her head back so he could deepen the kiss.

He couldn't deny the connection they had, and her confession was music to his ears. For the merest second, he allowed hope to overpower him.

Until self-doubt crept in. Perhaps he'd read it wrong. Was he really that lucky that someone as perfect as Jess would welcome his darker side?

With monumental self-control, he pulled away again. He wanted this so badly, but he didn't want to take advantage of Jess while she was emotionally unstable. 'Do you want this? I don't want you waking up with regrets tomorrow.'

She nodded. They were both panting, holding onto each other as if they were afraid to fall. But this was precisely the problem. Julian was falling, but he knew Jess wasn't in the right frame of mind to take him on.

'It's not that I don't want to. I think it's clear that I want to do a lot of things to you right now.' He was hoping his dick would behave like a gentleman, but it hadn't and was currently trying very hard to break out of his shorts and join the party.

'I had noticed. It's hard not to.' Her eyes darted from left to right, desperately avoiding eye contact while she chewed on her bottom lip. 'I'm going to take the bull by the horns.'

'You want to take the bull by the horns?'

She nodded. 'Yep.'

'Am I the bull? I thought I was a bear. This is confusing.'

'You're both. I'm sick of other people deciding what's right for me. I'm taking back control and that starts with telling you what I need.'

'Tell me, and I'll do it.'

'I really need to come.'

CHAPTER 15

JESS

Please (Single Edit) - Jessie Ware

The ache between her thighs was unbearable. It'd been building from the moment he uttered those words in the alleyway and no matter how much she drank, or how much she'd told herself it was inappropriate, her body wouldn't listen.

She lay in his arms and could think of nothing else but the feel of him over her, pressing his massive body against her. The size of the hard ridge visible beneath his shorts wasn't helping matters. She'd been drinking a demon's crotch all night, and now she had a beast's cock pressing into her.

It was too much.

She was only human.

Her future was uncertain. When she stepped off the plane in the UK, her life as she knew it could be over. They didn't have long left in Las Vegas, and she didn't want to go home with any regrets. So, when he asked her what he needed to do for her, she didn't mince her words.

'I need to come.'

The situation was serious. If he didn't sort her out, she was going to take matters into her own hands, but she'd rather he did it.

'Oh.' He was still, as if scared to move.

'You said you'd give me whatever I need. I need an orgasm. I want to be taken, Jay. I want to feel alive. I've been dead inside for so long, I can't bear the thought of going home and never feeling wanted. Your words tonight made me feel something, and I need more of it. Please, Jay.'

Something in his eyes shifted as he asked, 'Are you begging me, sunshine?'

The way he called her sunshine was anything but bright and breezy. His words were laced with sexual undertones and a promise of something carnal.

She wasn't above begging. She wanted him. She was done with keeping him away in fear of what her parents would say or do. They no longer had the right to control her, at least not for the next forty-eight hours. These days felt like her last and she was living them for herself.

'Yes. I'm begging. Please, Jay.' Her words were strained as she rubbed her thighs together.

He cupped her face, threading her hair between his fingers as he stared into her eyes. Was he looking to see the truth in them?

'Jay, please. Make me feel. Whatever you're willing to do. I want it all.' She swallowed down a desperate sob.

His lips curled up in a smirk. 'It all is a lot when you're with me, sunshine. I'm not sure you're ready for all of me.'

'Then give me what you can. I'll take whatever I can get.'

The smirk was gone, and his eyes turned serious. 'Do you want me to get you off with my fingers, my tongue, or my dick, Jess? You need to tell me what you want so I don't overstep.'

The conversation was frustrating. She didn't want to think; she wanted to feel. 'I want everything.' Her skin flushed at the prospect of what he could do with her when no one was going to stop them.

'I stupidly didn't bring any condoms.' She loved that he'd come along on this trip with zero expectations of getting her into bed.

Heat flooded her cheeks as she whispered, 'I did. I always have one in my bag, you know, just in case.'

He raised an eyebrow. 'You're such a good girl. Where's your bag?'

She pointed to the wardrobe. 'They're inside the zipped pocket.'

A rush of cool air brushed over her fevered body as he left the bed, but he was back within moments, tossing the packet on the bedside table.

He stood at the edge of the bed, a look of concern on his face. 'Are you sure? You can stop me at any time. You're in control of this, do you understand?'

She knew what he was saying. He understood others had controlled every move she'd made in the past, but tonight was for her, and her alone.

'Yes. I understand, and I'm telling you to stop being a gentleman and get on with it.'

A whoosh of breath left her lungs as he grabbed her ankles and spun her ninety degrees so she was facing him, dragging her until her arse was balanced on the edge of the bed. The ease with which he tossed her around impressed her and made her flutter in all the right places.

'Then let's start by removing this.' He ran his hands up her thighs as goosebumps erupted across her skin. His hands continued their path over her hips until he gripped the soft jersey fabric of her vest top and pulled it up her body. She arched her back and raised her arms as he peeled it off and dropped it to the floor. Propping herself up on her elbows, he surveyed her body.

'You're beautiful. Has anyone ever told you that?'

She shook her head, her blonde hair tickling her shoulders.

'Have you been with many men, sunshine?'

She cleared her throat. 'None. I've slept with a couple of people, but I wouldn't describe any of them as men.'

His eyes darkened as he nodded in approval. She shivered under his gaze, her core clenched at his obvious appreciation of her. 'I bet your pussy is nice and tight. Do you think you can take me?'

Here he was, the glimpse of Julian she'd seen in the alley. The fine hairs across her skin rose to attention as excitement washed over her, and her heart raced. She licked her lips as it curved into a smile.

'I'll make it fit.' She desperately wanted to try. She wanted a ride on his massive disco stick if it was the last thing she did.

His chest rumbled. Was he purring? 'You always like to do your best. You have an innate need to please, don't you?'

Jess didn't know what to expect from him when she asked him to help her out with her predicament, but it certainly wasn't this. Something had awakened in her, and she loved it.

'Yes.'

'Do you want to please me?'

Her nipples hardened in response to his words and her pussy pulsed as she felt her shorts soak up her arousal.

'I can see how much you want to please me.' He rubbed one of her nipples between his thumb and forefinger, sending shockwaves directly to her core. Lowering himself to the floor, he knelt between her legs as they dangled off the side of the bed. He tugged at the waistband of her shorts, dragging them down and throwing them to the side. As he bent his head, Jess expected him to lick or kiss her, but he buried his head in her mound and inhaled, long and slow.

And then he growled.

Deep. Low. Guttural.

Primal.

The vibrations had her core clenching and her hips bucking.

'You smell of desire. Your pussy wants to please me too. I won't rush you. I don't want to hurt you.'

Was it possible to orgasm from anticipation and words alone? She was on the precipice, staring over the edge of the best orgasm of her life. She was sure of it.

'Are you okay, Jess?' Where his earlier words were gravelly, these were softer, like he was coming in and out of character.

'Yes. I think I might explode, but other than that, I'm… god, I'm so desperate for you.' She'd had sex before. Gone through the motions, but this was something else. This wasn't sex, this was raw and pure, stripped down to their base needs. Who they were outside of this bed was forgotten.

'The only time you can explode is when it's on my fingers, my tongue, or my cock. From now on, you don't come until I say you can.'

'Fuck. Jay, please.' He was killing her. She'd never felt so alive and near death, and he hadn't even touched her clit. She fisted the sheets to stop her hands from reaching for her sensitive bundle of nerves and rubbing.

'Let's see what I'm working with.' He danced his forefinger over the perfectly manicured landing strip of blonde hair at her entrance before tapping her clit.

She bucked off the bed, her back arching almost painfully. 'Oh, god, Jay.'

'How long has it been since you came, sunshine?'

'Um… um, I don't know.' She thrashed her head from side to side as he continued to tap away.

He slipped a single digit inside her, and they both groaned in unison. 'Fuck, you're tight. Did you happen to pack any lube in your zip pocket?'

'No.' She didn't think to pack any, as she'd never needed it before. Just how big was Julian?

'Don't worry. We'll take this at your pace. You can say stop, and I'll stop. Unless you prefer a safeword?'

She almost laughed at that. Safewords weren't needed with battery operated boyfriends. 'I don't have a safeword.'

'I'll check in all the time, but tell me if it gets too much. Now lie back and close your eyes. Relax, sunshine. I'm going to take care of you.'

She released her elbows and sank onto the mattress, closing her eyes and trusting Julian. It was a strange feeling to trust someone like this. Usually by now, the guy she was with would've fucked her, rolled over and fallen asleep or left, not caring if he'd satisfied her. Her heart ached at the thought this might be the only time she'd feel like this. All thoughts of her future stopped as she felt his tongue swipe across her entrance. Firm strokes twinned with the scrape of his stubble made it impossible to focus on anything but what he was doing to her.

'You taste sublime. I'd put you on my personal menu du jour and devour you.' His tongue was hot against her flesh as he sucked her clit and dipped inside her with ravenous attention. She wanted to let go and grind on his face, but a part of her, ingrained from birth, wouldn't let her.

Her hips ached as he pressed his hands to her thighs, spreading her wide, and burying his face between her legs. He wasn't kidding when he said he'd eat her. He sucked, licked, and bit down on every part of her exposed flesh. Nibbled up her thighs and sucked on her clit as he slipped two fingers inside, curling them to stroke along her G-spot.

Self-control flew out the window as she ground her hips onto his hand and face and groaned out her need. 'Oh, please. Oh, Jay, please.'

He lifted his head, glancing up at her. 'Are you begging me again, sunshine? Do you need to come?'

'Yes. Oh, god, yes. I need to come.'

'Come for me,' he commanded as he continued the stroking motion on her G-spot and sucked on her clit. He flicked out another finger, toying with her tight, puckered entrance. The unfamiliar sensation lit the paper to her impending orgasm as she fisted the sheets and clenched her thighs against Julian's head.

'That's it. Let it go. Come for me. You're doing so well,' he whispered against her clit, languid strokes of his tongue punctuating his praise.

The sensation was so intense she feared for what it would do to her if she gave herself over to it. 'Ah. Fuck. Oh, God. Jay, please, I can't.' Her body was screaming for her to let go, but her brain was screaming louder to hold back.

'You can. You fucking are. You're perfect. Squeezing my fingers so tightly. I can't wait to feel you come on my cock.' He continued the assault on her senses as her orgasm rocked every cell in her body.

Her chest heaved, gasping for air as she unclenched her fists, releasing the sheets. She quivered beneath him as he slipped his fingers out. Instead of grabbing the condom and moving onto the next stage, he gently lapped at her pulsing entrance, devouring every drop of her release.

'You're delicious.' His stubble tickled at her sensitive skin, the bite of pain heightening her senses. He continued to devour her like a man starved of food, but she was too delirious to process how that made her feel.

He moved his attention to her navel, sucking and biting his way up her body until he was holding himself over her. And yet he still didn't push his way in. Her inner walls pulsed, desperate for something to grip.

She gasped as he cupped her breast and sucked it into his mouth, his tongue flicking across her nipple. He released it with a pop. 'I want to feast on these too. I want you covered in my bite marks. Can I mark you, sunshine?'

What did that mean? Did he want to give her a love bite? And why did the thought of being marked make her feral, even when she didn't really know what that meant? 'I told you, Jay, I want everything you'll give me.'

He raised himself onto his knees, grabbed her thighs and flipped her like a pancake. Before she could ask what he was doing, he gripped her hips and encouraged her to tilt her pelvis. 'I'm going to start with your arse.'

She lifted her head, eyes wide with fear. There was no way she was taking that dick in her arse. Absolutely no way.

'Don't worry, I said I'd be gentle with you, and my cock isn't going anywhere near your arse. I'd tear you in two.'

'Oh, thank God.' She rested her cheek against the sheets as she released a sigh.

'Don't thank God, thank me.'

She didn't know if he was joking but wanted to play along. 'Thank you, Jay.'

'Anytime, sunshine.' She didn't see his smiling face again for a while as he licked and sucked on her arse cheeks until two large love bites blossomed across her skin. As he worked, his fingers pumped inside her, stroking her G-spot until she was close to coming again.

Jess knew what it felt like to be horny. Not from any of the men she'd had in the past, but from the fictional characters she read, one hand on the book, the other, well, otherwise engaged. A quick play and she was sated. But what Julian was doing to her was on another level. As one orgasm subsided, her body craved more like it was riding a sugar high no amount of sweets could satisfy.

As if sensing her impending release, he withdrew his fingers. 'Not just yet. You'll come again before I fuck you, but this one is going to last. I need you nice and wet to take me.'

His words were a filthy delight to her ears. She wanted to turn over and see his face. Her hands were itching to claw at his back and roam over his perfect body. And she wanted to rip his shorts off and finally see the goods in all its glory.

'You good?' He hadn't forgotten his promise to check in with her, and that made her heart ache for him. No one had ever taken so much care of her, or her enjoyment, before.

'I need to see you.'

He immediately lifted and encouraged her to roll onto her back. 'Did you miss me?' His smile was gorgeous. Perfectly white, straight teeth and soft, full lips. Lips she could kiss for days. He always looked deep in thought, lines etched across his brow. She ran a finger across the faint lines that remained there. 'I did, actually.'

'I'm not going anywhere.'

She hoped that was true.

CHAPTER 16

JULIAN

Sweat - Isak Danielson

She was perfect. She responded to him as if the gods themselves had made her for him.

'I'm not going anywhere.' He meant it. Now he'd had a taste of her, there was no way he intended to let her go. The only way she was being married off to anyone else was over his cold, dead body. And even then, he'd find a way to stop it from happening.

Her begging him had broken the last of his resolve and there was no going back. And if she didn't believe he was here for the long run, he'd prove it in other ways.

He could see she was struggling with her demons. And by demons, he knew it was her parents. He'd fought his own demons, but he'd come to the realisation that he was worthy of Jess, and if anyone thought otherwise, they could fuck all the way off.

He climbed up the bed, leaning back and resting his head on the headboard, the many plump pillows supporting his back. 'Come and sit on me, sunshine.'

The way she crawled up to him had him biting his lip. She was effortlessly sexy as she straddled his hips and rested her perfect arse on his thighs.

He cupped the back of her head, pulling her lips to his, devouring her mouth as she mewled into his. His hands trailed down her body, feeling her shudder under his touch. He came to a stop at the dip between her hips and her waist and gripped, digging his fingers into her soft flesh, pressing her groin against his straining cock until her body took over, grinding her core against his in a slow rhythm.

'I want you to make yourself come like this. Take it from me. We're not stopping until you ruin my shorts with your cum. Do you hear me?'

She nodded as she gripped the top of the headboard and rocked back and forth. Her head fell back as she groaned. 'I'm so close, Jay. This feels too good.'

'Don't hold back. Let yourself go.' He watched as Jess closed her eyes and lost herself to the moment. Her body was perfect, from the small, pert breasts he could fit in his mouth to the silver stretch marks on her inner thighs. He salivated at the thought of sinking his teeth into them and licking away the bite of pain.

Her erect nipples were crying out to be sucked and pinched, so he did just that. Biting on one while he tweaked the other before swapping. She was right; it didn't take long before she was pressing down hard against his cock, so hard he was close to coming undone himself as her orgasm had her silently screaming, open-mouthed and panting for breath. Her body shuddered as her orgasm ebbed away.

She collapsed onto the bed beside him, but he wasn't done with her yet. He rolled onto his side and pushed the hair away from her sweat covered brow. 'You doing okay?'

'I'm in heaven.' Her eyes were heavy and her movements slow as she licked her lips.

'Not quite, but you will be.' He passed her the glass of water from her bedside table. 'Here, drink.' As she lifted her head and sipped from the glass, he trailed a finger down her torso and slipped it inside her pussy with ease. 'Are you ready for me, Jess? You can always say no.' He didn't want her to feel pressured, but he hoped to God he could fuck her now. His balls were crying out in agony.

'I'm ready, Jay. I want this. I want you.' With his free hand, he took her glass away.

He slipped in two more fingers, stretching her as she bucked under his touch, her eyes closed. He would've preferred some lube, but he'd make do. He shucked off his shorts, grabbed the condom from the side and climbed between her legs, knocking them wider with his knees. He tore open the packet and rolled the condom down his shaft. It was tight. He made a mental note to always make sure he had one of his own in his wallet from now on.

Spitting into the palm of his hand, he stroked it along his shaft. As his balls tightened, he breathed through the need to come. It wasn't an ideal lubricant, but it was better than relying on the condom's lube alone.

He braced himself with one arm as he sucked her bottom lip into his mouth before releasing it to graze the tip of his nose along her cheek. 'Eyes on me, sunshine.' She lifted heavy lids as he guided his tip to her entrance.

She hissed in a breath and clawed at his back as he eased himself in, inch by inch. 'I'm trying really hard... not to sound... like a cheesy erotic novel... but fucking hell, Jay, you're... massive.' Panting breaths punctuated her words.

It took every bit of self-control not to bottom out in one thrust, but he could feel she was struggling to take him. If it had been as long for her as it had been for him, this would be difficult for both of them.

'Am I hurting you?' He wasn't sure how much longer he could hold himself back. Sweat trickled down his spine as he clenched his jaw.

'It's good. I need you to go for it. Please don't hold back. Fuck me.'

In one long, slow thrust he felt her open for him and sank in to the hilt, the sensation almost too much to bear. She wasn't a virgin but she was so tight she felt like one. He paused, giving them both time to adjust. 'Christ, Jess. You feel too good. I can't hold back, but I don't want to hurt you.'

'Stop treating me with kid gloves, Jay. I can take it. Please, I need it. Now.' Any playful tone had gone and in its place was desperation.

He pulled out to the tip as he sat back onto his heels and tugged at her hips until she wrapped her legs around his waist, her feet on the bed behind him. He thrust into her with firm strokes, keeping a steady rhythm as he sucked on this thumb before he pressed it to her clit and swirled it in ever decreasing circles. Her thighs gripped onto him as he upped his pace, hammering into her and bringing her close to climax. Beads of sweat coated his skin as he ground his teeth, fighting the need to come, not ready for this to end. He watched as her perfect tits bounced with each thrust, the sound of her mewls like music to his ears.

He could feel her clench and tighten around him.

'That's it, sunshine. Are you going to come for me?'

'Yes. Please keep doing that. Oh fuck, yes. Please, please.'

He felt his orgasm build from the base of his spine as his balls tightened. There was no holding this back. 'Jess, I need you to come for me.' He pressed his thumb to her clit, increasing the pressure as he thrust at an angle that hit her G-spot repeatedly.

He could feel her tighten around him as she cried out. 'I'm coming. Oh god, I'm coming.' Her hands grasped at the sheets, balling them in her fists as her mouth fell open as she moaned in pleasure.

With one more thrust, Julian was coming so hard he couldn't hold back the guttural roar that left his lips, any thoughts of keeping quiet for their friends long forgotten. He slowed his pace, thrusting until he was spent. It was his turn to collapse to the bed, careful not to crush Jess. He slipped free before lying next to her.

They turned to face each other as Julian stroked a hand down her back, pulling her in for a hug, wrapping his leg over hers. They lay like that, gazing into each other's eyes as their panting breaths slowed to a steady rhythm.

He needed reassurance he hadn't hurt her. 'Are you okay?'

'I feel like such an idiot.'

That wasn't what he was expecting to hear. 'Why?'

'I can't believe we waited all this time. We've wasted so much time just being friends when we could've been doing that.' Her face fell and Julian had a feeling he knew why. 'And now we might not get a chance to keep doing it.'

'Hey, stop talking like that. I told you I don't lose, and I meant it.' He tried to lighten the mood by hitting her with a megawatt smile. 'You can ride this dick for as long as you want to. It's yours if you want it.'

'It's a very nice dick.' He could see her chewing the inside of her cheek, trying and failing to hide her grin.

Was that the best she could do? 'Nice?'

She batted at his shoulder with a giggle. 'All right! Your dick, your throbbing member is glorious in all its pulsing, veined glory, and I would very much like to stake my claim to it, for now, at least.'

He growled at her use of words. 'You keep talking like that and I'll have you over my knee.'

She raised an eyebrow at him. 'That doesn't sound so bad.'

'You won't be saying that when you can't sit down. But fear not, I'm not into spanking.'

She reached around and stroked a hand over her round backside as she craned her neck to inspect the mottled pink love bites. Her gaze moved to the crescent-shaped bite marks along her inner thighs. 'No, spanking is not your thing, biting is.'

'I'm into a whole lot, but we can talk about that another day. For now, I need to get rid of this.' He pulled the condom off, careful not to spill its contents. 'And then we need to get some sleep.'

'Hang on a minute.' Her eyes were wide as she pointed to his dick. 'Is that the tattoo?'

They'd been so caught up in the act she'd not noticed the tattoo that sat at the base of his cock. He looked down at it, which was unnecessary, as he knew exactly what it looked like. It acted as a reminder of his past life every time he took a piss. Nestled on his groin, just above the base of his penis, and only visible because he kept his hair well-trimmed, was a tattoo of a shield. The outline was filled with a geometric image of a wolf's head, and nestled on the wolf's forehead was a circle divided into three, a bit like the yin and yang symbol, but with an additional section.

Julian cleared his throat, knowing he had a lot to explain. 'Give me a minute.'

After disposing of the condom and washing up, he settled himself next to Jess in bed. While he'd been in the bathroom, she'd dressed in a fresh set of pjs and was sitting upright, tucking the sheets around her hips. She looked at him expectantly, but said nothing.

'The long and short of it is that I used to be part of the scene.'

'The scene?'

He didn't feel ready to explain all this to her. He didn't want to scare her off, but he didn't want to lie to her either. This was going to be the shortest fling he'd ever had or the start of something from his dreams. He could only hope that her passing comment about enjoying the thrill of the chase was a positive sign of how she'd take what he had to say.

'There's a reason the Lombardis invited me to their hotel opening party, Jess. They're old friends, but not in the way you may think.'

Realisation dawned across her face as her mouth formed an O shape. 'Did you used to go to kink clubs with them? Did you go to Katia's place?'

He shook his head. 'No. This tattoo is a mark of my status in a...' He tried to find the most appropriate term that Jess would understand. 'Club. My tattoo tells people I'm the master of a particular kink house.' He pointed to the wolf. 'And this tells them my preference as a primal dominant. The circle is called a BDSM triskelion.'

She blinked a few times as she stared at the tattoo. He covered himself with the sheets, not used to someone scrutinising the base of his cock like that, and it made him feel uneasy. He should've put on some shorts before getting back in bed.

He waited silently for a reaction. A few seconds ticked by before she said, 'You're the master of a kink house and you're a primal Dom. Like... that's a real thing?'

'Yeah, it's a real thing. Do you have questions? Ask me anything and I'll answer truthfully.'

She glanced down at her hands, interlaced in her lap, as her brows knitted together. After a second of processing, she looked up at him. 'What do you mean, you're the master of a kink house? What exactly is that? Do you have a secret club like K's somewhere? And if you're a primal Dom, does that mean that you want to chase me around and fuck me in bushes?' Before Julian could explain, she slapped her hand to her forehead. 'Oh-my-goodness. That's why the others said you're a pro at hide and seek. Is it really like it is in the books, where you hunt me down in a car park and shove my face in the dirt?'

Well, she didn't immediately run away, so he took that as a win. The chance of getting to sleep now was slim to none. Julian rolled onto his side and settled in for a long night of chatting. He sucked in a long breath, held it for a few beats, and then puffed it out. 'All right, get comfortable. I'm guessing you don't want the short story.'

She snuggled in next to him, her face resting on his chest. It felt good to be this close to someone again, and for the first time in a long time, he felt comfortable being vulnerable and opening up.

He started the conversation with an explanation of why he no longer took part in primal scenes. He figured if she was still interested in him after he admitted what happened with Chloe, then that was a good sign.

He skipped the gruesome details of Chloe's injuries, but that didn't stop Jess from reeling back in horror, her hand covering her mouth to stifle the shocked gasp before she pulled it away to squeeze his forearm. 'Jay, that's awful. Is she okay now? Are you okay?'

He nodded. 'Yeah, I heard she's doing well now, but it messed with her head for a long time.' He shook his head as he picked at the seam of the bedding. 'It messed with both our heads.'

People say that talking is the best therapy, and he had to admit, it felt good to be open about it all with Jess. He didn't feel the weight of guilt crushing him like he did before.

Jess pursed her lips. 'Christ. It can't have been easy to see her in the hospital, and I understand why it got under your skin too.' She shrugged and twisted her mouth to the side. 'I can't believe she put herself in danger like that but... I guess we've all fallen foul of thinking we can handle more than we actually can. It's not your fault though, you know that, don't you?'

Jess stroked his forearm and he was surprised by how much her delicate touch soothed him. He wasn't sure he deserved her understanding but he appreciated it nonetheless.

'Logically, I know I wasn't the one to abuse her, but I still feel responsible for her. I introduced her to the scene, so a part of me feels like I let her down. I failed to teach her fully about the safety aspects and then I couldn't provide her with what she wanted. As master of the house, I should've done more to protect her. As soon as she asked me to overstep my limits, I should've known what she was going to do. I'm a primal Dom, but I don't get off from the dubious consent side of the kink. I like the hunt, and I want to work for my reward, but I don't get involved in roleplaying non-consensual scenes, so we never openly discussed the safety aspects of that side of the kink.'

'I don't think you're being fair to yourself. She made the decision to explore outside what she had experience with, and she didn't take steps to research it thoroughly. I'm pissed off it meant you stopped living that lifestyle. It's not fair to you that you've denied yourself what you need for so long.' Jess cupped his face in the palm of her hand, grazing her thumb over his stubble. He leaned in to her touch. 'Until that drunk guy showed up earlier, I was loving the game. But I also understand why you went a little crazy when you saw me with him. It must have reminded you of how you felt about the whole Chloe situation. I'm sorry, I won't put myself in danger again. I promise.'

He kissed the top of her head. 'Thank you. And thanks for understanding. Is there anything else you want to know?' His instinct for aftercare was telling him she needed to get some rest, but it felt too good to have someone to share his demons with, so for as long as she was willing to listen, he was willing to talk.

'What I don't understand is how you can be the master of a kink house if you don't own a club like Katia does. Where would you do the, um, clubbing?' She shrugged. 'If you don't own somewhere to do it in?'

He yawned, covering his mouth with the back of his hand. 'Sometimes I'd hire somewhere like the kind of place you'd have for private weddings. They're always popular as the grounds are perfect for our needs. I had options. That's the benefit of primal play. It's better to be out in the wild instead of in a club. As long as there is space, we can make a place work.'

She buried her face in his chest as she mumbled, 'I wouldn't mind it if you wanted to play with me, you know, like that.'

A rush of emotions hit him like a tidal wave. The thought of introducing Jess to a primal scene filled his veins with ice, but something in him burned at the prospect. What if she tried it and hated it? What if she left him because she wanted more than he could give her? He recognised his train of thought was a hang up from Chloe, and one he needed to get over, but his body and mind were too tired to comprehend it all now. 'I'd love to explore that with you, but for now, I think we need some sleep.'

She snuggled up, rubbing her cold feet against his shins. 'True.' She yawned and her breathing evened out within minutes, but sleep didn't come for Julian. Thoughts of how to get Jess out of her father's clutches preoccupied his mind.

CHAPTER 17

JESS

Scared to Start - Michael Marcagi

As Jess rolled over, she reached out her hand expecting to find a large, warm body, instead she was met with a cool space next to her. Cool enough to tell her she'd been on her own for a while.

She picked up her phone from the bedside table and squinted at the time. She didn't feel like she'd slept for hours, so when she saw it was only nine-thirty, she wasn't surprised.

'Three hours sleep, ugh,' she mumbled to herself as she threw the covers off and rubbed the sleep from her eyes as they adjusted to the hazy sunshine streaming through the windows. She strained her ears to work out if Julian was using the bathroom, but she heard nothing. Her heart ached as she considered maybe he regretted what they did last night. She couldn't blame him. The situation she was in hardly made for a great relationship. They had no future as far as she could see, so why would he want to get involved with her? She only hoped it didn't make the rest of the trip awkward.

A wince formed on her lips as she stood, a sore reminder of last night's events between her legs. She opened the door to a silent suite, so she knew everyone was still in bed. Julian must have left her after she fell asleep and gone back to the sofa bed. She tried not to feel bad about this. He didn't owe her anything, and she was the one to beg him to make her come.

She cringed as she remembered her behaviour from last night. No wonder he left her. She'd scared him off. She was never drinking again.

As she rounded the corner into the massive communal space in their suite, she stopped in her tracks. Julian wasn't sleeping on the sofa bed like she thought. He was currently doing some sort of weird press-up where his feet weren't resting on the floor. What kind of trickery was that?

He was wearing a pair of grey sweatpants—of course he was; he was fucking perfect—and nothing else. She kept herself mostly hidden behind the wall and wasn't ashamed to admit that she was one-hundred per cent checking him out. He was simply stunning. She knew he had a well-built physique from their escapades during the night, and from the way he filled every item of clothing he owned, but seeing him work out was truly spectacular.

From her vantage point, she could see his biceps bulging and flexing as he ascended and descended into the moves with a grace and fluidity she couldn't believe. After a few press-ups he moved into a pose she recognised—the downward facing dog—before lifting himself into a handstand. And then her jaw dropped. To say she didn't know where to look would be a lie. Not knowing where to look first would be more appropriate. His front was facing her, and even though he was upside down, it was glorious. She did a double take as she counted not six, but an eight pack of heavily ridged abs as each muscle pulled taut with the exertion to hold him steady.

She chewed on her lip as she felt her temperature rise. This was the best way to wake up.

'Are you going to join me or just hide over there staring?'

She jumped at the sound of his voice, mildly embarrassed to be caught in the act. Holding her head up high, she walked over to the sofa opposite him and sank into the plump cushions. The leather was cool across her skin, causing goosebumps to erupt.

'Sorry. Didn't mean to perv.' She tucked her hair behind her ears and gave him a shy grin.

He dropped his legs and sat on the floor at her feet. His skin glistened with a sheen of sweat, and she once again felt the urge to lick him. She really needed to get a grip on that.

'Liar. You knew full well what you were doing. I don't mind. You can stare at me all you like.' His smile was warm and relieved the ache in her heart from feeling rejected. 'I didn't wake you, did I?'

She shook her head. 'No. I woke up and wondered where you were.' She rolled her eyes at herself. 'To be honest, I thought you might have regretted last night and come to sleep out here.'

He scooted over and ran his hands up and down her calves. She squeezed her thighs in response, the ache now in her core. 'I couldn't sleep. We should talk while the others are still in bed.'

His face had turned serious, and any sexy feelings flew out the window. 'Oh, yeah, of course.' This is the part where he'd tell her it was just a one-night thing.

'I'm going to be straight with you—'

Her spine stiffened and she cut him off, deciding she didn't need to hear him dumping her before anything had even begun. 'It's okay, Jay, really. I understand that I'm a walking red flag right now. You've been through enough and you don't need me complicating your life.'

He held up his hand. 'First, don't interrupt me when I'm talking. I may have said I'm not into spanking, but that doesn't mean I won't punish you in other ways.'

'O-oh,' she stuttered, shocked by his demeanour and shocked at how her pussy fluttered in response.

'Second, you're not a walking red flag. Your parents don't scare me. What I wanted to talk about was us. I'd like there to be an us, just in case you didn't get that from last night.' His lips formed half a smirk. 'I've avoided being with a woman for so long, but I can't keep my hands off you, Jess. And I know I can't stand back and watch some other fucker touch you. I love that you're up for trying primal with me, but I'm worried it might scare you off. If you don't enjoy it, you have to be honest with me so we can work around it.

I'm willing to curb it to be with you.' He huffed out a breath as if relieved to get that off his chest.

Her jaw dropped as she looked down at the unbelievably perfect man sitting at her feet. 'W-what? Um.' Butterflies erupted from her stomach as his words sank in. Was this really happening? Was she finally getting what she wanted?

She didn't want him denying any part of himself to be with her and from what she'd read about the primal kink; it sounded exciting. When she thought back to being chased down by him when they were playing in Cameron's garden, and when she was hiding from him, all she could remember was how alive she felt. How her heart raced and adrenaline coursed through her veins. She remembered his teeth sinking into her thighs last night and how he took her with a fierce need that drove her over the edge again and again. She didn't want him to water that down. She wanted more of it, all of it.

She climbed down from the sofa and sat on his lap, straddling his hips, her arms around his neck. 'I've denied myself of what makes me happy for as long as I can remember. I've lived my entire life with the sole purpose of making my parents happy and proud. But I will never make that mistake again. I'm done living in the image of a perfect daughter. I'm going to be true to myself from now on and I expect you to do the same.' His hands gripped her waist as she spoke, which only fuelled her fire.

'In fact, there's something I've wanted to do for so long. I'm just going to do it.' As she finished speaking, she leant forward and dragged her tongue from his collarbone to the sensitive spot under his ear. She closed her eyes as his scent mixed with the slightly salty taste of him. He smelt of sex, remnants of his cologne from last night, and something so delicious it made her flutter. She could only assume that was the work of pheromones.

A groan, deep and throaty, rumbled from his chest before he cupped the back of her head and kissed her lips with bruising force. His free hand cupped her arse and rocked her pelvis against his hardening cock.

He tore his lips away as he looked into her eyes. 'Let's make this clear. You're mine. You don't need to worry about your father. He's my problem now. Is that clear?'

Her heart fluttered and warmed her chest as she allowed hope to tiptoe in. Could he really take away her problems? Like a bird learning to fly, her hope crashed as a heavy weight landed on her chest. This was her problem, not Julian's.

'Jay, it's not fair to put that on you. What can you do?'

'Well, he can't marry you off if you're with me, can he? We go home and tell him together and take it from there. In the meantime, I have something more pressing to deal with.' He wasn't lying if the rock-hard trunk in his trousers was anything to go by.

A shiver tore through her body as a rush of emotions swallowed her whole. Excitement and fear warred inside her. Excitement at the prospect of a relationship that had so much to offer, unchartered territory, where she wouldn't have to hide who she was. Fear of what that meant for her life and her family. She wouldn't marry Will, but she didn't understand what that might mean for her family's business, and a part of her couldn't help but care.

She didn't have time to process her thoughts as a voice rang out from the other side of the room. 'Halle-fucking-lujah. The golden couple have finally got their act together.' Sarah followed her happy chorus with loud clapping. Of course, it was her who discovered them in a compromising position. At least that would save them from having to announce it.

Jess couldn't help the massive smile that spread across her face as Julian pressed his forehead to hers and muttered, 'Just what I need when I'm sporting a hard-on. We're out of here, sunshine.' With zero effort, he held her to him like a koala, wrapping her legs around his waist, stood up and walked away.

'Bye, Sarah.' He waved as they retreated to the safety of their room.

Before he closed the door, they heard, 'I fucking love you guys. Don't do anything I wouldn't do,' followed by a joyous giggle.

'That doesn't really leave a lot, does it?' Julian whispered to Jess. As he kicked the door shut, still gripping her to him, he said, 'Come on, I need a shower and then we'll have to join the others for the inevitable back slapping and hilarious remarks.'

If Jess was being honest, she was looking forward to being on the receiving end of back slaps and sex jokes. As long as she didn't think about the future, she believed that being with Julian was her chance at happiness.

For their final evening in Vegas, Cameron had asked everyone in advance to bring formal attire, and as they walked into the Michelin-starred restaurant, they could understand why. Joël Robuchon was the epitome of opulence, and Jess couldn't help but stare at the interior as they were shown to their table.

The ivory and purple swirls of the carpet swallowed the click-clacking from their heels. Jess's whole body calmed as the soothing background music replaced the hustle and bustle of the hotel and casino they were staying in.

In the centre of the grand room was a long, high-backed, plum-coloured velvet bench seat, four tables were pushed together to create a long table for eight and on the other side were four mahogany chairs upholstered in fine ivory silk. The artwork caught her attention, her eyes widening to take it all in. Some of the largest canvas she'd seen lined the walls, breaking up the shades of violet, lavender, and blue with splashes of gold, silver, and green.

Crystal chandeliers hung from the ceiling, casting a warm glow. Beautiful flowers in ornate glass vases scented the room. The restaurant was a classy gem, nestled between the garish lights and crassness of the main strip. Jess hadn't realised the constant state of sensory overload she'd been in until now.

As they took their seats, the ladies on the soft, plush velvet, the men on the chairs, Jess took the time to drink in the surroundings. She wanted an imprint of this perfect evening on her soul.

'What are you smiling at, sunshine?' Julian had taken his seat opposite her, and she took a moment to drink in the image of him wearing his suit, tailored to perfection, before she replied.

Julian's hand grazed over hers as she fiddled with the napkin artfully folded on the table. 'Hey, I asked what you were smiling at. You were miles away. Are you okay?'

'Bugger. Sorry, I was indeed miles away. Actually, I was fantasising about you wearing a bowtie so I could pull on it while I kiss you.' It felt good to say that out loud. She'd had thoughts similar to that for so long and keeping them to herself was becoming almost painful.

'Oh, I see. Well, I have something you can tug on while you kiss me.' His lips curved into a smile as a single eyebrow rose.

Jess looked around to make sure the staff didn't overhear. She leant over the table and whispered, 'You can't talk like that here. You'll get us kicked out.'

Each course that arrived surpassed the last until the waiter placed delicate petits fours along the table. The drinks had flowed freely, and Jess was drunk enough to feel like she could rule the world, but sober enough to know not to try it in a minidress and five-inch heels.

Cameron had arranged with the manager for them to have access to a private bar so they could carry on their evening away from the hustle and bustle of the main strip. None of them would openly admit it, but they'd tired of the never-ending action and flashing lights. She was desperate to get on a horse and ride off with only an audiobook to keep her company.

Where the restaurant was fresh and calm, the bar was sultry. The carpets, walls, and furniture were all a deep red, with the only relief coming from the multicoloured bottles of drink lit up along the glass shelving.

James looked at the bar menu as the others took their seats and settled in for a long evening. 'I know just what we need.' James's smile was mischievous as he stepped up to the polished wooden bar. 'We'll have a bottle of Don Julio 1942 tequila, please, and eight glasses. Thank you.'

He unbuttoned his jacket as he sat down on the red leather two-seater sofa next to Sarah.

'James, you know we always get ourselves into trouble when we drink tequila,' said Lucy, as she put her head in her hands.

'I know. I thought it fitting that our journey to each other has always involved tequila, and so I wanted to mark the coming together of Jay and Jess with a bottle of the finest.'

The barman set a silver tray on the table and placed what looked like a mini champagne flute in front of each of them.

'What, no shot glasses?' asked Sarah.

'If I may explain, Mademoiselle, these are tequila glasses, designated as such by the Consejo Regulador del Tequila and are designed to enhance your tequila drinking experience. I think you will notice the difference. Please, enjoy this fine drink.' He poured the amber liquid into each glass, bowed and retreated to the bar, disappearing out of sight.

Sarah worked hard to contain her giggle, but as soon as she looked over to Jess, she collapsed into semi-drunken giggles. 'We've gone upmarket now, wouldn't you say, what, what?'

Cameron rolled his eyes and raised his glass in the air. 'Let's toast to true love, shit-storms, and tequila. Pinkies out.' They all followed suit, holding their little fingers out, and promptly downed the tequila.

Sarah refilled the glasses and cleared her throat. 'And well done to Jess and Jay for getting together without the aid of murderous villains, the mafia, or a formidable Mrs Jones.'

Everyone apart from Jess and Julian raised their glasses. Sarah scrunched her face. 'Hey. Why aren't you joining in? Please tell me you're not being chased by the mafia as well?'

Jess looked over at Julian, but he kept his face neutral, giving her the option to spill the beans. She let out a sigh. 'No, we're not being chased by the mafia, but I'll be facing a shit-storm when I get home.'

Imogen shuffled forward in her seat. 'Has this got something to do with your parents by any chance, and their need to set you up with someone?'

Jess rolled her lips and nodded. 'Yep. In a nutshell, my dad has promised I'll marry Will to grease the wheels of a deal. I don't think he'll be pleased when I tell him that's not an option.'

A chorus of 'what the fuck?' erupted as Julian said, 'Too right, it's not a fucking option.'

Tom held his hand up. 'Hang on, everyone. Jess, are you serious? This is ridiculous. What kind of deal?'

Jess shrugged. 'I don't know the details, as I was listening in on a phone call.' Jess repeated what she'd already told Julian. She felt his grip on her thigh tighten as she talked.

Sarah scoffed. 'That's utter wank, Jess. This isn't an episode of bloody Bridgerton. You're not a commodity to be traded in a bank deal. Your dad needs a bloody good slapping, if you ask me.'

'I know, hun. But here I am regardless.' Jess shrugged.

No one could argue with her. Cameron looked at Julian before asking Jess, 'Have you got any idea how badly your dad needs the money, or how much money? I'd like to think he's not selling you off for a few hundred thousand.'

Jess shook her head. 'I have no idea. He keeps me and my mum out of all bank business, so I have no idea what kind of money we're talking about.'

Julian cleared his throat. 'Don't worry, Cam, I intend to get to the bottom of this. Jess is mine now. No one's trading her, so he's going to have to come up with a Plan B, or come through me.'

Jess looked at her best friends, all of whom had a face that said, 'Why didn't you tell us this sooner?'

Looks like an evening of tequila and explanations was on the cards.

CHAPTER 18

JESS

River - Bishop Briggs

As expected, Jess spent the rest of the evening apologising for keeping her friends out of the loop and fielding random suggestions of ways to get her away from her parents. The most insane was contacting some of Tom's old mafia buddies to sort out the Wilberforce family and her father. Jess shut that one down immediately, although Julian looked as though he was on board.

Cameron and Julian had plenty of hushed conversations, but Jess put that down to Cam not wanting to berate his cousin in front of everyone. Cameron took the safety and welfare of his friends and family seriously and wouldn't take too kindly to Julian keeping this news from him.

By the end of the evening, they'd all forgiven them both for keeping secrets and demanded to be kept in the loop over what happens when they get home. Jess could live with that.

As they closed their bedroom door back at their suite, Julian stepped up behind Jess and danced his fingers over her exposed shoulders, sending welcomed shivers across her skin. She leaned back, pressing into his chest, desperate to feel more of him against her.

He stroked her hair before gripping it in his fist, tugging her head back, opening her neck to him. He brought his lips to her ear, her pulse thundering through it as she felt him brush against the sensitive skin.

'I have a feeling you need to hit the off switch to your thoughts. Am I right?'

'Yes,' she whispered with a heavy exhale as his free hand tugged on her zip. She felt safer being with Julian, but the thought of travelling home in the morning still filled her with dread.

'I'm in charge tonight, sunshine. Understand?' He tugged on her hair again.

'Yes, please. I need you.'

He bit her lobe; the pain shooting straight to her core. 'You've got me.'

'What are you going to do with me?'

His free hand drew lazy circles up her thigh until it skirted under the fabric of her dress. 'I'm going to do exactly what I want with you. Is there anything you don't like? What are your limits?'

She had no idea. There was so much she had yet to try. 'I don't know. Are you going to Dom me tonight? What do I call you? Do I have to call you sir?' Her breaths were shallow as her body warmed at his touch and his words.

'I don't care what you call me, as long as you call me yours.' He released her hair and twisted her around, lips crashing to hers in a fierce kiss that stole the air from her lungs. As they kissed, he returned his attention to her zipper, pulling it down and letting her dress crumple at her feet.

Certain her heart had stopped beating, she pulled away from his embrace. 'Do you really want me? My future is so uncertain. You have no idea what we're walking into tomorrow. Do you really think being together will work?'

His jaw ticked as he listened. 'Have you finished?'

She blinked at his bluntness. 'Uh-yes, I guess I have.'

'Good, because if you don't stop spouting bullshit out of that pretty little mouth of yours, I'm going to plug it shut with my cock.'

'Oh.' *Fuck. That was hot.* Saliva pooled at the prospect. A smirk formed on her lips. 'I might carry on spouting bullshit.'

His eyes burned as he slowly and deliberately unbuttoned and unzipped his trousers. He pulled them down, tugging them off along with his socks, leaving him in only his boxers. 'Is that what you want, sunshine?'

She didn't need to ponder the question as her head nodded. God damn, she'd never tire of seeing him topless, bottomless, any way she could get him.

'Then I suggest you get on your knees. You can start with taking these off.' He tugged at the waistband of his boxers.

She was on fire as she lowered to her knees, her eyes never leaving his. He towered over her, but she didn't feel small. In this position before him, she felt powerful. Chosen. Safe.

She tucked her fingertips into his boxers, dragging them down his thick thighs. He kicked them out of the way; the movement made his cock bob in front of her face. Mimicking what he'd done to her the first time he went down on her; she pressed her face to his groin and breathed in his scent. It was like a drug; addictive, making her heart race and her nerves spark to life.

There was no way she could fit all of his cock in her mouth. He was perfectly proportioned, and that proportion was massive. She'd had a few sexual partners in the past; some were long, but lacking in girth, some had all the girth but were stumpy, rendering it useless. Julian was unmatched in both. Her core ached as she remembered how much he filled her, so much so, they'd not had full sex since. He wanted to give her time for the glorious soreness to dissipate.

She breathed him in one last time, running her tongue along the base of his cock until reaching his tip. His fingers gripped the hair on the back of her head.

'Fuck. That feels good.'

She smiled as she glanced up at him, pressing the tip of her tongue into his slit, lapping up the pre-cum that tasted mildly salty and a little sweet. Her taste buds tingled in response, asking for more. 'Jess, you know I like it rougher than you're probably used to, but if it gets too much, tap out, okay? Just tap m—' Jess wrapped her lips around his head, swirling her tongue around the ridge. 'Ah, fuck. Jess, this is important.'

'Mm-hmm,' she mumbled.

'Tap my thigh if you need me to stop.' He looked down to make sure she understood what he was saying.

She pulled away with a pop. 'Okay. Now, do you want to stop talking and fuck my mouth?' She had no idea where that had come from, but being with Jay made her feel adventurous. She didn't want to act like a lady. And she didn't think he expected her to.

Once again, she took his tip in her mouth as he gripped her head and thrust his hips. Her mouth stretched; the corners of her lips burned, but she didn't tap his thigh.

She flattened her tongue and swallowed as she moved her head to meet his next thrust, inching him in until he hit the back of her throat. Her eyes watered as she struggled to take any more.

She felt him grow impossibly hard as he fisted her hair and flexed his hips, driving his cock deeper. She pulled back, taking a moment to breathe as she licked along his shaft, sucking up more of his pre-cum, before opening as wide as she could and taking him straight to the back of her throat. His groan pulled a smile from her lips as his thrusts became short and frantic.

As he pulled out, she gasped for air. 'You're perfect. I wish you could see what I can see. You were made for me.' He wiped away a tear with the pad of his thumb, bringing it up to his lips and sucking. 'They're the only tears you'll cry when you're with me. You'll cry for me, sunshine, and only me. Stand up.' She felt protected, special, and owned in all the right ways. She wanted to give herself to him, knowing she'd have all of him in return.

He held her under her arms, lifting her until she could wrap her legs around his waist. 'Time for me to get my fix.'

He walked them over to the bed and dropped her onto her back. Her stomach lurched as they landed. Before she could catch her breath, he grabbed her ankles, pulled her to the edge, and spread her knees, pushing them up to her shoulders. He'd spread her wide, and she was exposed in the most intimate way.

'Are you particularly attached to these knickers?'

She craned her neck to look down at him. 'Not really, although they are Agent provocateur, so I do quite like—'

The sound of ripping and a bite of pain stopped her in her tracks. Within seconds, she didn't care about her shredded French lace underwear as he sucked her clit into his mouth and found her G-spot with two fingers in an instant. This man did not mess around.

Within moments, her hips were rocking, meeting the pace he set. Her orgasm coiled around her spine; white hot flames licked across her core as she found her sweet release.

'That's it. Let it go. Ah god, I want to feel you clench like that around my dick.'

'Do it. I want you to. I need it.'

As Julian coaxed the last wave of her orgasm from her, he wrapped his coated fingers around his cock and stroked along its length. And then his face fell. 'Fuck.'

Jess propped herself up on her elbows and dropped her feet to the floor, her legs hanging off the edge of the bed. 'What's the matter?' Had she done something wrong?

'I didn't have time to buy condoms today.'

'Oh.' Oh bugger.

She was on birth control. Her mother had made her go on the pill as soon as the doctor would prescribe it. It would help with acne, she said. It didn't occur to Georgina that Jess might not have wanted to be on the pill, but for her mother, looks were more important than health.

'I'm on birth control. And I don't know if you've noticed, but my parents have been very effective cock-blockers of late.' Her next thoughts were definitely from her brain and not from her vagina. 'I trust you, Jay.'

He scrubbed his hands through his hair. 'I've never gone bare. I've never had a desire to. But with you, I can't think of anything more perfect than fucking and filling you. Jess, I have to warn you, you do something to me. I'm a primal Dom. I like to lose control and get lost in the moment, but with you, that scares me. I want to protect you, but at the same time, I want to destroy you. I want to take you hard, fast, and everywhere. I want you to do dirty things with that mouth of yours. I might be a gentleman, and you are a lady, but in my bedroom, you're my whore. When I fill you with my cum, it means I own you. Ring or no, you're mine. You don't get to question if I want you. Understand?'

She nodded so fast she was sure she felt the burn of whiplash. 'I want all of that, Jay. I've spent my whole life living a lie. On the outside I'm straight-laced and perfectly presented. Underneath, I want to be fucked. I want my mascara running down my face. I'm sick of being so fucking pristine. So clean and wholesome. Take it away, Jay. Fuck it out of me. I want everything you want. I want it rough. I want it real and raw.' A tear escaped as she took a breath.

He snaked his arm around her as he lifted her up the bed, nestling himself between her legs.

He rested his forehead on hers as he inhaled, long and deep. 'Jessica Chatwin. You're. Mine.' On the last word, he thrust in to the hilt, filling her so completely, she felt owned, safe, and well and truly sullied in the best way possible.

CHAPTER 19

JULIAN

Fall At Your Feet (with Dean Lewis) – CYRIL

'Flight VS156 to London Heathrow is now boarding.' As the announcement played out over the speakers in the airport lounge, Julian squeezed Jess's hand a little tighter. Shit was about to get real.

Last night, something shifted in Julian that took him by surprise. He'd never had sex without a condom, so he was unprepared for the way his heart locked onto Jess.

He felt connected to her in a way he'd never felt before, and he had to admit to himself that it scared him. He knew he'd do whatever it took to keep her safe. He had no intention of letting her go.

'I wish we didn't have to go home.' Jess attempted to smile as she slipped on her denim jacket and slung her bag over her shoulder.

He wrapped his arm around her, pulling her in close. 'I know, baby. It'll be all right. We'll head straight to your parents' house to tell them about us, and I'll be with you the whole time. I'll do the talking, if you want me to.'

She looked up at him, and her smile widened. She was petite and delicate in his arms, a stark contrast to him. And yet they were perfect for each other.

'Hey, hun. It'll be okay,' said Imogen as they walked together to the gate.

'I second that. No one messes with my friends or my cousin and gets away with it. If your dad tries anything, or this Will guy, then we'll sort them. We're basically the Scooby-Doo gang.' Cameron wasn't wrong. Julian hadn't been that involved in their problems in the past, but he knew his cousin wouldn't let anyone suffer under his watch.

'Oh, can I be Fred Jones? I think I'm definitely the debonair one,' said James as he caught up with them.

They all laughed at him as Tom replied, 'Mate, you're Shaggy, for sure.'

'Fuck off.'

Julian knew they were trying to lighten the mood and distract Jess, and he was thankful for that. It didn't help with his impending feeling of doom, though.

Jess took full advantage of the complimentary champagne as they boarded the plane, and quickly settled into her seat, an audio book playing in her ears. Thanks to the configuration of the seats, he was opposite her, and didn't take his gaze off her for long. He rolled his eyes at himself as he could only see her legs from his seat, but it was enough. He'd never felt this protective over a girlfriend before, although to be fair, they'd never been offered up for sale by their father as part of a business deal, so he wouldn't be too hard on himself.

After what felt like forever, the captain announced they were coming in to land. Julian recognised the anxious look that came over Jess's face, so he reached across and held her hand until it was time to unbuckle their seats.

The journey back to Cameron's house was quick and quiet. Julian could feel the tension build in the luxury people carrier as they neared their destination, with talk turning to everyone wanting constant updates from Jess when she got home.

After tight hugs that lasted a little longer than normal, the others let Jess drive off, with Julian following closely behind. There was no way he'd let Jess go home alone. He promised he'd be with her every step of the way, and he meant it. What he didn't tell her was how concerned he was that her dad wouldn't take this lying down.

Best-case scenario, her parents admit defeat and leave them to live happily ever after. He wasn't stupid, however, and had a feeling that her dad would lose his shit. He didn't know the man, but using your daughter as a bargaining chip in a business deal wasn't exactly standard practice in the twenty-first century.

He was clearly up shit creek without a paddle, and Julian doubted he'd let Jess walk away. What was clear to Julian was that Peter Chatwin valued money and his bank more than his daughter.

Jess pulled up to a set of iron gates set between two stone pillars topped with horse statues. Within seconds, the gates eased open at a leisurely pace. With each inch of progression, Julian's stress levels rose. Jess led the way up the gravel drive, lined with shrubs. She pulled over under a carport, but Julian parked near the front door. He was quick to reach her, grabbing her bags for her.

'You doing okay?' From just one look at her, he knew the answer. Her usually glowing complexion had been replaced with a decidedly grey pallor and the shine had gone from her eyes.

'I'm shitting my pants.' She attempted a grin but failed. 'My dad has no idea I know what he's up to, and I don't know how he's going to react.' She looked down at her feet as she said, 'I've never feared my dad until now. He's never been bothered about me enough to care.'

Julian kept a lid on his rage. She didn't need to see his anger. What she needed was his strength. He caught her chin between his thumb and forefinger and lifted her head to look her in the eyes. 'You don't need to fear your dad. I'm here and I'm not letting anything happen to you. Okay?' She nodded. 'Come on, let's get this over and done with. I'm not leaving your side until you feel comfortable.'

He gripped her hand in his, grabbed her bag, and took a deep breath.

Jess pressed her thumb to the pad on the door and slowly stepped into the house. The tip-tapping of shoes on the wooden floor broke the momentary silence.

'Jessica Chatwin, where the hell have you been?' Her mother's words echoed in the vast space, only adding to her shrill tone.

Seconds later, an image straight out of a Home and County magazine appeared from down a hallway.

Dressed in cream jodhpurs, tan leather boots, a navy polo top, and a Barbour gilet, Georgina looked like she'd just got back from a hunt.

'Mum, hello to you too. Have you been out riding?' Sarcasm laced Jess's words. Jess had previously mentioned to Julian that Georgina liked to look the part, but didn't like to ride. He assumed horses weren't as easy to control as daughters.

Georgina's shoulders visibly bristled as she said, 'What? No, of course not. I went out to lunch at the Polo club. And you'd do well to watch your tone, especially…' She scanned her eyes over Julian, no doubt judging him and the size of his bank account. 'As you have a friend here.'

Julian had never heard someone make the word friend sound like an insult before. Georgina was a grade-A bitch, that was for sure.

Remembering his manners, and that he needed to at least try to start out on the right foot, Julian stepped forward, right hand outstretched. 'Good afternoon, Mrs Chatwin. Pleasure to meet you. I'm Julian.'

Georgina didn't take his hand at first. He could see the cogs turning in her mind, trying to weigh him up. He knew her to be a woman who held social standing and decorum in high regard, and he revelled in the fact she was clearly warring between ignoring his handshake and following the rules.

He held his gaze and his hand remained outstretched. Julian didn't lose, and he wouldn't be beaten with a handshake.

Decorum won out as she took his hand in one of the limpest handshakes he'd ever experienced. It was half-arsed, but he took it as a win. One-nil to Julian.

'Pleased to meet you.' She forced the words out through gritted teeth. 'Now, Jessica, I believe you owe us an explanation as to where you've been. Your father is on his way.' She looked at Julian. 'Are you just dropping off my daughter?'

The inference was loud and clear. *You can fuck off now.*

'Actually, we were hoping to speak to you both.' As the words leave his mouth, her mother glances between Jess and him, her eyes widening.

Ah, there they were, the alarm bells ringing in her head. He'd been waiting for that. He had the measure of Georgina Chatwin. She'd had him judged from the minute he walked in the door. He wasn't good enough for her daughter, but she didn't know him. If she did, she'd be rolling out the red carpet. But that was the beauty of the rich and entitled. They didn't give others a second thought if they didn't fit the mould, and he broke the mould long ago, hiding in plain sight.

'Oh.' Her shoulders bristled again. Her eyes squinted at Jess, who'd visibly crumpled in stature since getting home. 'I suggest we take a seat in the drawing room. Your father will be there shortly.' Jess obediently nodded and turned to walk down the corridor to the left. Georgina gave him a final scan before leading the way.

'Hey, it's going to be okay.' Julian spoke low enough so only she could hear, as he linked his hand in hers. Her lips formed a wan smile as she nodded. What he didn't tell her was that he was increasingly uncomfortable leaving her here. The Jess he knew—strong, witty, exuberant—didn't exist in these four walls. It crushed him to think that for the past year, he hadn't noticed. None of them knew what she was going through, and it broke his heart.

'I apologise in advance for my parents' behaviour.'

Julian stopped in his tracks and stepped closer to her. Lowering his head so their eyes were level, he fixed her with a determined stare, the muscle in his jaw twitching. 'Never apologise for them.' He nudged his head in Georgina's direction. 'You are not responsible for your parents' actions.' He resisted the urge to grab her, kiss her, grip her throat, and take her out of her mind. Now wasn't the time for that.

Peter didn't leave them waiting for long, and evidently hadn't been warned Julian was there as he stormed into the room. Julian hovered near a seated Jess. She'd taken the uncomfortable-looking chair in the corner of the room as Georgina paced, worrying her fingers together. The scent of lilies cloyed the back of Julian's throat.

'Jessica! You've pulled your last stunt. You—oh, who are you?' Julian was the one being questioned, but he directed the angry stare straight at his wife.

Julian pulled his hands free of his pockets and repeated the dance of earlier. 'Mr Chatwin, pleased to meet you. I'm Julian. Jess's boyfriend.' May as well rip the Band-Aid straight off. It was remarkable how his skin changed colour, going from a healthy tan that spoke of trips to St. Tropez, to a grey-green tinge then another quick change to red. Peter's expression changed at a similar pace, from indifference to blind rage.

He didn't waste his time offering his hand as Peter had promptly slid his into the pockets of his red chinos. Chinos that currently matched the colour of his face, contrasting with the white cotton shirt he wore, unbuttoned at the collar, allowing grey hair to poke out the top.

'I'm sorry, did you just say, boyfriend?' He spat the last word out, the colour deepening on his cheeks.

Jess stood up, taking a step towards him. 'Dad, we—'

'I suggest you sit down and shut up. You have no idea the trouble you've caused.'

Stepping between them and turning his back to Peter, he said, 'Jess, do me a favour and go pack your things. You're coming home with me.'

'Like hell she is. She'll be staying right here where I can keep an eye on her. And if you two think you're staying together, you can think again.' He turned his ruddy face to Julian. 'I don't know what she's told you, but Jess is already with someone, and I don't think they'd take too kindly to you parading her around like you own her.'

Julian nodded along, taking in everything Peter had to say. 'Okay, I can see you're not too happy with our announcement, but here's the thing. Jess isn't with anyone else; she's with me. Jess, pack any essentials you don't already have and meet me by the front door in a few minutes.'

Jess went to walk past as Peter stepped in her path. 'Don't you dare leave. If you walk out that door with this...' He looked Julian up and down with a sneer on his face. 'Man. You'll be turning your back on your family. Think very carefully before you take another step.'

Jess sucked in a long breath and shook her head. 'You turned your back on me the moment I was born without a dick. Bye, Daddy.' She dashed out of the door, her mother, who was panic-stricken, close behind.

As soon as they were alone, Peter turned on Julian. 'I don't know who the fuck you think you are—'

Julian stepped forward and held his hand up to stop Peter's rant. 'I'm going to have to stop you there. I'm afraid it's you that doesn't know exactly who I am, but you'll come to find out soon enough. Jess is no longer yours to use as you please. She's mine.'

'I'll cut her off. She'll walk out this door with nothing.'

This guy was a piece of shit, a grade-A arsehole. 'That's where you're mistaken. She'll walk out of here with everything. Her freedom, her pride, and her independence. You'll no longer have a hold over her and that kills you, doesn't it?' He turned to leave. He'd wasted enough of his time. Now he wanted to get Jess out of there.

'Looks like you need to find another way to seal your deal,' were his parting words as he walked through the door.

As he entered the hallway, Jess was running down the stairs, a bag slung over her shoulder and a pile of clothes still on their hangers over her arm.

'Come on, sunshine. It's time to go.' Julian took the bag and the suitcase still in the hallway from earlier and opened the door to leave.

Georgina ran up to them and quickly grabbed Jess, pulling her into a hug. Julian swore he could see a tear in her eye as she said, 'I'm sorry, Jess.'

A stunned-looking Jess faltered for a moment then hugged her mother back before running out the door.

'Georgina! Get in here, now.' Peter angrily barked from the drawing room.

Georgina wrung her hands together, looking between Julian and the room where Peter was waiting, conflict written on her face before she grabbed Julian and hurriedly whispered, 'Please look after her. You must keep her safe. Please, keep her safe.'

He nodded. 'I will.'

He'd had a feeling there was more to this than what Jess had overheard, and this confirmed his suspicions. What exactly was Peter Chatwin mixed up in?

CHAPTER 20

JESS

Midnight Ride - Orville Peck, Kylie Minogue & Diplo

Julian wasted no time throwing her belongings into the back of his car and driving off, his engine revving as stone chips flew from his tyres and skittered across the driveway. It wasn't until they were on the main road that Jess allowed herself to breathe.

She'd finally done it. So why didn't she feel good? An anxious knot formed in her stomach, sitting like lead. Her mother's parting hug threw her off kilter. Memories of being sent off to boarding school popped into her mind, the days where her bags were loaded into the car, ready for a new school year, and didn't warrant a hug. She now felt unsettled and entirely unsure of herself and her future.

'Are you okay?' Julian had stayed quiet, but it hadn't escaped her attention that his eyes darted to her every few seconds, and his hand hadn't left her thigh since they'd got in the car.

'I don't know. My mum's never hugged me like that before. It's like she doesn't expect to see me again.' She didn't want to admit that she felt guilty about leaving, or that she was having second thoughts. 'What did my mum say to you as we left?'

It shocked Jess that she'd gone from cold and unwelcoming to grabbing him like she didn't want him to leave.

'She told me to keep you safe.' Something about the tone of his voice, muted and hesitant, told her he was worried too.

'Is that all?'

'Yep. And I intend to do a better job at protecting you than your father did.' The whites of his knuckles as he gripped the leather steering wheel told her how angry he was.

'Protect me from what, though? That's what I can't figure out.'

'That's what I intend to find out. I promise I'll keep you safe, Jess. You won't need to worry about anything.'

Throughout her life, her father had made her feel like nothing more than a burden. Leaving home should've felt great, freeing, but she'd become a burden to another man in her life. Her heart sank. Was he with her out of a sense of duty? Was she just a damsel in distress? It wasn't fair on Julian to be lumbered with her.

'I don't have to come and stay at yours. I'm sure Sarah wouldn't mind putting me up while I try to find somewhere. I don't need my dad's money to get by. I've done well out of my business. I just need some time to get set up. Julian, it's not fair to force this on you. I know you like your space and—'

Jess stopped speaking and grabbed the seat to steady herself as Julian swerved the car down a sharp turn on the left that took them into what looked like a country park. The dirt track was lined with trees and ferns, and the only sign of light came from the headlights. He skidded to a stop, cut the engine, and practically threw himself out of the door. Jess's heart raced, not knowing if she felt scared, confused, or a mixture of the two.

He pulled her door open and practically growled, 'Get out.'

She wracked her brain, trying to work out what she'd said that would upset him so much. His chest heaved, his hands clenched tight at his side. He was pissed off, and she fleetingly wondered if he was about to leave her in the middle of a forest.

With shaky hands and unsteady legs, she unbuckled the seatbelt and twisted, getting out of the car. As soon as her feet hit the dirt track, he grabbed her hips, pushed her to the side, and pressed her back into the rear passenger door.

'I'm a patient man, Jess, but I won't listen to any more of your bullshit about what's fair to me. You've been raised to feel like less than you are. That much is obvious after meeting your parents, but I won't stand for it.'

Jess's heart raced and her skin heated as adrenaline pumped through her system. He towered over her, so close she had to crane her neck to see his face. He visibly fought to calm his breathing as he cupped her face with one hand, the other digging into her hip.

'I've grown up surrounded by girls who drain their parents of every penny, demanding the world be handed to them on a silver platter. They're fucking princesses and they make me sick. You're not like them, sunshine, and I won't have you belittle yourself again.' He traced his fingers down her cheek before wrapping his hand around her throat, the pressure making her gasp and lean in for more.

'Let me make myself perfectly clear. I'm a Dom; the women in my life submit to me, but from now on, I serve you. I'm not with you out of a misguided sense of duty. I'm with you because I fucking care for you. I've watched you from afar for too long, deciding I wasn't worthy of someone like you, but I cannot—will not—stand by and let you feel like anything less than the queen you are.'

Any minute now, she was sure to pass out. Her breaths weren't coming quick enough as arousal fought the tide of emotion that hit her, battering her heart and breaking down her defences.

He released her throat as he sank to his knees, gripped the hem of her skirt and draped one leg over his shoulder.

'Julian?' She tried to grip his hair to pause his movement, but he batted her hand away.

'Put your hands behind your back.'

Obeying immediately, she stopped her line of questioning and rested her rear against her hands as they pressed onto the cool metal of the car door.

He hooked a finger into her knickers, pushing them to the side, and swiped his tongue up her opening before sucking her clit between his teeth.

Her back arched at the sudden onslaught, a moan leaving her lips on an exhale. She forgot to think, only able to feel what this man was doing between her legs. Seconds ago, she felt like her life was over. Disowned by her family and worthless. Now, she didn't care. She was chasing a high she could feel building in her core already.

She heard cars approach and saw their headlights zooming past, but no one came down the track as Julian devoured her. Thrusting his tongue inside, he dug his fingers into her thighs, tugging until she was pressed firmly onto his face. Her hips ground against his mouth as her core clenched, seeking something to grip on to.

He slipped two fingers inside her with ease as he said, 'I'm on my knees for you, but you don't get to come until you tell me you're a queen.'

'Julian, please.'

He twisted his fingers, hitting her G-spot as she cried out.

'Now isn't the time for begging, sunshine. Are you a queen?'

Her body was on fire, her legs weak as he flicked every switch in her body.

'I asked you a question.'

'Yes,' she whispered.

'Yes, what?'

'I'm a queen.'

He sucked on her clit as his fingers stroked inside her. She could feel her orgasm readying itself to detonate as he paused. 'I think you can do better than that. Tell me to make you come. Own me, sunshine.'

She gripped the back of his head and looked down into his eyes, illuminated by the car's interior light. 'I'm a fucking a queen and I demand you make me come.' She felt power course through her veins, adding strength to her orgasm. This man was on his knees for her. She cried out with exhilaration. Tears ran down her cheeks as realisation struck. She was free.

The journey to Julian's house was silent as Jess came down from the events of the last hour. She felt like a zombie, her brain was scrambled from the immense low of walking out on her parents and the unbelievable high of Julian on his knees confessing the depth of his feelings for her. She was grateful he didn't push her for conversation, no doubt understanding her need to sit with her feelings, trying to make sense of them.

Jess knew Julian had a cottage near his restaurant, but she'd never been there before. He was a private man and moving in with him, however temporary it may be, felt incredibly personal, like she was encroaching on his space.

As he parked the car outside the house, she couldn't help but feel nervous. They'd had the occasional date in the past, and they'd grown incredibly close in Vegas, but now the holiday bubble had not only burst, it had positively exploded.

'Here we are.' Julian slapped his hands on his thighs as he turned to face Jess. He looked as nervous as Jess felt. 'Full disclosure. There may be a load of laundry draped everywhere to dry. Don't judge me, my cleaner quit before we went away.'

His rueful expression was a breath of fresh air to lighten her mood. She held her hands up. 'No judgement here.'

He insisted on carrying her bags into the house, which left her nothing to distract her hands from fidgeting.

His house was beautiful. She assumed he'd live in a modern detached house decorated to be minimalist and clean, perhaps all the furniture black leather or glass. But it was nothing like that. He lived in a picture-perfect English country cottage, complete with a thatched roof and trailing wisteria.

When he said he lived close to the restaurant, what she hadn't considered was that he lived on the grounds of the restaurant. As they walked through to the kitchen, having left all the bags and clothes in the hallway, she looked out of the windows to see the same river that flowed past the restaurant, running along the bottom of his back garden. As her eyes followed the banks of the river, she could just make out the outdoor seating of the restaurant if she craned her neck.

'Bloody hell, Jay, don't you ever leave work behind?'

He huffed out a laugh as he grabbed two bottles of beer from the fridge, opening one and passing it to her before opening his own. 'It wasn't intentional. My family owns this property, so when I moved out, I came here. When I decided to open a restaurant, I struggled to find the right location. I knew exactly what I wanted, but nowhere was just right. In the end, it was Cam who suggested we use some of the land here to build my dream. And so, here we are.'

She watched as he brought the bottle to his lips, his throat bobbing as he drank. She had a sudden urge to nibble on his neck. What was it about this man that made her want to devour him in the literal sense?

'I guess it saves on the commute to work.' Beer wasn't her go-to drink of choice, but she glugged it down out of desperation for something to keep her mind off what was happening. To her surprise, it was refreshing and light as she realised just how thirsty she was.

'That was the biggest plus side. I love my bed. Getting up doesn't come as easy for me as it does for Cam. I think he got the early-bird genes. Lounging in bed the day after a busy shift is one of my favourite things to do.'

Her cheeks flushed as she imagined spending the day in bed with him. His eyes locked with hers and from the way they twinkled, she reckoned he was having similar thoughts.

'Right, let me give you the tour.' He took hold of her free hand and led her through the various rooms downstairs. His home was warm and welcoming, and she felt at ease as he pointed out where everything was. The house was classic with predominantly off-white walls, the woodwork natural, and the floors oak. She slipped off her shoes as they reached the bottom of the plush cream carpeted stairs, that she couldn't wait to feel under her bare feet.

'There are four bedrooms, all en-suite. The main bathroom is down there.' Julian pointed down the corridor. 'It has an extra-large jacuzzi bath. It's bliss.'

She hummed loudly. 'You'll have to show me how to work it. I could do with a nice soak.'

He raised his eyebrows. 'I would love to. First, let's get you settled.'

'Sounds like a plan. Where's my room?' She didn't want to assume she'd be sleeping with him, but that didn't stop her wishing for it.

'Same place as mine, if you're happy with that?'

She forced herself not to sigh with relief, but she was mentally performing fist pumps. 'As long as you're okay with that, I am.'

As they walked into his bedroom, she could see why he loved his bed. The oak four-poster was bigger than a king-size and dominated the room. She would happily stay in it all day. The rest of the room was very much like the rest of the house, classic and clean.

'You have a beautiful home, Julian. Thank you for taking me in.'

He took her drink from her and placed it along with his own on the enormous chest of drawers before holding her in a tight embrace, breathing her in.

'It's my pleasure. I couldn't leave you there, not with how your dad was behaving. Is he always like that with you?'

'No. Any kind of emotional outburst from him would involve him giving a shit, which he doesn't. What you saw today was because he's worried about himself and the bank. My happiness isn't his priority.'

He pressed his forehead to hers and growled.

Her vagina purred back in response. *Down girl, now is not the time.*

'I'm so sorry you've had to live with that. You deserve so much better.'

If he'd have said that a few weeks ago, she'd have laughed it off. She didn't believe she deserved better. If her own parents didn't want her, then no one else would. But now she let the vulnerable part of her believe maybe she wasn't so bad.

She sighed as she gripped onto the back of his t-shirt. 'Well, I might not need to worry about my parents anymore. Once my dad gets over himself, he'll be glad to see the back of me, I'm sure.'

'Well, he's a fool. His loss is my gain. That is, of course, if you're happy to have me?' He pulled back and walked over to the bed, sitting on the edge. 'There's a lot you don't know about me, Jess.'

She didn't believe that for a second. 'I know all I need to. You've explained your...' She cleared her throat. 'Sexual proclivities, and I'm okay with that. Actually, I'd quite like to have a go. A proper go at it.'

He smiled. 'A proper go?'

Heat blossomed across her skin. 'Yes.' She sat down next to him. 'I'm assuming you like to run through the woods like a wild animal and pin your sub down and do all sorts of things to her? I want that. If you're willing to do it.'

He flopped onto his back, and rested his head in his hands, exposing an inch of his abs, sending heat to her core. 'I used to like that. I used to fucking love it. There's nothing better than the thrill of the chase. The sound of leaves and branches breaking underfoot as you search for your prey. The bite of pain as your knees press into the unyielding ground beneath you before you drive, balls deep, into your willing prey. '

'And you don't anymore?' She tried to ignore the disappointment that reared its ugly head.

He shrugged. 'Promise not to take this the wrong way?'

That didn't fill her with confidence. She was one hundred per cent likely to take whatever he said next in the wrong way.

'I'll try.' That was the best she could do.

'That night, in the alleyway, I could feel it stirring.'

'It?'

'Yeah, I call it the beast.'

Her pussy pulsed as she flooded her knickers with arousal. She clenched her thighs as she said, 'Oh, okay. Carry on.'

'Finding you in that compromising position triggered my baser nature and I could've easily lost control. I like it rough, Jess. I could've hurt you. But then images flashed in my head of Chloe, of how she looked in the hospital, and that stopped me.'

It hurt more than she cared to admit that he was thinking of Chloe when he had his hand wrapped around her throat. No one wants to hear your partner say they were thinking of someone else when you're getting up to sexy stuff. However, if there was anything her friends had taught her, it was that recovering from trauma wasn't a logical process.

'That's understandable. You're still working through the trauma.' Brownie points to Jess for taking the high road.

'I used to think I was broken for liking what I liked. Now I think I'm broken because I can't follow through on my desires.'

She didn't reply straight away. Instead, she flopped down next to him, turned onto her side, and rested her head in her hand. She ran her fingers up and down his torso, feeling the hard ridges beneath his clothes. She wanted to dig her nails in and hear him growl again. Perhaps there was a little beast inside her too.

'If it helps, I'm new to it all. I have no expectations and you'd have to start slowly to introduce me to it, so why don't you use me?'

He sucked a breath in through his teeth. 'Use you? Have you any idea what those words coming out of your mouth do to me?'

She looked down at his crotch. 'I think I can tell what it does to you.'

He closed his eyes and sighed, still lying on his back. 'But what if we try it and I break you?' His voice was thick with emotion, and it tugged on her heart.

'Maybe I want you to break me. At least if I'm broken, you can piece me back together. Form me into something new, something stronger, like Kintsugi. My scars will gleam in gold.'

He rolled onto his side to face her and cupped her face in his hand. 'Okay. But we'll take it slowly, start small.' He kissed her tenderly before pulling away and lying back down.

Warmth spread from her heart down to her core at his words. 'Can I ask a question?'

He nodded. 'I've already said you can ask me anything.'

'Have you ever been on the receiving end? Sarah said that James is a switch and that mostly he dominates, but occasionally he likes to hand the reins over to her. Have you ever done that?'

'No. Would you want me to?'

'I don't think so. I'm not as fast as you, or as strong. I'd never be able to hunt you down or get you on the floor. But I do often fantasise about licking you or biting you. Am I allowed to do that?'

He squeezed his eyes closed and groaned at hearing her admit her desires. 'I would never say no to you doing whatever you want or need, sunshine. Like seeks like, after all. Lick, bite, and suck on me whenever you want. Especially the last one; you can do that whenever you fancy.' Jess licked her lips. 'But not right now. I want to get you some food, then a bath. We can see how you feel after that. I have an idea.'

Jess soon discovered another benefit of living next door to Julian's restaurant, a fully stocked fridge at all times. After one phone call and twenty minutes, Julian walked back into the house carrying two plates filled with chicken in a creamy parsley sauce, roasted potatoes, and green veg. It smelled divine. And from the look of the glossy sauce flecked with fresh herbs, and the crispy potatoes, it was full of calories. Positively sinful.

'You'll feel like a new woman after a proper meal and a soak.'

'I'll feel like a bloater, is what I'll feel.' She hadn't meant to say that out loud, but her mother's words were always there, just below the surface.

'Bollocks. This meal has the perfect balance between nutrition and taste. Sometimes, sunshine, you have to feed your soul.' Living with Julian was going to take some getting used to, but she smiled to herself as she considered how happy and at ease she already felt.

They ate at the dining room table in comfortable silence. Julian had picked out a bottle of perfectly chilled white wine from his personal cellar, and she appreciated the relaxed buzz it gave her.

He gripped the stem of his wineglass between his thumb and forefinger, rolling it back and forth as he watched her finish the last of her delicious meal. She placed her knife and fork down with military precision as she looked up at him. 'You look like you want to say something.'

'I do. I was waiting for you to finish first.'

'Why? Is what you have to say going to put me off my dinner?'

'It might.' He lifted the glass to his lips and sipped.

There was that lead ball again, weighing heavily. 'What is it?'

'I want to check in, make sure you're doing okay.'

She shrugged. 'I'm doing as well as expected, I guess. To be honest, I'm more worried about Teddy and my car than anything else.' She'd left Teddy for days at a time before, but this felt more permanent, and she already missed him and the joy she got from riding him.

'Don't worry about your car, you can use mine until we sort out picking yours up. Your horse, leave that with me. I obviously don't have stables, but I know somewhere that does and they'll have room for Teddy. Let the dust settle a bit, find out what the state of play is and then I'm happy to talk to your mum about moving him.'

'You'd do that for me?'

'I'd burn the world down for you, remember? I'm the perfect morally grey boyfriend. Taking a horse is child's play.' His face turned serious as he fixed his eyes on hers. 'So, you're doing okay? It's all right to be feeling a bit shit right now. I just need to know where your head is at.'

She sipped her wine as she mulled over her response. He was doing the right thing by checking in with her. She was asking him to be vulnerable and let out his inner beast, but he needed to make sure she could cope with all that entailed. She'd spoken to Sarah enough to know that you had to be in the right headspace, as things could go wrong otherwise, but she also knew that playing with him could give her the release she needed.

During a scene, Sarah had explained how she could forget about the world around her. It's what got her through the court case. If James could learn to give Sarah what she needed, then surely she could learn to take what Julian offered.

'I love my parents. I can't help it. They're the only ones I have.' Her smile was weak as she tried to inject some humour. 'But I don't like them. I know they're toxic and I'm better off away from them. Tonight, I chose to walk away from them and leave with you. I trust you, Jay. I've grown up in an environment where I may as well have not existed. I coped with that by putting my feelings in a box and ignoring them. As long as I smiled and remembered my manners, life was easy enough.'

Taking another sip and swallowing down the lump forming in her throat, she blinked back the tears as she spoke. 'But when I'm with you, I feel so deeply. It's like I'm experiencing life for the first time... or at least, living. Yeah, I feel a bit shit. My dad tried to use me for financial gain, and I've left everything I know behind, but that's just noise in the background. I don't doubt that when I have quiet moments to myself, that noise will seem louder. It might bother me, but when I'm with you, you drown it out. You're louder.'

He drained the last of his wine, the glass ringing as he put it back down. 'In that case, it's bath time. And then we play.'

CHAPTER 21

JESS

Lust for Life (feat. The Weeknd) - Lana Del Ray

Julian wasn't kidding when he said the jacuzzi bath was massive. She watched as he stripped off his clothes and sank into the warm water. She couldn't help but chew on her bottom lip at the sight of a wet Julian.

Within a few seconds, she was in the water, nestled with her back against his chest. The water jets bubbled around them, not that she could feel them as he cocooned her.

'This is bliss. I don't want to return to real life just yet. Can we stay here for a few more weeks?'

Julian trailed his fingers lazily up and down her arms, her collarbone, and her chest. Despite the warmth of the water, goosebumps prickled across her skin. He hummed low and slow. 'I think we'd get too wrinkly if we stayed in here for a few weeks.'

She sighed as she swayed her bent legs from side to side, watching as the roiling water sploshed over her knees. 'I suppose I can't hide away from my life forever. Tomorrow is a new day, the start of a new life.'

They discussed what she needed to do for work. Thankfully she was sourcing artwork for the Lombardis and a few new clients that approached her after the hotel opening, so she could work from her laptop and phone.

'I don't like the thought of you being here on your own while I'm at the restaurant.' Julian's hands were stroking her hair and massaging her temples. She was in heaven. 'Do you think it would be a good idea to work with the others in their office? I'm sure James and Cam will have somewhere you can set up. You're basically a member of staff there now, anyway.'

She danced her fingertips across the surface of the water as she thought about it. It might be just the distraction she needed, and she'd always felt left out with them all working together. 'Actually, I like that idea. I'll drop James a text and see what he says.'

They sat in silence, their hands trailing over each other, enjoying the moment of calm. Jess felt so at home here. She realised during dinner she didn't feel judged for eating everything on her plate and enjoying every morsel. Maybe at the next meal, she'd put her elbows on the table and see if Julian scolded her. A light giggle escaped her lips at the thought.

'What's funny?' He pressed a kiss to the crown of her head.

'I was just wondering if you'd tell me off for putting my elbows on the table at dinner.'

'Would you like me to?' He palmed her breasts, her body coming alive under his touch.

'Well, that depends on what you'd do to me.'

'Oh, is there a little bratty Jessica coming out to play?'

'There might be.'

He ghosted his lips to the shell of her ear. 'I'd probably have to bend you over the table and bite your peachy arse until you're dripping and begging for my cock. And then I'd make you run.'

She writhed with need as she imagined herself at his mercy.

'Next time you want to start something, sunshine, just put your elbows on the table.'

Noted. She was very much looking forward to her next meal.

The water cooled and a shiver danced over the surface of her damp skin. 'Come on, time to get out,' said Julian.

He held out a bath sheet so big it swamped her in its fluffy, lavender scented softness.

'Do you still want to play?' Julian had efficiently dried himself off and was standing in front of her in all his naked glory. Soft skin taught across his muscles as his cock hung heavy between his thick thighs. She resisted the urge to get on her knees and worship at his feet.

'What are we playing?' Her voice was husky as her throat dried with anticipation and nerves.

'Tell me, what have you enjoyed most about what we've done together so far? Think about how you felt when I chased you down at Cam's house, or when you knew I was hunting you in Vegas.'

She rolled her lips together as she tried to put her feelings into words. 'You know when you're watching a horror movie and the victim is about to run upstairs and meet a stabby end? You get this buzz. You want to look, but at the same time you don't, but the excitement and adrenaline rush get too strong, so you peek through your fingers at the screen. Your heart is racing and you feel alive.' She nodded. 'That's how I felt every time we've done something together. I want more of that. The fear. When I feel that fear, it makes me realise I'm alive, but more than that, it's that I want to be alive, to have something to live for.' She shrugged a shoulder, her cheeks turning rosy at the admission. 'That probably sounds a touch dramatic. What can I say? I read a lot of romance.'

He stepped closer, pulling the towel away from her. The rush of cool air made her hair stand on end before he took her in his arms. 'I think that explains it perfectly. People describe themselves as adrenaline junkies and fling themselves off bridges or planes. I get the same result but also get to have great sex. It's a win-win.'

'Maybe we could jump out of a plane together and fuck on the way down?'

He looked down at her and raised an eyebrow. 'I think that might be a step too far... obviously I'm going to search for that on the internet later.'

She hugged him, pressing her face into his chest. Her shoulders were no longer around her ears. Her heart was beating a steady rhythm in time to his. She felt safe and comfortable and like herself. She shut the lid on how she felt about her family and promised herself to concentrate on what she wanted.

'So, what's the game then? You've kept me waiting long enough.'

Jess stood in the middle of the living room, naked, with only a blindfold on. Julian had given her a few minutes to remember where all the furniture was, but still warned her to tread carefully to avoid bruising her shins.

He'd drawn the curtains and turned all the lights out, which in itself would've scared Jess, but being naked and blindfolded added a vulnerability to the mix.

'We can't go outside to play while the restaurant is open; I don't think the locals would appreciate it if we went further afield. Although I think Roger down the road would want to join in, so best avoid him.'

'Okay. Avoid Roger, unless he's handsome.'

'Trust me, he's not. I want you to feel the anticipation and fear of a hunt without the hunt. You'll know I'm in the house, you'll hear me, feel me, but you won't know what's coming. I need you to tell me a safeword.'

She swallowed, the fear already creeping in at the mention of needing a safeword. 'Oh, um, can I use… oyster?'

'Oyster?'

'Yep, they're so gross. Guaranteed to put a stop to a sexy night.'

'Fair enough. I'll make a note not to serve you oysters. Are you happy with biting, scratching, me holding your throat, edging, praise, and rough sex?'

She didn't need to consider her answer as she felt her inner thighs grow slick. 'You know I'm happy with all of those. That's the sexiest wish list ever. Can I do the same to you?'

'I expect you to. I enjoy the chase, but I'd love for you to fight back. If you feel the urge to claw and bite me, then do it. Make me earn your surrender, sunshine.'

'Okay. Let's do this.'

'I'm going to go upstairs for twenty seconds. While I'm gone, I want you to move somewhere else. You can keep moving. I'll be able to find you easily, but the purpose is for you not to know what's coming.'

She nodded as she heard his footsteps leaving the room and started counting in her head. Her breaths quickened as she put one foot in front of the other, her hands outstretched, feeling for furniture. She remembered there was a large dresser unit against the wall in the dining room with a gap near the corner big enough for her to squeeze into. She tried to count to twenty while focusing on not tripping over, and within ten seconds, she felt the doorframe that led into the dining room.

At fifteen seconds, she felt the corner of the unit.

Eighteen seconds and she was tucked behind it. Her heart was beating out of her chest as she tried to calm her breathing and remain silent.

Twenty seconds she heard a creak on the stairs. And then silence.

She kept counting, giving her brain something to focus on. She had no idea what to expect. Would he grab her straight away?

Twenty-five seconds.

Would he touch her, bite her or leave her waiting?

Thirty seconds.

Still silence.

She resisted the urge to move from her safe corner, protected on three sides.

Thirty-five seconds.

These were the longest seconds of her life. Without her sight, her other senses were working overtime as she listened for his approach.

Forty seconds.

A rush of warmth brushed across her face. 'Run.'

She thrust her hands out, meeting a hard wall of muscle and flesh. She heard him grunt as she pushed past him and stumbled out of the room, her hands frantically searching for signs of where to go. As she made her way back into the living room, she ran her left hand along the wall, tracing a path to the kitchen. She'd hide under the kitchen table and hope that staying low would slow him down. She'd be harder to get to between the chairs.

She reached her hands around, finding the rounded edge of the table and grasped onto a chair, easing it out of the way. She bit her lip to stop herself from crying out as she clunked her head on another chair as she tucked herself under the table.

He must have given her time to escape, as she heard a movement coming from the living room. And then she knew he was near her. She could feel his presence humming in the air like an electrical current.

She wrapped her arms around her knees, hugging them close to her chest. She heard the faint noise of joints creaking before something soft ran up her leg. It wasn't his hand, and she hoped to God it wasn't a spider.

A hand gripped her ankle and suddenly she was pulled from under the table, her back slamming on the floor, the air from her lungs expelled.

And then nothing.

She couldn't feel him near her. Couldn't hear him breathing.

Should she move again?

She slowly rolled onto her side, then froze, waiting to see if he reacted. Nothing.

Getting up onto her knees, she shuffled along, trying to reach out with one hand while not losing her balance. Her knees were sore from the hard floor and her palms were sweaty from the panic she felt.

Where was he? And how was he so silent? It wasn't natural.

She crawled back into the living room and could feel the warmth of the rug under her hands and knees. She was thankful for that, at least. Something soft stroked along her spine, freezing her in her tracks.

Was he stroking her with a feather? Or maybe it was one of those floggers that Sarah raved about all the time. He'd said he wasn't into spanking, but maybe he liked to do it with props?

The stroking sensation worked its way up her thigh as her legs quivered and her back bowed, her hips opening.

'I can smell you from here, sunshine.' He was behind her now. Flames erupted across her skin as his hands gripped her hips. Her pulse pounded in her ears and her heart raced with exhilaration. Was he going to fuck her now? Part of her wanted him inside her, part of her wanted to make him earn her.

She pushed off from the floor with all her strength and tried to sprint off, but before she made any progress, he grabbed her calf as she tumbled; the sofa breaking her fall as she landed face-first onto the cushions.

'Are you going to fight me, sunshine?' His voice was low again, like it was in the alleyway in Vegas when she glimpsed his beast for the first time. The prospect of him letting down his guard and going full throttle on her, thrilled her. He flipped her onto her back and dragged her off the sofa, holding her back so she didn't slam into the floor.

He pushed her legs apart and pressed his hips into hers. She could feel his erection sliding between her slick opening and forced herself not to buck into him. Instead, she reared her head up and clamped her teeth onto his neck causing him to release his grip on her and cry out. She didn't know how hard to bite. What was acceptable? She didn't have time to think on it any longer before he pulled himself away, her mouth detaching with a pop.

'I can see I need to keep myself away from your mouth. That shouldn't be a problem.'

He had the size advantage as he gripped her wrists in one hand and pressed them into the floor above her head. His other hand kneaded one breast and brought his lips to her other one. He sucked her nipple into his mouth and bit down.

Molten hot pain lanced across her nipple, and she couldn't help but cry out. He released her, blowing cool air across her already pebbled flesh. As soon as the pain subsided, she craved more.

He answered her prayers as he repeated the action with her other nipple. 'Are you good?'

She panted as she answered. 'Yes. So good.'

'You ready to submit?'

She rolled her head from side to side. 'No.'

'Then I suggest you fight back, sunshine. Only one rule, don't knee me in the dic—'

Before he could finish his sentence, she seized the opportunity to roll and tug her hands free of his grip, only he didn't release her and now she was on her side, her wrists pressing into one another painfully. She grunted out a frustrated breath.

He was too big and powerful for her to escape that way. She needed to try something else. Rolling onto her back, she manoeuvred her legs until her knees were pressing to her chest. She knew Julian was going easy on her. He could have easily halted her movements.

'Careful. I like to fuck in this position. Are you giving yourself to me? Are you ready to feel me drive into you, hitting places you didn't know I could reach?'

Yes. She was entirely ready for that, but she also didn't like to go down without a fight. Having ridden horses since she could walk, Jess knew she had strong thighs. It was the strongest part of her besides her iron will. Driving her legs up, pressing her feet to his chest, she forced Julian away until he had to release his grip on her wrists.

The sudden movement had left him unbalanced, so she shoved again until she heard him land on the floor with a thud. She decided to hell with the rules and ripped the blindfold off as she sprinted back into the dining room.

'I knew you were a fighter the minute I laid eyes on you,' he called out to her as he followed. 'Like calls to like.'

He'd cornered her at one end of the large table. He moved to the left, so she dodged to her left. He dodged to the right. She mirrored him.

'This could go on all night, sunshine. And don't think you taking off your blindfold has gone unnoticed.'

'You didn't say I couldn't take it off.' She raised her eyebrow, feeling smug at finding the loophole.

He growled at the defeat; the sound sending waves of pleasure through her. She didn't want this lasting all night, so she took a chance and legged it to the door. She'd only just made it over the threshold before he crashed into her, gripped her body to his and twisted as they crashed to the floor.

Within a second, he rolled them over and once again he'd pinned her, his body pressing down onto hers.

But this time, she had a plan. She knew her small hand wouldn't reach around his throat, but her thighs could.

'Do you submit?'

She remained silent, unsure of the etiquette of agreeing. If she said yes, would she be breaking the rules if she continued to fight?

'I'll take your silence as a no.'

He bucked his hips into hers, his length sliding over her clit and sending sparks through her core. She wanted to submit. Maybe she could get a taste before enacting her plan. She lifted her knees back up, as if to push him away again, but this time, he pushed his head between them and forced her legs back and open with his shoulders. He'd fallen for her trap.

With her calves around his neck, she was in the perfect position for him to slide home, but she could also squeeze. Maybe she'd let him have a little fun first.

She thrust her hips up as he ground into her, his cock sliding in with ease. 'Fuuuck.' He growled out, filling her to the hilt and pausing while they both acclimatised to the sensation. She could've easily let him fuck her, but she wasn't done with him yet.

Twisting her feet behind his head, she locked her ankles together and squeezed. His face changed colour almost immediately, the veins at his temple bulging with the pressure she applied to his neck.

But he didn't let go. Instead, he withdrew his cock to the tip before driving back in, hitting her cervix with force. It was beautifully painful. She bucked her hips, using his shoulders for leverage.

'That's right, fight while I fuck you.' His words were raspy as he struggled for breath. She eased off, not wanting him to actually suffocate. That would be a terrible waste of an erection.

He thrust into her relentlessly until she felt her orgasm build. And then he pulled out.

The sudden emptiness caused her to lose concentration and her thighs relaxed. He seized the moment to pull away from her, his weight no longer on her body.

'Submit. I'm done playing.' She could tell from his tone that he meant it. 'You've put up an exceptional fight. I can't wait to take you outside, but for now, I need to fuck you.'

She lay there, panting and elated and ready to be fucked. 'I submit.'

Within seconds, she was over his shoulder, the world upside down, as he carried her back into the dining room.

'I'm going to fuck you on this table, sunshine, to make sure you enjoy every meal in here going forward.' He lifted her off his shoulder and gently laid her down on the table. Was it a coincidence that the table was the perfect height for him to fuck her? She briefly imagined him walking around furniture showrooms standing next to all the tables until he found one at cock height. Her wandering thoughts were halted as he spread her legs and ran his nose up the inside of her thigh, breathing her in.

'But first, I'm going to have *my* meal.'

It didn't take long for her to feel her arousal trickle down and pool on the table between her legs as he licked and sucked an orgasm out of her.

'I told you I'd have you dripping for me, didn't I, sunshine?'

'Yes. And now I'm begging for you to fuck me.' She was tired. The hunt had drained her, her legs shaky. She needed him to take her. To finish her.

He leaned her over, taking her mouth with as much passion as he'd just eaten her out with. Her arousal coated her chin as he devoured her.

He straightened and draped her legs over his shoulders before sliding between them. He took his time entering her, at first only a few inches, before pulling back to the tip. With each thrust, he sank in another inch until he was fully seated. His strokes were languid, like he had all the time in the world. She moaned with desperation, clawing at his arse to encourage him to thrust deeper, harder.

Her skin was damp with perspiration, causing her to slide on the table with each thrust, the friction warming her back, blending with the heat radiating out from her core. He raised her hips off the table so the ridge of his head stroked across her G-spot with perfect precision.

'You feel so good, sunshine. You were made for me. You take me so well. Are you going to come for me?'

She fluttered around his length as she cried out, 'Yes. I'm going to come like this. Just like this.' She didn't want him to change anything. Usually when she was close, the guy would pump harder, or faster and come before she could. Every. Single. Time. But Julian knew what he was doing. His face was strained, holding himself back.

He kept the same deliberate pace, hitting her spot with precision until she felt the rush of heat across her body, felt the pressure build in her core until the pulsing turned erratic and she came with a cry.

'Oh, yes. Fuck. Julian.' She'd never come like this before. This orgasm was different to any she'd had before. It rocked her core, warming her and then she realised the warmth was spreading from between her legs and under her arse.

'Fuck, sunshine. You're coming so hard; you're soaking my cock. I'm dripping with you.' He leant over her, released her legs from his shoulders as she wrapped them around his waist. He gripped onto her shoulder with one hand as the other pressed against her throat. 'I'm going to fuck you hard now. You okay with that?'

She locked eyes with his and nodded.

'Say it.'

'Yes. I want you to fuck me hard, Julian. Break me.'

He drove into her, chasing his own release. Her back burned as he forced her onto the table. His skin slapped against hers as the sound of her arousal filled the room. She didn't care. She wasn't embarrassed. He was the reason they were drenched with her orgasm.

He growled, 'I'm going to fill you with my cum,' before he sucked in as much of her breast as he could into his mouth and bit down, only letting go when he roared out his release. His cock throbbed as his heat filled her and leaked down to mix with the evidence of her own orgasm. She never felt so claimed and it felt fucking amazing. She wanted to cover herself in his cum, wanted to feel it all over her body.

He slowed his thrusts and then stood, his eyes hazy and a smile on his face. 'Look at how beautiful you are, slick with sweat and cum. I can't tell you what seeing my cum all over you does to me, sunshine.' He traced a finger from the table to her opening, pushing it back inside her. 'I want you full of me all the time.' He dragged his wet fingers across her stomach, leaving a glistening line behind as it cooled her skin. 'I've never wanted to fuck anyone bare before, but with you, it's not a want, it's a need.'

Her heart thundered in her chest as she steadied her breathing. She understood what he was saying as she felt it too. If she was in a fantasy novel, she was sure she'd just bonded with her mate.

CHAPTER 22

JULIAN

Iris - The Goo Goo Dolls

Julian's heart didn't recover after their mini hunt, as Jess liked to call it. Medically, his organ was in top-notch condition. Emotionally, it was irrevocably altered. He loved her. Not some surface level love that you thought you felt at first, when the romance was fresh, and you see everything through rose-tinted glasses. This was real love, where each breath when you're apart was painful.

Dragging himself away from her the next morning was agony. And every morning after that. A week and a half had flown by and they had plans to catch up with everyone at Cam's house. Jess had mostly stayed in the house, working from his home office, arranging meetings with artists and clients. She'd pop over to see him and eat lunch at the restaurant. That was his favourite part of the day, apart from when he got home and buried himself balls deep in her needy pussy.

He hoped that spending some time with their friends would give her the opportunity to open up about how she was feeling. It hadn't escaped his attention that focusing on work, or his dick, was how she coped with warring emotions, but when it was quiet and she didn't know he was watching, he saw the pain on her face. Just fleeting moments where she let her guard down. He knew what it was like to put a lid on your emotions, how it can eat you up on the inside. He didn't want that for her. He also wouldn't push her to open up to him. He was her safe space where she was finding her feet again. He was happy to let her best friends give her the support she needed.

He strolled into their bedroom where Jess was applying the finishing touches to her makeup. 'You nearly ready, sunshine?'

He let his thoughts fast forward to her in a wedding dress, and then with a swollen belly. He'd kept his fantasies to himself, knowing that all her life she'd been told she was only good for breeding. He doubted telling her he now had a breeding kink would go down well. But fuck, he got hard just thinking about it.

'Yep, I'm ready.' Her beauty was effortless. Wearing black jeans and what he'd learned was her favourite V-neck sweater, black with gold wings emblazoned on the back. She stood and walked over to him. He ran his finger down the V-neck and pushed it to the side, revealing his recent bite marks. An involuntary growl rumbled from his chest.

She glanced down at his dick, which was straining against his indigo jeans. He hadn't felt the need to wear his usual armour of black jeans and grungy T-shirts. Instead, he'd paired these blue ones with a white polo and a bottle green half zip sweater. He'd switched out his chunky black boots for chunky brown ones. He felt cheesy thinking it, but being with Jess, teaching her about his primal kink, made him feel like himself again.

She knew the real him, but he doubted she'd see it that way when he admitted who his family was. That was the problem. He wasn't hiding who he was from her; he was hiding from the life he'd left behind. But he couldn't keep it from her any longer. He wanted to be sure they were right together, that she could cope with him before he opened up to her completely.

She ran her fingers around his collar, straightening it as she said, 'From the look of it, you're the one that isn't ready. Need some help with that little predicament in your trousers?'

He cleared his throat as he stepped into her space, forcing her back until she reached the foot of their bed. 'There is something you can do for me before we leave, now that you mention it.'

She licked her lips. 'Do you want me on my knees?'

'Not in the way you're thinking.' He ran his fingers through her hair, pushing it to one side as he ran his nose up the column of her neck. 'I need to fill you before we leave. You're not allowed to clean yourself up. I want to be between your legs all night. Do you understand?'

He felt her chest heave as she licked her lips. 'Do it.'

'It's going to be quick and hard. You may not come, but I'll reward you later.'

She pulled her bottom lip between her teeth as she sighed. 'I think I might come just from the thought of it.'

He smiled at how perfect she was before spinning her round. 'You're going to want to grip the bed frame, sunshine.' He unzipped her jeans and, with her knickers, pulled them down to her knees. It was going to be a tight fit with her legs restricted like that, but he knew it would help speed up the process. They were already running late.

He unbuttoned his jeans enough to release his cock, spat in his hand and stroked his length before forcing it between her legs. She lifted her hips, giving him as much access as she could. 'Good girl. Ah, fuck. This won't take long. Are you hungry for my cum, sunshine?'

'Hmm-mmm, yes.' She thrust back, impaling herself as he lost control. He pumped into her, not caring about his technique. He was only interested in marking his scent all over her like an animal.

Jesus-fucking-Christ. She was so tight. 'I can feel you grip me. You really are hungry for me, aren't you?' His heart swelled, and so did his cock.

'Jay, please. I need to come. I'm so close.'

He didn't want her to come. He wanted her desperate for him all night while she sat with him leaking into her delicate lace knickers. 'Not now you won't.' He abruptly stilled, panting hot breaths on the back of her neck. He could feel the rapid and tight pulses of her eager pussy ease, and only then did he thrust again.

'Press your thighs together.' He needed to come before she did. Tonight was for him, to sate his beast. Tonight she'd learn what it was to be his sub. The added friction of her thighs rubbing along his cock as he withdrew caused his balls to tighten with their impending release.

'Fuck, Jay. Oh. Fuck. Please.' Jess rocked her hips against him, trying to take control and push herself over the edge.

With great effort, he pulled out. 'Stop it,' he growled. 'You'll move when I tell you to move. Do you understand? Your job is to take my dick. If you're a good girl, you'll get yours later.'

She nodded. 'Yes. Okay,' her words were quick and breathy.

He slammed into her without warning. The way her body reacted to the scene drove him closer to the edge. His clothes clung to his back as he held her hips in place, his fingers no doubt leaving bruises, and pounded into her with unrelenting force.

'Fuuuuck.' He ground out through clenched teeth as he collapsed over her, bracing himself on the bed frame. The force of his orgasm draining him of his energy.

He cupped her sex with his hand, feeling his seed drip into it. He wiped his palm over her entrance before sliding two fingers inside, pushing his cum inside her.

With his free hand, he grabbed her jeans and underwear from around her knees and dragged them up her thighs, careful not to waste a drop. With her clothes safely in place, he ran his fingers through her mussed hair, kissing her gently when she turned to face him. 'Thank you. You were perfect. You took me so well.'

Her cheeks were flushed and her eyes gleamed. 'It's a good job I wore my black skinny jeans. I'd be mortified if I was wearing a skirt, and your swimmers ran down my leg.' The look of horror on her face was delightful. The image she'd given him was enough to make him hard again.

'You've given me ideas.'

She rolled her eyes and said, 'Come on, you horn-dog, we're late.'

'Yeah, but it was worth it.'

The smile didn't leave his face until Cameron opened the door to them when they arrived at his house. 'I can tell there's no need to ask you what kept you two.' Cameron slapped him on the back as he stepped aside.

They made their way into the kitchen where everyone had congregated.

'Oh, at last. You two took your time.' Sarah bounded over to them, gripping Jess in an overzealous hug. Julian inwardly grinned at the blush creeping up Jess's neck. He had a feeling part of him had just been squeezed out of her.

He shook the image out of his head before he'd have to take her upstairs.

'Sorry, hun, I had to help Jay with something important.'

'Oh, what was that then?'

Cameron cleared his throat while attempting not to laugh, which caused Tom and James to give him a sly look. James winked as he brought his drink to his lips and sipped. Tom just nodded his head before sticking it in the fridge to get Julian a beer.

'U-uum, well…' Jess clearly hadn't thought this through and didn't know what to say.

'Oh my god.' The penny had dropped. 'Let's pretend I didn't ask.' Sarah sidled up to Jess and whispered, but still loud enough for him to hear, 'I need to know all the details later.'

Opting to change the subject, Julian said, 'So, Sarah, how is the interior design course going?'

And just like that, he'd taken the attention away from their sexual exploits.

As usual, Cameron had cooked them all a delicious meal, this time it was chicken curry with all the trimmings. He'd even made naan breads, which was impressive.

After their bellies were full, the men retired up to the bar and games room, while the women sat in their usual places on the large sofas and perved over fictional men. He couldn't lie. He was hoping she'd talk about him tonight. The thought filling him with pride.

James racked up the balls on the pool table as Tom opened more beer, this time an alcohol-free one for Julian as he was driving.

'Any word from Jess's parents?' Julian instantly felt ill at ease at the mention of her parents. Their lack of communication had him worried, as there wasn't a part of him that believed it was over.

'She's not heard a word. Not even a text message from her mum. I can't say that I'm surprised. The toxicity in their place was leaching out the walls.'

'So, what's going to happen now?' Tom said as he chalked up his cue.

Julian shrugged. 'No idea, mate. I'm worried though.'

That caught Cameron's attention. 'What about?'

'Jess's mum told me to keep her safe. She looked scared as she told me. And she hugged Jess.'

'What's wrong with that?' asked James as he sent the white smashing into the triangle of balls at the end of the table. They scattered, bouncing off the edges and clinking into each other.

'Jess said she didn't even get a hug when she left for boarding school. Apparently, Georgina isn't a hugger.'

Tom walked around the pool table, assessing his shot. 'So, you think there's more to this than her dad greasing the wheels of a deal?'

'I have no idea. From what I've seen of Peter's behaviour, I suspect it has more to do with us pissing him off.'

Cameron raked his nails across the stubble on his chin. 'That would make sense. Maybe Peter's a tad unstable. We've all seen what happens when unstable men don't get what they want. But I can't see her dad hurting her. Surely, he wouldn't go that far?'

Julian thought about it for a moment. 'Yeah, you're right. I don't think he'd hurt her. Jess mentioned the name of who the deal was with: Wilberforce. I don't know who they are, but this Wilberforce guy is the only other person with something to lose if the deal doesn't go through.'

'Well, him and the fuckwit that she was supposed to marry. He might not take too kindly to losing his bride.' James shrugged as he lined up his next shot.

Tom nodded. 'That's true, but for now assume the deal is off. If anyone's going to take the brunt of this, it'll be her dad. I think it's about time you two enjoyed yourselves. And from the looks on your faces when you arrived, you've been doing plenty of that.

How's it going in that department? She helping you work through your demons?'

Julian couldn't help the grin that formed on his lips. He sipped from his bottle to hide it. 'Those demons are fully exorcised. We've been working hard on those.'

James clapped him on the back. 'Good for you. I'm happy for you, mate.'

Cameron didn't look so happy, and Julian had an idea of why. 'Have you told her everything?'

The others looked quizzically at them before James said, 'What are you two on about? Told her what?'

Julian pinched the bridge of his nose between his thumb and forefinger. It was going to come out eventually. He'd wanted to tell Jess first, but he didn't feel like he could avoid this any longer. He'd have to thank Cameron for that later, and by thank him, he meant sucker punch him.

'Fuck. If I tell you guys, promise not to say anything to the others until I've told Jess. This feels so wrong.' He huffed out a breath.

James and Tom held up their hands as James said, 'Scouts honour, we won't tell. Bro-code and all that. No matter how much Sarah offers to suck the truth out of me.'

Cameron closed his eyes and shook his head. 'Thanks for the imagery, James.'

James rocked back on his heels. 'Welcome.'

Tom sat down on the leather sofa, resting his arm across the back. 'You can trust us. We've all got skeletons in our closets.'

Julian took a seat next to him as the other two leant against the pool table, their arms crossed as they sipped from their bottles.

'Okay. I'll start with my name.'

'Mate, we know your name.' James said with a scoff.

Cameron piped up. 'Not his full name, you don't.'

Tom turned to Julian. 'Jay, what the fuck is going on?'

His shoulders slumped as he said, 'Hi, I'm Julian Albert Hadley, future Lord of Easthampton. Pleased to meet you.'

A millisecond later, James sprayed Julian with beer as he took an ill-timed swig of his drink.

'Well, I wasn't expecting that. How the fuck did we not know that? This makes no sense. We've known you both for years,' said Tom, a look of shock on his face.

'It's quite simple, really.' Julian shrugged. 'My parents wanted me to have a normal life, as much as I could while going to the best schools, but to everyone else, I was just some rich kid. The school staff were under strict instruction not to discuss my heritage with anyone, and my parents weren't around enough to meet the other parents. Then I got to a point where I was sick of the life, the pressure I was under to be a certain way. I'm much like Jess in that respect. I'll become a Lord when my dad passes. Giving up the title isn't an option. I can't do that to my family, but I told them I wanted a normal life before then. The pressure is on me to marry and produce an heir.'

'Ahhh.' James said, as he understood the issue.

'Yeah. If I don't have a baby in wedlock, preferably a boy, then the title passes to someone else. I don't want that to happen, and I want to have kids. Fuck, being with Jess makes me want them now.'

'Jesus, mate, that's fast going,' Tom said with wide eyes.

'I know, but I can't help it. After everything Jess has been through, I can't tell her that. I wanted her to fall for me, the real me. Not the version of Julian everyone else will see when I'm a Lord. But I've fucked up. I don't know how to tell her without her running. She's literally just escaped from being forced into a marriage and bred like a horse, for fuck's sake. How do I prove to her it's not like that with me?'

'I think you'll just have to trust her, mate. Right now, I'm feeling pretty hurt neither of you told us.' James pouted.

Cameron held up his hands, his bottle left abandoned on the edge of the pool table. 'Hey, I was sworn to secrecy. It wasn't my story to tell, and I respected his wishes. My aunt and uncle are never in the country because it all got too much for them. They've gone into retirement and Jay is well within his rights to have a chance at a normal life before he has duties and shit.' He waved his hand through the air.

Tom sighed. 'I can understand why you did it, but you're going to have to tell her soon. And now we're all incriminated. You know we're all getting denied blow jobs for a long time after it gets out we knew?'

'Jay, can you placate the ladies by buying them all ponies or something?' said James with a laugh.

Tom winced. 'It's the only thing they'll be riding for a while, lads.'

James glared at Julian. 'You're lucky I love you, because right now I'm pissed. When are you going to tell her?'

'I'll tell her soon. I just want to make sure we're in the clear with everything else that's going on.' She'd had enough to deal with, and he didn't want her running away from him before he knew she was safe. Her mother's words replayed in his head and his gut said this wasn't over.

For once, Julian was glad when James turned the conversation back to his sex life, and he had to admit, it felt good being able to discuss his primal side with people who would understand.

After a few games of pool, they heard the padding of feet up the stairs as, one by one, the girls appeared and wrapped themselves around their other halves. Julian breathed in the scent of Jess's hair, his cock stirring at the memory of it wrapped around his fist.

Imogen unfurled from Cameron's arms and said, 'Did Cam tell you our news?'

'No, I didn't. I thought I'd leave that up to you, beautiful.'

'Really? What have you been talking about all this time?'

James bristled. 'Guy stuff. Never you mind.'

Imogen raised her eyebrows. Julian had a feeling he knew what she was about to say. He was smiling before the words left her mouth.

'We have something to celebrate, but it's too soon to make it public.'

Lucy clasped her hands together as Sarah brought her hand to her mouth. Jess squeezed Julian's hand.

'Cam and I are having a baby.'

In a rush of movement, everyone was jumping up and scrambling to hug the happy couple. Finally, they had the chance to celebrate something truly happy and pure.

'Easy, guys.' Just as Julian expected, Cameron was wrapping his arms around Jen, protecting her from the onslaught of celebratory hugs. He'd have to keep an eye on how Cam coped with the pregnancy. Cam's mum was attacked when she was pregnant with his brother. She lost the baby and the chance to have another child. It changed Cam into the fiercely protective man he was today. He just hoped he wouldn't suffocate Jen with his need to keep her safe.

They calmed down and let Jen breathe as Julian embraced Cameron in a tight hug. Lowering his voice, he said, 'She's going to be okay. This is the best news and you're going to be the best dad on this planet. But you need to let me know if it gets too much.'

Cameron's grip tightened as he said, 'Thanks, Jay. You're like a brother to me, and I appreciate your support. You're going to have to keep me sane on this one. Be my barometer for the crazy.'

'You got it.'

'Hang on a minute,' said Sarah as she scratched her head. 'You've been drinking wine all evening. How far along are you? We've not been back from Vegas that long.' Everyone's brows creased as they looked at Jen.

'Ah, about that. I've been sneaky. I filled empty wine bottles with alcohol-free wine for tonight, and in Vegas—because we were actively trying—my cocktails were virgin and Cam sneakily downed my shots. I can't tell you how pissed he was every night. And to answer your question, I'm only about two weeks, so it either happened just before or during Vegas. I've got my first midwife appointment booked for next week. We didn't know for sure until the other day when I peed on a stick and the display said two weeks, so that's why we haven't said anything sooner. Don't be mad at me, my hormones can't take it and I'd probably cry. Oh, and don't tell anyone. We haven't even told our parents yet. We wanted you lot to know because it's going to get tricky hiding the lack of drinking.

I don't know if you know this, but our lives revolve far too much around booze. We're going to need to find a new hobby.'

It wasn't long after the announcement of the year that Imogen was yawning, so everyone took that as their cue to leave.

Julian smiled as he steered his Range Rover along the winding back country roads.

'I'm so happy for Cam and Jen. Aren't you?' said Jess with a smile on her face.

'It's great. Couldn't have happened to a more deserving couple.'

'Can I admit something to you?'

He turned his attention to her for a moment, before casting his eyes back on the road ahead. She looked hesitant, as if he wouldn't like what she had to say. 'Of course. You can tell me anything.' It's not like he had any right to judge with the secret he kept from her.

'Before we got together, I would've been happy for them, don't get me wrong, but part of me would've resented their happiness. When the ability of having a baby is how you're deemed worthy, it rather takes the shine off the prospect. But I'm free of that now. If I choose to have a baby, it's because it's the right thing to do at the right time, not because it's expected. And don't worry, this isn't me putting any pressure on you, but now I think I want a family. I can see a future where I'm happy and have children, and I couldn't see that before. Jay, I finally feel like I get to live.'

Julian felt the colour drain from his cheeks. Holy fuck. He was in so much trouble.

Julian had been quiet all week. His thoughts turned to telling Jess the truth about his family without scaring her off. He felt the weight of guilt on his shoulders, knowing he was betraying her, but doing so because he didn't want to lose her. He avoided initiating any kind of sex, primal or otherwise, to lessen any chance of her feeling tricked into sleeping with him.

He was needed at the restaurant more this week, as Sam had taken his girlfriend away to propose. Julian was glad of the distraction, and equally happy that Jess was working at the office with Cameron. She'd be safe there.

It was a busy lunchtime service; it always was when the sun shone as people loved to sit outside on the riverbank. Only a few guests occupied the tables inside. He froze as he watched two women walk inside, one of his waitresses sitting them in the far corner.

Was it a coincidence that Georgina Chatwin was one of the women? He didn't think so.

'Let me handle that table, okay?' he said to the waitress as she walked past him into the kitchen.

'Sure thing, boss.'

He grabbed a tablet from the nearby stand and strolled over to her table.

'Ladies, can I take your drink order while you peruse the menu?' He kept his tone light and professional; he didn't want to scare Georgina off until he found out why she was here.

'Thank you, we'll take a bottle of the Perrier-Jouët, please.' It looked like Georgina was playing the same game, acting like she didn't know who Julian was. 'No need to give us time with the menu. I did extensive research before coming here, and we'd like the Lobster menu for two, please.'

She'd done a lot of research? Was he being paranoid, or was she trying to tell him something? He could only hope her reasons for coming here became clear soon.

'Of course, I'll get that ordered for you both. In the meantime, I'll have some bread and olives brought over.' He collected the menus, Georgina gripping onto hers a little longer than natural. He couldn't tell if the look in her eyes was trying to convey a message or if she'd just come from a Botox appointment. He figured he'd find out soon enough.

As they ate their lobsters, Julian noticed Georgina's eyes rarely left him when he was in the room. And then all became clear. She slipped with the claw while cracking it open and sprayed herself with lobster juice, melted butter and herbs. Dabbing at her face with a napkin, she excused herself from the table and approached Julian on the premise of asking where she could get cleaned up.

'Follow me.' He kept up the act until she followed him into his office and shut the door. He handed her a stack of paper towels which she used to dab at the mess on her top.

'I don't have long, so you need to let me speak.'

He nodded, his lips pressed firmly closed into a thin line.

'Is Jess okay?'

'She's doing well.' He decided not to add no thanks to you.

Her shoulders visibly sagged as she breathed what he assumed was a sigh of relief.

'My husband thinks me stupid, Julian, but I can assure you I am not. I know you despise me. You think of me as an incompetent, uncaring mother, but I'm here to prove to you that while I am potentially incompetent when it comes to raising a child, I care very deeply.'

'Really?' He crossed his arms over his chest, enthralled by the bullshit about to leave her lips.

She looked around the office. 'Can we please sit?'

He shrugged and pointed to the chair opposite his. He walked around the desk and sat.

'When I was eighteen, I was forced to marry Peter. We were deemed a good match and my father played golf with his. Judging by the new golf clubs, cars, and a new wing added to the house, I'd say my father did rather well out of the deal. Me; not so much.'

'Does this story have a point?' He couldn't contain his contempt for her any longer. If what she said was true, then she, of all people, would know what Jess was going through.

'Please, listen.' This time, he could tell the look of desperation in her eyes was real. 'What was expected of me was made very clear on the wedding night. I was to look pretty, keep my mouth shut, and my legs open.'

Julian couldn't keep the look of horror from his face, but to her credit, she straightened her shoulders and carried on. 'I'll spare you the details. Don't worry. I want you to know I never wanted children. I know I don't have what it takes to raise another human being. I didn't play with prams and dolls growing up. I am not maternal. And then I gave birth to Jessica. The day she was born, my heart ripped in two. One half fell in love with her, the other died. She was a girl. She was meant to be a boy. If I'd have had a boy, my work would've been done, and he'd leave me alone.'

She shuddered, her eyes going glassy. 'As soon as I was able, the process began again. Only Mother Nature wouldn't play ball the second time around. And he soon gave up. But he's never forgiven me for letting him down… like I had a choice,' she scoffed.

Julian felt sick. Her life sounded like an episode of *Game of Thrones*. Jess was never going back there, of that he was certain.

'So why did you go along with setting her up? Surely you were allowing her the same fate?'

'No.' She shook her head. 'I was trying to find someone that Jess could live with. I shipped her off to boarding school so she didn't have to live with the hatred that poured from Peter. I didn't want her to suffer the way I had. I thought if I could just find her someone with the right standing, who would be kind to her, then I would have done just one thing right. And then Peter got into trouble with some unpleasant customers at the bank. I listen to everything. He thinks I don't; that I'm too stupid to understand what he's talking about. More fool him. I knew he was in financial difficulty, and that's why he was asking the Wilberforces to invest. But that money paid someone else off. I had no idea he was using Jess in that way; I promise you, I was in the dark. I've been listening in on his conversations since you took Jess away. They want their money back, but he doesn't have it. I'm scared, Julian. What if they try to hurt Jess?'

Shit.

'I didn't recognise you at first, but something about your eyes had me thinking. I was sure I'd seen you somewhere before, so I did some digging, Julian Hadley.'

'Ah, so now you know who I am, you've come here. Why?'

'I'm begging for your help. Peter doesn't have the money.'

'And I do?'

'Yes, you do.' Her face had morphed from desperate to determined.

'How much are we talking?'

She didn't miss a beat, throwing a number into the air like it was nothing. 'Fifteen million.'

Julian nodded. 'If I get you the money, do you promise Jess will be out of it? You'll both leave her alone unless she decides otherwise?'

'Yes. Absolutely.'

He considered what she'd said, and he believed her. He could read people and he saw nothing but genuine concern for Jess and a need to help her out of this situation. Someone like Georgina Chatwin doesn't ask for help unless it's a last resort.

'Okay. I need to call my father. I can't withdraw that amount of money without him being made aware. Arrange a meeting in the next few days. I want to speak with Peter before I do this.'

She stood, straightened her outfit, and offered her hand to Julian over the desk. 'I know you hate me, but please tell Jessica that I'm sorry and that I love her, in my own way. I know you'll make her happy. You're a good man.'

'You barely know me.' He understood she was paying him a compliment, and even though he felt a level of sympathy for the life she ended up with, her opinion of him meant nothing to him.

'I know your parents. They're good people. It's a shame they're never around. We used to have fun at the tennis club. We lost touch after I married Peter. I lost a lot of friends thanks to him, because frankly, he's a pompous twat.'

Julian couldn't contain the shocked laugh that flew from his mouth. He never would have pegged her to be a swearer. He figured that must be where Jess got it from—well, that or Sarah.

'Now, if you'll excuse me, I must share a wonderful lobster with a vacuous shell of a woman. Please believe me when I say I tried my best to keep Jessica out of this life. I may not agree with how her friends live their lives, but I am happy that she is surrounded by people who love and care for her. Goodbye, Julian. I'll let you know when you can meet with Peter. God only knows how he'll react when I tell him what I've done.'

The gentlemanly side to Julian couldn't ignore the last comment. 'Georgina, are you safe?'

As she reached the door, she turned slowly and smiled, but her eyes were glassy. 'He's not a good man, Julian, but he's also not a violent one. That is his saving grace. I'm safe in that regard. Thank you.' She opened the door, straightened her shoulders, and left.

'Bollocks.' He ran his fingers through his hair as he sank into his chair, head in his hands. He pulled his phone from his back pocket and made a very expensive phone call.

CHAPTER 23

JESS

Shadows - Talia Rose

Little Willy: Cute move, Jessica, but I don't appreciate being played.

Jess dropped her phone into her bag, rolling her eyes at Will's audacity. She assumed that was his way of telling her he knew she was with someone, but she couldn't bring herself to care that his nose was out of joint. He'd soon get over it.

She rolled her shoulders and turned her attention back to her friends. 'I'm so happy I get to join you two on your trips for mac 'n' cheese.' Jess, Imogen, and Sarah were sitting around their regular table at the cafe local to the Spencer and Black offices. It was a cosy cafe, decorated with floral print, mismatched furniture, and crockery. It was famous for its homely dishes, and Jess could understand why. The scent of baked potatoes, freshly roasted coffee, and sweet chocolate cake filled her nose with every inhale.

'I can't tell you how jealous I was when you'd constantly talk about how it was like a hug in a bowl,' Jess said around a mouthful of the sinful pasta dish.

'So, why didn't you just join us?' asked Sarah.

'Well, for starters, my mother would go mad if I ate this stuff. She'd know for sure. I bloat like a whale when I eat too many simple carbs, and this is basically one hundred per cent simple carbs.' Jess pushed aside the heavy feeling she got in her heart every time she thought of her mother.

'No, it's not,' Imogen said as she waved a sprig of parsley in her face. 'This is a herb and therefore healthy. Also, it's the only thing staying down at the moment, so it's a vital food group.'

Jess and Sarah gave Jen looks of sympathy before Sarah said, 'Well, fuck your mum. You don't need to worry about her anymore. I want to hear all about you and Julian. Don't leave any details out.'

Another sinking feeling made itself a home in Jess's heart. Julian had seemed distracted all week, and Jess didn't know if it was because of her confession about wanting a family, him feeling forced into living with her, or something else entirely. He'd reassured her many times that he was with her because he wanted her, but a lifetime of thinking the worst about yourself wouldn't go away overnight. It was a knee-jerk reaction; one she was working on. She'd also never lived with a man and didn't know if maybe they, too, had mood swings. Part of her worried she wasn't enough for him sexually. She was willing to take his primal side further, but he wouldn't or couldn't fully let himself go. He was like a caged animal, and she held the key.

'I think I've either scared Jay off.' She was blurting the words out before she could stop herself. 'Or he's realised being with me isn't all it's cracked up to be.'

All eyes were on her as Imogen asked, 'What makes you say that? He's totally smitten with you.'

'I admitted to him on the drive home from yours that I could see myself having a family, and he went a bit quiet after that. He's been distracted all week. And then the other day, he came home from work and was in a strange mood; really quiet.' She bit her lip and shrugged her shoulders as she tried to stop her chin from quivering.

Sarah swiped her hand through the air. 'Puft. He's just being a man. James has been jumpy and scared to initiate sex all week because he thinks I'm going to ask for a baby, too. He's just being a normal bloke; I wouldn't worry about it. I bet Tom has been the same with Lucy. And don't give his mood the other day a second thought. He probably had to deal with a shitty customer or something. This happens when you live with your boyfriend. You get to see them during their highs and their lows, but it doesn't mean you've done something wrong or they love you any less.'

'Do you think so?'

'Yep. I know so.'

Some of the weight lifted from her shoulders. A sliver of self-doubt remained, but it was a start. She returned her focus to the delicious carb on carb meal in front of her, not caring if she bloated later.

The house was dark when Jess parked Julian's car and made her way inside. She'd grown used to him already being home, but he'd mentioned he was taking the evening shifts this week.

She dropped her bags in the hallway, kicked off her shoes and made her way into the kitchen, turning on every light on the way. She didn't normally have a problem with the dark, but lately she preferred not to see any dark corners. The events of the last year or so had made her somewhat paranoid and, being on her own, gave her the jitters.

As she opened the fridge to work out what she could make herself for dinner, she noticed a covered plate with a note on top.

Jess, I'll be home late, so I've made you some dinner.
Be a good girl and eat it all.
J
xxx

She smiled as she traced her finger across the three little kisses. Jess never pegged him as a man to leave little notes with kisses, but there was a softer side to him she felt privileged to see. She made a promise to stop questioning his feelings for her. In truth, he'd not said anything to warrant her doubt, and it wasn't fair to deflect her demons onto him.

After changing into her sweatpants and hoodie and reheating the food, she settled down in the living room with her latest book. An hour later, the empty plate forgotten at her feet, the main characters had just got to the hotel and there was only one room, classic admin error, and better yet, only one bed. She did a little fist pump as these enemies were about to become lovers. The doorbell ringing interrupted her excitement.

She quickly checked her watch. It was only eight-thirty. The restaurant was still open and why would Julian ring the doorbell?

Should she open it?

None of the girls had mentioned they were popping over tonight, so she didn't know who could be here. Her parents didn't know where Julian lived, so she doubted it was them.

She ducked her head around the corner of the living room door to see if she could make out who it was through the glass panes in the door. She saw a man as tall as Julian, but with grey hair. He didn't look like an axe murderer, but then, isn't that how they made their way into the victim's home?

'Julian, son, are you home?' She jumped at the sound of his voice, but quickly recovered, realising it was in fact not an axe murderer, but Julian's dad.

She attempted to make her outfit look smarter, before realising it was pointless and pulled the door open. 'Hello…' Shit. It occurred to her she didn't know Julian's dad's name. 'Mr Hadley, please do come on in. I'm Jessica… Jess.'

'Ah, yes, Jess. What a pleasure to meet you.' She placed her hand in his outstretched one. It engulfed hers as he cupped his other hand over their clasped ones. They were warm and reminded her of Julian's in how they made her feel safe. These weren't the hands of an axe murder, that was for sure.

'Please call me Albert or Al. No need for formalities.' The delicate skin around his green eyes crinkled as he smiled, again another feature he'd passed down to his son.

'Nice to meet you, Al.' She could see where Julian got his good looks from. He had a thick head of silver hair, but where Julian's was wavy, his was poker straight and looked as soft as silk threads.

'I must admit, I had rather hoped you'd be here. I've been dying to meet you.'

She blushed at his genuine pleasure of seeing her. 'Oh, well, here I am. Can I make you a drink? I'm afraid Julian is at the restaurant tonight for another couple of hours, but you're welcome to wait.' She thought he wasn't in the country, so she had no idea why he was here or where he was staying.

'A cup of tea would be marvellous, thank you. We arrived back in the country today and I haven't stopped for a second. There's always so much to do when we come home, although Julian does a good job looking after the estate.'

The estate? Just how big was the family home? Julian had mentioned it before, but he'd never used the word estate.

She made his tea, adding two teaspoons of sugar and a healthy glug of milk, the act bringing her joy as it made her feel rebellious, even if it wasn't her drinking it. Actually, sod that; she was having one too.

As they took their seats in the living room, she couldn't help but notice Albert was staring at her, an enormous grin on his face. She allowed a smile to flash on her face before she looked around the room, feeling a little uncomfortable, as if under a microscope.

'How are you finding living with my son?'

Oh blimey, what was she supposed to say to that? Are they allowed to be sleeping together? Does he even know they're together?

'Oh, it's great, thank you. Julian is making me very welcome.'

There was that beaming smile again. 'Oh, I don't doubt that. I must say Pen—Julian's mother, Penelope—and I were over the moon when he called to say you'd moved in with him. We were a little worried that his ex-girlfriend had scared him off women for life. Goodness, that would have put the future of the Hadley title in jeopardy.' He chortled, pulled himself together and carried on.

'But now we don't need to worry, because here you are, and I get the feeling you're here to stay.'

Okay, what the actual fuck was going on here? Her mind was working at a million miles an hour trying to understand what he meant by the Hadley title, while looking entirely unphased and not like she was in the dark. And she'd already ascertained that she no longer liked the dark.

'You make a lovely cup of tea. You can tell a lot about a person by how they make the tea. Chloe,' her name was laced with venom as he said it, 'couldn't make a decent cuppa for love nor money. Pen will kill me for telling you this, but neither of us liked her. We couldn't tell Jay that, of course. He had to find out the hard way that she wasn't suitable. We don't like to interfere with his love life, but that doesn't stop us from wanting him to be with the right person. You know, I believe Pen and I used to play tennis with your mother, Georgina. She used to be such fun.'

'Oh, really?' Oh god. She couldn't tell if knowing her mother was a good thing or bad. This entire conversation was making her feel uneasy. 'Isn't it a small world?' Hopefully not so small that he knew what was going on with her dad's plans to sell her off.

'When Jay phoned me the other night, I must admit I wasn't entirely shocked to hear what he had to say. Please don't take offence, but it didn't come as a surprise that Peter was in trouble. He's known for his less than squeaky clean dealings on the golf course. I was reluctant to release the funds at first, fifteen million is a large sum afterall, but having met you, my dear, I can see why Julian wants to help. I believe that the future Lord of Easthampton has found himself a beautiful Lady. Pen will be pleased, and will no doubt go looking for the perfect mother-of-the bride outfit, but please don't let that put you off, she has a tendency to get a little carried away, but you'll soon realise it's all part of her charm.' His eyes twinkled as he spoke of his wife, but all Jess could focus on was the word 'Lord'.

It all fell into place as she mentally kicked herself for not seeing it sooner. She obviously knew of Lord and Lady Easthampton but had rarely heard of them by their full names, and therefore hadn't associated Julian's name with them. Why would you? Plenty of people share a surname, and Cameron had never mentioned having family in those circles. But then his words came back to her, *the family home*, and *there is more I need to tell you*. She should have known simply because his family owned this house and all the surrounding land. She'd been so distracted by what was going on in her life that she hadn't considered the level of his wealth and where that came from.

He'd lied to her.

He'd kept her in the dark.

Lords had to marry and produce heirs, otherwise they lose the title.

She'd jumped out of the frying pan and into the fire.

And he was paying fifteen million to her father for her. Julian was planning on buying her. It seemed so unbelievable, but here she was, listening to it from the horse's mouth.

She swallowed the rush of saliva and blinked in an attempt to stop the room from spinning.

Julian had made her feel wanted. Owned. And she'd loved it. But now she felt dirty and used because he did own her, literally. And in a move she never would've seen coming, he owned her father too. She didn't know how to process that, only able to focus on her immediate situation.

Albert placed his cup and saucer on the side table and stood. 'Well, my dear. I won't keep you from your book any longer.' He gestured to where it was draped over the arm of the chair. 'I popped by to let him know I'm happy to release the funds. Can you let him know I'll do it tonight?' She could see his mouth moving but the words were rolling into one as she forced herself to stay upright.

'Pen's set me up with a new banking app. Very fancy. You don't need to worry any longer. You're with the Hadley's now and we'll look after you.' Within a few strides, he was in front of Jess and embracing her in what was clearly a Hadley hug. 'It's been a pleasure meeting you. I look forward to seeing you soon. Sit back down, I can see myself out.'

She stood, frozen, as she watched him leave.

She felt sick, clammy, and was overheating. Her cosy hoodie was suffocating her as she clawed at the neckline, trying to get some air.

The physical symptoms were nothing compared to the feeling of betrayal that weighed so heavily on her heart she felt like it would break under the strain.

She was stupid. Her car was still at her parents' house, so if she wanted to leave, she'd have to take Julian's. Was he planning on that to keep her? She shook her head, getting carried away with her thoughts. No, he wouldn't do that. But then she didn't think he'd try to buy her for fifteen million, either.

She needed to get out. She made her way upstairs, packed a bag, slipped on a pair of trainers, and grabbed his car keys.

As she started the engine, she unlocked her phone. Her hand shook as she deliberated over what to write.

> **Jess:** I met your father today. I hope he didn't think me rude when I didn't curtsey for his Lordship. Apparently, I am worth fifteen million and he'll release the funds tonight. Well done, you've just bought me. I won't be at home tonight. Please don't message me. Don't look for me. I am not an object to be bought.

She didn't know where to go, but she knew she needed to get away. She couldn't go home, or to her friend's houses as they'd all call Julian. She certainly wasn't going to Cameron's house. He knew who Julian was all along and didn't mention it. Maybe they all knew and kept it from her. She couldn't trust anyone. She was truly alone.

She drove for miles, in no particular direction, following the winding roads of the countryside. She had no destination in mind. All she knew was that she wanted to get as far away from her life as possible.

The sun traced its well-worn path below the horizon as her headlights came to life. She was so focussed on blinking away the tears to see the road ahead of her; she didn't notice the lights that followed her every turn.

She didn't see them get closer and closer. She didn't spot them until she felt something clip her rear bumper. Within mere moments, too fast for her to rectify, the road was no longer in front of her as the car swung to the left. It careened off the road, hitting the damp leaves of the unforgiving terrain of the forest before skidding down a ditch.

The seatbelt locked into place, but her body didn't get the memo to stay put as it tried to burst its way to freedom through the belt, leaving her winded and gasping for breath.

Everything slowed as the contents of the centre console flew through the air as if someone had hit the anti-gravity button. A muffled explosion was the only warning she received before a soft white cloud engulfed her, the airbag taking the brunt of her immediate halt as the car landed, nose first. As the bag deflated, she slumped onto the steering wheel, dazed and confused.

She was aware of her door being pulled open before she felt the burning pain of someone gripping her hair to lift her head.

'Hello, Jessica. I've come to collect my end of the deal.'

Once again, her head hurtled towards the steering wheel, but this time, the airbag wasn't there to save her. Bright lights burst into her vision before popping out of existence.

She no longer felt any pain.

She no longer felt anything.

CHAPTER 24

JULIAN

Medicine - JC Stewart

'Mother fucker,' screamed Julian as the glass he was cleaning flew through the air, hitting the kitchen wall and smashing, the pieces skittering across the tiled floor as the wait staff recoiled in horror.

'I need to go.' He pointed at the new head waiter and said, 'You're in charge.'

He ran back to his house, hoping Jess was still there, but as he flung the door open, he could tell the place was empty. He couldn't feel her energy, couldn't smell her perfume. He looked out onto the driveway to see his car was gone. That was the only saving grace; he could track it.

She wanted to be alone, and he needed to respect that. But for how long? He was about to tell her everything, but he was too late. Why the fuck did his dad decide to call in at the house? He couldn't blame his dad, this was his mess. He'd fucked up again and now she was out there, alone and hurting because of him.

He didn't know what to do, so he called the only person who might be able to help.

'Cam, I need you.' There was no point in hiding the desperation in his voice.

'Jay? What's the matter?'
'She knows. And she's gone.'
'Fuck. I'm on my way.'

In record time, he heard Cam's car screech to a halt outside his house. He hadn't bothered shutting the front door, so Cam came running straight in, Imogen close behind.

'Jay, are you okay?' Cam grabbed him, pulling him into a hug.

'No. No, I'm not. Dad came over while I wasn't here. She knows, and she's left me.' He pulled on his hair. 'Fuck. Why does Dad have to be so bloody chatty?'

'She'll be okay. She just needs time to get used to the idea and then she'll be back.'

Julian looked at Imogen, who was standing in the doorway, her arms folded across her chest. 'It's not just the whole Lord thing, Cam. It's worse than that.'

Imogen stepped forward. 'What's worse than building your entire relationship on a lie?'

Wow, how to kick a man when he's down.

Cam looked apologetic as he said, 'Sorry. I gave her the abridged version on the way over. She's not happy with either of us right now, and her hormones are making her pretty ragey.'

'Do not blame my hormones for this,' growled Imogen as she pointed at them with an accusing finger. 'I can't believe you didn't think it was important to tell her who you were earlier, like before you started something.'

'It's complicated. I was trying to do the right thing.'

As Imogen huffed, Cam said, 'What's worse? What's happened?'

'Her mum came to see me at the restaurant the other day, long story short, Peter is in financial trouble with the wrong people. He had to raise fifteen million to pay them off, hence why he had the deal with Frank Wilberforce. Only problem is, now Jess isn't part of the deal they want to withdraw their offer, and their money.'

Cam nodded. 'And let me guess, Peter doesn't have it.'

'Bingo. Georgina worked out who I am and came to ask if I can give him the fifteen mil.'

Imogen threw her hands up in the air. 'You have got to be fucking kidding me.'

'Sweetheart, please calm down.'

'Do not tell me to calm down, Cameron. Your cousin has just admitted to paying Jess's dad fifteen million. How do you think Jess will take that? She's just left her family behind because they tried to sell her as part of a deal and are trying to force her into having babies because they need an heir. She's just been told the boyfriend she trusted…' That earned Julian a hard stare. 'Has not only lied about being a Lord, which by the way requires him to marry and produce an heir, but that he's also paying a huge sum of money for the privilege.'

Julian sank to the floor, his head in his hands. 'I've fucked up. I just wanted to keep her safe and show her she's worthy of so much more than she's been given. I wanted her out of that house, that was all. I have no intention of forcing her into marriage, or into having kids, but I hoped she'd want to do that with me. I've lost her, but worse than that, she's out there alone. What if something happens to her?'

Imogen's face softened. 'She needs time to get over this. Give her some space. Give her a couple of days and then I'm sure she'll be back.'

'I can't just sit here and wait. I need to find her and explain.'

'If the hardest thing you have to do is nothing for a couple of days, then I'd say you're doing all right.' Imogen looked pissed off again.

Cameron crouched down next to Julian. 'Use this time to sort the mess with the money. I get the impression that Georgina didn't take the decision to come to you lightly. We don't know what might happen if Peter doesn't come up with the money and there's no sense letting this carry on if you can pay off his debt. He may be an arsehole, but he's still Jess's dad.'

'I'm meeting with them tomorrow to complete the transfer.' He felt hollow, detached from his body and operating purely on autopilot. He'd vowed never to hurt Jess, and once again, he'd let someone he cared for down because of his misguided belief in what's right. He deserved every one of the fiery, rage-filled stares he was getting from Imogen. And he had a feeling this was just the beginning.

The next morning, a secretary showed Julian straight up to Peter Chatwin's office. Cameron had offered to go with him, but he needed to sort this mess out on his own. He was tired, the dark rings around his eyes announcing the lack of sleep.

He'd tossed and turned all night, worrying about Jess. The others had all messaged her, but they were left unread. Something wasn't right, but he couldn't put his finger on it. According to Cameron, Imogen wasn't surprised that Jess ignored her messages. Jess had probably assumed Imogen knew the truth already, and Imogen was quick to point out that she, too, would've expected her husband to have filled her in a long time ago.

He'd done his best to dress like he wasn't falling apart. His shirt and chinos were at least ironed, and his shoes polished. He'd run a brush through his hair and slapped at his cheeks a few times before getting out of the taxi. If anyone asked why he wasn't driving, he'd simply tell them it was because Jess had borrowed the car. He certainly wasn't about to tell them she'd disappeared. He didn't want them knowing she was alone and vulnerable. Until he knew she was safe, he'd keep that information to himself.

Peter was sitting behind his desk and an equally plump man in an ill-fitting suit was sitting opposite. Julian assumed it was Frank Willberforce.

They certainly looked like a bunch of bankers. And by bankers, he meant *wankers*.

They both stood as Julian walked over. He had no intention of dragging this out any longer than necessary and couldn't bring himself to shake their hands. Instead, he sat in the empty chair next to Frank.

'Okay, shall we get this over and done with?'

'Um, yes, of course.' Peter was red faced and clearly embarrassed by the whole situation. Julian wished he could've been a fly on the wall when Georgina told him she knew what was going on and that she'd found the solution.

Julian clasped his hands together in his lap and twisted around to face both men. 'Who am I transferring the money to?'

Frank cleared his throat. 'You'll be transferring the money directly to me. It's fair to say Peter can't be trusted.'

Julian pulled his phone from his pocket and opened his banking app. 'Before I transfer you fifteen million pounds, I want to be sure that you'll leave Jess out of any future dealings. She is no longer part of any deal and neither of you, nor your son, are to approach her again. Is that clear?'

Peter huffed a yes, while Frank said, 'I don't have a problem with that. My son was only part of the deal because I needed him to have a new toy to keep him occupied. The boy's a liability with ideas above his station.' Frank shook his head in disgust at his own son. 'Delusional, that boy. I blame his mother. She always pandered to him and gave him what he wanted.'

Julian clenched his fist, desperately trying not to punch Frank in the face.

'My son won't be an issue. He didn't take the news of the deal being off well, but once he gets over his tantrum, he'll move on to something, or someone new. He'll soon come crawling back with his next grand plan.'

Seething, Julian calmed himself enough to move the meeting along. 'Okay, Frank. Let's get this over with. Give me the details and I'll transfer the money now. Neither of you will bother Jess again. Agreed?'

Peter muttered something about him still being her father, but nodded in agreement. Frank shifted in his seat.

'About the fifteen million. That was how much I paid for my shares in the company. I did so expecting a return on my investment. Maybe I'm not happy to roll over and accept the original investment. I'm due some return for the inconvenience, at the very least.'

Julian saw this coming. As soon as they knew who he was, they knew he could pay a lot more. He leaned back in the chair and crossed one ankle over his knee. He sighed, trying to look bored, but on the inside, he was burning with rage and a need to get away. He was glad he made the taxi driver wait outside.

'Okay, Frank. Tell me, how much it will take to get you to walk away and keep a leash on your son?'

Peter had the decency to look embarrassed as he kept his head down and his mouth shut. Frank, however, looked like a spoilt brat at Christmas.

'Twenty million.' He quirked an eyebrow, looking ready to barter. Julian didn't have the time or the inclination.

'Done.' He tapped on his phone and handed it to Frank. 'Put your bank details in and we're done here.'

Frank couldn't keep the smug look off his face as he entered his details. Julian snatched the phone back and walked out of the office without another word.

Julian threw his house keys on the dresser in his hallway, and kicked the door closed behind him.

The house didn't feel right without Jess in it, as if the atmosphere was angry at him for lying to her, not trusting her with the truth. Or was that just his own self-hatred poisoning the air around him?

How long was he supposed to leave her alone? It was taking all his self-control not to check the location of his car, but he had to respect Jess's wishes. He couldn't fuck up again. He was on everyone's shit list, but he didn't care about anyone else, he just needed to know Jess was okay. The air felt heavy around him as he stood in the hallway, head hung in shame, unable to walk any further into the house. He couldn't be there without her. He needed to work off some frustration.

He stripped out of his clothes, swapping them for the safety and familiarity of his black jeans, T-shirt, and boots. He needed to get out, to run, to find somewhere away from everyone else, to scream out his frustration.

As he pulled open the front door, he was halted by two policemen getting out of their car, notebooks in hand, as they walked up to where he stood.

'Mr Hadley?' said the taller of the two, his brown hair cut into a buzz cut.

'Yes.' Was it possible for him to still be standing, speaking, when his heart had stopped beating? 'Oh god, is it Jess? Is she okay?'

'Jess?' said the other. 'We're here about your car, Mr Hadley.'

'My car?' Oh fuck, she'd had an accident. He couldn't suck in any oxygen. His lungs burned with the effort.

'Can we come inside? We need to talk to you, sir.'

He stepped back, silently allowing them entry. They strolled in, making their own way to the living room, and took a seat next to each other on the sofa. Buzz cut pointed at the sofa opposite. 'Take a seat Mr Hadley. You don't look so well.'

His legs gave way, the sofa taking the brunt of his landing. 'Can you please tell me what this is about? What about my car? Is Jess hurt?'

'I'm afraid we don't know who Jess is, sir. We've discovered a car registered to yourself in a ditch about forty miles from here. Are you the owner of a black Ranger Rover? Was Jess driving it?'

He nodded. 'Yes. She was borrowing it as hers is still at her parents. Please, where is she?'

They looked at each other and then flicked through their notes. Buzz cut said, 'No one was at the scene of the accident. Initial investigations show the car went into a skid and lost control. Debris on the road leads us to believe there was another car involved, but that it left the scene.' He pulled his phone from his pocket and brought up some photos on the screen. He leant forward and showed them to Julian.

'Do you recognise this bag? It was all we recovered from your car.'

'Yes. That belongs to Jess.' He collapsed back onto the sofa, rubbing at his eyes as he fought to maintain some semblance of control. 'We need to find her. I think he has her.'

It was the only explanation he could think of. Frank's words filtered into his thoughts; he's off having a tantrum. What if that tantrum involved him tracking Jess down and doing something to her?

'What do you mean, Mr Hadley? Who is Jess and who has her?'

'Jessica Chatwin, my girlfriend, and Will Wilberforce has her.'

Buzz cut looked incredulous. 'I'm sorry, are you saying you think Miss Chatwin has been abducted? Are you sure she's not just crashed your car and ran off to avoid the consequences? Is it possible she was drunk or on drugs and didn't want to get found out?'

'No, she wasn't fucking drunk.'

The other policeman flipped open his notepad, his pen poised. 'Okay, Mr Hadley. Let's start at the beginning with why Miss Chatwin was in your car, forty miles away. Do you know where she was heading, who she was meeting perhaps?'

How was he going to explain this whole sorry mess to Tweedledee and Tweedledumb in a way they'd understand and that didn't incriminate him?

An hour later, he closed the door after showing the policeman out. He was light on the details, simply explaining that she'd recently fallen out with her parents and had needed to get away. She'd gone out for a drive to clear her head. They didn't look convinced but said they'd look into her whereabouts. He knew that meant they'd ask around and leave it at that. They didn't consider her a missing person yet. Julian knew that by the time they took this seriously, it could be too late for Jess.

He pulled his phone from his pocket and dialled Tom.

'Mate, I need your help, or more specifically, I need you to call in a favour from your mafia friend.'

He didn't have time for pleasantries and Tom must have understood that as he said, 'What do you need?'

'I need to find Jess.'

He heard Tom sigh. 'Mate, I get that you miss her, but I really think you need to give her some time on this one. She'll come back when she's ready.'

'The police have just paid me a visit; they found my car in a ditch and they think another car was involved in the accident and left the scene. Tom, I met with Frank Wilberforce today and paid him off. He said Will was off having a tantrum. My gut instinct tells me he's got Jess, and I can't rest until I know for sure. Can you help me?'

'Fucking hell, Jay, are you sure?'

'No, but I don't know what else to think. Will is missing, Jess is missing, and my car is in a ditch. I won't sit here and do nothing while she could be with him.'

'Okay, I'll call Andre and see what he can do. He has some friends on the force, maybe he can dig up some info. What did the police say?'

'They don't consider her a missing person and from the looks of things, they think I'm involved somehow. They won't help.'

'Okay, I'll call Andre now. I'll keep you posted. And Jay, get Cameron round. This is one of those times where you need us all involved. This isn't all on you.'

He pulled in a deep breath. 'Yeah. I'll call him now.'

A little while later, the sound of tyres crunching on stones announced the arrival of Cameron and he felt an easing in his chest. He wasn't alone in this, and he would find her.

CHAPTER 25

JESS

Bring Me to Life – Evanescence

Black dots danced in her vision as Jess winced from the pain. She tried to bring her hands up to cup her throbbing skull, but her movement came to an abrupt halt as hot metal burned at her wrist.

She blinked rapidly, trying to clear her vision to work out where she was. The floor beneath her was hard and cold, but she could feel heat radiating out from somewhere nearby. With her one free hand, she rubbed her eyes with her thumb and forefinger and brought herself up to a sitting position. The room spun as she took some steadying breaths.

Where the fuck was she? It was dark, there were no windows and only a faint light shone under the crack in what must be a door. The burning at her wrist grew worse as she tugged at her restrained arm. She felt along her arm until her fingers landed on a metal loop around her wrist. She followed its path until she touched a hot, smooth surface. Was she handcuffed to a towel rail radiator? She tried to hold the cuff away from her wrist for a moment of reprieve. When that didn't work, she blew on it as she gingerly felt around the radiator for the thermostat. She sighed with relief when she felt the ridged dial and twisted it in what she hoped was the right way. 'Righty-tighty, lefty-loosey', she whispered as she hoped that the logic of turning this radiator off was the same as loosening a screw.

Once the burning pain remained at a steady state, she turned her attention to the pounding in her head. She ran her fingertips along her forehead where she could feel something warm and sticky—blood. She had a vague memory of losing control of the car. The road morphed into trees and bushes, and then she remembered the biting pain as her head hit the steering wheel.

Then she remembered his voice and what he'd said. It was Will. That trumped up little fuckwit had run her off the road and knocked her out. Then handcuffed her to a hot radiator with metal cuffs. He was either into causing her pain or was just a total idiot. Maybe both.

Jess couldn't believe this was happening. Like seriously, just how evil was she in a past life? She had to give it to Will; she never thought he'd have the backbone for something like this, but here she was, she assumed from the presence of a towel rail and cool tiled floor, on his bathroom floor.

She brought her knees up to her chest and rested her cheek on a knee, one hand trying to massage her temples as the other hung limply from the radiator. The room spun as she swallowed down a rush of saliva. There was a fair chance she had a concussion.

She focused on the light from under the door until her blinking slowed, her eyelids growing heavy with the effort of staying open. She gave in to the tiredness and let the darkness swallow her once more.

'Wakey, wakey, sleepyhead.' Hot breath laced with the scent of alcohol pulled her from her blessed slumber. She tried to open her eyes, but the harshness of the spotlights in the ceiling felt like hot pokers in her eyeballs.

She felt a clammy hand grip her face, and droplets of spittle hit her cheeks as he spat out his angry words. 'Open your fucking eyes and look at me, bitch.'

She forced her eyes open. Will looked like death. His eyes were bloodshot, pupils blown, and the remnants of white powder dusted his nostrils. 'There you are. Forgive the heavy-handed approach, but it's not like you answered my messages, is it? Did you honestly think you could walk away from me?'

She tried to reply, but her dry lips split as she opened her mouth, her throat too hoarse to form words. How long had she been shackled in his bathroom for?

'You were my ticket to the big time. Your dad and his fucking antiquated ways gave me the perfect way in to take over the bank. So fucking simple. I fuck a baby in you, and boom.' More spit landed on her face, revulsion souring her stomach. 'The bank becomes mine until our son is old enough to take over when I retire. Don't worry, I didn't have any plans to keep you around.' His lip curled in a sneer as he rubbed at his nose with his index finger.

'But you thought you could run off into the arms of that posh twat, Julian-bloody-Hadley. What? Did you think I'd just roll over and let you embarrass me like that?'

She forced the words from her lips. 'Yes, I did.' She may as well be honest with him. 'Believe it or not, you don't own me.' Her throat felt like she'd eaten glass shards, but she wouldn't let that stop her.

She tried not to think about what he was going to do to her, but she knew she wanted to survive it. She had no idea how much time had passed, but she remembered getting into Julian's car and feeling like giving up altogether. But now, she wanted to see Julian again. She wanted to feel his arms around her, keeping her safe.

'Oh, you think you're so clever, don't you?' He put on a mocking tone as he said, 'Oh, look at me with my fancy art career, too good for marriage. Well, I bet you don't feel so clever now, do you?'

She wanted to scream a massive 'fuck you' to the universe for screwing her over yet again. This was her punishment for finally feeling like she could live. She'd dared to believe that she could have a normal life and become something.

'Fuck you.'

'Oh, no.' He shook his head as he laughed. 'It's me that will be fucking you.' He pressed his forehead to hers as he gripped her throat, crushing her windpipe. His grip tightened as he said, 'I hear Julian is a kinky fucker. Likes to play rough. Is that what you like about him, slut? Do you like it rough?' He ran his nose along her cheek and she recoiled from his touch. 'I can make this rough for you.'

She wouldn't cry, wouldn't give him the satisfaction. Squeezing her eyes shut to hide her fear, she tried to swallow but couldn't. Her lungs burned as she ground out her words in defiance. 'You could never compete with Julian. He doesn't have to take women against their will and handcuff them to radiators.'

He pulled back, standing to his full height and paced back and forth, tugging at his hair. His shirt clung to where sweat patches darkened the light blue linen. He'd rolled his sleeves up to his elbows and the telltale bruising of puncture wounds spoke of how he'd spent his time here. She took the opportunity to breathe deeply, replenishing the much needed oxygen until she felt dizzy.

'That's what he said, my dad. He said I couldn't compete with a Hadley and that if I'd have been a better man, this deal would still be on. Well, I'll show him.' He lunged forward, his nose almost touching hers as his eyes darted from side to side, looking into hers. 'Who's got you now?'

She tried to turn her head, to give herself as much distance as possible as she said, 'No matter what you do to me, you'll never have me.'

Chills swept over her as she faced the realisation that she was unlikely to escape this unscathed. She couldn't reason with him. It was all her fault. She was so quick to lose faith in Julian because she couldn't believe for one second that he genuinely wanted to be with her, or that she was worthy of true love without conditions.

Her breathing slowed, her mind jumbled as Will throttled her. She tried to pull at his wrist, but it didn't budge.

She told Julian to leave her alone.

Her father didn't love her and had disowned her.

No one was coming to look for her.

She willed the darkness to take her as his clammy hand slid under her top.

Shooting pains and a tugging sensation. That was all she could feel as she tried to blink her eyes open. He was still there. She could feel his weight pressing down on her, feel his hot breath against her bare skin.

When had he taken her top off?

She tried to move, but her arm was still shackled to the radiator, hanging, useless. She could no longer feel her fingers, or anything from the elbow up. If only that were true for the rest of her body.

She felt a sharp pain in her ribs as he ripped at her bra, the lace tearing like paper. His damp hands mauled her exposed breast, his nails digging in, the bite of pain enough to stop her blacking out again. She would get no refuge from the darkness she was praying for.

'Oh goody, you're awake.' He was breathless, his words slurred. 'I thought I'd squeezed too hard and killed you.' He laughed, the high-pitched noise assaulting her ears. 'I'm not into necrophilia, but for a moment there I was willing to give it a go. Such a waste otherwise.'

The weight lifted off her as he sat back on his haunches. She tried to take some deep breaths, but her ribs screamed in protest. She couldn't bite back the whimper that escaped her lips.

'Oh, yes, sorry about that. I had some rage to work through and you were such a pretty punching bag.' He looked up at the ceiling as he pulled in a long breath. 'Are you ready to play nice?'

Her back pressed into the hard tiled wall as she tried to shift, but she was numb. Her joints had seized from the hours, days, she didn't know, sitting in the same position.

Will knelt down, one knee on either side of her hips as he dragged a tongue along his bottom lip. 'I'm going to take my time with you. I could just fuck you and be done with it, but where's the fun in that?' He rocked his hips against her as he grabbed clumsily at her breasts, pinching at her nipples and twisting like he was tuning a radio.

He repulsed her. He may have overpowered her, sucked the life from her and will probably kill her, but she wouldn't take it that easily. 'You're a pathetic excuse for a man, do you know that? I'm glad I walked away from the deal. I would rather die than be married to you.' It hurt to speak, but this might be her only chance. She wanted to rile him up, she wanted to make him angry, because then he might bring about the darkness. 'Rather die than have a lifetime with you and your pencil dick.'

He swung for her, the contact snapping her head to the side. Her cheek hit the edge of the radiator and white hot pain shot across her face as her skin split. Her ears rang from the impact, the room spinning. He grabbed her face, his fingers digging in, her teeth cutting into her cheeks until she could taste the metallic tang of blood on her tongue. He pulled her to face him as he leaned over her, his breath more potent than smelling salts. 'Pencil dick? Sounds to me like you're desperate to see my dick, you filthy bitch. You think you're so fucking special, don't you, with your fancy career? Did you really think you could make something of yourself? You're good for one thing and one thing only. You're a fuck toy. You'll take my dick, however I see fit and you'll thank me for it.'

He pressed her head into the wall before releasing his grip. She flexed her jaw and spat the blood from her mouth.

'Pencil dick,' he muttered. 'I'll fucking show you.' His hands went to his jeans, releasing the button and pulling down the zipper. A few seconds of fumbling later, he pulled his flaccid cock from his boxers and tugged on it.

'You like art so much; I'm going to paint you into a pretty picture with my cum.' He writhed and groaned as he tugged and stroked his dick barely to life. She twisted her head and squeezed her eyes shut, not wanting to witness the scene unfolding.

'You're so fucking useless; you can't even get me hard.'

'I think that's a you problem.' If she was going to die at the hands of this wanker, she was certainly going to attack him the only way she could.

'Shut up, you fucking bitch!' He panted as he slapped her across the face. 'Ah fuck, yes. Ah god, yes, that felt good.'

She wanted to vomit. She wanted to die. 'Is that the best you can do? Your dick is like a shrivelled chipolata.' Blood dripped from her lip as she stared into his bloodshot eyes, daring him to take it further. Her mouth curved into a satisfied smile as he wrapped his hand around her throat and squeezed. She closed her eyes and pressed her neck into his palm. He may think he was in control, but he was giving her exactly what she wanted, a way out.

The room closed in around her as she heard the rhythmic slapping of his hand against his dick, his guttural moan, before she felt hot liquid spatter across her ribs.

CHAPTER 26

JULIAN

To Die For (Bonus Track) - Sam Smith

Cameron had spent the last three hours trying to keep Julian calm, and it was safe to say it wasn't working. He hadn't stopped pacing the length of his living room while gripping his phone, willing it to give him the answers he was desperate for. The second it vibrated in his hand, he put it on speaker. 'Tom, please tell me Andre has information on Will?'

'Will has an apartment in London. Andre thinks he may have taken her there. It's the only other place he had a connection to other than his house out near you guys.'

Jay didn't need to hear anymore before he was walking to the front door, Cameron understanding what he needed to do as he followed closely behind, his car keys ready.

'Can you send me the address?' As Jay asked, both his and Cameron's phone dinged with a message.

'Already sent. I'm on the other side of the city. You're probably going to get there before me. Julian, do I need to tell you to stay calm?' They were already in the car, the engine roaring to life. This was one of those moments where he was thankful for Cameron's love of fast cars.

'Don't waste your breath. I won't do anything that could put Jess in any more danger than she's already in.'

Cameron sped out of the village as Julian tapped the address into the sat nav.

'Andre's contact in the police has said he's ready to move on this. What do you want me to tell him?'

He knew what Tom was asking. Does he want the police there, or is he going to handle this himself? 'Give us a head start. I want her safe before the police swarm in and spook him. I'll send you my live location. When we get near, call them in.'

Cameron gripped the wheel as he nodded at Julian. 'She's going to be okay, Jay.'

'She has to be. There isn't another option.'

For once in his life, the traffic gods were looking down upon them as they made it to London in record time. Cameron parked up close to the address, but out of sight in case Will was watching.

Julian felt like a coiled spring ready to go. He was desperate to break the door down and find her, but he knew he needed to be cautious. They didn't know what state Will or Jess were in, and he didn't want to make the situation worse.

They hurried to the back of the building, where they saw an entrance to an underground garage. Thankfully, the only security was a barrier that might deter someone from trying to steal a car. It didn't stop them from walking straight in.

Julian spotted a car in the corner with a missing front bumper and a personalised licence plate that read, BIG WILL.

He pointed to the car as he said, 'That motherfucker is here, and I'm certain he has her.'

'How do we get to her? The only entrance I can see is the elevator, and it looks like it needs an access card to open it.' Cameron looked around, trying to find another way in. His eyes landed on something, and Julian followed his line of sight.

Julian allowed a moment of hope to filter in. 'The fire escape.'

The fire escape didn't come all the way to the ground floor, ironically, to stop people from using it to break into the apartments, but if Cameron gave him a boost, he was tall enough to reach the railings on the first floor.

Cameron looked up at the side of the building. 'I'll give you a boost. There'll be a leap of faith moment, but if you can grab the bottom of the ladder, you can climb up, release it, and I can follow. We'll figure the rest out along the way.'

Cameron planted his feet wide apart and interlaced his fingers. 'Ready?'

Julian stepped into Cameron's hands and launched off with the other foot. He stretched his arms out as much as possible and gripped hard as his fingers wrapped around the ladder. Heaving himself up, he pulled himself over the railings onto the balcony of the first-floor apartment. He unlatched the ladder and watched it descend.

As Cameron climbed, Julian carried on up to the next floor, Will's floor. He was careful to stay out of sight as he cupped his hands around his eyes and peered into the spacious living area.

His element of surprise was ruined as he heard sirens in the distance and Cameron uttering, 'fuck,' from behind him.

It wasn't hard for Julian to find a picture of Will online. One quick search had resulted in hundreds of photos of him out and about with the IT crowd and so he recognised him instantly when he saw him making his way to the fire escape, obviously spooked by the sirens.

Julian and Cameron pressed themselves up against the brick wall and as they heard the click of the door open, Julian jumped in his path, pushing him back inside.

Cameron took over, grabbing Will and throwing him onto the floor, restraining his wrists behind his back. 'I've got him. You find Jess. He's off his face.'

Will barely put up a fight as Julian ran from the room, pushing every door open until he found what he was looking for.

'Jess,' he screamed, desperate to see any sign of life from her. He skidded to his knees, the hard tiles sending shooting pains up his thighs, but he didn't care. Jess was lying on the floor of the bathroom, her face bruised and bloodied, unconscious. Her hoodie was half removed, dangling from the arm that was cuffed to the radiator.

'Jess. Jess. Can you hear me?' He shouted her name through the sobs he could no longer control. 'Jess, please.' Her body lay limp in his arms, a dead weight.

He heard the crack of wood giving way as the front door crashed to the floor and a team of police swarmed the apartment. He could hear them shouting at Cameron to back away as he screamed at them to go into the bathroom.

Feet thundered in his direction as he covered her body with his. He didn't want them seeing her like this, her skin covered in marks, her bra torn, but still in place.

'Sir, you need to step back and let us get to her.'

'Sir.'

But he couldn't let go. He let go once before and he vowed never to do it again.

A strong hand gripped his shoulder as a familiar voice said, 'Jay, it's okay. You need to let them get to her. She needs their help.' He was tugged away, collapsing into Cameron's arms. His world crashed down around him. He'd let her down, and just like Chloe, she paid the price with her body.

He watched as a policeman pulled out a tiny metal key and released her cuffed wrist. Heard the thud as it landed on the hard floor.

CHAPTER 27

JULIAN

Die With a Smile - Lady Gaga & Bruno Mars

Beep.
Beep.
Such an innocuous little sound, but one that carried the power to bring grown men to their knees. One little noise was the difference between life and death. He'd grown to hate that noise, but needed to hear it.

Beep.

It was the only signal that Jess was alive. That, and the slow rise and fall of her chest, now covered in a hospital gown. Her clothes removed and stuffed into a plastic bag for evidence.

He hadn't left her side. The hospital staff had tried to have him removed when visiting hours were over, but one call from his father, who was now a benefactor of the hospital trust, and he had a large chair rolled in so he could sit at her vigil for as long as needed.

He wasn't leaving her alone. The others arrived as soon as they could, forcing him to take care of himself. He refused to pee unless one of them was holding her hand when he left. He'd probably caused irreparable damage to his bladder as a result, but he didn't care.

Sleep was a distant memory. So were clean clothes, hot food, and her smile. He missed her smile and the way her eyes would light up when he kissed her.

Now, when he pressed his lips to her battered skin, there was nothing. Not a spark of recognition.

Fucking Will. He should've ripped his throat out with his bare hands. He remembered saying that he'd burn the world down for her, and instead he stood back and watched the police cuff him. He was motionless as Will was escorted out of the building where he'd no doubt spend some time in a holding cell and then have an expensive lawyer get him off. But it's all well and good proving your love with grand gestures like murder, but the reality of the situation is that he would end up in a prison cell and Jess on her own. That didn't stop him from feeling like the world had burned down anyway, and he couldn't promise Will's throat would remain intact if he ever laid eyes on him again.

The doctor on shift knocked before walking in. 'Mr Hadley, how are you doing today?'

'That doesn't matter. Do you have an update on Jess?'

'I'm sorry, but you know I can't discuss her medical records with you, Mr Hadley.' His eyes were apologetic, but it did nothing to tamp his anger at the absurdity of the situation

His jaw ticked as he rubbed his thumb over the lifeless knuckles of Jess's hand. 'Can you tell me anything? I'm losing my mind.' He didn't know what was worse, not knowing what that fucker had done to her, or knowing and it being his worse nightmare.

Images of what Chloe had been through had replayed in his mind every time he closed his eyes, but now, Chloe's face morphed into Jess's. He couldn't bear for Jess to have suffered a similar fate. Once again, it was his fault that someone he cared for, someone he loved, had been hurt. If only he'd trusted her with the truth from the start; none of this would've happened.

The doctor made some notes on her records and sighed. He lowered his voice. 'From what I can tell, she'll regain consciousness soon.' He must have sensed Julian's turmoil as he reassured him. 'She's going to be okay. The bruising is the worst of it.'

He nodded as he scrubbed at his face with his free hand, the other still firmly clutching onto Jess's. The doctor squeezed his shoulder before leaving him alone.

He needed Jess to wake up, needed to know what he was dealing with. No one else could give him answers as to what Will had done to her. It was clear he'd taken his anger out on her with his fist, but the rest was a mystery. He was so high on drugs when the police arrested him, they had to hold him for hours before he could string a sentence together. He hated to think about what Will would've done if they hadn't showed up when they did.

After the doctor had left, Sarah called. Julian put the call on speaker, hoping the sound of her friends would bring Jess around. Sarah said she and James were on their way. He could hear James shouting that they'd also brought clean clothes and a shower in a can—body spray and deodorant—for him. Apparently, it was his smell that kept her unconscious.

'You smell… pretty… bad.' The words were so quiet he thought he'd imagined them. He lifted his head from her lap to see her eyes blinking open and her licking her lips.

Like a spring, he was up and next to her. 'Jess. What do you need? Do you need pain relief?' He pressed the call button next to her bed, never taking his eyes off her.

'Water.'

He grabbed the cup and straw the nurse had left and half-filled it from the jug.

'Here.' He watched as she wrapped her lips around the straw, closing her eyes as the liquid hit her tongue. 'Just little sips. Don't take too much on too soon.' He didn't know why, but he'd seen this scene so many times in movies that he figured some of it had to be based on fact.

A moment later, the doctor and a nurse came running in.

As the nurse fussed with the various tubes coming out of Jess arms, the doctor flashed a light into her eyes as he said, 'Miss Chatwin, I can't tell you how pleased we are to see you awake.' The doctor gave her a brief summary of where she was and the circumstances surrounding her being in the hospital and then he turned to Julian. 'I'm afraid, I need you to step outside while I speak to Miss Chatwin.'

Before Julian could respond, Jess croaked, 'No. Please, I want him here. You can discuss everything in front of him.'

The relief he felt at hearing that was immense. She wanted him. All was not lost.

'Very well. We were able to run various tests while you were unconscious and can confirm that the CT scans show no signs of brain damage or internal bleeding.' The doctor looked between Julian and Jess before continuing. 'Miss Chatwin, when you arrived here, we found evidence of sexual assault on your torso, but your clothing from the waist down remained in place.'

That was his polite way of telling her Will had shot his load over her chest. Julian had seen it when he found her and wanted to vomit every time he thought about Will's cum marking her skin.

He cleared his throat as Julian clutched onto Jess's hand, willing himself to stay calm. 'Preliminary external examinations showed no signs of localised bruising or bleeding, and therefore we did not believe an internal examination was necessary. Miss Chatwin, I must ask, would you like for us to perform an internal exam to look for evidence of further sexual assault?'

Jess's hand flexed in Julian's, squeezing it tightly. 'Um, I'm not sure. I don't know what to do. I don't know how long I was unconscious for.' A tear slipped down her cheek.

Julian sandwiched her hand between his as he swallowed down the heartache so he could speak. 'If you aren't sure, Jess—if there is any doubt—I think you should have the test. You need to know for sure.' It wasn't a lie, he knew her well enough to know that the doubt would eat away at her, but selfishly, he needed to know.

She nodded. 'Okay. You're right. I need to know. I'll have the test.'

The doctor gestured at the nurse, giving her the go ahead to get the test ready. 'Mr Hadley, could you wait outside, please?'

Jess's eyes grew wide. 'Please,' she croaked. 'I don't want... him to leave.'

'It's okay, sunshine. I'll be just outside that door. I won't go any further.' He was struggling to hold it together, and this was the excuse he needed to take a breath.

She gave a tentative nod as Julian squeezed her hand and stepped out of the room. He leaned against the wall, pressing his head back as the stress of the events hit him. He sucked in a ragged breath, the first proper lung-full since he'd found her on the bathroom floor and let his emotions out. As his knees gave way and he sank to the floor, he allowed his tears to fall.

'Jay?' Sarah was running down the corridor, James close behind her. 'Jay, what's happened? Is Jess okay?' She dropped the bags at his feet as she crouched down.

'She's awake.' His eyes met hers, glassy and full of concern. 'She's okay…' He swallowed. 'The doctor is with her now, checking on her.'

Sarah slumped to the floor, tears streaming down her face as she looked up at James. 'Everything is okay, James. She's going to be okay.'

James looked up to the ceiling, his Adam's apple bobbing as he swallowed. 'Thank fuck for that. Come on, mate.' He held a hand outstretched for Julian to take. 'Let's get you cleaned up.'

He shook his head. 'I promised her I wouldn't move. I'm not leaving this spot.'

James pursed his lips and nodded. 'Fair enough.' He rummaged around in the backpack he was carrying and pulled out a can of deodorant and a white T-shirt. 'You can freshen up here, then.'

Julian nodded his thanks and stripped his top off, sprayed his armpits, and pulled the clean tee over his head. Sarah turned her head, finding something on the wall fascinating.

Once he was covered up, she turned back to face him. 'Has she said anything? How is she?' The words she wanted to say hung heavy in the air but were left unsaid.

'She's literally just come round. She wanted water. That's all I know right now.' Sarah squeezed his shoulder and nodded. They'd tackle whatever was thrown at them.

She'd asked him to stay, though, and he clung to that glimmer of hope they'd be okay. He wasn't naïve enough to think he was off the hook. He had so much to say to her, so much to apologise for, but for now, he would be here for her in whatever way she needed.

'Did you call her parents?' Sarah couldn't keep the venom out of her tone.

'Yes. I told her mother they weren't welcome here. She agreed to stay away. I don't want Jess seeing them until she's ready.' So many choices had been taken away from her and he wasn't about to carry on the trend by letting the people that got her in this mess see her without her consent.

Julian looked at James. 'Have there been any updates on Will?'

He shook his head. 'No. He's being evaluated by a psychiatrist. Looks like Jess isn't the only one who's been screwed over by their parents. Not that it gives him an excuse. I'd still like to get my hands on him.' He ran his fingers through his hair. 'I don't know how you didn't kill him when you got there.'

Julian shrugged. 'He wasn't my priority.'

The door opened and a smiling doctor stepped out. 'She's all yours, Mr Hadley.' He looked at the others. 'May I suggest you two wait out here? She's feeling a little overwhelmed.'

Sarah wrapped her arms around James and pressed her face into his chest, but Julian could see the rise and fall of her shoulders. He knew that feeling all too well.

He stepped into the room, keeping his fingers on the door to slow its progress as it swung shut.

'Hey, you.'

'Hey.' Her voice was quiet, unsure.

In three strides, he was next to her, reaching his hand out to hers. 'May I?' He wasn't going to assume she wanted him touching her. He may have held her hand earlier, but there was nothing to stop her from changing her mind about what she wanted now.

'Please. I need to feel something other than… him.'

He couldn't bring himself to say his name out loud, but that twat didn't deserve to have that power over her. He didn't get to leave his mark on her. She was his. His to mark. His to own. He forced back the growl that threatened to escape.

He wrapped his large hand around hers, so small and cool to the touch. Careful not to move the tube in the back of her hand, he gripped onto her. 'Jess... I... are you all right? Shit, I don't—'

'He didn't rape me, Jay. Ol' pencil dick didn't have it in him.' Her smile didn't reach her eyes.

The shockwave of relief sucked the air from his lungs as tears sprang from his eyes. He pressed his lips to the back of her hand as he silently thanked every god he could think of.

'Jess, I'm so sorry. Can you ever forgive me?'

She shook her head, a single tear falling from her eye. 'Please, I don't want to have this conversation now. There are things we need to talk about, but for now, I just want you to hold me. You're still my safe place, Jay. He didn't take that away from me.'

CHAPTER 28

JESS

Rise Up - Andra Day

The days after she woke up had been awkward, not knowing what to talk about, but Julian seemed content to just be present, to hold her hand and press his lips to the delicate skin at her wrist every once in a while, kissing away the burn.

She slept a lot, napping between the nightmares. She no longer welcomed the darkness. It was back to being her foe, but she couldn't evade it as sleep took hold of her.

Julian hadn't asked for the detail of what happened to her, even though she could tell he was desperate to know. She didn't want to think of it again, but the day after she came around, the police needed to take her statement. She demanded Julian left the room while she spoke to the police. She needed to tell them everything without worrying about how he'd react, and she wasn't ready for him to know. A small part of her worried that his feelings towards her would change when he knew the details.

They sat in silence after the police had all the information they needed, or at least, all that she could remember. Julian stroked her hair or just sat, stoic, waiting for her to take the lead and open up to him about what happened.

'I blacked out frequently.' She'd start there. Seemed like as good a place as any to start, and she wanted to get this conversation over with. She watched as every muscle in Julian's body froze. Every muscle apart from the one in his jaw, which was currently twitching.

'I didn't feel like he'd done… that…I couldn't be sure. But the doctor confirmed it. I needed to know. I needed to hear it.' Julian's grip tightened around her hand, but he remained silent.

She tutted and rolled her eyes. 'He couldn't even get that right; he'd taken so many drugs he struggled to get it up. Of course, he blamed me for that. I told him it was his problem.' She ran her finger along a faint bruise on her cheek. 'That earned me this. My mother always said my smart mouth would get me in trouble.'

She smiled, an attempt to reassure Julian that she'd be okay, but he didn't smile back. She watched as something inside him shattered; the light in his eyes puffed out.

He dropped his head, chin to chest. 'I let you down. If I'd just told you everything from the start, we wouldn't be here now.' She could feel him withdrawing, but she wouldn't let him. He didn't get to shoulder the blame for this.

'You don't know that. Will's unhinged and you telling me about your family wouldn't have changed that.' Julian shook his head, refusing to believe what she was saying.

'He would've got to me, eventually. Julian, I can't be with you if you're going to spend the rest of your life blaming yourself. I don't blame you. I'm pissed off that you didn't tell me sooner. Be angry at yourself for that, learn from it and promise never to keep me in the dark going forward, but do not blame yourself for this. I can't bear to see what happened to me reflected in your eyes every time I look at you.' She sat up, taking the moment to steady her breathing. 'I won't put myself through that.'

She shook her head as she picked at her fingernails, finding the courage to voice the feelings she'd locked in a box. She raised her head, her defiant eyes meeting his heart broken stare.

Her voice softened as she said, 'While I was lying on the bathroom floor, I realised I was utterly alone. I thought I was going to die.'

'Fuck, Jess, please don't say that.'

She squeezed his hand, needing to keep his attention focused on what she was saying and not on his feelings. 'You need to hear this. For a split second, I wanted to give up. I didn't see a way out of the situation, but then I decided that if I survived, I'd start living.'

She leaned forward, and said loud and clear, 'Did you know that to make a plant grow stronger, you snip off the new shoots from the top?'

Julian's brow creased. 'No.' He shook his head.

'Well, you do. Pinch it right off.' She made the motion with her thumb and forefinger. 'I'd just started to live my life, thanks to you, but Will came along and pinched off my new shoots. Is that going to make me weaker? No, it's not. I'll come back even stronger for it.' She slapped her hand down on the bed.

'When I leave this room, we're going to pick up where we left off.' She waved her hand back and forth between them. 'I won't accept you moping around, wracked with guilt on my behalf. I don't have time for it. When we get out of here, we're going to have one hell of an argument about you keeping something so important from me, then we're going to have make up sex. And then I'm getting on with the rest of my life. Do I make myself clear?'

His lip curled into a half smile. 'Abundantly. Am I allowed to kiss you now?'

'Yes, please. And then you can get me a cup of tea with milk and two sugars.'

They hadn't discussed it, but when it came time to leave the hospital, Julian had taken her back to his house, or as he'd referred to it, their home.

As she'd feared, he treated her with kid gloves, scared to touch her, or come on too strong. She let him off while her bruises were still evident and her ribs sore, but after another week, she was healed and feeling great. Better than great. She was ready to live her life free of her parents' control.

Being at home with him, sleeping in his arms every night, and breathing him in, healed her in so many ways. Her nightmares lessened when her lungs were full of him, like he'd climbed inside her to keep her safe.

Her lady parts were unscathed, and they felt neglected. She sat at the kitchen table watching as Julian prepared her a feast for breakfast, a ritual he'd started as soon as she was back from the hospital. He claimed she needed feeding up, and that he was the man for the job.

She didn't mind. If she'd known he did it topless, wearing only his baggy lounge shorts, she'd have pulled herself from their bed to watch sooner. Today's breakfast was a special request. She'd asked Julian to prepare American buttermilk pancakes with crispy bacon, blueberries, and maple syrup so she could satisfy her craving for them since returning from Vegas. She should have known he wouldn't just knock up a packet mix.

His morning run included a trip to the local farm to buy fresh buttermilk and bacon, and he was currently mixing the batter. His back was to Jess and she couldn't take her eyes off the way his back muscles flexed as he whisked the batter.

She released the lip she was biting down on as her phone vibrated on the table with an incoming message from the Book Club Besties WhatsApp group.

> **Sarah:** How you doing J? Has he fucked you yet?

Jess may have vented her frustration in the group chat last night when chapter updates inevitably turned into sex life and pregnancy updates. Her friends gave her a therapy session, checking in on her mental state and asking her to be sure she was ready. She'd never been surer about anything in her life.

> **Jess:** No. He's still focusing on my nutrition, apparently. He's in the

kitchen whipping up a batch of buttermilk pancakes. TOPLESS. FML.

Sarah: You could tell him his batter has loads of nutrition in it.

Imogen: You just had to go there. I need to throw up.

Sarah: Soz, Jen. You know you used to love it before you got preggers. Nom nom nom. Don't worry, your gag reflex will improve after birth.

Lucy: I walk away from my phone for one minute...

Jess: It's too much. Instead of just using squirty cream on my pancakes, he's using some fancy piece of equipment like they have in bars. You know that thing they use in cooking shows?

Imogen: You mean a whipping siphon?

Jess: Yes! I knew you'd know. He's giving it a right good wanking, and it's jiggling his package, as apparently, he cooks breakfast topless and commando. I'm just going to pounce on him. He's smiling at me. He knows what he's doing.

Sarah: Save a siphon. Wank a chef?

Sarah: Sorry, couldn't resist.

Lucy: I have nothing... But Jess, if you want him, just go get him.

Imogen: I agree.

Sarah: A wise woman once said to you, take the bull by the horns. Go get his horn.

Jess: Okay ladies. I'm doing it.

She placed her phone down on the table and tapped her nails on her case, gaining Julian's attention.

'Everything all right?' He'd washed the blueberries and was now extracting the ones that were slightly too squishy. There was nothing worse than a soft blueberry.

She plastered the most demure expression she could muster on her face as she planted her elbows firmly and deliberately on the table, one eyebrow raised. 'Jay, could you come here? I need some help with something.'

Blueberries forgotten, he walked over. 'What is it, sunshine?' He stood, hands on his hips, emphasising all his hard lines and ridges, his gaze drifting down to where her elbows rested on the table.

Fucking hell, he was too much.

She twisted in her seat and gripped onto his hips before looking up through her lashes at him.

'Miss Chatwin, what are you doing?' He smirked, and the glint in his eyes told her he knew exactly what she was doing.

'I need something.' Her heart thundered in her chest.

'What do you need?' She watched as he swallowed, his hands resting gently on her shoulders, sending warmth down her spine.

'I need to taste you.' She pressed her nose to the spot above his navel and breathed in her personal heaven. She could detect the scent of eucalyptus, ginger, and lime from his body wash, but the underlying scent of him was what called to her; earthy, leather, and musk.

She parted her lips on a sigh and dragged the tip of her tongue up one line of the V. She veered off the path as she followed a vein that pulsed under her touch.

'Jess, are you sure?' Arousal, hope, and the slightest touch of trepidation laced his words. 'I don't want you doing something you're not ready for. You've been through a lot and you need to focus on recovery. I'm not going anywhere. You don't need to rush.'

'Julian, my body has healed. My mind? When I close my eyes, I can still feel his hands on my skin.' She shuddered. 'He was so clammy and gross. I don't want to feel him on me anymore. I want to feel you. I'm going to do what I need to in order to make you mine again. Claim you back.' She hummed a laugh. 'My parents are quite diabolical, but they've taught me one very important life lesson. Resilience. Yes, I've been through a lot, but it's by no means enough to defeat me. Please don't take away the one thing that makes me feel alive.'

He squeezed her shoulders. 'Jess. I'm so sorry—'

'Give it a rest, Jay. Now shut the fuck up while I suck your cock.' She didn't want to hear another apology. He'd said it a thousand times with every glance at her, every meal he fed her, every touch and caress.

Her fingers traced along the edge of his shorts as she rested her forehead on his abs. She tugged on his waistband, pulled his shorts down his thighs, and let them drop to the floor. She leaned back just enough to run her forefinger over his tattoo. His cock bobbed under her touch, growing firmer as she ran her fingers along its length.

Gripping the base, she lifted it up to her mouth and licked around his head.

'Ohhh fuucckk.' He growled out as his hips thrust and she took him to the back of her throat. It was the only time she'd be able to fit so much of him inside her mouth. She felt it lengthen and harden as she dragged her tongue around the ridge, her hand twisting at his base.

'So fucking good.' His hands drifted up from her shoulders, his fingers combing through her hair, holding it back from her face.

She released his cock, now fully erect and jutting angrily upwards. She licked from base to tip, coating him in saliva. With both hands, she gripped him, twisting and stroking as she sucked and nibbled on as much as she could fit in her mouth. Salty liquid dripped onto her tongue.

She closed her eyes, pulled away and hummed. 'You taste so good. I've missed this.' She widened her mouth until the creases of her lips stung with the stretch. Flattening her tongue, she took him to the back of her throat, tilting her head to take just that bit more.

Holding her head, he thrust his hips, fucking her mouth as he moaned intelligible words. 'So... deep. You... take me... so well.' Each word was punctuated with a thrust. He was careful not to push her too far. She could tell he was still holding back. Wanting this to step up a gear, she kept one fist gripped around his cock as she brought her other hand up to his face and pushed two fingers into his mouth.

She pulled herself off his cock, stroking her hand up his shaft. 'Suck,' she demanded.

He closed his eyes and swirled his tongue around her fingers, sucking them and lapping at them with delight.

She pulled them out with a pop as she said, 'Good boy.'

He looked down at her, one eyebrow raised. She returned his what the fuck look with a double eyebrow wiggle as she lifted the hem of his old band T-shirt she'd taken to sleeping in and pushed her slick fingers into the waistband of her knickers.

Her opening was wet and ready for her as she slid her fingers over her clit, a soft moan escaping against his crown, her tongue licking at the pre-cum on his tip.

'Christ, sunshine, you're driving me crazy. I won't last long at this rate,' he said through gritted teeth as he watched her grind her hips against her hand.

She felt life and power surge through her veins. She'd had enough of people thinking they knew better and taking control. Julian had once again tried to do what he thought was best for her, but she was taking control of this situation; she was tending to her needs and he would fall in line this time.

She pulled away until her lips circled his tip before leisurely drawing more of him into her mouth. Her head bobbed at a languid pace, his grip tightening in her hair. She smirked around his cock; he was barely containing his need to take over, to fuck her face.

She pulled her hand out from where it was bringing her close to orgasm and gripped his hips, pulling herself up to standing. She pushed with one hand, twisting him. 'Sit down.'

The back of his knees hit her chair, forcing him to sit. 'Yes, ma'am.'

She shimmied out of her knickers, discarding them under the table. 'I'm going to fuck you now, my Lord. I'm going to take what I need. Okay?' She straddled his thighs and pressed her hands into his rock-hard chest, dusted with dark hair so soft she wanted to nuzzle into it.

'Fuck, Jess. Wait.'

She froze. Had she gone too far? 'What is it? Sorry, did I do something wrong?' Her bravado left her as she went to lift off him.

He gripped her hips, holding her in place. 'No, you're perfect. It's just hearing you say those words… it does something to me. I need a second.' He closed his eyes as he took a deep breath. 'It makes me want to throw you up against the wall and fuck your brains out until you scream my name.'

She guided his throbbing cock to her entrance, sinking down onto it. 'I look forward to you doing that, my Lord.' She pronounced his honorific clearly. 'But for now, this is for me. I'm going to fuck you until I come, and maybe then I'll let you do whatever you want to me. I remember you promising to bend me over the table.'

He ran his hands up her thighs, sweeping them over the rise of her hips before digging his fingers into the globes of her arse. 'Ride me, sunshine.'

She leaned down, pressing her chest to his as she tenderly kissed him, her pelvis grinding against his in a slow, steady rhythm. The way he stretched and filled her was perfect. She needed him to possess her inside and out.

She panted as she pulled her T-shirt over her head, throwing it to the floor, her skin already flushed and damp. Every part of her body was in contact with him, her tongue, her skin, her core. With every thrust, she felt more alive.

'Take it, sunshine. Take your pleasure from me.' His hips rose to meet her, deepening their connection, bringing her to the edge of her pleasure/pain threshold.

Steadying herself with her hands on his chest, she gripped with her thighs and bounced on his cock with an urgent need. 'Jay, I need to come. Oh god, I need to come.'

Giving her the help she needed, he rubbed her clit with the pad of his thumb. 'You need to come.' He panted. 'You're fucking amazing. Giving it to me so well. I can't hold out.' Beads of sweat glistened on his forehead. 'It's too good. Fuck.'

He kept rubbing her clit as he gripped a breast, tweaking her hardened bud. The bite of pain as he pinched her nipple once more had her grinding harder and edging closer to blessed release.

She arched her back, reaching a hand behind her and between his legs, gripping and rolling his balls as her middle finger rubbed along his perineum. 'Fuck, oh fuck.' He bucked his hips. 'Come for me, sunshine. Come, now.'

She clamped down on him as her orgasm tore through her, her thighs shaking and her chest heaving as wave after wave shook her.

'Shit, Jess. Hold on.' Julian grabbed her arse and stood. Before she knew what had happened, he'd pulled out, flipped her, and bent her over the table. Her breasts pressed into the cool surface as he drove into her with punishing thrusts. 'I'm sorry, I can't hold back.'

In answer to his apology, she tilted her pelvis, taking him deeper and meeting him thrust for thrust, egging him on, begging for more. He released a strangled moan, folding over her and sinking his teeth into the base of her neck. His fingers dug into her hips as he pounded into her, sweat making their bodies slide with every thrust.

He roared as he came, his dick pulsing inside her, filling her.

He licked at where he'd bitten her, humming to himself with apparent satisfaction. Her breath misted over the varnished surface as she fought to fill her lungs.

He ran his fingers down her spine, leaving goosebumps in their wake. 'You holding up, okay?' He pulsed his hips once, twice, making her pussy flutter. She bit down hard on her bottom lip and let out a gentle moan, overwhelmed by a feeling of being owned. Like that little thrust was him marking his territory.

Jess lifted on her forearms, just enough to twist her head to look back at him. She was already breathless, but the image of him looming over her, sweat slicked and balls deep, left her deceased.

'Never better.' She wasn't entirely sure she could stand, but standing was highly overrated.

He sighed, a low rumble vibrating in his ribcage. 'I need to feed you.'

He'd sated her carnal need, so she'd allow him this. 'Okay. Let me clean up while you finish cooking the pancakes.' She went to get up but found her back pinned beneath his hot palm.

'Not a chance, sunshine. You'll sit in this chair and keep your legs crossed while I cook.' He stepped back, slipping free of her, and slid the chair to the back of her knees. He ran his hands over her shoulders as her bottom hit the seat. 'Good girl.'

She giggled as he reached for an apron, tying it around his waist. He looked like one of those butlers in the buff you could hire for parties with his beautifully pert buttocks bared and a little square of fabric protecting his modesty.

'You may laugh, but my cock is well and truly in the danger zone in front of this gas hob. I'm cooking pancakes, my love, not sausage.' He set to work cooking, and Jess couldn't help but stare at the apron that resembled a tent, pitched to perfection.

'How are you still hard? You're an animal.'

'I can't help it.' He pointed at his groin with the spatula. 'This is what you do to me. You call me Lord with that mouth, a mouth that does very unladylike things to me, and it drives me crazy. My dick can't get enough of your perfectly tight pussy, either. Right, breakfast is served.' He plated up and placed the plate on the table, the siphon of cream next to it.

He stood next to Jess and waved his fingers in an up motion. 'Stand.'

He whipped the apron off and sat in her seat. 'Sit. Facing me, on my cock.'

As she straddled his hips, she slid down easily on his shaft, his cum leaking out as she moved. How was she supposed to eat now? It was safe to say she was full.

He picked up the siphon and shook it before piping two perfect swirls of cream on her nipples. She gasped as the cool cream hit her fevered skin. 'This is how we should eat every meal. From now on, mealtimes are a strictly no clothes zone.'

He bent his head and licked the cream as it warmed from her body heat. 'I'd like to see you cover me in beef gravy and make it as sexy as this.' She gasped as he sucked her other nipple and bit down.

'Don't challenge me, sunshine.'

Having him fill her and not move was driving her crazy. She flexed her hips, grinding her cum covered clit against his pelvis.

'Be a good girl and sit still while I feed you.' He put the cream down and cut a slice of pancake with a fork, spearing it and bringing it up to her mouth. 'You need your energy, but I intend to be on you, in you, all over you as often as possible until it's only me you feel. If that means I'm inside you whenever we're alone together, then so be it. When we're apart, I want the imprint of my cock inside you to act as a reminder of who owns you and who you own in return.'

She wrapped her lips around the fork and closed her eyes as the fluffiest pancake ever to pass her lips hit her tongue. She groaned as she chewed and swallowed. 'More.'

He smiled as he broke off another piece, this time including some bacon. She had to hand it to him; this was her new favourite way to eat. As he fed her the last piece of pancake, he dragged his finger across the plate, wiping up the remnants of the maple syrup.

He pressed the tip of his finger to her lips. 'Suck.'

Her eyes flared as she dutifully did as she was told. The rich sweetness of the syrup complimented the saltiness of his finger. She sucked hard, her cheeks hallowing as she watched him close his eyes, part his lips, and growl. She squirmed as she felt him thicken inside her. He pulled his finger out and sucked on her bottom lip before kissing her with a tenderness that made her heart ache for him.

'You're amazing. Do you know that?' His eyes danced between hers as a damp curl of his hair flopped down over his forehead.

She wrapped the wayward strands around her finger, combing them through the rest of his hair. 'Am I?'

'Mmm-hmmm. Only you could use my future title against me in a way that makes me blow my load. Speaking of which, are you ready for round two? I can feel my cum all over us, but it's not enough. I need you to take more of it.'

'I'm ready.' She wanted his cum to cleanse away the invisible scars Will had left behind. He lifted from their seated position, turned one-eighty, and placed her down on the edge of the work surface. Her head pressed against the overhead cupboard, holding her up.

She felt a gush of heat as he pulled out to the tip and dragged his fingers through the hot liquid before sliding back in. The lewd sounds of him thrusting into her turned her on in a way she didn't expect.

He rubbed his fingers across her torso, spreading his seed over her, marking her.

'Mine,' he growled.

'Yours. Only ever yours.'

CHAPTER 29

JULIAN

Banks - Jordan Davis & NEEDTOBREATHE

'Come on, I'm taking you home to officially meet my parents.' Julian cleared away their plates from lunch as Jess finished the last of her water. He'd been putting off seeing his parents since they got home from the hospital, but it had been a couple of weeks and they were getting a tad demanding. He just wasn't ready to share her yet.

He'd kept his promise of being on her and in her at every opportunity, and he knew it was going to be tough sitting next to her for the afternoon without at least getting a semi. An erection in the presence of his parents would be inappropriate and disturbing in equal measure. But he couldn't put it off any longer. They had given him full access to their bank account, no questions asked and were twenty million lighter for it, but they'd never hold that over him, so he figured the least he could do was keep his dick in his pants and pay them a visit.

'Well, I've met your dad already, remember?' She looked up at him with raised eyebrows as he closed the dishwasher door.

He leant back against the counter, hands gripping it on either side. 'Yeah, true, but you've not met my mum, so let's focus on that. She called this morning while you were in the shower and has demanded I bring you over. Apparently, I've kept you to myself for long enough.' He shrugged. 'They need to talk to me about something, too, so I said we'll pop over. That's okay with you, isn't it?'

It hadn't dawned on him to ask if she was okay with meeting his parents. He figured that was a big step in any relationship, or at least it was when he was with Chloe. He'd dreaded taking her over to meet them, so much so he met them at the restaurant instead. She never got to know the real Julian. But with Jess, it felt natural. He was actually looking forward to showing her where he grew up, and where one day they'd raise their family. He'd keep that last bit to himself for now, though.

Jess pushed her chair under the table and straightened out her black denim dungarees, sliding her hands under the front to pull her plain, white T-shirt into place. 'I can't wait to meet your mum; she sounds amazing. Do I look all right though? Should I get changed into something more befitting meeting a Lord and Lady?' Her head shot up, her eyes meeting his, wide with terror. 'Oh fuck! Do I need to learn some protocol? Do I curtsey or have to address them as my Lord and Lady?'

Julian stepped forward and pulled her into his arms. He pressed his nose into the crown of her head, breathing in the floral scent of her until his lungs were at capacity. His hands swept around the curve of her hips and came to rest on her bottom, giving it a squeeze. 'The only time you refer to anyone by my Lord is to me as I fill you with my cock. Is that clear?'

He smiled as her face flushed. His sweet Jess; so easily scandalised one minute and the next, she's begging for his cum. Perfection.

'Crystal clear, my Lord.'

That earned her a growl and slow, delving kiss that nearly derailed their plans to head out.

As they pulled up to a massive set of black iron gates, Jess did a double take. 'Hang on a minute.' Julian tried to keep the smile off his lips. 'This is yours?'

'Yes.' He clicked a button on a keyring and the gates opened. The stone crackled under the tyres as he slowly made his way up to the main house. Open fields surrounded the road as far as the eye could see. He knew Jess would love it here.

'I didn't think anyone actually lived here. I thought it was one of those stately homes you could hire out for weddings and TV remakes of period dramas.'

'Well, we do those things occasionally, but mostly, this is a private residence.'

'Fuck, Julian.' She looked at him, a mix of wonder and worry crossing her face as it scrunched, wrinkling her button nose. 'You're basically royalty, aren't you?'

He laughed. 'Royalty? No. Not in the slightest. I promise, we're a completely normal family who just happen to have a title passed down the generations.'

Jess looked around the Porsche Cayenne that Julian was driving and raised an eyebrow. 'And a fleet of luxury cars on hand. Yep, totally normal.' She added air quotes around normal, emphasising her point.

Julian shrugged. 'Okay, maybe not normal, but having a dad who collects cars is handy.' He tapped the dash. 'I like this one. Might keep it.'

He squeezed her thigh as a few minutes later, the house came into view. 'Do you understand why I choose to live next door to the restaurant now? This house is beautiful, but when you're on your own, it's a bit much.'

'Jay, this isn't a house. It's a bloody castle.' Her words were a strangled whisper as she leaned forward in her seat, taking in the impressive building in front of her.

The house-cum-castle was three storeys high, with a turret flanking the building on each end and a square structure in the middle that had a massive set of wooden, double doors. A pathway led around the house, lined with lavender and roses. Julian breathed in the scent and realised it was the same as Jess's shampoo. That explained why she smelt so calming; she smelt like home.

'Jay, this place is stunning. But you're right, I bet it can feel pretty lonely on your own.'

Julian took her by the hand and led her away from the front door, taking the path to the right.

'Are we not going in?'

He shook his head and pointed to the end of the building. 'No, these front doors look impressive but are a total ball ache to open. There's a smaller door down here.' As they reached the door, almost hidden behind two large bay trees, he pressed his thumb to a pad. 'Dad put this in so he didn't have to remember door keys. He's quite forgetful. Oh, and my mum's a bit of a hippy. You know those herbal teas you love to drink at home?'

Jess gave him the side eye as she said, 'Yes.'

'That's my mum's brand.'

'Right.' She nodded, pulled her hand away and faced him head on. 'Is there anything else I need to know about you or your parents before I step inside this door?'

He stuffed his hands in his blue jeans, rocking back on his heels as he looked at the sky. 'Nope. That's everything.' And then he added with a murmur, 'I'm fairly sure, anyway.'

Jess rolled her eyes and clasped his hand. On a deep inhale, she said, 'Come on then, let's get this show on the road.'

He pushed the door open and led her inside. He wasn't prone to nerves, but as his feet stepped over the threshold, his stomach fluttered, and his temperature rose. He chastised himself for doing away with the comfortable black band T-shirt in favour of a light blue, long-sleeved polo top.

Now the word was out about who he was, he didn't feel the need to hide behind unassuming clothing. He'd gradually found himself reaching for his other clothes, wanting to look good for Jess. She deserved the best. But right now, the fine knit of the top was making him hot. He pulled at the collar as he prayed his parents didn't embarrass him. They weren't like people imagined them to be: stuffy, old-fashioned, and covered head to toe in tweed. No, his parents were new age. They loved life, each other, and positively hated tweed. He loved them. He was never made to feel like he wasn't enough, or that he was strange. They supported and understood why he wanted to shy away from who they were. They didn't know exactly what he got up to in his personal life, but he knew they'd support it.

He figured he got his tendencies from somewhere, and he suspected it was his mother.

They walked hand in hand in silence as he led the way through the many corridors and rooms until they made it to the back of the house. 'I have a feeling you'll love it here, for this room alone.'

Having met Jess's parents and seen how they were with her, he understood her love of wide open spaces. He could also understand where her primal side came from. She'd spent her life being forced into a box, told to behave like a perfect lady. It was only natural that her subconscious would rebel and want to run, want to debase herself in the best way possible. That's what made them a perfect match. Their upbringings were polar opposites, but the result was the same.

'Hey, Mum, Dad. We're here.' Jay called out as they stepped into the orangery. Jess's eyes lit up as she took in the glass room, filled with citrus trees reaching up to the tall glass ceiling, and other lush green plants from warmer climates. The room spanned two storeys and stretched along a large proportion of the back of the property. The fresh scent of lemons and limes filled the air.

Julian could see her breathing deeply and smiling. 'See, I knew you'd love it.'

'It's like being in St Tropez.'

'Julian, my darling, welcome home. And this must be the firecracker Al has been telling me about. Jess, it's such a pleasure to meet you. Do, come and sit.'

Penelope had bounced over to them, dressed in a multicoloured, multi-patterned dress that floated to the floor. Her bare feet padded across the room with bright pink nail polish peeking out from under the fabric. Her silver hair fell in long waves, reaching her chest and her face was clean of makeup and glowed as the skin around her eyes wrinkled from her smile.

Al eased himself up from the chair he occupied and came to stand behind her. He cleared his throat. 'Jess, it's lovely to see you again. May I start by apologising profusely for the way I handled our previous meeting? I feel responsible for what happened.' His cheeks were red as he clasped his hands behind his back.

Julian was about to tell him to not worry, but Jess beat him to it, stepping up to him and wrapping her arms around him.

'Please, don't apologise. This wasn't your fault. Thank you for bringing the truth to light and being the catalyst that put an end to the situation.'

Julian watched as his father squeezed her just a little tighter and closed his eyes. 'Welcome to the family. We're delighted to have you.'

As they parted, Jess ran a finger under her glistening eyes, with only a second to spare before Penelope's arms engulfed her. 'I second what Al said. I can't tell you how happy we were when Jay told us about you.'

As they sat down, Jay next to Jess on a two-seater sofa, their hands clasped, it was Jess's turn to clear her throat. 'I'm very sorry for what my family has done, and I just want you to know that I'll pay you back.'

Julian hadn't considered that Jess would think she needed to pay back the money he'd used to make the Wilberforce family walk away. 'Jess, you don't need to worry about that.'

Al spoke up. 'Jay's right. There's no need to pay us back. I don't want to sound crass, but the money really means nothing to us. We'd rather know you were safe and well.'

'Is there any news on what's happening with that monster, Will?' It was just like his mum to move the conversation along. She wouldn't want Jess feeling the need to shower them in thanks.

Julian wrapped an arm around Jess, pulling her into his side as he reclined. 'He's been sectioned and is undergoing assessments. Apparently, he had a psychotic break. I don't know where that leaves the case against him.'

Penelope's face fell. 'Oh goodness. Another child of this environment being pushed too far. I think we need some tea.' She made her way over to a table adorned with cups, jars of herbs and dried flowers, and a pot of water heating over a candle.

Julian rubbed at the back of his neck. 'Mmm, I don't know about that, Mum. I get the impression his father has arranged it all. I wouldn't put it past him to pay someone off to keep him out of prison.'

Jess wrapped an arm around him. 'I don't know. I think he had it just as hard as I did, but I have an incredible group of friends to support me. I've had time to come to terms with what he's done, and whilst I still have the occasional wobble, on the whole I just feel sorry for him.'

'I think that's the right attitude to have. I hope he gets the help he needs,' said Penelope as she poured water into a glass teapot with a metal strainer. 'How do you take your tea?'

After an hour of chatting, drinking chamomile tea sweetened with honey, and listening to embarrassing stories from Julian's childhood, mostly involving the mischief he and Cameron would get involved in, Al cleared his throat once more.

'Jay, we wanted to see you today to let you know we're moving to France. Permanently.'

'Oh.' He had a feeling this was coming. They were spending more time there, each visit longer than the last.

'Yes. We're going to invest more time in the vineyard. We've had a successful harvest in the last few years and the locals have finally accepted that wine grown by a foreigner is drinkable.' His dad laughed.

'Well, that's great, Dad. Jess and I will have to come and visit. You love France, don't you, sunshine?'

'I do. And I love wine.' Her eyes lit up.

'There was something else we wanted to ask.'

Julian had a feeling this was coming. It was no coincidence that him being in a relationship coincided with them leaving the country on a more permanent basis.

Penelope sat forward in her seat. 'We need you to take over this place. We're going to be kept plenty busy looking after the vineyard, and we'd like it if you could manage the portfolio. We think it's time you came back into the fold so we can enjoy our semi-retirement.'

Julian waited for the sinking feeling to fill his stomach, but it didn't come. Jess looked back up at him, waiting for his answer.

'What about the restaurant though, Mum?'

'You have a competent manager there. I see no reason you can't take a step back like Cam does. Sweetheart, we'd love it if you two lived here and filled it with children and happiness.'

He looked at Jess, panic making his heart skip a beat, but thankfully, she was smiling.

'I think that's a wonderful idea, Penelope. We've been telling Jay for ages he needs to take a break from the restaurant.'

Visions of them living in his family home, their kids running around breaking the antique vases filled his mind as a need to grab her, kiss her, fuck her crept along his skin like a rising tide. He needed to wrap up this visit and get her home.

'Okay, well, if Jess is happy, then I am too. I'll make arrangements at the restaurant.' It felt right. Everything felt like it was falling into place.

Penelope clapped her hands together. 'It's about bloody time you came home. This is your house, after all. Okay, now that's out of the way, it's time for my yoga session. Jay, I'll let you show Jess around.'

They all stood as Penelope hugged Jess goodbye.

Julian had a surprise for Jess, and he couldn't wait to show her any longer. 'Come on, I'll give you a brief tour, but there's something in particular I want to show you.' He wrapped his arm around her shoulder as she looked up at him, a questioning look on her face.

'I hate to think what else you can show me.'

'Don't worry, you'll like this surprise.'

He walked her through the property, pointing out the drawing rooms, ballroom, main dining room, and private dining room until they reached a door that led out into the gardens. They strolled hand in hand along the winding pathways that meandered along the river, the same river that flowed through the grounds of Julian's house and restaurant.

As they rounded a corner, a long brick building appeared, wooden doors dotted along it at regular intervals. She heard him before she saw him.

Jess turned to him, a beaming smile on her face. 'Is that Teddy?'

He nodded. 'I spoke with your mother; I hope you don't mind? I know you missed him, and she agreed to transport him over.'

The air was forced out of his lungs as she threw herself at him; her legs wrapped around his hips, her arms wrapped around his neck like a boa constrictor as her lips crashed to his in a bruising kiss. 'This is the best surprise.'

As quickly as she'd latched onto him, she'd jumped down and ran over to where Teddy was huffing and neighing. As he watched her hug his head to her shoulder and stroke down his neck, he felt happy. Settled. And he hoped to God nothing came along to fuck with it.

After promising she could come back tomorrow to take him for a ride, Jess agreed to leave. He was desperate to take her home and do some riding of his own.

Plans to fuck her the minute he got her inside flew out the window as he parked his car outside the small cottage. Sat on the low brick wall outside his front door sat a familiar woman, one he didn't think Jess was prepared to see.

CHAPTER 30

JESS

Primal - Vo Williams & Vyceroy

'Mum? What are you doing here?' Jess felt sick at the sight of her mum, but something seemed different about her, and that alone encouraged her out of the car and to approach.

Georgina didn't look as well put together as usual, wearing beige trousers, a black T-shirt, and were they trainers? Gucci trainers, but still. Her hair wasn't coiffed into perfect waves, and her makeup was minimal. Something was off.

She stood by the front door, clasping her hands together, and seemed unsure if she should take a step closer or stay where she was. 'I'm sorry for coming. I know you hate me and don't want to see me, but I needed to see you, to make sure you're okay.'

Jess huffed out a laugh. 'It's a bit late to care about my welfare, isn't it?'

Georgina had the decency to look at her feet, her face guilt ridden. 'I deserve that. I admit, my abilities as a parent should be called into question.' She looked up at Julian. 'Did you explain to her what I told you about my situation?'

Jess looked at Jay, her expression asking him what her mother was talking about. A feeling of unease crept over her as she wondered when he'd seen her mother, and why they'd had a heart-to-heart conversation. And more importantly, why didn't she know about it?

He had the decency to look sheepish. 'No, I haven't mentioned it. Shall we all go inside? I think you two need to talk.' He looked at Jess for her permission.

She supposed she couldn't ignore her mother forever. 'Okay. Let's talk.'

Julian poured them all wine as Georgina repeated the story of how she came to be married to Peter.

'Jessica, please know that I am truly sorry. I had no idea what was going on, and when I suspected your father, I tried to find out as much as possible. I understand you probably never want to see me again, but I wanted you to know that I love you, and there isn't a day that I don't regret how badly I behaved, however misguided I was in my treatment of you.'

Jess took a sip of her red wine. It soured in her stomach, so she placed it down on the coffee table and looked at her mother. 'I can't say that I forgive you, or that I'm able to forget, but I don't hate you. Maybe, in time, we can build a better relationship.'

Georgina sniffed. 'Thank you. I'd like that. I have some news to tell you.'

Oh god, why did that fill her with dread? Those words had never meant good things were to follow. She remained silent, letting her mother carry on.

'I've left your father. He's... well... he's just such a bastard. I hate the man. Jessica, you've been through so much and come out the other end so strong. You inspired me to take back control of my life. That man isn't capable of love. He cares about money and his bank and that's all. I went with Teddy to Al and Pen's to drop him off, and it gave me a chance to reconnect with them. We were old friends, you know, and they reminded me of the fun we used to have before Peter came along. I've agreed to travel out to France to visit them. I need a break, a chance to find myself again.'

Jess didn't know what to say. Stunned at this new side to her mother she'd never seen before. Her mother looked lighter, happier, and she believed there was a chance they could mend their broken relationship.

'Where are you staying?' Jess knew full well that Peter wouldn't leave the house.

'I've moved into your old place in the village. It's rather nice there. I've joined a book club.' She shook her head. 'Not like yours, I might add. My fandango wouldn't know what had hit it if I read one of your books.'

Jess cringed as her hands flew to cover her face. 'Mum, you can't say that.' She turned her head, peaking through her fingers. 'Sorry, Jay. You'll have to excuse my mother; she seems to be having a moment.' Julian just laughed in response.

As she waved her mother off, she felt like a weight had lifted from her chest that she hadn't realised was there. She'd carried the feeling of being suffocated all her life, and now it was gone. It was a strange sensation. She rubbed at her chest as she closed the front door.

'Hey, you okay?' As always, Jay was right there at her side.

'You know what? I am okay. I'm finally doing okay. There's just one thing missing.'

He pressed her up against the wall, avoiding the coat hooks, his groin providing her with a perfect level of pressure and friction.

'You've been holding out on me. I want it, Jay. I want the hunt. Can we do it?' She could feel her core calling out for it. Her body sang with longing.

'Are you sure?' From the way his hips rutted into hers, and the erection pressing against her in a most delicious way, she guessed he was thrilled to hear her request.

'I wouldn't ask if I wasn't.'

He ran his fingers through her hair as his brow creased. 'I can't think where we could do it. Are you happy to wait for the restaurant to close? We could hunt here then.'

'Yes.' She couldn't wait as excitement zipped up her spine. 'I might take a nap and then get ready. What do I need to do?'

He'd gone upstairs with Jess, settling her under the covers.

'Wear comfortable clothes, nothing too restrictive like skinny jeans. They're a fucker to pull down in a hurry. Don't wear your designer leggings; I make no promises that your clothes will survive.

You'll need some lace up trainers. I expect you to run. Don't make this easy. The more you fight, the harder I'll fuck you.' Her underwear grew damp as he spoke. She wanted it now, not later. This was going to be a hard few hours to get through.

His face turned serious. 'Jess, are you sure you want this? What you've been through may have given you triggers you're not aware of.'

She considered what he was saying, and he was right. She didn't know how she'd react to what he did to her until he did it, but she wanted this. Deep in her core, she yearned for this, long before the events with Will, and that feeling hadn't gone away. If anything, she wanted it more.

'I want it, Jay. I at least want to try, and I know I can use my safeword if it gets to be too much.'

He nodded, deep in thought as he chewed on his lip. 'Okay. I promise not to hold back, but you have to use your safeword if you need to. Don't go being a kinky hero on my account. I have to know that you're okay or I won't be able to do it. What about limits? Do you want to introduce any new ones?'

'No. I told you; I want it all.'

Julian's phone pinged with a new message at eleven o'clock. He read it before dropping his phone on the bedside table. 'It's time. They've closed the restaurant. We officially have the grounds to ourselves.' His eyes darkened as he walked over to his wardrobe and changed into black combat trousers, a black T-shirt, and his chunky black boots.

'You look like you're about to go on a S.W.A.T. mission,' Jess said with a nervous giggle. She was ready to go in a pair of old leggings she used for riding and one of Jay's T-shirts. Her running shoes were by the back door. What Jay didn't know was that she'd forgone underwear.

As they made their way outside, he recapped. 'Okay, so when I say run, you go. I don't mean jog a little down the lawn. You need to get as much distance from me as possible. I'm fast, sunshine.'

He pointed over to the woods in the distance. 'Head for those trees. They back onto the main house, so if you get lost, walk in one direction. You'll either end up with my parents or you'll come back here.'

'I really hope I don't get lost and end up having to knock on your parents' door. Can you imagine? "Hi, don't mind me. I was hoping to get fucked in the woods by your son, but I guess I took a wrong turn." I don't think that would go down well.'

'Yeah, probably best avoided. Okay, you'll get ten minutes before the hunt begins.'

She pursed her lips and nodded, bouncing from one foot to the other. 'Okay. Ten minutes.'

'When I've had enough of the hunt and need to fuck you, I'll say "enough." That's your cue to stop fighting and take my dick like a good girl. Got it?'

Yep, she was definitely ready to take his dick right now. Instead, she just nodded.

Julian grabbed her hips and pushed her back against the cold, hard stone of the cottage. His body surrounded her as he pressed his forearms on the wall, either side of her head and took her mouth in a passionate kiss. It was hot, needy and a sign of what was to come. His stubble scraped across the delicate skin around her lips as he bit down, drawing her bottom lip into his mouth. His lips traced a path down her neck, biting and sucking as her body pressed into his. She was seconds away from cancelling their plans and dropping to her knees when he pulled away enough to bring his mouth to her ear and growled, 'Run.'

It was music to her ears as her fight-or-flight mode kicked in, giving her the energy she'd been lacking all day to take off on a sprint. She refused to look behind her. Her eyes were fixed on the treeline in front of her and knew she could make it there easily in the allotted time, and have plenty of time spare to hide. She didn't have the speed or strength advantage over Julian, but she could hide.

Her lungs ached as her legs pumped. The familiar burn in her thighs reminded her of when she'd ride Teddy for hours.

Exhilaration, fear, excitement, and need warred inside her as she ran and ran and ran. As she crossed one of the bridges over the river and hit the treeline, leaves, roots, and fallen branches replaced the soft, bouncy grass. Her legs protested as her feet pounded against the hard, uneven terrain, twisting her ankles. This is where she'd lose time, not willing to risk falling and ending the hunt before it began.

She took a moment to catch her breath, resting her hands on her hips as she sucked in a lung full of damp woodland air. The scent of earth and pine reminded her of Julian, and as if thinking of him had conjured him, she heard the crack of a branch at the edge of the woodland. Shit, had it been ten minutes already?

She surveyed her surroundings, barely making out anything in the moonlight. The further she'd gone into the woods, the darker it had become, no longer lit by the lamps dotted along the river's edge.

She saw a large shadow cast by a tall, wide based oak tree and carefully made her way over to it, not daring to give her location away by stepping on a branch. She felt her way around the base of the tree. It was wider than her arm span, so she was confident she could hide behind it. She didn't see another option.

Crouching down, she pressed her back against the deep ridges of the bark and breathed as slowly as possible, which was tricky considering how out of breath she was. She tried to remember the Wim Hof breathing technique she'd seen in a documentary recently. She heard movement, but it echoed all around her, impossible for her to know which direction it had come from.

Moonlight filtered down through the canopy of the trees, and she noticed a shadow move close to where she was hiding.

Shit, she mouthed silently to herself. He was already so close. He wasn't kidding when he said he was fast. She pressed the backs of her arms into the tree, lifting herself to standing as slowly as she could, before sidestepping around to the other side of the tree. After she'd reached the other side, she took a deep breath and pushed off the from the tree, sprinting as fast as she could while not being able to see the ground beneath her feet.

Immediately, she heard thundering footsteps behind her as she released a squeal. She tried to pick up speed, but just as she did, her foot caught on a root and she came to an abrupt halt, her chest, then her face making their acquaintance with the ground. The air left her lungs, leaving her winded and disorientated as she scrambled to her hands and knees.

Before she could get back on her feet, a hand clasped around her ankle, yanking her across the ground. Her T-shirt bunched up under her arms, the damp earth sticking to her back as the woodland debris clawed at her skin.

She kicked out with her ankle, trying to shake him off, but his grip was vice-like.

'Look what I found hiding in the woods.' His voice was deeper, if that was even possible. He sounded out of breath, his words raspy and tinged with darkness.

She tried to twist onto her front, to kick away and pull her body out of his reach, but her hands found nothing to grasp onto. Within seconds, he'd pinned her hips to the ground, settling between her legs. She pressed her hands into his chest and pushed with all her might, but he didn't budge. Instead, he grabbed both of her wrists with one hand and pinned her arms above her head. His other hand slipped inside the waistband of her leggings, his fingers sliding straight inside her.

'Fuck, sunshine. No knickers and soaking. You really are quite the find.'

All fight left her as he forced two fingers into her, pumping without finesse. As her hips thrust, desperate to find some friction, he pulled his hand out.

'I don't think so. You'll do as you're told, and you don't get to come until I tell you to.'

He pressed his groin to hers, rubbing his erection over her clit as he brought his two fingers up to her mouth. She could smell her arousal as he pushed them between her lips, forcing her teeth apart until she nearly gagged with how far he was pushing them in.

'Suck me clean.' His words were harsh, and it turned her on. There were no airs or graces now. Thoughtful, gentle Julian was nowhere to be seen.

She sucked her musky flavour from his fingers before biting down on them. The fight hadn't totally left her.

He pulled them out with a growl as his hand went for her throat. And then he stopped.

She froze beneath him, her eyes locked with his. 'Why are you stopping?'

He stared at her, his mouth in a grim line.

'I said, why are you stopping?' She couldn't keep the hurt from her voice.

'I saw the marks on your throat. I know Will strangled you until you passed out.' He dropped his eyes from hers.

She pushed his chin up with her finger and looked him in the eyes. 'I love how you hold me there. The feel of your palm and fingers around my throat, applying the perfect amount of pressure to make me feel claimed. Do you really want Will's hands to the be last to touch me there? Do it.' She tilted her head back, opening her throat to him. 'Claim me. Mark me. Make me yours again, my Lord.' She knew she was playing dirty. She didn't care.

With a nod, he pressed her wrists into the ground, his lips to hers and his with his free hand, traced her jawline with his thumb before sliding his hand into place around her throat. She could tell he was taking it one step at a time. He exerted no pressure as he kissed her, just held his hand in place. She moaned in encouragement and rocked her pelvis against his.

He released her throat just long enough to tug her leggings down to her knees and unbutton his trousers. He pressed his hot tip to her entrance but didn't push inside. Her core clenched and pulsed, trying to pull him inside.

His palm was back on her throat, and this time he gave it a gentle squeeze. Pressure built behind her eyes as she tipped her head back and closed them. Soft lips pressed to the other side of her neck as he pushed himself inside her, just the tip.

She felt the bite of pain as he sank his teeth into her flesh in the dip at the base of her neck, certain he'd broken the skin.

His mouth was at her ear, his hot breath tickling the column of her neck. 'Have you given up already, sunshine? I don't remember giving you the cue to stop.'

He wanted her to fight back? But she didn't want to. His dick was right there, taunting her.

'If you want a good fucking, earn it.' He leaned back on his haunches, releasing her wrists. She didn't have time to think about what to do, so she flipped onto her hands and knees and tried to crawl away, her leggings around her knees hampering her movements.

He was toying with her. 'Has anyone told you it's rude to play with your food?' she said over her shoulder.

'Playing is the best part.' He let her crawl a few paces before he grabbed her leg and tugged. She collapsed to the floor, her naked arse in the air.

'Perfect. Just how I want you.'

He climbed over the top of her, but she reared back, pushing him away as she clambered to her feet, catching him off guard. She half ran, half side-stepped as she tried to pull her leggings up as she heard Julian laughing behind her.

Before she'd made it to a full run, she felt his chest collide with her back and his arm wrap around her torso as he lifted her feet off the ground, her spine cracking as he forced her into a slight back bend. She paid a fortune for a chiropractor to do what he'd just achieved in a matter of seconds. Who knew primal had health benefits?

He walked them over to a tree, pressing her chest into the bark, the sharpened ridges cutting into her nipples. With one hand holding her in place against her spine, he tugged her leggings down and kicked at her feet, widening her stance.

He gripped at her throat with one hand, pressing her face into the tree while the other pulled at her hips as he nudged his cock at her entrance. 'Enough.'

He slammed inside her with a growl as her scream echoed through the woods. Somewhere in the distance, she heard the frantic flapping of wings.

'Get on your hands and knees.' With his cock still inside her, he gripped her hips as he swung her round, his knees pushing into the back of hers until her legs collapsed and they fell to the ground. As her hands landed, she gripped onto the earth and rotten leaves beneath her as he grabbed her shoulders, continuing his punishing thrusts, hitting her cervix over and over.

'You feel so good. So fucking tight. So wet. Perfect.' He muttered words of encouragement and praise through gritted teeth as he pushed her T-shirt up her back. He leaned his body over hers, biting her back, sucking her skin into his mouth. The pain enhanced the pleasure. He was like a wild animal, out of control and chasing his release. He was no longer second guessing every move, worrying that he might hurt her or trigger her.

This is what she needed to feel alive again. This is what she needed to put the past behind her.

'Jay, I need to come. It's too much. I'm so close it's painful.' Her core was twisting and tightening. Every time he sank his teeth into her, or battered her inner walls, she wanted a release, but it wasn't coming. His cock thrust against her G-spot, but it still wasn't enough. She was almost crying now, desperate to fall off the edge. 'Please. Please, I need more.' She rocked her hips, meeting his thrusts.

'Limits, Jess. We good?'

'Yes. Good.' She couldn't form complete sentences.

She heard him spit a split second before she felt his finger slide along his dick, forcing its way inside her, stretching her to her limits. Her opening was on fire, and she was sure she was close to tearing, but she wouldn't say her safeword. She loved it, the pain, the knowledge he was fucking her so completely. After a few thrusts, the burning turned to something far more extreme, an intense pleasure she didn't believe possible. 'Fuck, Jay, that's… oh, God, yes.'

'You like that, sunshine?' He ran his finger along her G-spot as shockwaves pulsed along her spine. 'Don't worry, you'll come. But only when I tell you to. I'm going to grab your throat and squeeze. I need to know you're okay.'

'Jay, I'm good. Please. I need this.' She might die if he didn't finish this.

He ran a hand up her spine as he pulled his cock out all the way to the tip. He pumped his finger as he gripped her throat, dots flashing on the back of her eyelids. He thrust harder and deeper, setting a relentless pace, the shockwaves of which she felt throughout her body. His finger caressed her G-spot, his dick hit her walls, battering her with pleasure so intense she couldn't breathe. Her blood turned to fire as heat spread throughout her.

She felt the rumble from his chest before he released a growl, loud and long and unlike anything she'd heard come from him before. 'Come for me. Grip my cock, sunshine… yeah, that's it. Grip it harder. I want you to milk every fucking drop out of me. I want you gushing for me. Fucking soak me, sunshine. Don't hold back.'

He released her throat and she gasped in air. His hand reached down and pinched at her clit. 'Oh. Oh.' She couldn't form words. Her ohs became whimpers. She was no longer Jessica Chatwin, her soul had left that body. She was something so much purer and debased. Her mind switched off, the ground beneath her knees no longer cutting into her skin. She could no longer feel the chill of the night air against her damp, exposed body. Jay's words no longer made sense, they were sounds, somewhere in the distance. She lifted a hand, bringing it to her nipple and pinching.

The sensory overload exploded around her. She detonated, arousal gushing from between her legs as she screamed once more into the canopy.

Julian's carnal groan competed with her screams as hot jets of cum filled her, leaking out and spilling between her thighs. He pulled his finger from her as he finished himself off with languid, lazy strokes. 'Fuck me, sunshine. You were made to take me.'

Her arms collapsed as she fell to the floor. Julian quickly grabbed her, lifting her up and against his chest. He sat back on his haunches, his erection at half-mast through the zipper of his trousers.

She rubbed her nose against his neck, breathing him in, entirely too spaced out to form words.

'Are you doing all right? Did I give you what you needed?'

She couldn't believe he needed to ask. The evidence spoke for itself. His trousers were wet beneath her bare arse. 'I've never come like that before, Jay. I'm not sure I can walk, and from how hot my insides feel, I think it's safe to say I'm full of your seed. It's going to be a messy walk back.'

He brought his knees up and pushed off from the ground, once again demonstrating his sheer strength as he brought them to standing, carrying her bridal style. 'I'll walk us back like this. I've got you, sunshine.' He pulled her leggings up as best he could. She was useless, unable to coordinate her limbs enough to lend a hand. She felt drunk and like they were walking through mist. Before she knew where she was, they were stepping up to the house.

As he closed the back door, he pulled her shoes off and dropped them to the floor, her leggings not far behind. He took the stairs up to their room slowly, peppering her with kisses with each step.

As he rested her on the bed, he pulled her T-shirt over her head, flinging it to the side. 'Don't move.'

She heard the water run in their bathroom as he washed his hands. She took the moment alone to collect her thoughts. Pressing her hand to her chest, she could feel her heart beating against her ribs, like a drum announcing the resurrection of Jessica Chatwin. A smile tripped from her lips, before they parted on a contented sigh.

Within moments, he was back at her feet, spreading her legs. He ran his fingers up her opening, spreading his cum across her clit. His dick glistened with their combined arousal as he stroked his length. It grew thicker and longer with each pass.

'This turns me on, seeing you like this. Full of me. I've never experienced this before,' he said as he stripped out of his clothes. 'I can't put into words how I feel. Just know that I vow never to hurt you. You mean everything to me. I need to make love to you, Jess, and then we can shower.' He climbed over her, his arms bracing on either side of her, the beat of her drum getting louder and faster.

He nudged her legs apart with his knee. 'I want to give you the world.'

He pressed a kiss to her forehead. 'You'll never want for anything. Your dreams are my dreams.'

A hot kiss to her cheek. 'You run; I'll find you.'

Another kiss to her collarbone. 'I will always find you, Jess.'

He pressed his cock to her entrance, sliding up to the hilt in one smooth thrust. 'Mine.'

CHAPTER 31

JESS

Stand By You - Rachel Platten

'Can you believe we're all back together, sat around this table in the very pub where it all started?' said Sarah as they took their seats at the dark wood table in the window. The pub had been the location of their weekly book club, in the village where at one time or another they'd all lived.

Lucy rested her chin on the heel of her hand. 'It's crazy. We've gone full circle, only the circle was more of a swirly pathway.' She wiggled her finger through the air. 'My mum always used to say the path to true love never ran smooth, but holy shit balls, ladies, we had to work for it.'

'True story,' said Jess with a laugh.

Imogen rubbed at her temples. 'We all made it, though. We're stronger for the shit we went through. Let's toast to being awesome friends.'

They raised their glasses, clinking them together. The difference this time was the absence of booze. In solidarity with Imogen, they'd all promised 'to go dry.' Sarah wasn't overly sure it was necessary, but she'd come around in the end.

'Okay, do any of us want to talk about the book we're reading, or do we all want to hear about what's going on with Jess, her primal-fricking-dom boyfriend who also happens to be a fucking billionaire future Lord?' asked Sarah, her eyebrows getting increasingly closer to her hairline with each word.

Lucy shrugged. 'The book was good. That's my review. Let's move this along to Jess.'

All eyes were on her. This was new. She wasn't used to being the centre of attention. She was the strong stable friend in the background. The friend where nothing remarkable ever happened.

Well, she was certainly making up for it now. 'All right, ladies, you know I've told you everything there is to know.'

Sarah pouted. 'So, you're not giving us exact measurements?'

'No.' Jess lifted her glass of Coke Zero to her mouth to hide her smug grin.

'How's your mum? Have you heard from her since you last saw her?' asked Imogen.

'I called her the other day. She's doing well, happier. I guess we're both a lot happier without Dad.' She bit her lip as it threatened to quiver. It was ridiculous. Her dad wasn't a good man. He'd never treated her with kindness or love, but that didn't stop her from wishing she had a father she could be proud of, a father who made her feel wanted.

Lucy gripped her hand, giving it a squeeze. 'It's okay to feel sad, but don't lose sight of the fact you have us, and a whole troupe of Hadleys who've chosen to love you. They say blood is thicker than water, but...' She shrugged. 'I think that's bollocks.'

Sarah was leaning on her elbows, her mouth agape. 'Wait, is that it? Seriously, chick, I thought you were going to say something truly enlightening.'

'What? It is bollocks. We've all bagged ourselves men that are top tier, but that's not because we don't deserve to be with Britain's hottest men.' The others nodded along. 'It's because we're top tier.' Lucy waved her hand in the air. 'I don't mean that in a big-headed way, I just mean... well, we earned happiness. We've all hit rock bottom and climbed our way out, and these amazing, hot, talented—'

'Big-dicked,' added Sarah.

Lucy nodded. 'Yes, big-dicked men chose to love us. So, basically what I'm trying to say, Jess, is that you shouldn't judge yourself by the behaviour of your family, but by the quality of the people that choose to love you.' Lucy's words caught on the last few words as emotion seemed to take over.

Sarah raised her glass. 'And we fucking love you, you classy bitch.'

Imogen covered her face with her hands and burst into tears. 'I love you guys,' she sobbed, and then flapped her hands at her face, trying to regain control and dry her tears.

Jess leaned forward, wiping under her eye with the pad of her thumb. 'You okay, hun?'

'Ugh, fucking hormones. I can't keep up. The other night—I kid you not—I was so bloody horny I climbed Cam like a tree the minute he'd finished in the gym, and then the orgasm was so amazing that I burst into tears and cried for a solid five minutes. Cam didn't know what to do and just stood there like a deer in the headlights.'

'That is a confusing situation to be in, to be fair.' Sarah raised her index finger in the air. 'But I have a question. Are you saying that being pregnant makes sex better?'

Imogen pulled herself together, leaned forward and ducked her head like she was about to share a secret related to national security. 'Ladies, the sex is mind blowing. I did some internet research, and it's a fact. There is so much going on,' she waved in her general crotch area, 'down there, and so much extra blood flow, that everything is more sensitive. And I've started having mega sexy dreams, so I wake up raring to go. Cam thought I was like a dog in heat while we were trying, but it was nothing compared to how I feel now. It helps that I'm nearly at twelve weeks, so I'm less pukey. Side note, morning sickness is a lie. You'll feel like shit twenty-four-seven. The sickness does not magically disappear mid-morning.'

Sarah rubbed at her belly as she groaned. 'At least you don't have to worry about periods for nine months. Mine are doing my head in. I swear they get heavier every month, like they're punishing me for all the orgasms.' She looked at Jess. 'That was the good thing about living with you, Jess. Our periods were in sync, so we knew to stock up on ice cream. James is clueless about all that. How's Jay with it all? Does he bring you hot water bottles and chocolate? I bet he's so caring and cooks you lush dinners.'

Jess felt the blood run from her face as her friends all turned to stare at her.

'Hun, are you okay? You've gone a weird colour,' asked Lucy.

'Yeah, no. Um.'

Sarah's eyes widened as her jaw dropped to her chest. 'Oh, fuck!'

Imogen was quick to say, 'Right, okay. Let's not jump to conclusions. Jess, you've been through a lot, and your body has been through a lot of trauma, and that can disrupt your cycle. Anyway, you're on birth control, right?'

Jess nodded. 'Yeah... apart from when I wasn't. Will didn't exactly tend to my sexual health needs when he handcuffed me to a radiator—a hot fucking radiator, I might add—and I didn't really take any while unconscious in the hospital. Have I just become my least favourite trope? Seriously? Accidental fucking pregnancy.' She mouthed the last word silently, unable to vocalise it. Fear and excitement caused her belly to flutter.

'We don't know this for sure. I'll pop to the shops down the road. Grab a test,' said Sarah. She pointed at Jess's drink. 'Down that while I'm gone. You're gonna need to pee when I get back.'

The next few days went by in a blur. Jess's emotions flipped from scared shitless to surprisingly excited. She'd sworn the others to secrecy. They were to tell no one. Julian and the boys were allowed their secret about his past. She was allowed one tiny secret about their future. She just needed to get her head around it before she could consider telling Jay. And work out how to tell him.

The complication was that she knew he wanted to have children, but he wanted to be married first. He was a traditional guy, and she didn't know the finer details or loopholes, but it was probably rooted in the requirement to be married to pass his title down to his children. Regardless, she'd just gone and pissed on those plans. It took two to tango. She understood that, but she really should've realised that you can't skip birth control and continue to have unprotected mind blowing sex. She was certain that with the way he fucked her, even birth control wouldn't have stopped his swimmers from hitting their target.

She'd wanted to wait until the weekend to tell him. He no longer worked weekends, so he'd be more relaxed, and have more time to freak out before having to put on a professional face and deal with hungry people. That was tomorrow, and she couldn't be sure if the butterflies in her stomach were anxiety, excitement, or a sign she was about to vomit.

'I have a surprise for you today.' Julian said as he rolled over in bed, pulling her into him, breathing in her hair the way he always did in the mornings.

I doubt it's as surprising as what I have to tell you, she thought to herself as she pressed her rear into his morning wood.

'No sex this morning, sunshine.' He slapped her on the arse. 'Come on, quick rinse in the shower and then we're heading to the main house.'

That wasn't what she was expecting. Maybe he'd brought a horse, so Teddy had a friend?

He wasn't kidding when he said he was eager to get out. As soon as she was dressed, he ushered her out to his car, a sweet pastry wrapped in kitchen paper shoved in her hand and a cup of tea in a travel cup already sitting in the cup holder. She side-eyed Julian as he drove, hoping he didn't notice her surreptitiously dusting puff pastry off her chest and onto the floor of his car.

As they made it to the main house, however, he kept driving until he parked outside a row of barn buildings she'd not seen before.

As he turned the engine off, he said, 'Look at me.' She removed her seat belt and twisted to face him.

'What's going on, Jay?'

'You'll find out soon enough, but first...' He pulled a strip of black silk from the back pocket of his jeans. Her mind instantly went to kinky-fuckery. Surely, he wouldn't want to get sexy first thing in the morning at his parents, well, his house?

He covered her eyes with the cool fabric and tied it behind her head. She could feel his warm hand cup her face before his lips pressed to hers in a chaste kiss. 'Stay there, I'm coming around.'

She heard his footsteps crackle against the stone chips as he made his way to her before the door popped open. 'Okay, twist around. Here, take my hands. Careful.' He ran his hands up her thighs as she planted her feet on the ground. 'Mind your head.' She ducked before he gripped her hands and pulled her to standing.

'Okay, there is nothing between you and where we're going, so hold my hand and take slow steps forward.' He sounded excited but also there was an edge to his voice. What on earth was the surprise?

'Jay, what have you been up to?' Her heart thudded in her chest as she tentatively stepped forwards.

'You'll see. We're nearly there. Okay, step up here. Yep, like that.' She'd stepped off the gravel and was standing on hard concrete, or so she assumed. She heard a click and then warm air surrounded her as he guided her inside a building.

'Right.' He took hold of her shoulders and moved her into place. 'Okay, I'm going to take your blindfold off, but keep your eyes shut until I say you can open them.'

'Okay.' Excitement washed over her, the hairs on her arms standing to attention as she felt him untie the knot of the blindfold. She kept her eyes tightly closed, not wanting to ruin the surprise. She'd never seen Julian behave like this before, so it must be something big.

'On three, open your eyes. One. Two. Three.'

She blinked rapidly as her eyes adjusted to the light that flooded into the space. White walls, three of them. As she turned to face the direction they'd just walked in, she looked out over a large courtyard through large glass panes, which explained why the air was so warm. She still didn't have a clue what was going on.

'Jay, what is this place?' She continued to turn in a circle before facing him.

'This,' he held his arms out wide, 'is your art gallery.'

What the fuck?

'W-wh… my what?' Did he say her art gallery?

'Your dreams are my dreams. You're used to people saying you can't have what you want. Well, that's changed. If you want an art gallery, you've got one. If you prefer working for James, you can do that. I'm not forcing anything on you, but I want you to have a choice.' His Adam's apple bobbed as he took her hands in his. 'If you want it, all you have to do is come up with a name. This place is yours to do with it as you wish. Gallery, office, whatever.'

'I don't know what to say.' She wanted to cry, she wanted to laugh. She wanted to sit down. He was just too much, too perfect.

'You can take your time to think about it. This building isn't going anywhere. I do have something else to ask, though.' The cheerful smile faded on his face, and his brow creased. He stepped back, but didn't release her hands.

'Jay? What's the matter?'

He rolled his lips. 'I don't know how to say this. I've been thinking about it a lot lately, but I don't know how you'll react.'

Oh shit, did he have another secret to tell her? What the hell could he have to say?

'Just spit it out, Jay.' She wanted to know, but also could happily live the rest of her life in this happy bubble.

'Yes. Good plan. I'll just come right out with it.'

As if in slow motion, he looked into her eyes and then he was sinking. It took a second for her brain to catch up to what was happening, but as he went down on one knee, she knew.

'Jessica.' He craned his neck to look up at her. 'I love you. Have done from the minute I walked into Cam's kitchen and laid eyes on you. I wake up every day feeling like the luckiest man alive, and I never want that to end—'

She pulled her hands away, stepping back. 'Julian, stop. This isn't right.'

CHAPTER 32

JULIAN

Rescue (Stripped) - Tyler James Bellinger

'Julian, stop. This isn't right.'

He dropped his hands, letting them hang by his sides as he stood up, his jeans catching on his thighs, but he didn't care.

He knew he was moving too fast. Knew Jess had been through a lot, but he didn't want to wait any longer. He was moving back to the main house, taking over from his parents at managing their sizeable portfolio, and he wanted Jess by his side. He needed her by his side.

He considered that perhaps he'd not made this romantic enough. He wanted to prove to her he wouldn't demand she give up her life for him, and it just felt right there and then to do it. He didn't have a ring with him. Was that the problem? He didn't think so. Jess wouldn't care about a ring.

Fuck. He'd messed this up. Her face was crumpling up in that way that told him tears were imminent. When proposing to a woman, tears were acceptable, but they were usually tears of happiness. These were not that.

Panic set in as sweat formed on his top lip. 'Shit. Jess. I'm sorry. I didn't mean to upset you. It just felt right.' What he wanted to say was, please don't leave me.

'No, Jay. You've done nothing wrong. This is definitely a me problem.' She flapped her hands as she paced back and forth. 'The gallery is amazing. Thank you so much.' She placed her hands over her heart. 'I love it and I can't wait to open it.'

He was confused and a little hurt at her reaction. He stuffed his hands in his pockets and perched down on the window ledge. 'I don't understand, then. What doesn't feel right? Are you not happy with me? Is that what you're saying?'

She stepped closer to him. 'I'm trying to find the words. Can you give me a minute?'

'Okay.' The seconds ticked by as he watched her chew on her nail. She kept going to say something, but then thought better of it. After what felt like an eternity, but in fairness was around sixty seconds of pacing, she came to an abrupt stop in front of him, a newfound look of determination on her face.

'Julian.'

'Yes, Jessica.' He wished he'd kept the door open. It was growing increasingly hot in the gallery. He pulled on his neckline, fanning his top to cool his skin.

'I've never had any control over my life. I didn't get to plan my meals or my outfits. I couldn't date who I wanted. Moving out didn't work, as my parents soon dragged me back home. I'm free now. I get to make my own choices.'

He knew all this. This is why he'd offered her the gallery, no strings attached. 'Jess, I'm not trying to take away your control.'

'I know. You're perfect. Honestly, Jay, I love you. I'm just trying to tell you how I feel.'

'Okay, sorry. Shutting up now.'

She smiled at him, and he realised all was not lost. 'I wanted some time to do things on my terms. Make some decisions for myself.'

Oh, he understood. Because of circumstances, she had to move in with him. Now they're moving to his family home, but she didn't get a say in that. He kept his mouth shut, though, choosing to nod.

'You saved my life in more ways than one. I decided not to give up on life because I wanted to be with you. You kept me going when Will was determined to break me. You found me. You cared for me and made me feel safe. You didn't just make me feel like myself again, you made me realise who I am. I'm a better version of myself.'

He slid his hands under his rear to stop himself from wrapping her in his arms. She needed to say her piece.

'Basically, what I'm trying to say is...'

Hang on, why was she getting on one knee? His heart tried to beat out of his chest, ready to ask what she was doing.

It was her turn to take his hands. He couldn't lie. This felt weird. Usually, if a woman was on her knees in front of him, it wasn't to do the talking.

'I don't want you to propose to me. I don't have a swoon-worthy speech planned. I wasn't planning on doing this at all, but now that I think of it, it's probably great timing. Or would you say serendipitous?'

He chewed on the inside of his cheek, stopping the chuckle from escaping. Now wasn't the time to laugh at how much she rambled when she was nervous.

'Focus, Jess.' She mumbled to herself before clearing her throat and saying, 'Julian, will you marry me?'

The back of his nose burned as the edges of his vision blurred with tears. He sniffed and blinked as he lowered to his knees. 'Yes. It would be my honour to marry you.' Unable to wait any longer, he grabbed her and hoisted her legs around his hips. 'You scared the shit out of me. Never do that again.'

He fisted her hair as he sat down; her straddling his thighs and their lips crashing together in a hot, messy kiss. As he came up for air he said, 'You're happy taking my name, though, aren't you? I'll understand if you don't want to, but it really would be an honour if you did.'

'Yes, Jay. The Chatwin name isn't one I want for much longer, that I'm sure about. It saves arguing over what surname to give our kids, anyway.'

He closed his eyes. Hearing her talk about kids was making him hard. 'Christ, Jess. Don't talk like that. If I had my way, I'd be fucking a baby into you as we speak.' He pressed her down into his lap so she could feel the effect she had on him.

'Did you have a date in mind for the wedding?'

He'd not thought that far ahead. He'd marry her tomorrow if he could. 'I'll leave that up to you. You're in charge of the wedding. Whatever you want, you can have it.'

'I'd quite like to have it before I show.'

Show? Was she talking about horse trials or something? 'What are you showing? Are you taking Teddy somewhere?' He was half smiling, half wondering what the fuck she was talking about.

'Not horses.'

He half shook his head. 'Not horses?'

'No. Jay, prepare to come in your pants.'

'You've really confused me now.' His heart was thundering in his chest.

She ran her nose up the column of his neck, and sure enough, his dick twitched, pressing painfully against his zipper. She sucked his earlobe into her mouth, a groan rumbling from his chest. 'Jay?' She whispered into his ear.

'Mmm.'

'You've already fucked a baby inside me. Brings a whole new meaning to "fuck me, Daddy."'

Hang on. The room span as he digested her words. 'What? How—no, I know how it happened. But you're on birth—' His eyes widened. 'Jess, I'm so sorry. I didn't even consider that you'd had a break in birth control.' He bit down on his lower lip. His eyes scanned her body, her face. She wasn't crying, she was smiling. Smiling was good, right?

He couldn't make sense of the million thoughts and feelings swimming around in his brain. 'Are you okay? How pregnant are we?'

'Well, it can only be a few weeks at most. I haven't worked it out yet.'

'Do you feel okay? How long have you known? I have so many questions, when all I want to do is pull your jeans down and fuck you here. We're going to have to be gentle from now on.' *Wow!* That was all his brain could come up with. He was still recovering from getting engaged, and now he was going to be a dad. There was a baby growing inside the woman he loved, and it turned him the fuck on.

She placed her hands on his shoulders. 'Jay, calm down. I'm fine. Let's not be too hasty with the going gentle thing. I'm incredibly horny at the thought of carrying your child and if you don't fuck me hard, I might explode. And not in a good way. Oh, and I've only known for a few days. Don't be mad, but the others guessed during book club before I did, and Sarah made me pee on a stick in the pub toilets. It wasn't quite how I imagined that going.'

They all knew before he did and that took the shine off, just a little, but still. 'Oh. So, am I the last to know?'

'No, I swore them to secrecy, so you get to tell the boys. I'm sorry, Jay. It only came about because we were talking about periods, and I realised mine hadn't arrived.'

He shook his head. This wasn't even worth discussing. 'Don't worry, we've got more important things to worry about. Are you happy to tell my parents all the news, or do you want to wait?'

'I can't wait to tell them.'

'Come on, spit it out. What's going on?' James said as the waitress took their menus and left.

Julian had asked Cam, Tom, and James to meet at their local pub and everyone was suspicious as to why. Julian wasn't the one to initiate lads' night, but he wanted to tell them everything in person. Jess had agreed not to announce the engagement until he'd spoken to them. He figured that was a fair deal.

'Jess proposed to me.' He couldn't keep the smile from his face. His cheeks ached from how much he'd smiled in the last few days.

A chorus of 'Ah, nice one,' and 'congratulations' rang in his ears.

'Thanks. We're not waiting around to get married either.'

James scoffed. 'Oh eh, shotgun wedding?' He wiggled his eyebrows as he licked the frothy head of his beer from his top lip.

'Not a shotgun wedding, no, but we are having a baby. That was my other news. The engagement came before I knew about the baby.'

'Holy shit. Sorry, mate. I didn't know.' James looked sheepish. 'But wow, that's awesome. Congratulations.'

Cameron pulled him out of his seat to hug him, his hand slapping him hard on the back. 'This is amazing news. I have someone to go through all of this with. Brace yourself, shit's about to get real.'

Tom, followed by James, lined up after Cameron for the obligatory back-slapping hugs.

Tom rubbed at his temples as they sat back down. 'I reckon, James, it won't be long before our two get broody. I'm not ready for kids. We haven't even finished building our own playroom. I wanted a few years of sexy play before the cameras and handcuffs get replaced with plastic shit that makes far too much noise to be legal.' With an apologetic look, he glanced at Cameron and Julian. 'Sorry, guys. Obviously, it's going to be great, and you'll still get all the sexy time.'

Julian squinted his eyes at Tom. 'You raise a valid point. I'm going to need to hire a discreet nanny who works evenings. Someone will have to watch the baby while I chase their mother through the woods. Actually, Tom, do you know anyone who can advise me on safe primal play during pregnancy? Jess is basically feral, and I'm scared I'm going to harm her or the baby.' He'd been away from the scene for so long, he didn't know of anyone that had a baby.

'I'll ask around.'

The rest of the evening was spent discussing the wedding plans. As Julian got out of the taxi, he took a moment to breathe. The scent of roses and lavender filled his lungs and made him ache to hold Jess. For the last few months, he'd felt like his life was a rollercoaster ride, but he finally felt settled. A vibration from his back pocket interrupted his thoughts.

> **Wifey**: Are you nearly home? If so, I want you naked. Oh, and bring pickles.

Thankfully, his parents had gone out to France to buy the wine for the wedding, so they had the house to themselves. Not that it mattered. The place was so large they rarely bumped into each other. He smirked as he tapped out a reply with one hand, unbuttoned his shirt with the other.

> **Jay**: I have a better idea. I'll give you 5 mins. Run.

CHAPTER 33

JESS

Love The Hell Out Of You - Lewis Capaldi

'You look beautiful. I'm so grateful I get to share this moment with you.' Georgina dabbed a tissue under her eyes as she stood with Jess in her bedroom.

Penelope had pulled out all the stops and got everything in place within a month. A tiny chapel on the boundary of their land was to host the ceremony. The reception was back at the main house. The ballroom was a sea of round tables, adorned with cream tablecloths, tall vases filled with the last of the season's lavender and roses scented the air. Most importantly, Jess had requested a disco dancefloor, and that had been installed at one end of the room.

Julian had to be removed by force the night before and had stayed at their old cottage with Cam and the others. The girls had stayed with Jess. They'd spent the night being pampered by the team of beauticians Georgina had arranged. It turned out that Jess rather liked her mother. She was funny, carefree, and had some incredibly filthy stories to share about her time on the circuit. Their relationship wasn't perfect, but it was enough.

Peter Chatwin didn't get an invitation. He was currently being investigated for fraud. When that had come up in conversation over dinner one evening, Albert and Julian had both mumbled about not knowing anything about that, and the conversation quickly moved on.

'I think it's time I got you to the church, Jessica.' Georgina checked her makeup one last time before fussing over Jess.

'You look stunning. I simply can't believe you could source this dress on such short notice. I guess being the future Lady bumps you up the list.' She raised her eyebrow before smirking.

'Yes, well, I only had to drop the title a few times. Needs must and all that.'

Jess stroked her hands over her stomach as she stared at her reflection in the mirror. She wasn't showing yet, and they'd chosen not to tell everyone. It was still early in the pregnancy and Jess was nervous to share the news far and wide. The baby hadn't really had the healthiest start in life and she couldn't deny she was worried. But, so far, so good, so she tried to manifest the most positive of positive thoughts.

Her A-line dress was ivory silk with a Bardot neckline. It hugged her curves to perfection, skimmed her waist, and flowed out to the floor. It was simple, elegant, and befitting a Lady. Two shoe boxes sat next to the door. One held the matching ivory silk three-inch peep toe heels. The other contained her custom Converse. She already couldn't drink on her wedding day; there was no way she was spending it wearing heels. Absolutely not.

The makeup artist had followed the brief, and Jess looked natural and glowing. The artist couldn't believe how little she had to do to add a glow. Jess kept her mouth shut.

Her hair had grown out enough to allow for a simple updo, tendrils of hair falling loose around her nape. She'd clipped an antique French lace veil at the base of her head. Her dressmaker had shortened the veil to be the same length as her train. It ticked the something borrowed and old box as Penelope had insisted she use it as had been the tradition in her family. Only Julian would get to see the something blue.

A horse and cart awaited them outside, pulled by Teddy. Jess had to include her beloved horse on her big day. She allowed the gentle sway of the cart and the clip-clopping of Teddy's hooves to calm her mounting nerves. The others had gone ahead, leaving the final journey to just her, Georgina, and the man controlling the cart.

As they made it to the main road, she felt like a princess as she waved to the locals and the small crowd of press. They weren't celebrities by any stretch of the imagination, but the nation had fallen in love with the classic story of the Lord and his Lady. She hoped they'd get bored with them soon enough.

Albert, looking dapper in his morning suit with tails, was standing with Imogen, Sarah, and Lucy, who all looked stunning in their dresses. Jess had chosen dark lavender tea dresses, the neckline matching her own. It was the only style that would suit all three of them and give Imogen room for her small but perfectly formed baby bump. Imogen was already dabbing at her eyes as they watched her roll into the grounds of the chapel.

Albert held his hand out, ready to help them out of the cart. After a quick peck on the cheek, he announced he was going in.

As she stood at the doors, ready to walk down the aisle, she sucked in a steadying breath. After years of doubt, she was finally getting her happily ever after.

After a quick change from heels to Converse, Jess was ready for the party to begin, but she had something to do first. As soon as she'd set eyes on her husband—she was still getting used to how good it felt to say that—she'd been thinking incredibly naughty thoughts, which made her feel a little uneasy stood before a vicar in a chapel, but she blamed the hormones and the incredibly sexy man she was marrying.

Julian, like his father and the rest of the wedding party, wore the traditional morning suit. His waistcoat was made from the same silk as her dress, and the lavender tie at his neck brought out the deep olive tones of his skin. His hair had been trimmed and styled, so it sat in perfect waves, and he smelled good enough to eat. She fully intended to eat him later.

But nothing, absolutely nothing, compared to how hot he looked with a ring on his finger. Her core pulsed at the thought of it. New kink unlocked.

The wedding breakfast was over. The guests were milling about as the DJ was getting ready for the first dance and reception. There was a lull in the proceedings, and she intended to fill it. Her mother had explained the importance of taking some time away together to enjoy their wedding day, but she probably didn't mean what Jess had planned.

She grabbed a napkin and stole the pen from the guest book to scribble out a message to Julian as they'd inconveniently left their phones alone for the day.

Dearest husband,

Give me a 5-minute head start from when you read this.

Then run, (we don't have long).

Love from

Wifey
xxx

She looked around for someone she could trust to not read the note before handing it to Julian, and her eyes snagged on his other cousin, Miles. He was definitely not the sort to pry into other people's business, but he was a good sport. She sidled up next to him at the bar.

'Miles?' she asked in her sweetest voice.

He leaned his elbow on the bar as he smiled. 'Hey, Jess. What can I do for you?'

He looked a lot like Julian, but not as tall. He was hot and a billionaire in the shipping industry. God help whoever ended up with him. They'd be batting away competition with a shitty stick for eternity. Anyway, she remembered her mission as she handed him the folded napkin.

'Could you please pass this message to Jay for me? No peeking? It's urgent, needs to get to him right away. If you don't mind?'

Miles bent at the waist in a bow and said, 'Anything for you, my lady.' He gave her a quick wink before casually strolling up to Julian, who was having his ear chewed off by a distant aunt.

Jess hid behind a large plant near the French doors where she intended to make her escape and watched for his reaction. He looked bemused as he took the napkin. Miles slapped him on the shoulder before walking away, spotting Jess and giving her a quick thumbs up.

Julian read the note and stuffed it in the pocket of his trousers as he looked around for her. He said something to his aunt before walking off like a man on a mission. He glanced down at his watch, and that was her cue to make a run for it. She hoisted up the skirt of her dress and legged it.

If anyone chose that moment to look out into the gardens, they'd see her skirt trailing in the wind as she ran with all her might to the treeline in the distance. Thankfully, the veil was safely packed away for another generation of Hadley to use. She'd underestimated how heavy her dress was. It was slowing her down considerably. She might only just make it to the trees before he'd find her, although a quick chase was required, considering they were to have their first dance shortly.

She jumped over the ferns that lined this part of the woodland, her pearl necklace hitting her in the chin, but she didn't have time to care. She pulled on her dress to lift it higher, the bulk of the train draped over her arm. She should've bought one of those convertible dresses. That would've been a far more sensible idea.

Realising she wouldn't get much further, she found the closest sizeable tree and hid behind it, with only seconds to spare before she heard heavy footsteps charging towards her.

'I know you're near, sunshine. I can smell you.'

Her heart thundered in her chest; her breaths shallow as she tried to recover from the run. She rested her back against the tree. Her arms were aching from holding her dress up, and it was slipping. A warm hand snaked around her throat, careful not to squeeze.

'Your dress couldn't be less suitable for a hunt if it tried. You made it too easy for me.' He let go of her throat and stepped in front of her. 'Is someone feeling a little needy, sunshine?'

'Yes. Jay, I couldn't wait any longer. Seeing you with a ring on your finger does things to me.' She felt empty and desperate. 'We need to hurry. Can you please fuck me, now? I need it quick and hard.' She bounced from one foot to the other. 'Christ, I'm so close to coming just thinking about it.'

'Fucking hell, Jess.' He said as he pulled down his zipper and released his cock. 'I have no idea how to tackle this.' He waved a hand in the air around her dress.

'It's a bit like when I need to pee. I have to sit facing the cistern while one of the girls holds my dress up. It's a bloody nuisance, and of course, I'm peeing all the time.'

'Hang on, what? No, never mind, now is not the time to consider how you pee. Turn around.'

She faced the tree and placed her palms on the trunk while draping as much of the dress as she could over her arm. Julian stepped up close to her rear, pushing the rest of her dress up onto her back. She heard him suck in a breath.

'Oh, sunshine. Your take on something blue is exquisite.' He ran a finger from the top of her thigh to the edge of her electric blue lace knickers. 'I'm guessing I can't rip these?'

'No, you're going to need to move them to the side. They match the corset and I love them.'

As requested, he looped a finger into her knickers and held them to one side as he nudged the head of his erection at her entrance.

She pushed back onto him, impatient. 'Jesus, you're so wet already. If I'd have known putting a ring on my finger had this effect on you, I'd have married you in Vegas.'

'If I'd have known, I would have let you. Now, my lord, will you please fuck me?'

He wrapped his left hand round to her front, sliding it under her knickers and stroking over her clit as he tucked himself close behind her, his knees pressing into the back of hers as he thrust into her with relentless power. She didn't want slow and sensual. She wanted him rough.

'Push back onto me, sunshine. That's it, just like that. I feel how close you are, so snug around my cock.' She knew he was laying it on thick, getting her there with his hand, his cock, and his words.

'Like that. Fuck, yes. Keep doing that. Jay. Jay, I'm close.'

'I know. Fucking hell, you're so fucking tight. Fuck. Jess. Fuck. Come. Now.' He was losing control, his words punctuated with his thrusts as she came with a cry, his release coming immediately after.

He slipped out of her, carefully tucking himself back in and checking his trousers for any sign of spillage, and she straightened her underwear. They were already hot and damp from his cum, but she rather liked that. He pulled the pocket square from his jacket and crouched down in front of her.

'Jay, what are you doing?'

'Cleaning you up, my Lady.' He lifted her dress and ran the piece of silk across her inner thighs. He straightened her dress, folded the pocket square and put it back in his pocket. He stood back and scanned his eyes over them both.

'Are we good to go?' Jess was still out of breath, but figured she could take her time walking back to the wedding.

Julian offered her his arm as he said, 'Come on, there's a first dance with our name on it, Mrs Hadley, and then I intend to rid you of this dress at the earliest opportunity.'

EPILOGUE

JESS

Feeling Good - Nina Simone

One year later:

Wifey: Harriet is down, the nanny is on shift. You have 15 minutes.

Jess smirked as she hit send and dashed down to their stables from the office in her art gallery. She'd finished her paperwork for the day while the nanny looked after Harriet. Julian hadn't lied when he said her dreams were his dreams. He'd interviewed over twenty nannies until he found one that was discreet and trustworthy. As soon as she felt ready, Jess returned to work with a waiting list of clients as long as her arm. The beauty of having her gallery and office at home was that she was never far away from her family.

She was already in leggings, trainers, and a baggy T-shirt over her sports bra. The benefit of being a new mum was that she wasn't expected to get dressed up, and she found she was ever ready for a hunt just as long as Harriet wasn't due for a feed. She'd also discovered that sometimes, she liked to be the huntress.

Teddy neighed as she approached his stable and, having asked her stable hand to get him tacked before he left for the day, she made quick work of getting him ready. She checked her watch. Six minutes to go.

The first time Julian agreed to switch, Jess had quickly realised she couldn't compete with him on any level. But on a horse, well, that was another matter. Julian demanded she wore a helmet, which made the whole thing a lot less sexy, but he wasn't about to take any chances.

She put her foot in the stirrup and hauled herself into the saddle. Her body came to life as she gripped the reins in one hand and ran her fingers through Teddy's mane. With a squeeze of her thighs, she dug in her heels and clicked her tongue, setting off at a slow pace until they reached the lawns. She checked her watch. One minute to go.

'Close enough,' she said to Teddy. 'Come on.'

He broke out into a canter as adrenaline pumped through her system. Within minutes, she'd reached the edge of the woodland. She raced up and down, scouring the trees for a sign of Julian. On her third pass, she spotted a white flash run between two large sycamore trees and pulled on the reins to head in that direction.

As she got closer to where she saw him last, he dashed out into a clearing.

'Found you,' she called out as Julian raced off in his trousers, dress shoes, and shirt. She loved it when she caught him while he was still working. He couldn't run as fast in his polished shoes, but fucking hell, Julian looked hot in a tailored suit.

As soon as his parents left the country, he stepped away from the day-to-day management of the restaurant and spent his days either on conference calls in the office at home or attending official meetings elsewhere, but he refused to work outside of office hours. He spent his free time running around after his daughter or chasing his wife.

Teddy's hooves pounded the ground as she rode into the clearing and gained on him. She shucked off a stirrup and swung her leg over Teddy's neck, so she was riding him side saddle. Well, she was a lady, after all.

Julian looked back and nearly stumbled as Jess leapt from the saddle and landed on him, forcing him to the floor. She scrambled to sit astride him, but before she could say 'enough,' he flipped her over onto her back.

Teddy rode off and busied himself chewing on a bush as she unclipped her helmet and dropped it next to them. The ground beneath her was cold as dampness seeped through the fabric of her top, but it did nothing to dampen the heat radiating from her core.

Julian raised an eyebrow. 'We're going to need to revisit the rules if you're going to throw yourself at me from a moving horse, my love. You could've hurt yourself.'

'Nonsense. Lucky for me, I landed on something hard.' She gripped his length to prove her point. 'I caught you fair and square, so now I get to have my wicked way with you.'

'I think you'll find that I'm the one on top. Do you surrender to me, or would you like to continue?'

He always did this. He knew she couldn't resist him for long.

'Okay. You got me. Now, what're you going to do with me?'

He unbuckled his belt, letting the two ends drop to his thighs, undid his trousers and pulled out his cock. 'I intend to breed you.'

Oh lordy, she knew this would happen, and she couldn't have been happier.

ACKNOWLEDGEMENTS

It goes without saying (but I'm going to say it anyway), thank you to my readers. Being an independently published author is hard work and I couldn't do it without your love and support. When you slide into my DMs to give me real-time updates, I love it. Keep it coming.

I want to say a special thank you to my Alpha readers: Laura, Sarah, and Hannah. Your feedback was invaluable, you knew what I wanted to achieve, and you helped me get there.

To my beta readers, and my personal cheerleader squad: Aimee, Beckie, Casey, Lynn, Kylie, and Tracy, you ladies keep me going and it makes my heart sing to know you love my characters almost as much as I do (although I think some of you might love Tom Harper more than me…).

Kerri, I value your aggressive proof reading, but not as much as I value your friendship. Love you, bestie.

Throughout this process, I've had someone cheering me on, and I call her *my last line of defence*. She's the first person to read the final version and I know when she gives me the nod, I'll be alright. Fi, thank you for reading my books and loving them. I hope you'll want to keep reading for me, but be warned, what I have planned is on another level.

My husband doesn't read my books, so he'll probably never see this, but I want to say, thanks. When I lock myself away in my office, thank you for supporting me. And thanks for helping me come up with different words for cock and cum, your eloquence is invaluable.

Kids, I'm sorry I write romance novels that your mates' mum's read. If I ever make millions from my books, I'll buy you all the fancy trainers you want. That's a promise.

THE BOOK CLUB SERIES

Imogen's Story
Lucy's Story
Sarah's Story
Jess's Story

Grumpy Sunshine (Book Club Novella One) – available to download for free at www.alifischer.com

And there's more to come…

To keep up to date with all things Ali, sign up for my newsletter at www.alifischer.com